# ROBIN'S FLIGHT

## BREANNE LEFTWICH

For my daughters, Sophia and Lila. I pray this inspires you to fulfill your dreams and never give up as you grow.

A special thanks to my cousin, Brittany, whose loving pushiness made this book a reality. Without it, this story would still be only in my head.

# CHAPTER ONE

The moon glistened in the reflection of the frothy waves that lapped the shore in front of me. The ocean was a dark, ominous presence, reaching as far as the eye could see. My toes scrunched up the silky, white sand beneath them, and I took a deep breath, inhaling the sea-salt scent while the light breeze brushed my hair back. This was happiness. This was peace.

"Robin," a soft voice whispered.

My head snapped up, and I looked around, trying to locate the source of the sudden noise. Who's invading my peace?

"Robin," the voice repeated louder.

I turned in a circle before spotting a woman in the distance. The warm air quickly turned frigid, causing me to shiver. The waves crashed together in a roar of chaos as the woman walked closer. My hands began to sweat, and my heart thumped rapidly. Who was this woman? The closer she advanced, the more frequently my name escaped her lips.

"Robin . . . Robin . . . Robin," she called. Suddenly, she appeared directly in front of me with her mouth wide open as if to scream. "Robin!"

My eyes flew open, and I gasped, shooting up in bed. I frantically looked around, trying to place where I was as my heart hammered in my chest and sweat dripped down my back.

"Robin!" my little sister yelled in my face as she jumped on my stomach. "It's time to wake up I said!"

"I'm awake, Dawn," I assured her in the hopes that she would lower her voice. This wasn't the first time I'd had that dream, and I tried to shake it off, but the faceless woman haunted my thoughts.

"Get up, get up, get up!" Dawn sang in her usual bubbly demeanor.

"Okay, okay, okay," I sang back, pushing her off me onto the bed. She giggled, and I couldn't help but smile at her six-year-old innocence. "Go eat. I'll be there in a minute."

She took off out of the room we shared, and I sighed heavily as I tore myself away from the warmth of my blankets. Pots banged around in the kitchen, and I cheered up, remembering it was pancake day. I pulled on my slippers and waltzed into the breakfast nook off the kitchen. My mom set a plate down in front of me, and I was surrounded by the sweet fragrance of the pancakes that sat atop it.

"Good morning, sweetie," she greeted me, kissing the top of my head before joining Dawn and I at the table.

Every Monday, she made a point of cooking breakfast and sitting down to eat with us so our week would start out with 'happiness and love.' She was insistent that a positive start led to a positive end. I wasn't so sure about that logic, but I did appreciate the sentiment behind it and never dreaded Mondays like most kids.

"Good morning," I replied, accompanying the greeting with a yawn as I drowned my food in syrup.

"Where's Daddy?" Dawn asked around a mouthful of eggs.

"He left early for work," Mom answered with a forced smile.

I glanced at her, knowing he'd never come home last night. She would never let Dawn know that though. As much as she tried to show us unconditional love and support, she couldn't make up for the absence of our father. Not for me at least.

He adored Dawn and spoiled her as much as a drunk with no stability could. For some reason, I didn't hold the same place in his heart. I could disappear into the night, and he wouldn't care—maybe he wouldn't even notice—but I'd come to terms with that a long time ago. Why did I need affirmation from someone who had no place in society?

"I won't be able to make it to your game today, Robin. I'm working a double," Mom informed me.

I tried to give her as much grace as I could manage, but it still hurt every time she missed something.

"I understand," I replied with a smile that looked more like a grimace. "Lizzie's coming to watch Dawn after school?"

"Is that even a question?" she replied, amused. "Yes, she is. You'll probably make it home before I do, so don't wait up. You can tell me about your game tomorrow."

"Okay," I said, despite knowing sleep would evade me until she was home.

Dawn took over the conversation for the rest of breakfast, informing us who had a paste-eating problem and what the newest game on the playground was.

*Oh, to be in kindergarten again with no real-world worries.*

Despite the silliness of the topic, Mom and I both listened intently with undivided attention. From the outside, Dawn would appear completely spoiled—and maybe she was in a way—but it was only because she was the glue that held our dysfunctional family together. Without her, we'd be in total disarray.

When we finished eating, I volunteered to clean the kitchen while Mom helped Dawn get ready for school. After washing the dishes, wiping down the counters, and taking out the trash, I rushed to my room to get myself ready for the day.

"If you're ready in the next fifteen minutes, I can give you a ride to school," Mom called out to me.

I made my way to my less than adequate clothing options and pulled out the first things my eyes saw: a pair of dark skinny jeans and my favorite light-blue blouse with long puffy sleeves. I pulled on my gray, mid-calf boots then headed to the bathroom.

The front door opened, and I turned to see my dad stumbling in. He was drunk. At eight in the morning. I shook my head, hoping he'd go straight to his room so Dawn wouldn't see the state he was in. He started to walk forward but didn't make it very far before he fell into the wall, knocking down a couple picture frames in the process.

"Are you okay?" I asked warily as I walked towards him. I reached for his arm to help steady him, but he shook me off.

"I'm fine," he snapped. His sour breath wafted over me, and I scrunched my nose in disgust as it was bombarded by the smell of booze.

"Mark!" Mom came up from behind me with heavy disappointment layered in her voice.

"Rebecca!" he mocked before breaking into a fit of laughter.

Mom ground her teeth together. "Mark, go to bed and sleep this off," she said, rubbing her hand across her forehead. "We'll discuss it later."

Dad rolled his eyes theatrically but thankfully didn't cause any more of a scene before slowly making his way to their room. Mom sighed as she knelt to clean up the mess he'd made. I bent down to help, picking up the frames that weren't broken so I could hang them back on the wall.

I examined the last photo in my hand. It was one of the few family photos we had of all four of us. In it, Dawn and I sat on a bench, mid laugh, while Mom looked on with eyes full of adoration. Dad had his hand lovingly rustling Dawn's hair with a subtle smile on his face as he stared directly into the camera.

I couldn't help but notice, as I often did, how different my features were to theirs. Both my parents stood tall and lean with dirty-blond hair and thin lips. Dad had chocolate-brown eyes, an oval-shaped face, and a long nose while Mom had honey-brown eyes, a triangular face, and an upturned nose. Dawn was the perfect mixture of the two of them sporting their dirty-blonde hair and thin lips. She had my dad's eyes and my mom's nose. No one could ever question who her parents were.

Then there was me. I was average height with broad shoulders and a curvy waist. My thick, chestnut-brown hair flowed down my back in waves and my piercing, sky-blue eyes were lined with thick lashes. My heart-shaped face featured high cheekbones, a slender nose with a high arch, and full lips that puckered out on the bottom. I had an olive skin tone that clashed with my family's fair colors. People often joked that I was adopted and, little did they know, I wondered if there was some truth in it. I didn't have the heart to ever bring it up to my mom though.

"I'm sorry, Robin," Mom said, cutting through my thoughts. I shook my head as she threw the remaining glass away.

"Don't apologize for him, Mom. Please. It's not your place, and you do it too often."

She tucked her hair behind her ears and rubbed at her nose as a sniffle escaped her. It pained me to see her look so defeated. "Go finish getting ready. I'll get Dawn rounded up, and we'll wait for you in the car. We might be a little late today."

I wrapped her in my arms, hugging her as tight as I could, then headed to the bathroom. Luckily, I never took very long. I washed my face and brushed my teeth before dealing with the mess atop my head. Deciding I didn't have time to tame it today, I yanked it into a loose bun with a couple shorter layers falling over my cheeks. I gave myself a once over in the mirror, making a face at the mess that stared back.

*It'll have to do.*

I headed for the car, picking up my book bag, jacket, and beanie along the way. Dawn stuck her head out the window, waving and smiling like we were being reunited after a lifetime apart. It warmed me to my core knowing how much love she held for me. I slid into the backseat next to her and buckled us both up.

"I'm mad at you," she informed me, despite still having a big smile on her face.

"You know, most people frown when they're mad," I replied, holding back my own smile. She quickly creased her eyebrows and pouted her lips. "That's much better. So, why are you mad at me?"

"You don't have your necklace on," she answered, her puppy dog eyes cutting through me.

My hand automatically reached towards my chest, and I realized she was right. "Oh, I'm sorry, Dawn."

Guilt ate at me over forgetting my half of the gift I'd gotten for us last Christmas. I struggled to remember to put it on, but Dawn was extremely attached to them. She hadn't missed a day of wearing hers since opening it that winter morning.

I noticed she was smiling at me again and eyed her suspiciously. "You have it don't you?" I accused her with a playful tone.

She giggled as she pulled it out from her jacket pocket. "You left it in the bathroom again, silly!"

She dropped it in my open hand as she grabbed hers from underneath her shirt, connecting the two half hearts to create a full one. Both were sterling silver with our respective birthstone gems lining the top—topaz for me and emerald for Dawn.

"You're such a responsible girl," I said, making her beam proudly. "Thank you for watching out for me."

She leaned over and rested her head against my shoulder.

"Well, someone has to," she replied as serious as could be, and I tried to suppress my amusement. "I love you, little bird."

"I love you too, my sunshine."

I kissed the top of her head then caught my mom's eyes in the rear-view mirror as she watched us. If only it was just the three of us.

# CHAPTER TWO

When I reached Milton High School, the halls were nearly empty. The first bell had already sounded, so I scurried towards my locker, pulling my books out of my bag as I went. As I rounded the corner to the junior hallway, I slammed into a solid barrier, falling back from the impact. My books scattered around, echoing in the deserted space as my backside hit the floor. I groaned as I looked up, a familiar face meeting my eyes.

"Are you okay?" Ben asked as he bent down to pick up my lost items.

I briskly picked myself off the floor, hoping he wouldn't notice the fiery red hue I could feel on my cheeks. "I'm fine, thank you," I replied curtly, avoiding eye contact.

He straightened up, towering above me, and I couldn't help but notice how much he'd grown since we'd last spoken. He had to be six-foot tall now and possessed a well-toned body that matched his size.

"I'm glad I ran into you," he said cheerfully, as if he hadn't heard my less than pleasant tone. He chuckled. "Well, actually, I guess you ran into me."

"Really? Why's that? Finally tired of blowing me off for your hotshot friends?" I finally looked him in the eye, unwavering in my accusation, and he ran his fingers through his long, raven-black hair as he shifted from foot to foot.

"Come on, Robin, don't be like that," he said. "I . . . Well, I want us to be friends again."

"I'm not the one who ruined this friendship, *Benjamin*." I emphasized his full name just to annoy him. "You did."

I nudged past him to put my bag in my locker. After grabbing what I needed for calculus, I closed the metal door and twirled the combination lock. When I turned around, Ben was still there, leaning against the wall. His light-brown skin and amber eyes shone in the sunlight that came from the skylights above us. He'd grown into his once too-wide nose and bushy eyebrows, and I swallowed around the dryness in my throat.

*When did he become so attractive?*

"Aren't you late for class?" I asked him.

"Yeah." He shrugged nonchalantly.

"Then why are you still here?"

"Because I still have your books." He grinned as he held them up.

"You couldn't have told me that *before* I locked my locker?" I scowled as his grin widened.

"Where's the fun in that?" he teased as I yanked my books from his hand.

The second bell chimed loudly, making me groan again. Being late wasn't something I was accustomed to, so I decided to just bring the books with me and walked past Ben.

"Meet me after school so we can talk!" he called out.

"No!" I yelled back without turning to look at him.

* * *

Calculus passed quickly, and luckily, Mrs. Cohen didn't comment on my late arrival. Even so, I made sure to arrive with plenty of time to spare for my next class. I slid into my usual seat at the table I shared with my best friend, Felicity, who was already there setting up our supplies.

"You're here early," she noted. Her first class was right across the hall from the art room whereas mine was on the opposite end of the building, which meant I was usually one of the last students to arrive.

"Yeah, well, I didn't want to be late to a second class," I grumbled, still annoyed at the interaction I'd had with Ben earlier.

Felicity glanced up at me and arched her perfectly sculpted eyebrow in amusement. "Someone is testy this morning." I made a face, and she let out one of her melodious laughs. "Why were you late?"

"A blast from the past came knocking," I replied as I organized our paints by color.

She scrunched up her nose as other students filed into the room. "What?"

"Ben," I clarified, resting my chin on my hands.

"Ah. What happened?" she asked, turning towards me with anticipation.

If Felicity loved anything, it was drama—not because she involved herself in it, but because she was a drama queen on stage and swore that other people's problematic states inspired her when she was acting.

"Nothing really." I shrugged, and she scoffed.

"Oh, come on! I need more information than that."

"All he said was that he was glad we bumped into each other, then he asked me to meet him after school so we could talk."

Her eyes lit up. "Are you going to?"

I gave her a look and shook my head. "No."

"Why not?"

"Why would I?" I asked, not understanding why she'd want me to.

"I don't understand why you wouldn't if he's trying to reach out," she said, her eyes scrutinizing me.

"Because it doesn't erase the past."

"Who's the drama queen now?"

I narrowed my eyes slightly. "I don't see how that's being dramatic. It's true."

"Okay," she replied sarcastically.

"What's your deal?" I asked, folding my arms over my chest.

"I just think you're being stupid."

"Well that's pretty rude."

"But it's true." She watched me intently, her brows furrowing. "For someone who's so levelheaded, you always get super irrational when it comes to him. It doesn't make sense to me. Why are you carrying such a grudge against him still?"

"I'm not," I answered with a scowl.

She rolled her eyes in reply and waved her hand to dismiss my attitude, then continued gesturing widely as she spoke again.

"Listen. Yes, he got to high school and made new friends. And, yes, he made some really poor choices with them and shut you out. But he only cut you off completely when *you* ratted *him* out to his parents. I get that he hurt you when that happened, but you also hurt him. And it's been two years. *Two years,* Robin. He's changed since then and so have you. It doesn't make sense for you to still be this angry. So why are you?"

I looked away, not sure how to answer. People grew up and drifted apart all the time. Our case was nothing special. We were just another classic story of lost friendship. But our last interaction all those years ago had left a hole in my heart that never healed. Ben had been my best friend since kindergarten, and I'd thought I could count on him for anything. I thought he'd always be there for me.

The last words he'd spoken to me that bleak day proved different, though, and they were always in the back of my mind.

*I wish you were dead instead of him*, he'd screamed at me.

I took a deep breath, trying to swallow around the lump that formed in my throat. I'd never told anyone he said that to me. If I had, I'm sure Felicity would be more understanding, but I knew I never would. I didn't know if he meant it or not, but I didn't want anyone to see him differently for it. I still cared enough about him that I'd protect his image.

I couldn't deny that Felicity was right though. He'd grown up since then, so why couldn't I? If he was willing to talk, why not give him a chance? It might even bring me a little bit of peace.

I felt Felicity watching me, waiting for an answer.

"I don't know exactly," I finally told her, kicking my foot against the leg of my stool. "I honestly don't."

Felicity smiled wide, a reaction I was not expecting at all.

"What's that for?" I asked warily.

"You liked him." She winked at me, and my mouth fell open.

"I did not!" My cheeks flushed with intense heat, not knowing how she'd made that mental leap.

"You *still* like him."

"I do not! I don't even know him anymore."

"He likes you," she said with a sly smile, and I nearly fell over in my chair.

"No, he doesn't!"

"He asks about you all the time."

"No, he doesn't!" I repeated as the heat rose to my ears.

Felicity's grin lit up her entire face as she enjoyed my humiliation. "Yes, he does. Whenever we run into each other at parties, or when the girls' and boys' teams are switching off on the court or—"

"Felicity, please stop!"

She pursed her lips as if thinking it over. "Okay," she finally said before slipping in a final comment as the bell rang. "But I wasn't lying."

Ms. Meers walked to the front of the room, her bold ensemble catching everyone's attention. She clapped her hands to silence the class as she began to speak.

"Alright, guys, we're going to paint some portraits. I've already stocked each station with all the appropriate necessities, and you'll be paired with the individual at your table. Today, one of you will be the muse for the other and tomorrow you'll switch. Any questions?"

When no one answered, she turned on some upbeat music and settled down to her art magazines, signaling us to get started.

"You can paint today if you want," Felicity offered.

I nodded happily, knowing she was giving me a way to relax after our conversation. Painting was a favorite pastime of mine. It was the only way I could drain my mind completely or, on the flip side, hone in on a thought and work through it effortlessly. Painting was my therapy time.

As the hour passed, my brushstrokes slowly brought Felicity's face to life on the white canvas, but it was hard to do her justice. She possessed the sort of beauty any girl would dream of having. With her petite body and delicate facial features, I often compared her to a fairy.

I painted the porcelain skin of her V-shaped face and highlighted it with light freckles. Then I looked down thoughtfully at my paints, mixing some together to accurately capture the shade of her auburn hair, which was cut just below her jawline. Once that was done, I grabbed a smaller brush and highlighted the delicate side bangs that framed her forest-green eyes. Before I knew it, Ms. Meers was announcing our time was over, and we needed to begin cleaning up.

"Place your canvases on the drying rack. If you didn't finish, you'll have time to complete them later this week." She looked at each one as they were brought up, giving feedback.

Felicity stretched as I got up from my stool to bring my painting to the front.

"Oh, my!" Ms. Meers exclaimed as I placed it on the drying rack. "Beautiful work, Robin. You've brought Felicity to life there."

"Thank you, Ms. Meers." I smiled happily, used to her kind words about my work. I did well in all my classes, but art was something I naturally excelled at. I didn't have to work hard to accomplish something great with colors and imagination.

Felicity helped me clean the mess I'd made, then we left for our next class together. As we walked down the hall, people greeted her every couple of steps, and she beamed infectiously as she returned each one. It never failed to amaze me how many people she knew. She held a high status of popularity due to her ability to befriend anyone and everyone. It also helped that she was president of the drama club, involved in two varsity sports, and her parents were on the town council.

Despite that popularity, though, she was extremely humble and compassionate—it was one thing I loved about her. She was single-handedly responsible for the school council passing a zero-tolerance bullying rule and had worked hard to help maintain that standard. It wasn't an easy job, but she did her best to make sure that all the students at Milton had a good experience there.

Every now and then, people threw greetings out to me as well, which I answered with a timid smile or nod of the head. Some people thought I swam in Felicity's shadow, but I honestly couldn't care less. I was content with where I stood in the school hierarchy, but that never stopped Felicity from urging me to be more interactive with people.

When I opened my locker, a folded-up piece of paper slipped out, falling to the floor. I picked it up as Felicity hovered over my shoulder.

"What's that?" she asked, opening her own locker as I unfolded it.

I shook my head, immediately recognizing the handwriting.

## Will you PLEASE meet me after school?

"Ben," I said with a sigh as I folded the note back up and tucked it into my binder. "He asked me to meet him after school again."

After grabbing her physics book, she closed her locker. "Have you changed your mind?"

"I don't know." I rubbed my hand over my face and sighed again.

"Look. I know I teased you before, and I personally think you should at least hear him out, but don't stress about it. If you really don't want to, he'll just have to accept that. But if you do, well, I'm here for it."

I offered her a small smile. "Thank you."

"I'm in your corner, girl," she said, throwing me a wink before we made our way to physics and settled in.

As I sat there listening to Felicity gossip, I suddenly broke out in a cold sweat, and a chill raced up my spine. Goosebumps raised on my arms, and my stomach churned slightly. I glanced around the room, trying to shake off the odd feeling, when I noticed Mr. Garcia speaking to a boy I didn't recognize.

A well-fitted, V-neck, black T-shirt revealed his tanned complexion and lean, muscular frame. He appeared rigid and serious with his brows furrowed deeply and lips down-turned in a seemingly permanent scowl. His shirt made his light-blue eyes pop, and his shaggy, dirty-blond hair fell over his temples in a way that highlighted his strong jawline and prominent cheekbones.

He glanced my way and our eyes met. My heart hammered in my chest as his piercing stare seemed to make its way to my very soul. I didn't know him, but there was a strange sense of familiarity anyway. It seemed to fill me up, becoming all consuming.

He cocked his head to the side as he appraised me. Chills continued to spread through me, and my body spasmed with a violent shiver. I tore my gaze away from his, breaking the spell.

*What just happened?*

I nudged Felicity, interrupting her conversation with one of our classmates.

"Who is that?" I asked, nodding my head his way.

She looked up to see who I was talking about.

"*That* is Matthew Alastair," she replied, looking him up and down. "He started almost two weeks ago after Christmas break."

"Two weeks?" I repeated. We didn't go to a very large school, so new students were always a big deal. "How have I not noticed him before?"

Felicity shrugged. "He hasn't been very consistent with being in class. And I know he was trying to get his whole schedule changed for some reason."

"Have you talked to him?" I kept my voice low and my eyes down as Mr. Garcia directed Matthew to a desk two seats away from me.

"Not yet. Julie and Annette both tried last week, and they said he was polite but short and that he seemed completely disinterested in them." She let out a little laugh, probably imagining their comical flirting being shut down. "Julie said he had to be gay to pass her up."

I snorted, distracted for just a second. "Sounds like Julie." I peeked at the new kid from the corner of my eyes, then blushed when I saw him still staring—well, more like glaring—at me. "He seems . . . menacing."

Felicity wiggled her eyebrows. "He seems yummy."

I rolled my eyes at her. "Looks aren't everything. Besides, have you seen that scowl on his face? He seems so angry."

"Maybe he just hasn't adjusted yet. Being the new kid can't be easy. Besides, you shouldn't judge a book by its cover."

"True." I knew she was right but still felt a strange discomfort with him being in the room. It was like pins and needles were trying to claw through my skin from the inside out.

"I bet he just needs some help getting adjusted to Milton High," she continued, tapping her finger against her chin. Her face lit up, and I knew what was coming next. "I'm going to introduce myself and help him out!"

"And if he doesn't want your help?" I asked just for argument's sake. If Felicity had her eyes set on him as a project, I knew she wouldn't give up until she was satisfied that she'd done everything she could to assist him.

She grinned. "Then I'll ask again tomorrow." She stood to go over to Matthew but plopped right back down as the bell rang. "After class."

As Mr. Garcia discussed Newton's second law of motion, my arm hairs stood on end. I looked towards Matthew then instantly regretted it when I saw him watching me with narrowed eyes. I quickly averted my gaze as the familiar feeling of heat crept across my face. I could feel his fervent eyes lingering on me as class progressed, making me squirm in my seat.

*Who is this guy? Why does he make me feel so unsettled? And why does he feel the need to glare at me?*

I wasn't sure I wanted to know.

# CHAPTER THREE

Felicity never did get the chance to talk to Matthew after class. As soon as the bell rang, he was up from his seat and out the door. He shared government class with me as well, and we repeated the same pattern there that we had in physics. I was on edge the entire time and eager to be away from him by the time lunch came around.

As I walked towards my locker to put my things away, I saw Ben leaning against it. His infectious smile lit up his face as I got closer, and I internally groaned. I was over this day.

"Hey!" he exclaimed in his usual bubbly demeanor.

Just then, Felicity came around the corner behind him. When she saw us, she stopped and raised her brows, mouthing the word 'help.' It took me a second to realize she was asking if I needed to be rescued. I shook my head very slightly, thinking about her earlier words. There was no need to be rude when he was just trying to be nice.

"Hi," I said, finally acknowledging his presence as I closed the distance between us.

Felicity stayed where she was and began chatting with someone nearby, closely monitoring the situation in case I changed my mind and she needed to swoop in with an excuse to pull me away.

"Did you get my note?" he asked, shoving his hands in his jean pockets.

It'd always been a nervous tick of his when we were younger, and it made me pause. I studied his face, and realized maybe he actually *was* nervous. It softened my hard exterior just enough to be a bit nicer to him.

"I did," I said in a kinder tone.

He must've noticed because his smile widened. "So? Will you?" When I didn't answer, he pressed on hopefully. "Will you meet me after school to talk?"

"Why now?"

His brow furrowed. "Why now what?"

"Why do you want to talk to me now? What's different today than the last two years?"

He chewed on his bottom lip and ran his hand through his hair before pushing it over his shoulders. His mannerisms hadn't changed at all, so I could tell he was wrestling with telling me something. I waited as patiently as I could as he opened his mouth then shut it again. Finally, he cleared his throat and took a deep breath.

"Therapy," he finally admitted, and my eyebrows raised into my hairline.

"Therapy," I repeated slowly.

He nodded, shifting from one foot to the other. "I've wanted to talk to you ever since we had our fight, but I just couldn't bring myself to. I was angry and couldn't figure out how to forgive you. Then I was ashamed and couldn't figure out how *you* could forgive *me*. I had a lot of issues I needed to work through, and I really didn't want to come to you before I was able to apologize and mean it."

I licked my lips, unsure what to say. Ben had always been confident and collected. Seeing him so unsure of himself was strange and finding out he'd been struggling behind closed doors—even while playing such a strong leadership role in school—was unexpected. It was something I'd never expected from him.

"If you'll give me a chance," he said, "I'd like to try to make things right."

He rubbed his lips together, and his eyes drifted away from mine. He suddenly looked extremely unsure of himself, and I couldn't imagine how hard it'd been for him to confide in me that he was going to therapy. His desire to talk—to reconnect—seemed genuine and I couldn't think of a reason not to give him the chance he was asking for.

After another moment of hesitation, I nodded. "Okay."

"You'll meet me after school?"

"I'll meet you after school." His eyes sparkled as his face radiated with joy, and I couldn't help but smile back. "But I have a basketball game today, so I have to be at the gym by five."

"I'll take what I can get," he said, throwing his hands up. "Besides, I have a basketball game after you, so I have to be in the gym by five as well."

"Oh, yeah," I mumbled. I didn't know what else to say, so before the silence could stretch uncomfortably, I waved to Felicity. "There's Felicity. I better go if we're going to have enough time to eat."

Ben looked over his shoulder and waved at Felicity as she walked up to us. "Hey, Felicity!"

"What's up, Ben?" she replied, jumping up to try to reach his outstretched hand for a high five. He laughed when she didn't even come close.

"Just have to grow a couple more inches," he teased as she playfully huffed and crossed her arms.

My eyes darted back and forth as I watched their banter. I knew they were acquaintances, but it was weird to see how effortlessly they interacted with one another. Maybe they were better friends than Felicity had ever let on.

A couple of Ben's baseball buddies called out to him, and he nodded in acknowledgement. Still smiling brightly, he said, "Well, I'll see you guys later," and turned to go.

The second he was out of sight, Felicity pounced.

"Okay, tell me everything!" she demanded as we walked towards the cafeteria.

"You first," I countered, arching a brow.

She looked over in surprise. "What?"

"How long have you and Ben been so buddy-buddy?"

"A while," she admitted, pushing her bangs out of her eyes as we walked into the cafeteria and grabbed premade plates of spaghetti and garlic bread. "Are you angry?"

We sat at our usual table before I replied. "No, I'm not angry. I don't get to dictate who you're friends with. But why didn't you tell me?"

"I knew it was a sore spot for you. I didn't want to rub it in your face or make you uncomfortable."

She seemed uncharacteristically worried about my reaction, but I really wasn't angry. I understood she'd kept it from me because she cared about my feelings. I couldn't be upset about that, so I offered her a reassuring smile.

"Thank you for trying to spare me, but you didn't have to."

She looked like she disagreed but didn't argue. "So, are you going to tell me what happened then?"

I gave her a quick summary, leaving out the part about Ben being in therapy. That wasn't something for me to share.

"He's been working on himself this whole time, and here I was holding a grudge and being mad." I shook my head. Sometimes reality had a way of slapping you in the face with a wake-up call, and this was definitely one of those times. "It seems so stupid now."

Felicity nodded. "Can't argue with you there." I rolled my eyes, and she shrugged her shoulders. "Just being honest."

"Just being blunt," I corrected, and she grinned.

As we finished our lunch, we started talking about our game that evening and the drama that went down at a party Felicity had attended over the weekend. I got invites to those parties all the time but had no interest in going. I tried to keep most of my weekends open for Dawn and me to do things together.

"I'll be right back," Felicity announced suddenly.

I watched as she strutted to one of the tables in the back, stopping right in front of Matthew Alastair. He stared at her with cold eyes that cut through me but didn't seem to bother her at all. His face remained stoic as she bounced around, gesturing widely with her arms as she spoke. Then she turned ed towards me and pointed.

My breath caught in my throat as Matthew's eyes met mine once again. Luckily, he looked back away as Felicity demanded his attention. They exchanged a couple of words, his facial expression relaxing ever so slightly. Then he nodded his head once, stood up, and headed towards the door as Felicity glided back to me.

"Wow, he's a hard cookie to crack," she said with a little laugh.

"He doesn't scare you?"

She snorted as she sat down. "Why would he?"

"I don't know. I just get a bad feeling about him." I couldn't explain how he made me feel, but I knew it wasn't normal.

"He's a little rough around the edges," she replied, "but I think he just needs a friend. Or maybe some guidance."

I shrugged as I rubbed my lips together. She was so trusting, but sometimes I worried it verged on naivety.

"What did you say to him anyway?" I asked.

"I just welcomed him to the school and introduced myself. I told him I understood how hard it can be to be the new student but that he'd adjust quickly, and if he needed anything, I would help. Oh, and I told him he already had two friends in this school."

"Two?" I asked warily, realizing what the pointing had been about.

"Yes, two," Felicity repeated. "Me and you. Stop judging and be nice if he tries to talk to you."

"Yes, Mom," I said mockingly, already knowing he wouldn't be conversing with me any time soon.

"I swear, you're on a roll today!" she exclaimed. I grinned as she looked at the clock on the wall. "Well, I must bid you adieu. Drama class is calling my name."

"Have fun."

"Oh, of course," she replied, giving a little curtsy, and I snorted. "I'll see you at practice?"

"Yep!"

"And you'll tell me how it went with Ben?"

"Maybe."

"Whatever. You know you will." I shrugged, and she narrowed her eyes. "You better tell me."

"We'll see," I responded coyly.

"Robin," she groaned, and I laughed.

"Yes, I'll tell you. Now get to class."

"Yes, Mom," she replied, mocking my earlier comment. "Bye!"

I shook my head as she pranced out of the room, then stood to take myself to Spanish. Only a couple more classes to get through.

# CHAPTER FOUR

My stomach churned with anxiety for the remainder of the day as I thought about meeting Ben. I typically had a more positive and laid-back demeanor, but I was no good in awkward situations. Realistically, I knew it wouldn't be that bad, but my mind was picturing it as the end of the world. It didn't help that Matthew was in both my classes after lunch, and we kept making eye contact.

I tried to keep my gaze forward, but my curiosity and yearning to understand why I found him so off-putting kept winning out. So, I would glance over and instantly regret it. We shared our free period as well but most every junior and senior did. He had gone from being nonexistent to omnipresent in my life and I didn't like it.

I spent my free period in the library, as I often did, making sure to finish all my homework so I wouldn't have to worry about it after our game. When I was done, I looked up at the decorative rock waterfall that'd been installed at the back of the library. I chose to sit across from it so I could hear the burble of the water as it glided over the rocks and hit the bottom. The tranquility of it always mesmerized me and relaxed me even after the worst of days.

As I watched it, a cool feeling crept over me. It started in my hands and feet but slowly trailed through the rest of my body. The sound of the water intensified in my head, encompassing all my senses. I stared at it intently as the tingling in my body heightened, then the water at the bottom of the bowl seemed to still.

"Hey, Robin."

The voice broke through my stupor, and the cool feeling left my body as suddenly as it had come. I glanced up and saw Ben, his hands in his pockets again.

"Hey," I replied.

"You okay?" he asked. "You looked like you were in a different world."

"Yeah, I'm good," I murmured, despite wondering what had just happened. Looking around, I realized I was the last student there. "Did the bell already ring?"

"About fifteen minutes ago. I waited for you at your locker, but you never came. I almost thought you had changed your mind."

He tried to hide it, but I could tell he'd been hurt by that thought.

"No, I haven't," I assured him as I stood up and gathered my things. "I just got distracted. I didn't realize school was over. Let me drop these off at my locker, then we can go." I stopped as a thought crossed my mind. "Where *are* we going?"

"Wherever you want," Ben replied. "Or we can stay here if you're more comfortable with that."

"After the day I've had, this is the last place I want to be," I told him, hearing the defeat in my voice.

Ben opened his mouth, but I shook my head ever so slightly. I wasn't ready to confide in him yet. His face drooped slightly, but he quickly masked it with a smile.

"Do you want to go to the park down the street? The one we used to go to all the time?" he asked.

"Sure."

I put my books in my locker before grabbing my phone and wrist wallet from my backpack. There was no point in bringing the whole thing home if I didn't have to. I pulled on my jacket, then placed my hat over my ears to protect them from the harsh winter wind before we headed outside.

The parking lot was almost empty, but Ben waved at the few guys who were still there hanging out by their cars. The snow that had piled up over the weekend was already melting, so we trudged through the slop as we headed down the street. It was only a five-minute walk to the park but neither of us spoke on the way.

I sat on one of the swings, letting the wind push me gently. Ben chose a semi dry spot in the pebbles next to me, leaning back against the swing's structure with his ankles crossed. For a moment, the only sound was the whining wind as it encased us.

"I bring Dawn here all the time," I finally said.

"Really?" he asked, and I nodded. "I haven't been here since . . ." He stopped to think. "Well, since we had our fight here, I guess. It just never really felt the same after that."

"I'm sorry," I murmured. It wasn't the first time I'd apologized since it happened, but I'd stopped trying long ago.

He snapped his head up and looked at me with a burning intensity. "Do not apologize to me about that."

I was taken aback by the anger in his voice. I opened my mouth to ask why he was so upset, but he held his hand up to stop me.

"You did absolutely nothing wrong," he said. "*I* did. I was stupid. So stupid." He slammed his fist into the ground, then stood and started to pace with his hands interlaced behind his neck. "You were always so much more mature than I was. So levelheaded, so smart about real life situations. You were just looking out for me, and there I was acting like a jackass with 'friends' who could've gotten me killed."

My eyes grew wide as I listened, not expecting our conversation to jump to this so quickly, but I didn't dare interrupt him as he continued.

"I didn't appreciate what you did for me back then. It's no excuse, but I was young and definitely stupid, so I was consumed by unwarranted anger instead." He stopped pacing and crouched down on one knee so he was eye level with me.

"I said some *terrible* things to you, Robin, and I've regretted it for a long time. I know I hurt you, and I can't change that no matter how much I wish I could. But I am *so sorry*. I'm so sorry for everything I said and all the pain I caused you. You have zero obligation to forgive me or be my friend again, but I need you to know how sorry I am for everything."

He looked so distraught that I had to fight back the urge to hug him as my emotions ran wild. I didn't realize how much I needed that apology until he said it. I always knew I did the right thing by going to his parents about his good-for-nothing, alcohol-drinking, law-breaking friends, but I'd never realized the guilt I'd been carrying around for it. His apology lifted a weight off my shoulders I didn't even know I was carrying.

"And I also need to thank you," he said, his eyes glazing over. "If you hadn't intervened, I don't think I would be here right now."

He was quiet for so long I wasn't sure he was going to continue. I opened my mouth to say something, but he held up his hand, stopping me once again.

"The night after my parents had found out about everything, I was supposed to go to a party with Mick and James," he said, and all the air left my lungs as if I'd been punched.

"The party where . . ." I trailed off, unable to finish, and he nodded.

He swallowed loudly. "Since I was on house arrest and being watched like a hawk, I couldn't even sneak out like I wanted to."

"Thank God," I whispered.

"I don't know if you ever knew the specifics, but they got wasted and wrapped their car around a tree. Mick died on impact but James . . . He suffered a lot before passing." Ben took a deep breath to compose himself as his voice began to waver. "If I'd been with them . . . If I'd been in that car . . ." He looked up at the sky, then cleared his throat. "So, anyway, thank you."

I inhaled shakily then let it out slowly as tears pooled in my eyes. I'd never known he was supposed to go to that party with them. He'd told me he was going but it never crossed my mind who was taking him. If I hadn't ratted him out, he could've died that night. I could've lost my best friend in a much more terrible way.

Without giving it a second thought, I got off the swing and knelt in front of him, wrapping my arms around his stomach tightly and burying my face against his warm chest. He stiffened for just a moment then hugged me back fiercely with his chin resting on the top of my head. The cold ground seeped through my pants, but I didn't care. All I cared about was the boy in front of me who'd gone through so much turmoil.

I wasn't sure how long we stayed like that but once my tears stopped, I finally pulled away. I looked up at him as the wind took hold of his hair, whipping it around.

"I forgive you," I told him as he swiped at his wet cheeks.

"You do?"

"Yes."

"That means a lot. Thank you."

"No. Thank *you* for apologizing."

"I should've done it a long time ago."

I shrugged slightly. "I'm glad you waited until you were ready. It means more." I paused for a moment. "Hey, Ben?"

"Yeah?"

"I'm happy you're still here."

"I am too," he replied quietly as he wrapped me in another strong hug, this one much shorter.

When I pulled back, I stared into his eyes and smiled softly. In that moment, I knew we were friends again. We'd have to work our way back up to the relationship we used to have, but this was a good start.

* * *

"Good luck in your game," Ben said as we were about to part to go to our separate locker rooms in the gym.

"You too," I told him, raising my hand up in an awkward wave.

He grinned at the gesture before walking away, and I bit the inside of my lip as I watched him go.

"He's such a hunk," someone said, and I turned to see three of my teammates heading my way.

"Hey, guys," I said as I followed them into the locker room.

"Hi," Amara replied quietly with her usual timid smile as Alli and Jordan continued gushing about Ben.

"I haven't seen you talk to him in ages," Jordan commented, her light-brown hair bouncing in its ponytail.

"Because they haven't been *friends* in ages," Alli said with an obvious 'duh' in her tone.

I pursed my lips, remembering the gossip that spread when we'd had our falling out. Something told me we'd be a hot topic once again when word got out about our rekindled friendship.

"Then why was she talking to him now?" Jordan shot back.

I rolled my eyes at Amara, and she grinned as the other two girls turned towards me.

"Well?" Alli demanded in a playful tone as she wiggled her eyebrows up and down. "Spill the beans!"

I pulled my jersey over my head. "Fine. Consider yourselves lucky to have the juicy details before anyone else. Ben and I are friends again."

They both stood there waiting for me to continue and groaned when they realized that's all I was going to say. I did my best to not feed the gossip mill if I could help it, and they knew that.

"That's really all we get?" Jordan asked.

"That's really all I got," I replied, and she groaned again.

"You're no fun," Alli said, and I shrugged.

"Sorry," I responded.

They started to converse amongst themselves as more members of the team filed in. I finished changing, removed my necklace, and sat down on a bench to tie my sneakers.

"Ben is sweet," Amara murmured, sitting down next to me as she braided her jet-black hair. "He always includes me in our tribal events because he knows I won't go alone."

I smiled. "Sounds like Ben."

"He talks about you a lot," she said. I glanced over at her, wanting to ask for more information, but decided some things were better left unknown. "I'm happy he has you back."

Before I could say anything else, someone attacked me from behind with a hug and Amara slid away.

"Hi, Felicity," I acknowledged without having to turn around to see who it was.

"I've been *dying* waiting to see you! I was going to ask how it went with Ben but, from what I hear, you two made up!" she said, basically squealing with excitement.

My mouth fell open as I looked at her. "Seriously? That quick?" I shook my head.

"The team has big mouths." She shrugged as she changed. "But you have to give me more details. I need word for word."

"Later, okay?"

Her red lips puckered, and she crossed her arms. "Fine. But if I die from a lack of information, I'm blaming you."

"You're such a drama queen."

"Thank you!" she exclaimed, her eyes lighting up at my unintended compliment.

"You're ridiculous," I said as I pulled out my phone.

I had texts from my mom and Lizzie, both wishing me good luck in my game. Lizzie had a bunch of emojis added to hers, and I smiled, knowing it was probably Dawn's doing. I put it away quickly as Coach Mayfield came in and started talking, pumping us up for our game against the Sentinel Bears.

"We are 11–1, ladies. Let's keep up that momentum and get that W!" she was saying when we heard the warning buzzer go off—our signal to get onto the court. "Time to warm up! Let's go!"

The game got off to a good start with Felicity scoring our first basket, and we held that small lead until after halftime. The third quarter was more intense with both teams scoring one after the other. Our team played like a well-oiled machine as we passed the ball effortlessly around our opponents. Despite that, they were up by two going into the final quarter, and time kept running down with neither team scoring. As the clock hit the three-minute mark, Coach Mayfield called for a timeout, so we ran up to her, sweating and panting.

"Amara, step in for June. Nancy, you switch out with Rachel," she instructed, trying to give us our best chance at scoring just one more time before the buzzer rang. "Three minutes left, girls. Go out there and push it! Get the ball in that net before the clock runs out."

The referee blew his whistle, signaling the end of our huddle, and we ran back onto the court before time started ticking down again.

"Two, two!" I called out, signaling what play to do.

Felicity dribbled the ball out of reach of the girl guarding her before passing it to Amara. They played the keep-away game between the two of them as Nancy and Tamika kept their girls away. The crowd was in an uproar, yelling and cheering anxiously as the clock hit thirty seconds.

Amara ran the ball in right under the basket. All five of the Sentinel girls rushed towards her, and she threw the ball in between them to where I stood unguarded behind the three-point line. I jumped up and launched the ball into the air as the buzzer rang out. Silence filled the gym as all eyes watched the ball in anticipation of its landing point.

*Swish.*

My team swarmed me, screaming excitedly. We'd won the game by one point. The gym echoed with the celebration of both the players and the spectators in the stands, and I happily joined in. Once things settled down, we lined up to high five the other team then headed to the locker room as the boys made their way onto the court for warm-up.

Coach Mayfield was thrilled with our performance, praising us endlessly. "That was an excellent game, girls! Way to drive it at the end! Keep this up and we'll definitely have a spot in the championship tournament. Now, get cleaned up and go support the boys' team."

We were all a bundle of energy, yapping loudly as we showered and changed. The adrenaline still hadn't worn off by the time we went out and sat in the front row to watch the boys' game. When it began, we cheered as obnoxiously as we could. Ben was one of the five starters, and he made sure we knew why as he racked up eighteen of the team's thirty points. He was a strong player and worked cohesively with each of his teammates. There was no doubt in my mind that he'd be nominated for MVP this season.

Their game came to an end with another win, and they all jogged off the court in an ecstatic, sweaty mess. The crowd slowly began to disperse, and I told my teammates goodnight as Felicity and I headed out. She drove me home, discussing the games the entire time. I thanked her as we pulled up into my driveway then headed inside. When I opened the door, I was hit with the sweet aroma of home-made food.

"Hey, Lizzie," I called out as I pulled off my jacket and boots.

She peeked around the corner and gave me a warm smile. "Hi, honey. How did your game go?"

I went into the kitchen and saw that a plate had been made up for me already.

"We won," I replied as I grabbed my food. "This looks delicious."

"Your sister sure thought so. She had seconds and then thirds!" She shook her head in bewilderment, and I grinned. "I don't know where she puts it all."

"Sounds about right." I shook my head then sat down at the table as Lizzie began cleaning the dishes.

She was my mom's oldest and dearest friend, and I couldn't remember a time in my life when she wasn't around. She came from a wealthier family, so she didn't have to work, but instead of being lazy, she took the opportunity to offer herself up as a babysitter when we needed help. During basketball season, that was often, but she seemed to look forward to it.

With her purple-streaked hair and heavy eye makeup, she was the polar opposite of my mom, but somehow it worked for them. Their differences seemed to bring out the best in each other, and I was thankful my mom had someone to confide in when she couldn't say certain things to me.

"I can finish the dishes," I offered, but she declined.

"You just sit there and relax. I don't mind taking care of you kids. You know that."

I nodded and said, "Yes ma'am. Did Dad go to work tonight?"

"As far as I know, yes."

"Good. Maybe last night was just a fluke then." I was sure my mom told her what had happened. "He'd been doing good there for a while. I don't know what caused him to go off and drink again."

Lizzie didn't say anything, so I glanced over at her, and she conveniently turned away to put some plates in the cabinet. She knew something but wasn't going to tell me.

"I'm sure it'll be okay," she said instead. I narrowed my eyes slightly, trying to read into her comment. "But you need to get ready for bed before your mom gets home."

I didn't push the topic, despite how curious I was. Instead, I gave her a hug before heading to my room. I quietly got into my pajamas then leaned over Dawn's sleeping figure. She looked so peaceful with her small mouth barely parted and her hair tucked under her head. This little girl was my whole world. I smiled down at her, giving her a quick kiss on the forehead before getting into my own bed and snuggling down with a good book.

Mom came home two hours later, and the sound of her and Lizzie conversing in the living room soothed me. I let out a loud yawn and put my book down as my eyes began to close, sending me off to dream world.

# CHAPTER FIVE

"You look tired," Ben remarked as he sat down to join Felicity and me at our lunch table.

"Is everyone going to tell me that today?" I grumbled, not even questioning why he was sitting with us.

I rested my head on my arms and closed my eyes. The image of the woman by the dark water flashed before them, giving me a headache. It wasn't enough that I'd dreamt about her again—she captivated my mind while awake as well.

"Ignore her. She's just grumpy," Felicity said around a mouthful of food.

"Yeah, well, you try getting almost no sleep two nights in a row." I sighed, rubbing my eyes as they burned from being so dry.

"Everything okay at home?" Ben asked, concerned as always. Of course, he knew firsthand how difficult my dad could be, witnessing more than his fair share of our complicated family dynamics.

"Everything's good," I replied. "I've just had this strange dream the last couple nights. It's really eerie and just leaves me feeling . . . off. I've had it before too and it's always the same exact thing."

"Want to tell us about it?" Felicity asked. "Maybe it'll make you feel better."

"I doubt it."

"Worth a shot anyway," Ben said.

"Okay, well." I stopped to gather my thoughts as I tried to figure out how to explain it. "It starts with me standing by a body of water. Maybe the ocean? I'm not sure. But it's beautiful. The water is so soothing, the moon is shining, the sand is warm between my toes. It's just really, really peaceful."

"That doesn't sound so bad," Felicity said.

"It's not. It's what always comes next," I replied.

"Which is?" she asked.

I opened my mouth to answer, but a small tingling ran through my stomach. I glanced around and saw Matthew hesitating near our table. Felicity and Ben followed my gaze and Felicity beamed.

"Hey, Matthew!" she said happily. "Did you want to sit by us?"

"No," he replied, his voice flat, before promptly stalking away.

"Wonder what that was about," Ben commented, his brows furrowed.

"I think he was listening to our conversation," I said.

"Maybe he was just trying to work up the nerve to talk to us," Felicity responded.

"If that's the case, why didn't he take you up on your offer to sit?" I asked.

"Maybe he's shy."

"I don't think that's it."

"Well, we wouldn't know because you keep scaring him off."

"I do not!" I exclaimed.

"He probably senses your hostile vibes."

"I am *not* hostile! I'm just a little wary of him, is all."

"Why?" Ben asked.

"I'm really not sure," I admitted.

"She has no good reason." Felicity stated. Before I could argue, she said, "Anyway, what happens next in your dream?"

"Oh, uh—" I thought about it more before answering. "Someone starts calling my name and when I look around, there's this woman standing far off in the distance. The second I see her, the whole atmosphere changes. The air gets really cold, and the water starts crashing around like a storm's about to hit. The woman keeps saying my name as she gets closer then all of a sudden, she's directly in front of me with her mouth wide open and she screams my name. Then I wake up."

They stared at me with wide eyes.

"Yeah, that's a little creepy," Felicity admitted. "What's she look like?"

"I don't know. I can't actually *see* her. It's like she's there but there's no solid features, just her shape," I explained. "I know it sounds weird, but I feel like she's trying to tell me something. There's something almost familiar about her."

"Even though you don't know anything about her," Felicity said, and I nodded.

"Maybe she's a spirit trying to communicate with you," Ben suggested, and I looked over at him with a blank stare.

"That's really helpful. Thank you," I said with a bite of sarcasm.

"I'm serious," he replied defensively. "You know my people believe in the spirit world. To us, it's the same as the real world. We can access all things spiritual as easily as we can climb a mountain or feel the wind on our faces."

I looked down and rubbed my lips together. "I'm sorry. I know you were just trying to help. I didn't mean to offend you, and I really didn't mean anything by it. I wasn't trying to dishonor your beliefs or anything."

"I know. Don't sweat it," he said, nudging my arm. "Just get the grump gone."

"I'll try."

"What if I go bribe one of the lunch ladies to give me an extra slice of chocolate cake for you?" he asked.

"Yeah, right," Felicity scoffed as she scraped the last of her piece of cake from the plate. "They're stingy as hell with these."

"Want to make a bet?" Ben challenged with a mischievous gleam in his eye.

Felicity looked him over with pursed lips before smiling slyly. "Fine. If you don't get it, you have to stand up on a table in the center of the cafeteria and profess your love for dancing while doing the hokey pokey."

I choked on the piece of food in my mouth as a laugh escaped me. "Oh, I'd love to see that."

"And if I *do* get it," Ben shot back, "you have to tell the entire audience at your next production that you wet the bed when you dream about pandas."

I laughed again as Felicity turned bright red.

"That only happened once," she muttered, "and I was seven."

"So, do we have a bet?" Ben asked, holding out his hand.

Felicity looked at it for a second, then shook it. "Have fun dancing," she said.

Ben grinned widely as he headed off towards the kitchen.

"You don't think he's really going to get it, do you?" Felicity asked, turning towards me so I could see the worry in her eyes.

I suppressed my smile as I shrugged my shoulders. We both watched the kitchen door intently, waiting for Ben to reemerge.

"No!" Felicity gasped, throwing her hands over her face. I laughed loudly as Ben presented me with a piece of moist cake. "How did you do that?"

"I have my ways," Ben replied with a wink. "So, when's your next production? I need to make sure I get a good seat."

Felicity crossed her arms, refusing to answer, so I grinned wickedly and told him, "Next Saturday."

"Perfect!" Ben exclaimed, and Felicity groaned.

I happily ate my cake, listening as they continued their banter until the bell rang.

"Can I walk you to class?" Ben asked after Felicity marched away from us.

"Um, yeah, I guess. If you want."

"Cool. I was thinking we could hang out outside of school again." He saw my hesitant look and raced to clarify. "I mean, we don't have any classes together and lunch is only forty-five minutes, so we really don't have any time to do anything or talk. Plus, you're always with Felicity at lunch. But if you don't want to that's totally fine. I mean, I'd like to get to spend more time with you, but if you don't want to—"

"Ben," I said, cutting him off. He looked down at me sheepishly with his hands in his pockets. "It's not that I don't want to. I just don't have a lot of free time after school. When I don't have games, I'm usually babysitting Dawn."

"I could help you with that!" he offered. "You know I love that kid."

I smiled as I remembered how they used to play together when she was just a toddler. Ben had been Dawn's favorite person back then.

"I appreciate it, but my dad wouldn't like it very much if he came home and found you there," I told him, which was true, but I also knew how sporadic my dad's mood could be. I never knew how he was going to act or what state he would be in when he got home. So it was easier to just never have people over.

"What about weekends?" Ben asked persistently.

"During basketball season, I try to leave those for family time since I don't get to see my mom much during the week," I replied.

Ben nodded, his face thoughtful. "What about home game days? We could hang out beforehand like we did yesterday."

"I usually go over to Felicity's house game days," I told him, and his face fell slightly. "But I'm sure she wouldn't mind me skipping sometime if it's to hang out with you."

"Really?" He smiled wide. "Okay, awesome! Only if you want to though."

I licked my lips before slowly saying, "I want to."

He arched a brow. "That didn't sound very convincing."

"No, I do. Really. It's just, the thought of hanging out with you again is . . ." I trailed off as I searched for the right word.

"Strange," Ben said.

"A little. Yeah," I admitted, hoping I didn't hurt his feelings.

To my surprise, he said, "I understand."

"You do?"

"Yeah. We've avoided each other for so long, it might take time to feel comfortable being around each other again."

"Exactly!" Relief washed through me. Knowing he understood what I was feeling and that he felt the same way somehow made it easier. "But . . . We'll be able to, right?"

"Be comfortable around each other again?" he asked, and I nodded. "I actually think it'll be easier than either of us realize."

"Really?"

"Really."

"I hope so."

"Well, we're doing good so far, wouldn't you say?" He nudged my arm playfully and I giggled. "I'm going to fight to hang out on a weekend at some point though."

"You do that," I said sarcastically.

We stopped at the door to the Spanish room, and I looked up at him as he stood there. His eyes sparkled as he watched me, and I dropped my head as heat rose to my cheeks.

"Robin," he started, sounding nervous as he took a step closer to me. I lifted my head and swallowed loudly. "I—"

"Excuse me," a deep voice interrupted.

Ben and I both took a big step back as Matthew walked between us. He looked at me coldly as he passed by, and his shoulder gently brushed my arm. My breath caught in my throat as an icy chill paralyzed me. Matthew paused, his usually emotionless face seeming puzzled as his eyebrows scrunched together.

The woman in my head screamed loudly, and I dropped my books as both my hands flew to my head to cover my ears. My stomach churned, and my sight blurred ever so slightly as Matthew took a step back, his eyes now wide. Ben nudged past him and gently grabbed my arms as I breathed deeply, concentrating on not throwing up that second piece of cake.

"Hey, are you okay?" he asked.

The woman's scream still echoed in my ears but slowly started to fade away. My hands and back were slick with sweat and my mouth had lost all moisture.

"Robin?" Ben pressed, his voice layered with worry.

I licked my lips and took another deep breath. "I-I'm okay."

"What happened? You're as white as a ghost."

Matthew was still in the doorway, watching me as well. He looked slightly confused and—dare I say—concerned? The bell rang, and Mrs. Sanchez got up from her desk to close the door and start class. When she saw the three of us, she stopped short with tense lips and crossed her arms.

"What is going on here, *estudiantes?*" she asked.

"Robin isn't feeling too well, Mrs. Sanchez," Ben answered, his hands lingering on me. "I think she needs to go to the nurse. I can take her if that's okay."

I opened my mouth to argue but shut it again, knowing I wouldn't be able to sit in class right now.

She took one look at me and nodded. "Si, Señor Toves, go ahead. Quick, quick. What class do you have right now?"

"AP Literature with Mr. Davitt," he replied.

"I'll call and tell him you'll be late," Mrs. Sanchez said. She then turned towards Matthew. "Y tú, Señor Alastair?"

Matthew appraised me briskly, his eyes heavily guarded once again. Without a word, he turned and walked away from us. Mrs. Sanchez spewed her irritation at his retreating back then slammed her classroom door shut as Ben returned his focus back to me.

"Can you walk?" he asked.

"Yes, but please don't take me to the nurse," I begged. "I just need to sit down."

"Are you sure?" His forehead scrunched as he observed me. I nodded and, after a moment, he let go of my arms and stood up straight. "I don't like it but okay."

He picked up my books then led me to the nearest empty room, watching me closely the entire time as if I were going to fall over. I sat down and rubbed my temples gently, trying hard to focus on reality.

*What is happening to me?*

"I'll be right back," Ben said before leaving the room.

I was thankful for the moment alone so I could ponder what had happened. None of it made sense. I had no explanation, only questions. Who was the woman in my dreams and how did she scream at me while I was awake? Was it my own imagination just thinking it was her? Either way, why did Matthew's touch fill me with such alarm and unease?

Ben walked back in with a bottle of water. "Drink up."

"Thank you," I said, thankful for the gesture. I sipped on it slowly, feeling more normal as the minutes passed.

After a while, Ben asked, "How are you feeling?"

"Better. Thank you."

"What happened?"

"I just got a ringing in my ears and felt lightheaded," I told him, but he eyed me doubtfully. "What?"

"It seemed like there was more to it than that."

I stayed silent. How could I explain something to him that I didn't understand myself?

"I'm okay," I said, running my hand over the nape of my neck.

"I know that's not entirely true." He shook his head as he leaned onto his knees. "But I won't press the matter. It sucks that you think you can't confide in me though."

"I'm just not there yet, Ben," I said as I placed my hands between my legs, unable to meet his gaze. "We both agreed it'd take time to be comfortable around one another again, and that includes being able to talk to you about some things."

"I know. It just sucks. You used to be able to come to me about anything."

I glanced up, remembering all the things we'd shared over the years. He'd been my biggest confidante through a lot of life events. "I hope I can again someday," I said.

"Me too." After a moment of silence lingered, he asked, "Do you want to go back to class?"

"Definitely not."

"We'll just ditch this hour entirely then."

"You don't have to stay with me. I'm fine. Really."

"I'm glad, but I'm still not leaving you alone. Just in case."

A timid smile crept over my lips. "Thank you."

"You're welcome." He returned my smile with his own soft one as his gentle eyes watched over me.

As the hour passed, he tried to make light conversation, but I had trouble focusing enough to respond. My mind was too busy racing with a thousand thoughts and questions, and, for some reason, they all came back to Matthew. Was it possible he held the answers I was seeking?

* * *

After school, I went straight home to meet Dawn as she got off the bus. Her face lit up when she saw me, and she ran to give me a hug.

"How's my little sunshine?" I asked her as we began the walk up the block to our house.

"So good! I won our class spelling bee *and* got a homework pass," she told me excitedly, swinging her hand in mine.

"Look at you go! You're just a smarty pants, aren't you?"

"Yes, I am," she replied, and I laughed at her young-minded honesty.

As we ventured closer to home, I was surprised to see our dad's motorcycle out front.

"Daddy's home!" Dawn squealed, running ahead of me.

I stopped inside the door to take my boots off and heard Dawn yapping Dad's ear off. He laughed at something she said, and I let out a sigh of relief that he was in a good mood. I walked around the corner into the living room and leaned against the door frame.

"Hey, Dad," I said, and he gave me a tight smile in return.

"Robin. How was school?" he asked.

"Fine." I knew he didn't actually care.

"Good." He nodded once then turned his attention back to Dawn.

I took that opportunity to get started on some chores. Once I was done vacuuming and cleaning the bathroom, I started on the dishes. As the water filled the sink, I found a song to listen to on my phone. When I looked back up, my eyes couldn't seem to leave the water as it rippled against itself. I was mesmerized, held captive by its motion.

I stared, transfixed, getting lost in the calming aura it produced. The cool feeling I'd felt in the library made its way across my body once again, and the sound of the water took over my senses. I instinctively reached out to touch it, but my hand never made contact. The water seemed to react to my close proximity, and I was jolted by a shock. I pulled my hand back with a gasp as electricity ran through my fingers.

"What happened?" Dad asked as he came up behind me with Dawn in tow.

"Just some static electricity, I guess," I replied. It was the only logical explanation. He grunted in reply, so I asked, "Did you need something?"

"No."

He walked away as Dawn jumped at me, attaching herself to my leg.

"Will you come play with me?" she asked.

I playfully shook her off. "As soon as the dishes are done."

She ran out of the room, yelling gleefully to herself as the front door opened. Mom walked in, shuffling some leftover snow off her shoes.

"Hi, Mom," I greeted, and she came up to give me a kiss on the cheek.

"Hey, honey. Where's everyone else?" she asked as she started rummaging through the fridge.

"Dawn just ran down the hallway to go play, and Dad's probably in your room getting ready to watch TV," I replied as she grabbed a bottle of water and closed the fridge door. "How was work?"

"Busy but rewarding," she said with a smile that reached her eyes, crinkling the sides of them.

"Really? Why's that?"

"Well," she paused wiggling her brows mysteriously before continuing. "I just ordered some pizzas, so once they get here, we'll all sit down, and I can tell everyone the big news together."

I gave her a look of feigned amazement as I brought my hand to my chest. "Delivery *and* eating together? Must be really big news."

She shrugged nonchalantly before going down the hallway to locate Dad. I finished the dishes, then went to mine and Dawn's room where she was lying on the floor playing with her barbies. When she saw me, she handed me one that was decked out in a geometric dress and go-go boots.

"You can be Trixie," she told me.

I happily accepted and plopped down next to her. A while later, the doorbell rang, and Mom called us out for dinner. We took our places at the table, filling our plates with the cheesy goodness of three-meat pizza.

"Dig in," Mom ordered.

As we ate, my parents kept up most of the conversation between them. Dawn was too busy stuffing her face to talk for once, and I didn't have anything to say unless I was asked a direct question. When we all finished our food, Mom cleared her throat, and we looked at her expectantly.

"I hope you guys enjoyed the food. I know we don't get to eat out very often, but that's going to change very soon."

"Yay!" Dawn clapped ecstatically.

"Why's that?" Dad asked her.

"Because I've just been offered a promotion at the hospital. It comes with a set schedule and a significant pay raise." The beam on her face showed me how excited she was. "So we won't be so tight on money here soon."

Big smiles broke out all around as we offered our congratulations.

"I'm so proud of you, Rebecca," Dad said, leaning over to give her a kiss.

"Thank you. And Dawn, that also means Mommy will get to spend every day with you after school!"

Dawn gasped. "We'll get to play like me and Robin do!"

Mom laughed and nodded in agreement. "That also means your afternoons are now completely freed up, Robin." She looked at me with soft eyes. "I appreciate how much you step up for this family, but now you can go do all the things you couldn't before."

"I don't mind helping," I told her as Dad got up and left the table.

"I know, honey," she replied. "But now you don't *have* to."

A smile crept onto my face. I really didn't mind helping, but if I wasn't needed, my world was suddenly open to a bushel of social opportunities I'd previously been forced to turn down. Felicity was going to go nuts when I told her.

# CHAPTER SIX

That night, the dream changed. I was still on the bank by the lapping waves in the moonlight, and the woman still broke through my peace. This time, though, I didn't just stand there. I walked towards her slowly. The thunder rumbled lightly in the distance but didn't come any closer as the temperature remained the same. The woman and I approached one another, and I saw her more clearly than ever before.

She appeared to be average height with a slender figure. Her chestnut-brown hair whipped wildly in the wind, and her wide blue eyes mirrored mine in color. I found this odd, considering how distinctive my eye color was. Her full lips turned up into a smile as I came closer. I looked down at my arms, then back up at her, realizing we had the same olive skin tone as well. It was almost as if I were looking at a future version of myself.

"Robin." Her voice was warm and inviting as she reached her hand out, inviting me to join her.

I lifted my hand to accept then hesitated and drew it back. That slight moment of hesitation was all it took. The approaching storm rapidly picked up its pace until it was directly above us. The waves crashed against one another angrily, and the wind pushed at me forcefully. A flash of lightning struck the sand directly between myself and the woman—whose face was nothing but a black hole again—and I fell back. Then everything faded to black.

* * *

"I'm so happy for your mom!" Felicity said in art as we worked on our portraits. "That is going to be so good for her!"

"I know. She deserves it," I agreed as I lightly painted the canvas.

"I can't wait to start my to-do list with you."

"To-do list?" I asked with raised eyebrows.

"Yes! It's everything I always had to ask someone else to go do with me since you couldn't. Sleepovers, shopping, movies. That sort of thing." She gasped, her hands flying up. "Oh! And you'll get to come see my plays!"

I smiled widely at how happy she was. This meant even more to her than I thought it would.

"Too bad this didn't happen during football season. The games are *so* fun." She gasped again and turned to me. "Does this mean you'll get to go to prom?"

"Uh, maybe. I hadn't really thought about it," I said, and she rolled her eyes.

"Of course, you haven't. But that's okay because we have *months* to plan. We could go to New York and dress shop at my favorite boutique!"

"I am absolutely positive that isn't in my price range, Felicity."

Felicity's parents were rich. And I don't mean well off; I mean *rich*. They lived in a beautiful Victorian-style home and often made weekend trips in their private plane to somewhere exotic. Felicity's closet was packed full of designer brands, and she wanted for nothing. Despite that, her family was some of the most giving, down-to-earth people I knew.

Her parents were involved in multiple charities and constantly held functions to promote positive changes for prominent social problems. Felicity had been raised going to these events and volunteering on a regular basis because her parents held high standards for her in terms of ethics and morals. But she was only human and sometimes forgot that others couldn't afford the luxuries she could.

"Oh hush! It can be your birthday and Christmas gift," she said. I opened my mouth to argue, but she held up her hand and gave me a look.

"We'll see," I replied, and she clapped gleefully.

When we arrived at physics, we sat down and started conversing with Alli. I kept a watchful eye on the door, waiting for Matthew to walk in. When he did, I felt the usual tingling I was becoming accustomed to. He glanced at me before sitting down, but for the rest of the hour, he didn't look my way even once.

Government played out in the same way, so I had my fingers crossed that he'd finally lost interest in staring me down. He sat alone at lunch, as usual, and I tried to remove him from my mind as I ate.

"Guess what?" Felicity asked Ben when he sat down next to me. "Mrs. Hayes got a promotion and gets to spend every day with Dawn after school!"

"What? That's great!" Ben exclaimed. "Does that mean—"

"She's all ours!" Felicity interrupted, and Ben's lips turned up. "Well, she's mine first, but I'm sure she'll give you a day or two."

Ben made a childish face at her that made me laugh.

"In two weeks," I reminded her. "That's when my mom starts her new position."

"You know what else it means?" Felicity asked slyly.

"What?" Ben questioned before taking a sip of his drink.

"You can ask her to prom, and she has no excuse to say no," she stated with a coy smile.

Ben choked on his water and started coughing as he brought his hand to his mouth.

"Felicity!" I cried out as heat ran up my cheeks.

Ben pulled his hair off the back of his neck as he turned a similar shade of red, but I wasn't sure if it was from embarrassment or lack of air.

"I'm just saying," she said, shrugging her shoulders.

I glared at her, refusing to look at Ben. "*Anyway,*" I muttered pointedly.

"Anyway," she repeated with a roll of her eyes. "Do you guys want to come to my house after school?"

"We can't today," I said, spooning soup into my mouth as she crossed her arms.

"Why not? Do you two have plans or something?"

"We do, actually."

She looked at me, feigning shock. "Is this how it's going to be? Me becoming second choice?"

"It just might," I replied, trying to suppress a smile at her pout. "But in this instance, no. You're part of our plans."

"I am?" Her brows furrowed.

Ben snorted as I grinned. "We have an away game to-day," I reminded her. "We have to load up on the bus right after school."

"Crap," she groaned, pulling her phone out of her pocket. "I totally forgot it was an away game. Better tell my mom."

Ben cleared his throat, still slightly red in the face, as Felicity put her phone against her ear. I looked over at him, shifting uncomfortably.

"So, uh, that's great that you'll have more free time now," he said.

"It is," I agreed. "It'll be nice to be able to do things with people outside of school."

"People including me?" he asked hopefully, and I smiled a bit.

"Yes, Benjamin, that includes you."

"You know, you're the only person who gets away with calling me that," he said while attempting a scowl. It looked unnatural on his usually happy face.

"Only because I'm special," I teased, not fully thinking about what I said.

"Yeah . . . You are," he said quietly, looking at me intently with those beautiful amber eyes.

I peered down at my plate as my heart fluttered and but-terflies swarmed in my stomach. Felicity hung up with her mom at that moment and rejoined the conversation, so I didn't have to respond.

The rest of the day went by quickly. On the bus, Felicity and I sat with the girls in the back while the boys' team sat up front. Ben kept sneaking glances my way, often catching me already staring at the back of his head. When we made eye contact, I'd look down, embarrassed, but he would just grin.

The small interaction sent me into a tailspin every time, and I'd rub my lips together to keep the smile off my face. Welcoming him back into my life wasn't as hard as I'd thought it was going to be.

The rest of the week, as well as the next, went by in the familiar pattern I was used to—aside from one big detail: now my school days included Ben. He met me at my locker and escorted me to all the classes I didn't share with Felicity, but he never intruded on the time she and I walked to our classes together. Our interactions became less awkward and uncomfortable and more enjoyable and gratifying. Seeing him turned into something I looked forward to—something I craved.

Matthew continued to give me uncanny feelings, but I did my best to ignore him whenever he was around. Something in the back of my mind nagged at me to talk to him, but I couldn't bring myself to do it. However, Felicity didn't seem to have the same problem.

"Hey, do you want to do something before the game today?" I asked her Monday morning. I looked into the bathroom mirror, pulling my thick hair into its usual ponytail.

"I can't," she answered as she touched up her makeup. "I'm going to grab some food with Matthew."

I nearly fell over, whipping my head towards her. "You're what?"

"I'm going to Elton's Diner with Matthew before the game," she repeated, oblivious to my reaction.

Questions attacked my brain in a frenzied swarm, and I sputtered as I tried to figure out which one to ask. She finally seemed to take notice of my distress and turned towards me.

"Relax," she said, only half serious. "Breathe."

I took a deep breath then let it out slowly before saying, "You don't know him or the kind of person he is. You should hang out with him here first."

"I already have been," she replied, waving her hand dismissively.

"What? When?"

"Almost every day since I first introduced myself. We've been spending our free period together."

I shook my head, blinking rapidly as I tried to fight away the feeling of hurt. "Why didn't you tell me?"

"He just didn't seem to be your favorite subject."

She purposely avoided my gaze as I eyed her with a suspicious stare.

"There's more," I accused, crossing my arms.

She sighed and leaned against the wall as her eyes got a faraway look in them. "He's just so *different*. He's not like the other guys in this school. It took him a little bit to warm up to me, but once he did, he was nothing like the hard, unkind image he gives off. He's definitely cautious, but I think it's because he hasn't had an easy life."

I stared at her as realization dawned. "You like him, don't you?"

"No!" she exclaimed, but after thinking about it for a moment, she bit her lip. "Maybe? I don't know."

My brows furrowed as she tugged at her hair. This wasn't like her at all. She was gorgeous, and she knew it. She had her pick of any guy she wanted, and she wasn't embarrassed about that fact because she knew what she wanted when it came to her relationships. I'd never seen her act so unsure about someone before. But why did it have to be with someone I didn't trust?

"He's still really closed off about a lot of things, and he shuts down sometimes if we accidentally land on the wrong subject," she said. "But he's so respectful of me and does little things most guys don't care about any more like holding a door open or giving me his coat."

"You didn't mention how good-looking he is," I observed as it stuck out to me like a sore thumb.

She wasn't necessarily shallow but physical appearance definitely played a main factor in who she dated.

Felicity grinned. "Oh, he's hot. There's no doubt about it. But he's so much more than that."

*Well, crap.*

I closed my eyes, not sure how to respond. I wanted to be supportive of my best friend the same way she always was of me, but I also needed to make sure she was safe.

"Are you sure you want to go to the diner with him?" I asked with a defeated sigh.

"Yes. I was surprised he even agreed when I asked him. I don't want to pass it up," she answered.

"Will you text me when you get there?" I asked. She gave me a look, but I didn't care if she thought I was being nuts. "Please?"

"Fine. If it'll make you feel better."

"And text me when you're leaving?" I pushed, and she rolled her eyes.

"Fine."

"Maybe a text every thirty minutes—"

"Robin!" Felicity cried out, giving me a pointed look, so I held my hands up in defeat, knowing I'd reached my limit.

"Just be careful. Please," I murmured, and she smiled softly.

"Of course I'll be careful. Thank you for caring. Even if it is ridiculous."

She gave me a hug, then we headed our separate ways for first period.

# CHAPTER SEVEN

"What's going through your mind?" Ben asked as we sat in the park.

The snow fell lightly around us, melting as it hit the ground, and I shivered as a cold gust of wind traveled through my thick jacket.

"Felicity," I replied, picking apart a dead leaf.

"She's fine, Robin," he said. "She's a big girl. She knows how to look after herself."

"I know that."

"Then what's the problem?" he asked gently before blowing into his cupped hands.

I rubbed my lips together then huffed as frustration built. "I truly cannot explain it to you in a way that will make sense."

My usually sound mind and judgement were a cavity of doubt and unease, toying with my sanity.

"Just try. I'm sure I can keep up."

He looked at me with patience as I tried to gather my thoughts so I could attempt to tell him what was going through my head.

"I don't trust him," I finally said. "When he's around, I get this strange feeling. It's like ice is traveling through me and I get all tingly and uneasy. I don't think he's who he says he is."

Ben ran his hand through his hair, trying to process my unusual explanation, and I could see him struggling with what to say back.

"Look," he said, hesitating before continuing, "I'm not saying you're wrong or that I don't believe you, but have you ever even talked to him?"

"No."

"You started having that recurring dream the night before you first noticed him, right?"

I frowned at the subject change, not seeing how he'd jumped to it. "I'd had it a few times before but that's when it became more constant."

"You know, sometimes we reflect things on other people. So, maybe you're using him as an outlet for your feelings about your dream," he said.

"I mean . . . Maybe." It was plausible enough, but I wasn't sure I bought it. Then again, I definitely didn't understand my dream or how it made me feel so maybe he was right. "I guess it's possible."

"Then you should trust Felicity's judgement. You know how good she is at reading people."

"I know."

"I'm not trying to downplay your feelings. I hope you know that."

"I know," I repeated.

"I just think maybe you'd feel differently if you gave him a chance. See what type of person he is based on a real interaction. Not a gut feeling."

I stayed quiet, nibbling on my lower lip as I fought with myself.

"What if we invite him to sit with us at lunch?" Ben suggested. "Start small and see how things go."

The idea didn't thrill me, but I couldn't think of a real reason to say no. "I guess it couldn't hurt anything," I reluctantly agreed, and he smiled.

"There's the optimistic Robin I know and love," he said teasingly.

"Ha. Ha," I mocked, pushing him over.

"Hey, do you want to come to my house sometime next week?" he asked.

My heart thumped a little faster, and my palms were sweating despite the cold that surrounded them. "Your house?"

"Yeah, my parents would love to see you." He let out an awkward laugh as he rubbed the back of his neck. "They've actually been bugging me for a while to bring you by."

"Oh." I smiled, the thought of seeing his parents after so long actually exciting me. Jeremiah and Kiona had been a big part of my life for a long time before our fallout. "Sure. I'd love to see them too."

"Great! Just let me know what day Felicity hasn't already claimed."

I grinned. He knew Felicity well. My first week with no after-school obligations was all she could talk about. It wouldn't surprise me if she had something planned for us every day for the rest of the school year.

The wind picked up heavily then, blowing the chilly snow in our faces.

Ben shivered and rubbed his arms over his brown hoodie. "Do you want to head back?"

"Definitely," I said as the cold bit at my already frozen nose.

Ben offered me his hand, helping me off the bench. As he released me, I jumped over a large puddle. My foot landed in the loose mud, and I fell backwards as my arms wildly clawed at empty air. Just as my butt was about to hit the mountain of slush, Ben grasped my arms and pulled me towards him.

I fell into his chest as his arms wrapped around my back to steady me. A sigh of relief escaped me, followed by a lighthearted laugh. I looked up to thank Ben for his heroics, but the words caught in my mouth when I realized how close his face was to mine. My smile faltered, and his grin diminished as he registered the same thing.

His eyes traveled over my face before landing on my lips. I opened my mouth, then shut it again as my heart thumped wildly in my chest.

*Is he going to try to kiss me?*

He cleared his throat and stepped away, making sure I wasn't going to fall before he released me from his grasp. He stuck his hands in his pockets, refusing to make eye contact as I stood dumbfounded.

"We should go," he said before turning around and walking ahead of me.

"Yeah," I murmured as I tried to slow my racing heart. "Yeah."

* * *

I drummed my fingers against my knee and eyed the locker room door as I waited for Felicity. Chatter buzzed around me from the other girls, but I was too focused to hear what they were saying. When I saw her all too familiar reddish hair, I pounced.

"How'd it go?" I asked, looking her up and down. She looked to be in one piece.

"It was really fun," she said joyfully. "Granted, I dominated the majority of the conversation, but he seemed to enjoy it as much as I did."

"That's good. What did you guys talk about?"

"He asked a lot about my life. Family, friends, upbringing, that sort of things." Her face clouded over just a bit. "It was a little weird actually. He seemed in awe of what I was saying or something. Sometimes he seemed a little sad or . . . jealous maybe?"

"Jealous? Like of your money?"

"No! Definitely not. It was like . . . like he didn't know what families did together."

My brows furrowed. "Huh? That doesn't make any sense."

Felicity shrugged. "I'm just telling you what it seemed like. Maybe he grew up in foster care."

"Maybe." I drummed my fingers on my leg as I thought.

Her words made me consider the possibility that I really had misjudged him. He could just be an awkward teenager who was bad in social situations, which would make a lot of sense if he'd grown up in an unhealthy environment. Maybe Ben was right, and I'd projected unrelated emotions onto him.

"I asked him to stay and watch our game, but he said he couldn't," Felicity said. "But he did tell me he'd like to see me outside of school again."

Even if I was in the wrong, I was glad he wouldn't be there to distract me on the court.

"Did he use those exact words? He'd like to 'see you' outside of school?" I grinned. "Normal people would call that a date."

"Well, he's not normal. He's—"

*"Different,"* I finished, batting my eyelashes as my hands interlaced under my chin. She swatted my arm, and I giggled. "When are you going on another date then?"

"This wasn't a date," she corrected me. "I'm not sure the next time will be either."

"Why's that?" I began changing into my uniform as she replied.

"Because I'm not sure if he likes me like that or not." Her lips drew downward. "I offered to be his friend and help him get adjusted to our school. He might think us being together is just that."

I nodded, my brows drawing together. "That's true. You don't want to be on different pages about it though."

"Definitely not," she agreed as she pushed her hair back with a red headband that matched our uniforms. "He seems interested, but he's a little hard to read sometimes. So, I figure I'll just continue meeting up with him but keep my feelings to myself for now. No point in making a fool of myself."

I averted my gaze, thinking of how forward she'd been with guys in the past. Matthew really must be on a different level to have her acting so sensible, which meant she really did like him.

It was at that moment I decided to give Matthew a chance. Whether I was right or wrong in my original feelings about him, I had to try to see what Felicity saw. My animosity would have to be placed on the back burner unless it was necessary to bring back.

"Do you want to invite him to sit with us at lunch tomorrow?" I asked.

Her eyes widened, and she broke out in a wide smile. "Really? You don't mind?"

Her voice was overflowing with happiness. Seeing how much this meant to her only validated my choice.

"I don't mind. It'll be nice to get to see what you see in him."

"Oh, you will! I mean, maybe not at first since he's so closed off, but just give it some time, and I'm sure he'll warm up to you like he did with me."

She continued to ramble on about the possibilities of introducing him to more people as I fixed my hair and took off my necklace. I didn't get a word in, but I didn't mind. She kept going until Coach Mayfield came in for our pregame pep talk, then we headed onto the court for another game.

* * *

"Sorry about the loss," Ben said as we walked to the parking lot. Felicity grumbled an unintelligible reply and stomped ahead of us. "Such a sore loser."

I snorted. "If I remember correctly, you're the exact same way."

"I'm just passionate," he replied with a wink.

"And Felicity is?"

"A sore loser." He wiggled his brows, and I shook my head.

"Because that's fair," I commented as he grinned. "So, Felicity's going to invite Matthew to sit with us tomorrow at lunch."

"Really?" Ben asked, his brows now launching into his hairline, and I nodded.

"I thought about what you said and decided you were right, so I told her to."

"I'm proud of you, Robin."

"Oh, thanks," I said dryly.

"No, really," he replied, stopping me with his hand. "I know it's not easy going against your instincts. I think it's commendable you're going to make an effort to get to know him instead of not liking him based on nothing more than a feeling. You never were one to judge people unfairly, and I'm glad that hasn't changed." He looked into my eyes, unwavering in his praise. "You're still one of the most caring people I know."

"You think too highly of me," I murmured. I looked down, kicking at a rock near my foot, but his warm fingers tipped my chin up so I was looking at him again.

"And you think too little of yourself," he said, just as quiet as I was. "Robin Hayes, you are so much more than you give yourself credit for."

My stomach flipped nervously, and heat washed over me as he seemed to stare right through the walls I'd built. His eyes slid down to my lips then back to my eyes as he took a step closer to me.

The wind whistled around us, but I couldn't feel anything except the beating of my heart. He leaned down slightly, lingering there for a moment to see if I would pull away or not. I took in a shaky breath but didn't retreat—an invite for him to finish what he had started. His bright eyes were gentle in the moonlight, and his lips parted slightly as he moved in closer. My head tilted up instinctually as my own lips followed suit.

"Robin!" Felicity called from the front of her car.

Ben snapped back to his full height and quickly took a step away from me as I turned towards her. Her eyes threw fierce apologies at me, and she grimaced as she realized what she'd interrupted.

"I, um, I better go," I managed to say around the dryness in my throat.

I glanced over at Ben, trying to fight the urge to run. He had his hands in his pockets, his face just as red as I'm sure mine was.

"I'll see you tomorrow?" he asked sheepishly as a grin made its way onto his face.

I smiled and nodded as I backed away. "Yeah. See you tomorrow."

I turned around and rushed to Felicity's car, burying my head in my hands with a grunt.

"Oh my gosh, I can't believe I just stopped that from happening!" Felicity cried out. She grabbed me by the shoulders, forcing me to look up. "I am *so* sorry, Robin. I didn't look before I called your name."

"It's okay, Felicity," I assured her, actually grateful for the intervention.

"No, it's definitely not! He was going to *kiss* you!" she exclaimed, her eyes wide and sparkling.

"I know. I was there."

"And you were going to let him!"

I put my hands in front of her heaters without answering. My head was clouded with emotions, and my heart refused to settle down as I thought about Ben and how close our lips had come to touching. Felicity was right—I was going to let him kiss me. But why?

"Well, crap," I groaned, banging my head into the head-rest.

"What's wrong?"

"I think I like him," I said quietly.

Felicity let out a laugh, and I glared at her, annoyed by her reaction to my dilemma.

"I told you so," she said slyly.

"Oh, shut up," I grumbled, buckling and slouching down in the seat as she began driving.

*"Ben and Robin, sitting in a tree, K-I-S-S-I—"*

"No one is kissing anyone," I interrupted.

"Not yet," she replied, grinning wickedly.

"You're impossible."

She continued her teasing the entire way to my house, and I was sure there would be more awaiting me tomorrow. Despite the day I had, I slept peacefully that night. The woman left me alone, and I was instead joined by Ben in dreams that left me feeling safe, happy, and complete.

# CHAPTER EIGHT

The next morning, I woke up feeling rejuvenated and got out of bed early enough to have a shower and get ready without rushing. My hair dried in wispy ringlets, and I was grateful it decided to do something presentable instead of settling into its usual straggly mess. I pulled the front layers up, connecting them at the back of my head with a silver French barrette then gave it a quick dousing of hairspray to keep the natural wave it possessed but rarely showed. I pulled on a fitted black T-shirt with a multicolored wool cardigan and a light pair of skinny jeans before clasping my necklace around my neck.

"Good morning, little bird," Dawn said as she came up behind me with a yawn.

I bent down to give her a hug. "Good morning, my sunshine. Ready for another day?"

"No. I don't want to go to school," she mumbled.

Her lower lip stuck out, and I got on my knees to look her in the eyes as concern filled me.

"What's wrong, Dawn?" I questioned, looking her up and down. I put my hand on her forehead. "You don't look sick, and you don't have a fever."

"I'm sick in here," she said, pointing at her chest.

"Your chest? Are you coughing?"

She shook her head as her eyes brimmed with tears. "My heart is sick."

I pulled her in for a hug. "Oh, don't cry, sweetie."

She wrapped her arms around my neck and began to sob, her entire body shaking. I brushed my hand over her hair, rocking us back and forth as I tried to sooth her. After a couple minutes, she quieted down, so I pulled her away from me to look at her tear-streaked face.

"What's the matter, Dawn?" I asked.

She sniffled and ran her arm along her runny nose. "John and Samuel told me nobody wants me to come back to school because everyone hates me."

It took everything in me to keep my face as neutral as possible despite the rage that now burned inside. Kids were so cruel to one another.

"John and Samuel don't know what they're talking about," I said as calmly as I could manage. "You are a kind, smart, selfless little girl. Anyone would be lucky to have you in their lives."

"Then why did they say that?" Dawn asked as her lips quivered again, and my heart broke as I stared at her sad face.

"Because they're bullies."

"What's a bully?"

"A bully is someone who's mean to someone else for no reason."

"But why?"

"I wish I knew," I replied, hating that she already had to learn about it. "This isn't the last time you'll have to deal with something like this, though, so listen to me very carefully. Don't ever let anyone make you feel bad about yourself. If someone is being mean to you, just turn around and walk away, okay?"

"Okay."

"Besides, you have *plenty* of friends," I reminded her. She smiled a little bit, so I kept going. "There's Cheyenne and Savannah and Adalynn and Colleen and Sophia." I poked her belly as I said each name, and she started to giggle. "And Gabriel and William and Shane and Fernando."

She was full-on laughing and squealing now as she tried to squirm away from me.

"Okay, I get it!" she exclaimed, still giggling.

I joined in before giving her another hug. "Do you still want to stay home today?"

"No!" she shouted proudly with her hands on her hips. "My friends would miss me."

"Darn right they would," I told her with a grin. "Now get!"

She ran away, and I picked myself up off the floor. Guilty formed in my stomach as I went to the kitchen to get breakfast. I wasn't bullying Matthew with words, but I was no better than one with the thoughts I'd been having about him. Today, that was going to change.

* * *

"Good morning," Ben greeted me as I arrived at my locker.

"Morning," I replied with a smile.

He leaned over me as I put my books up, and I was intoxicated by his woodsy, pine-like aroma. His head hung right by mine beside the open door, and it took everything in me to stay composed as my whole body reacted to his close proximity.

"So, about yesterday," he said, and I rubbed my lips together as I replayed the scene in my head for the ten thousandth time.

"Are we really going to talk about it?" I asked with a nervous laugh, pushing my hair behind my ear.

"Don't you think we should?" he countered as he rested his arm against the locker by my head.

"I'd rather we didn't," I replied, trying to squirm away from him.

His bashfulness from the night before was gone, and he grinned at my obvious distress.

"You're cute when you're embarrassed."

My eyes bulged and I hissed, "You can't say stuff like that!"

"Why not?" He was very clearly enjoying my misery.

"Because. People will think you like me or something," I replied, glancing around as students passed us by.

"But I do like you," he said, causing my breath to catch in my throat. "And I think you like me too."

"Please, don't say that."

"Why not? It's the truth. I care about you. Literally everyone can see that."

My heart hammered in my chest at his words, and I closed my eyes as I took a deep breath. "I can't do this, Ben."

"But *why?*"

"Because it'll change everything!" I almost yelled. I took a deep breath and continued. "I'm sorry. It's just . . . You can't take something like that back, and I don't want what we have to be ruined. I just got you back in my life, and I don't want to risk losing you again because of what we may or may not feel for each other."

Ben was quiet for a moment then he brushed my hair back over my shoulder, sending a shiver down my spine, before saying, "Okay."

"Okay?"

"Okay. I don't want to jeopardize having you in my life again either. If that means I have to play by your rules, so be it."

I let out a relieved sigh, the urge to hurl diminishing. He took that better than I'd expected.

He leaned closer and winked before murmuring in my ear, "But I think it's going to be harder for you than you think."

I pushed him away from me and playfully socked him in the arm as I scoffed. He grabbed at it with a pitiful groan of pain as we started walking to class, and I rolled my eyes at him.

As much as I wanted to deny it, I was afraid he was right. He unlocked feelings I'd pushed away for a very long time, and I wasn't sure I could keep them at bay as well as I once did. Over the years, he'd always held a place in my heart in one form or another. First as a best friend, a safe place, and a partner in crime. Then as a broken twinge of hurt and loss as we'd broken apart.

Now that we were together again, the place he held in my heart had manifested itself into something I'd never acknowledged before. It was stronger, more passionate, and it continued to intensify as time went on. A sudden realization hit me like a ton of blocks, and all the air left my lungs.

*I'm in love with Benjamin Toves.*

* * *

"I'm in trouble," I told Felicity as I sat down.

She looked up from her phone and gave me a once over. "What's wrong?" she asked, putting her phone away to give me her undivided attention.

"I have feelings for Ben," I answered seriously.

The corner of her mouth twitched as she tried not to smile. Instead, she nodded. "Okay. Why does that have to be a bad thing though?"

"Because this isn't something I do," I replied, my hands waving around. "I don't- I don't catch feelings for people. I don't date."

"Just because you haven't before doesn't mean you can't start."

"But I don't know how," I basically whined. Despite her best effort, Felicity's lips twisted up into a smile, and she began laughing loudly. I couldn't help but join in, hearing how ridiculous I sounded. "Okay, I admit it. I'm pathetic."

"Just a little bit," she agreed. "But I can help you! If there's one thing I know, it's dating."

"But I don't think I'm ready for that with Ben."

"Why not?"

"I don't want to ruin our friendship. Knowing me, I'll screw it up somehow, and then I'll lose him again."

"First of all, you're not going to screw anything up," she said earnestly. "All relationships have problems at some point; it's unavoidable. It's how you handle them and grow as a couple that matters. And secondly, your friendship is already ruined in some ways. You guys aren't just friends anymore because you both know the other has romantic feelings for you. The more you fight those feelings, the more strain you guys will have between you as time goes on, and that'll hurt your 'friendship' just as much."

The matter-of-fact tone of her argument left me with no room to question her. The words made sense.

"I guess you're right," I admitted.

"Of course, I am! So are you going to tell him how you feel?"

"No," I answered, causing her face to cloud over. Before she could ask, I quickly explained. "Not yet at least. I just need some time to process and figure out if I'm ready for it first."

Felicity rolled her eyes and sighed in exasperation. "You're impossible."

"Well, we aren't all as confident and open as you," I pointed out with a shrug.

"Whatever," she dismissed my subtle jab as Ms. Meers called our attention to the front.

The hour passed slowly as we sculpted clay and talked about next week's after-school plans. When we got to physics, Felicity spent the five minutes before class started leaning on Matthew's desk and yapping away at him about joining us for lunch. He looked my way, and I managed to give him a small smile, hoping it looked inviting. As he turned back to Felicity, I noticed his body language change completely.

He appeared more relaxed and open as he looked up at her with his full attention, hanging on to her every word. I even thought I caught a glimpse of a smile as Felicity let out an embarrassed giggle about something and smoothed her hair back. They were in their own little bubble, and they both seemed content to ignore the rest of the world as they stared at each other.

Felicity could draw out the best in anyone, so I wasn't surprised she'd been able to crack Matthew's hard exterior. However, I *was* surprised at the intensity of their demeanors in the scene I was witnessing. I felt as if I were peering into a private moment of intoxicating euphoria and had to avert my eyes.

There was no doubt in my mind that Matthew felt the same way about Felicity as she did about him. I was also convinced she felt something more for him than she'd let on to me in our past conversation. I made a mental note to talk to her about it later as Mr. Garcia began his lesson.

* * *

When lunchtime came around, Ben and I were the first at the table. I took my plate of pizza off the tray as he set our cups of water down. Soon, Felicity waltzed over with Matthew in tow, and he slid into the seat next to her without a word.

"Ben, Robin, this is Matthew," Felicity introduced as she beamed. "Matthew, this is Robin and Ben."

"Good to meet you officially," Ben said, holding out his hand, and Matthew looked at it for a moment before shaking it in greeting.

"You too," he replied, his voice low and smooth. He glanced my way, as if to see if I shared Ben's sentiment.

I smiled and followed Ben's lead, holding out my hand to greet him.

"Welcome to our school," I said lamely, internally cringing as Ben gave me the side eye of judgement.

"Thank you," Matthew replied, grasping my hand.

The moment his skin touched mine, a surge of cold energy soared through my veins. Our handshake lingered longer than necessary as we both examined the other. His brows knitted tightly together but his eyes were slightly wider than usual, making him look thoughtful and even a little bit hopeful.

The energy continued to build inside me, threatened to consume all my senses, so I finally yanked my hand away from his. A wave of frigidness bolted from my fingertips and all four cups of water simultaneously fell over, spilling the liquid across the table.

"What the hell?" Felicity said, jumping up as it flowed over the side onto her seat. We all grabbed at our napkins, trying to clean up the mess.

"That was weird," Ben commented.

"Someone must've bumped the table," Matthew murmured, watching me expectantly.

It seemed like he was waiting to see if I was going to agree with him or not. Since I wasn't about to try to explain what I'd just felt, and I couldn't think of any other explanation, I decided his was best.

"Probably," I replied.

"Maybe," Ben said with a shrug, but I could tell he wasn't quite convinced. We finished cleaning the table as he started conversing with Matthew.

"So, where did you move here from?" Ben asked, and Matthew's eyes hardened slightly.

"California," he replied.

"That must be a hard transition. Sunny California to Wisconsin's winter wonderland."

"I don't mind the snow."

Ben nodded his head slowly before asking, "What brought you here?"

Matthew sat rigidly, his jaw set tightly as he looked away from us. Ben glanced at me as we both realized he wasn't going to answer.

"Felicity said you don't like talking about yourself," I said after the silence drug on, surprising myself. I hadn't planned on saying anything, let alone something so forward. "Why is that?"

Felicity narrowed her eyes at me slightly, then turned to Matthew. "You don't have to answer that."

"It's okay," he said, his eyes boring into mine. "I just don't have much to say about myself."

"When you meet new people, you're usually expected to talk about yourself," I replied with a small bite.

Ben and Felicity exchanged glances, but I ignored them as Matthew raised his brows and frowned.

"What would you like to know?" he asked flatly.

"Do you have any siblings?"

"Not that I know of."

"Pets?"

"Never had one."

"What do your parents do?"

"Don't have any." That stopped me cold in my tracks, but he continued. "I didn't have the best childhood, I have no family that I know of, and I never went to public school before this. I don't socialize well or really know how to be anything but defensive."

I looked down at my hands as guilt wafted through me.

"But now I'm here," he continued, "and I'd like to leave my past in the past and try to have a normal life. If you can't accept that, then we have nothing left to discuss."

He stood to leave, and Felicity shot me a panicked look. I knew I needed to fix what I'd done.

"No, wait," I said to Matthew, throwing up my hands. "I'm so sorry. Please stay. We're a rough bunch, but we can make for good friends if you give us a chance."

With his face completely devoid of expression, he said, "Seems like you're the one who has to give me a chance."

I licked my lips and nodded slowly, wishing I could take it all back. This impertinent, untrusting person wasn't me. I was acting completely out of character and had been since I'd first laid eyes on him. It wasn't fair to him, and I didn't like myself for it.

"I'm sorry," I repeated. "I'm not normally this rude to people."

"She's really not," Felicity added.

"You've done nothing to deserve that, and if you'll let me, I'd like to show you that I'm actually a pretty nice person and can be a good friend."

We all waited, watching him expectantly as he frowned, mulling over my words.

Finally, he shrugged. "I can't promise you that *I'll* be a good friend."

Felicity smiled widely, and I could tell that was the closest thing I'd get to a confirmation that he forgave me. I looked over at Ben, and he gave me a nod of encouragement.

"We'll accept you either way," I said. "Besides, you have the queen bee of the school as your right-hand woman. Soon enough, you won't even remember what it was like to be antisocial."

Ben laughed as Felicity nodded, completely unashamed. They started talking about her ever-growing popularity while Matthew and I looked on, remaining largely silent. I peeked up and caught him observing me. The cold eyes I was used to seeing were replaced by ones that swam with questions.

After a moment, he gave a slight nod of his head, then shifted his focus to Felicity as she laughed rambunctiously. I wasn't sure what that interaction was supposed to mean, but I took it as a sign that we were moving forward. Hopefully that wouldn't be too hard to do.

# CHAPTER NINE

Despite having all our after-lunch classes together, Matthew and I didn't speak again the rest of the day. It was an awkward and forced start to a friendship, and neither of us were ready to interact with the other alone yet. But I was hopeful it would evolve into something better as time passed. We made polite conversation at lunch the next day while Felicity and Ben kept up the majority of the conversation, in which I was informed that I had a busy week ahead of me after the coming weekend.

Felicity had made plans for the two of us on the three weekdays when we didn't have a game, but Ben fought tooth and nail with her until she finally gave up one of those days so I could go to his house for dinner. Then they both begged and bribed Matthew and I to agree to go to a small bonfire that weekend. If nothing else, it would be nice to have someone as reserved as I was to be tortured alongside of.

When the weekend rolled around, my mom took Felicity and I to the mall to help her shop for an updated wardrobe for her new position at work while Dawn spent the day with our dad at the zoo. Felicity encouraged my mom to step out of her comfort zone by having her try on different business suits with crazy designs and colors. Much to Felicity's disappointment, she ended up purchasing ones that were neutral and modest instead.

We ended the day on a sugar high as we gulped down a gallon of ice cream with churros. As much as I loved my little sister, it was nice spending time with my mom without her. After we dropped Felicity off and got home, we were ambushed by a squealing, hyper child and to our surprise, Lizzie.

"What are you doing here?" Mom asked, giving her a hug.

"Dawn called me and asked if I'd come over. She said Mark had to leave," Lizzie replied.

Mom brought her eyebrows together. "What do you mean? He was supposed to watch her all day," she said as she pulled off her coat. "Where did he go?"

"I'm not sure," Lizzie answered hesitantly.

Mom paused at her tone. "What aren't you telling me?"

Lizzie glanced at me, and I could tell she was uncomfortable as she said, "Mark wasn't here when I got here."

Mom and I both stared at her with wide open jaws.

"Wait, what? He left her here alone?" Mom asked in bewilderment. "For how long?"

"Dawn said he left right after she called me, and it took me about thirty minutes to get here." Lizzie looked like she wanted to say more but held her tongue as my mom pursed her lips.

"Robin, get your sister ready for bed please," she told me.

I quickly rounded up Dawn and led her into the bathroom as Mom banged dishes around in the kitchen. I knew she needed time to be angry without having to worry about what she was doing or saying, so I made sure to keep Dawn preoccupied with loud music as we changed into our pajamas.

After reading her a bedtime story, Dawn fell asleep, and I carefully tucked her covers in around her. I climbed into my bed and waited, but Lizzie was still there when I finally drifted off and my dad was not. Whenever he did show up, I knew it wasn't going to be a pretty scene, and I just hoped Dawn and I were nowhere near to witness it.

* * *

"So, uh, what are you gonna do after school?" I asked Matthew awkwardly as we walked to Spanish class.

Lunch just ended, and Felicity and Ben had conveniently suggested we go to our next class together since they both had prior engagements. Icy goosebumps spread over me at our close proximity, but I ignored it, getting used to the feeling. I didn't want to disappoint Felicity or Ben, but Matthew and I were now in a tricky situation since we were both quiet by nature. It didn't help that I couldn't ask any personal questions without setting us back.

"Studying," he said, looking straight ahead.

"That's usually what I would be doing too. But now that I don't have to watch my little sister, Felicity is demanding almost all of my after-school time." Matthew nodded slightly but didn't say anything, so I continued rambling. "Not that I mind. It'll be a nice change to have fun like a normal teenager."

He gave me the side eye, and his mouth twitched slightly, as if amused, but he still didn't speak.

"But knowing Felicity," I continued, "she'll try to drag me to parties and stuff which is really not my scene. I'm sure you'll be in the same boat as me with that though. It doesn't seem like that's something you're into either."

I looked over at him, but he just shrugged. I sighed and stopped walking, which caused him to pause and glance back at me.

"Listen," I said, rubbing my forehead. "I'm really trying here, and it isn't easy for me. It would mean a lot to Felicity for us to be friends, but it can't be one-sided. You have to give a little, too, otherwise it isn't going to work."

"I apologize," he said, his tone formal as he bowed his head slightly. I gave him a look of bewilderment, wondering if he'd time traveled here from the past. He noticed my expression and changed his posture as he cleared his throat. "Normal teenage interactions aren't something I'm particularly accustomed to."

"Clearly," I stated with raised brows. "Can I give you a couple pointers?"

After a moment, he slowly said, "Yes, I suppose that would be alright."

I started walking again, glancing back to make sure he followed. "First of all, relax. Don't be so uptight, so . . . proper. I'm not sure who you grew up around, but teenagers don't talk like that. At least, not teenagers from this century."

He nodded slowly, his brow furrowed as he absorbed what I was saying.

"And secondly, add to the conversation. If someone is speaking to you, reply. Preferably with a kinder tone than you typically use."

He peered at me as we reached our class and said, "I guess I can try."

"Okay then." I nodded once before turning my back to him and heading to my seat.

While Mrs. Sanchez spoke too loudly about how you conjugate verbs, my eyes were drawn to Matthew. He seemed deep in thought, and a couple times, I caught him mouthing words to himself. He might not be the person I'd originally thought he was, but there was no denying he was weird. There was something very different about him.

When the bell rang, I gathered my books and headed to the door, expecting to see Ben as I'd grown accustomed to. To my surprise, he wasn't there. I frowned, suddenly sad. I'd got used to him walking with me.

I accepted the fact that I'd be walking alone when someone cleared their throat behind me. I turned to see Matthew standing there with narrowed eyes and a heavy frown. I internally shivered, wondering if my earlier words had made him angry.

"Would you care to walk to class with me again?" he asked.

"I'm sorry, what?" I questioned, blinking rapidly.

"Would you care to walk to class with me?" he repeated, and I let out a single, breathy laugh.

"S-sure."

It took everything in me to follow as he stalked away, the warning bells in my head not quieting. From the corner of my eye, I noticed him looking at me.

"May I ask you a question?" he asked.

"Yeah, of course," I replied.

"Why did you react like that when I asked you to walk with me?"

My mouth lifted in a smile, and a surprised laugh escaped me.

"Are you serious?" I asked, trying to process his odd nature. He nodded once. "Because you looked *pissed*. I thought you were about to cuss me out in the middle of the hall."

"Oh," he murmured. "I didn't intend to appear that way."

"Well, you might want to work on that RBF then," I told him jokingly. His brows furrowed so I explained before he could ask. "Resting bitch face."

I was hoping he would laugh, or at least smile, but he remained as serious as ever. "Apparently, I need to work on everything to fit in with people here."

I wanted to question what he meant by that but refrained. I didn't think I'd understand even if he tried to explain.

In AP Literature, Mr. Julian paired us up in groups of four to read, dissect, and rework a scene from *Romeo and Juliet*. I was put in group eight with Matthew, Amara, and a loud-mouthed jock named Zack.

"Group one, you'll have Act One, Scene One. Group two, you're going to do Act One, Scene Four," Mr. Julian said, assigning us scenes, and I groaned when we received Act Five, Scene Three: the tragic conclusion of the story that contained the goodbye kiss. "Get with your groups and get started. We'll be performing the scenes at the end of the week, and your group essay will be due on Monday."

The room echoed with the sound of desks scraping the floor as people rearranged their seats to face their groups.

We ended up in the far back corner, and I opened my book, ready to get started.

"Okay, so first things first. Who wants to play who? There's Romeo, Juliet, Paris, and the friar," I said, glancing from one person to the next.

Matthew looked confused, and Amara kept her head down, her hair a blanket of protection. With her shyness, I knew this was the worst possible situation for her.

"I call Romeo," Zack replied, raising his hand up with a smirk.

"Okay. I guess that means Matthew will be Paris?" I asked. He shrugged his shoulders slightly, and I rolled my eyes. "Paris it is."

"Now which one of you ladies gets the pleasure of kissing me?" Zack asked, flexing his arms.

I turned my nose up in disgust as Matthew's head snapped towards him, his mouth a tight line. I looked at Amara, wanting to make this as painless as possible for her.

"Which one will be better for you?" I asked gently. "The friar has more lines, but Juliet has to get kissed."

Amara peeked out from behind her hair to look at Zack, and her cheeks instantly flushed bright red.

"It's just a quick peck though," I assured her.

Zack snorted, leaning back in his seat with his arms raised behind his head as he wiggled his eyebrows. "Sure. That's all it's going to be."

"What is that supposed to mean?" Matthew hissed, his eyes blazing.

Zack laughed loudly, unfazed. "Chill, dude. They'll be begging for more of the Zack Attack after getting a taste."

Matthew's jaw tensed, and the muscles in his neck rippled. In one fluid motion, he was on his feet with Zack pinned against the wall, his arm pressing violently into his throat. Zack attempted a swing at Matthew but ended up with his arm pinned above his head instead. Our classmates stared on in shock as Zach spit at him.

Zack was burly, towering over Matthew by at least a head, but Matthew didn't appear to be struggling in the slightest to hold him there. Mr. Julian jumped up from his chair and ran our way.

"Learn some respect," Matthew wildly spat at Zack, whose face was beginning to turn red. "Otherwise, I'll be forced to teach you a lesson."

"Hey! Break it up! Now!" Mr. Julian yelled. He was usually laid-back and friendly with all the students, so it was alarming to hear him speak in such a tone.

Matthew stared at Zack for a moment longer then released him, his face emotionless. Zack coughed violently, his hand reaching for his throat while actively glaring at Matthew.

"You two to the office *now!*" Mr. Julian said angrily.

Matthew immediately turned around and waltzed away with his head held high while Zack stumbled out a couple steps behind him. Amara and I stared at each other with wide eyes and open mouths, unsure how to proceed, when Mr. Julian approached us.

"Can one of you please tell me what that was all about?" he asked.

"Um . . ." I trailed off uncertainly. "I think Matthew was defending our honor."

Mr. Julian raised his brows, and I knew it sounded as ridiculous as I thought it did. "I beg your pardon?" he asked.

"Zack was being a pompous, patronizing pig about the kissing scene, and Matthew didn't like it. He told him to learn some respect."

Mr. Julian nodded slowly before saying, "Good for him." He grinned then gave us a wink before turning to walk away. "I'll assign Zack to a different group. Oh, and nice use of alliteration, Ms. Hayes."

"Thank you," I replied, amused by his tranquil reaction. I turned back to Amara and mouthed the words *"Holy crap."*

"That was insane," she said, and I nodded. "Can I tell you something?"

"Of course."

She picked at her fingernails without meeting my gaze. "I, uh, I didn't like Matthew very much before now."

"Why not?"

"No real reason. He just looked like a troublemaker. I thought he was going to cause problems here."

I smiled a little bit, feeling less guilty about my own first impression of him.

"Can I tell you something?" I asked, and she watched me expectantly. "I thought the same thing."

"Really?" She relaxed her shoulders and let go of her hair. "I'm glad I wasn't the only one!"

"What do you think of him now?"

"Well, after what just happened . . . I think he's probably a person with good intentions but goes about things in the wrong way. You don't meet many people who will stand up for others or call someone out for being nasty. But I don't think hurting someone like that is the way to get your point across."

"I think I'd have to agree with that," I remarked quietly.

Matthew really was as chivalrous as Felicity claimed. Without even knowing Amara, he'd protected her from Zack's subtle threats. The way he'd contained Zack so quickly, without even a hint of struggle, made me think he'd been in situations like that before, and it made me wonder where he'd learned to do that and why. Did he learn it to protect others from something or to protect himself?

"Still," Amara added, "I have to admit I'm grateful for the intervention, even if it was physical."

"Me too Amara. Believe me . . . me too."

# CHAPTER TEN

"Hello, Robin," Annie Larson greeted me as Felicity and I walked into their grand, two-story foyer. She was a mirror image of Felicity—only older—with auburn hair swept into an elegant updo and green eyes lightly coated with dark makeup.

"Hi, Annie," I replied, welcoming the hug she wrapped me in.

"I hear we should be expecting you more often than usual." Her bright-red lips lifted in a smile. "Tell your mom I said congratulations. We really should have her over for dinner sometime soon."

"I'll relay the message," I said, and she nodded then turned to Felicity.

"I'm meeting your father and the Andersons to start planning our fundraising campaign. Then we're having dinner with them and the Durhams. Would you like us to bring you home anything?"

Felicity shook her head. "No, thanks. Robin and I are going to pick something up after our mani-pedis."

"Okay. You two have fun and be safe." She kissed Felicity on the forehead and gave me a wave before exiting the large double doors.

"Mani-pedis?" I asked as Felicity led us up the spiral staircase. I admired the intricately carved mahogany railing as I always did when my hand slid over it.

"Of course!" Felicity exclaimed. "You can't have a girl's day without a mani-pedi."

"But it's basketball season. I don't think fake nails would be very wise."

"You don't have to get fake nails. Just let them pamper your hands and paint your real nails."

She had me there. Her hands were always lovely with fresh styles and paint. Mine most definitely were not, so this would be a treat for me. We walked to her wing of the second story, and I paused to take in the sights, which always left me wowed.

Two bedrooms had been redesigned and molded together to create a massive bedroom off an open common area. The original crown molding and hardwood floors were refurbished throughout the entire home to keep the authenticity, but Felicity's space was anything but charming.

The wood was covered by a plush, blood-red carpet with bright-white couches and a modern coffee table sitting upon it. A sixty-five-inch television was mounted to one wall and framed with red, black, and white shelves.

Pillows in the same color scheme accented the bay windows, and bookshelves full of items lined the back wall. Speakers hung strategically so the sound was evenly distributed throughout the entire wing, and a collection of retro guitars and old records decorated the walls.

"I will never not be in awe of your house," I told her as I turned in a circle.

She smiled and looked around as well. "Yeah, it's pretty great." We walked to the far side of the room and entered her bedroom, which was decorated in the same colors as the common area, but these walls were lined with pictures of friends, family, and herself in the various productions she'd acted in. "I'm just going to change, then we can head out."

"Okay," I said, flopping myself onto her bed.

"Matthew told me he was sent to the office today," Felicity called out from inside her closet.

"Really?" I hugged a fluffy, red pillow.

"Yeah. He was late to our meeting place during free period, and he apologized and told me that's where he was."

"Did he tell you why?"

She popped her head out the door with a sheepish look. "I was actually going to ask you since you guys have that class together. All he said was he and Zack got into it."

"You could say that," I said slowly.

Felicity emerged from her closet wearing a lavender sweater and name-brand black jeans that showed off her small figure. She sat down on the upholstered chair in the corner and started to pull on her sandals before looking at me expectantly. I explained the events that took place earlier that day, and her eyes got wider and wider as I continued.

"Wow," she said. "Zack has always been such a jerk. It's about time someone put him in his place. But I wonder why Matthew didn't tell me himself."

"Maybe he thought you'd be upset."

"No," she responded, looking deep in thought. "I don't think that's it."

"What do you think it is then?"

"I think he's the type of person who doesn't see the good he does. Or when he does, he doesn't want praise for it."

"I mean, maybe. I guess you would know better than me," I replied with a shrug.

"Well, I'm just glad he didn't get hurt." She walked to her vanity and began touching up her makeup.

"I don't think Zack could've hurt him even if he tried. Matthew had him pinned pretty easily. Zack wasn't getting out of it."

Felicity cocked one brow. "Really? Dang. I know he has some muscle on him, but I didn't know he was *that* strong."

"I don't think it was just muscle. He had him, like, *strategically* held. Like he's been trained in self-defense or something."

She raised both brows now as she looked at me in the mirror. "What, like a ninja or something?" she asked with humor in her voice.

"No, more like an assassin," I shot back, and she rolled her eyes.

"Maybe he's taken karate or martial-arts classes," she suggested. I pondered that, knowing it was a pretty reasonable option. "Lots of people do."

"That's true."

She smirked and got a sly look in her eyes. "Not that I mind him being all badass and protective. I think it's sexy."

"Of course, you do." I suddenly remembered the questions I had for her. "Speaking of which, is there something more going on between you two?"

"What do you mean?"

"Are you guys dating?"

"No, of course not!" she exclaimed. "You know I would tell you. What makes you think that?"

"It's just that you two are very . . . comfortable around one another," I said, choosing 'comfortable' for lack of a better word.

"Is that a bad thing?"

"No."

"Then?"

"It just seems intense," I blurted out. "The vibe you give off is all-consuming. You both get so absorbed in the other, and your whole demeanor changes. And the way he looks at you . . ." I trailed off, coming to a conclusion I didn't know if I should say out loud.

"The way he looks at me?" Felicity pressed, hanging on my every word with wide eyes.

"He looks at you . . . like he's in love," I finally said. Felicity looked down at her hands as a timid smile crossed her face. She sat quiet for too long, and I grew impatient, so interrupted her thoughts. "Well?"

"Well, what?" She looked at me with an expression I'd never seen from her before.

"What do you think?" I asked, trying to figure out what was going on in her head.

"I think that it's way too soon for the 'L' word," she replied, but there was a sparkle in her eye, and I could tell the thought entranced her. "But I would be lying if I said the feelings I have for him aren't intense."

She sat down on her bed before continuing. "I've liked plenty of guys in the past. And I've wanted even more. But this . . . This is something so different. When he's not around, I just think about being with him again, and when I am with him, I feel so content. It's like he takes a piece of me every time he's gone, and then when he's back, he returns it . . . and I feel whole again."

I swallowed around the dryness in my throat then licked my lips. "Wow, that's . . ." I paused, then we both finished my sentence together. "Intense."

"I know," she groaned, throwing a pillow over her head. "We spent all weekend together, and it still wasn't enough time."

"Just because it hasn't been very long doesn't mean you couldn't feel something stronger than just liking him," I pointed out. "Sometimes people get lucky, and they know right away."

"It just doesn't seem realistic."

"None of the best love stories are." I offered her a warm smile that she returned. "Don't focus on the time frame. If it feels right, that's all that matters. It's not like you guys are confessing anything to each other anyway, so just keep doing what you're doing now—hanging out and being friends. At least until one of you owns up to what you're feeling."

"I guess you're right."

I winked at her and said, "Of course, I am."

"Whatever." She pushed me off the bed, joining in on my laughter as I picked myself up from the floor.

She hopped after me, an enthusiastic ball of energy, and started discussing our outing as I replayed our conversation in my head. I had the feeling her 'friendship' with Matthew wouldn't last much longer before one of them took it to the next level. He was clearly important to her, so I needed to make sure I took more initiative to interact with him. Matthew and I would be friends before he knew it.

# CHAPTER ELEVEN

"Do you guys want to go to the movies with us tonight?" I asked Matthew and Ben in the hall the next day.

Felicity gasped. "That's a great idea! We could get dinner before too."

Matthew hesitated, so I added, "Come on, it'll be fun! No different than when you're with all of us here."

"Yes, I suppose that's true." He thought it over a moment longer then said, "I'll join you."

"Great!" I looked over at Ben. "What about you?"

"I wish I could, but I'm attending a powwow with my family today," he replied, looking less than pleased at the idea of missing out. "I could try to skip out of it this time around though."

My stomach churned at the idea of him not coming. I'd been planning on him and Felicity being our usual buffer. Without him there, Matthew and I would have to help hold up our sides of the conversations. Maybe this hadn't been such a good idea after all.

"No, that's okay," I said, trying to assure myself as much as him. "I know how much those mean to your family. We can plan something for the four of us to do some other time."

"For sure!" Felicity agreed eagerly. "But until then, the three of us will have to have fun without you."

"You'll have to try awful hard to make up for my absence," Ben teased, nudging her shoulder with his arm.

"I'm sure we'll manage," I said sweetly, ignoring my inner turmoil.

"Well," he said with a wicked gleam in his eye, "when you end up spending all night missing me, I don't want to hear your cries about it tomorrow."

I rolled my eyes. "And I don't want to hear your cries about it when we tell you how much fun we had without you."

He brought a hand up to his chest in feigned shock, shaking his head in disappointment. "I am appalled at you."

"The feeling is mutual," I replied, forcing my mouth into a pout.

Felicity snorted. "And here I thought *I* was the drama queen," she remarked with an amused smirk as Ben and I grinned.

Matthew looked on with thoughtful, observant eyes—as he often did—then said, "It appears these two are trying to give you a run for your money."

We all stared at him, shocked. It was the first time he'd added anything to a conversation without being prodded or coaxed. Felicity beamed at him and put her hand on his shoulder.

"Don't worry. They'll never reach my level," she told him playfully.

He gave her a tight smile and a nod of the head. "I have no doubt."

"I'll pick you both up around five then," she said.

"I can drive us," Matthew offered, surprising me again as Felicity automatically agreed. "I'll just need your address, Robin."

I hesitated. The situation with my parents had grown heated last night, and I didn't want any outside eyes subjected to a brawl if they were at odds again.

"If you're uncomfortable with that arrangement, we can decide on something else," Matthew said, sensing my discomfort.

"No, no," I replied quickly. "It's not that. It's just . . . It's nothing. That'll be fine. Felicity can give you directions to my house."

The first bell rang so we parted ways in pairs with Felicity and Matthew going one way and Ben and I in another.

"Matthew seems to be coming around to the idea of friends," Ben said.

I nodded. "Slowly but surely. Do you ever wonder what kind of life he's had for high school to be so foreign to him?"

"All the time. But it's not my place to pry into that, and it isn't yours either." He gave me a pointed look, seeing through my question.

I sighed heavily. "Yeah, I know. But sometimes I just get so curious."

"I do too. But whatever is in his past doesn't change who he is to us right now."

"And who is he to us?" I asked for argument's sake.

"A friend who just needs help adapting."

I couldn't help but stare at him in admiration, taking in his physical features as I thought about the ones that couldn't be seen—his kind heart, his selflessness, his drive to help others. If more people possessed even one of those traits, the world would be such a better place. Even with the mistakes he'd made in the past, he was the epitome of a pure soul.

He noticed me looking at him and one corner of his lips turned up. "What?"

"You just amaze me," I said.

He stuck his hands in his pockets, and the smallest hint of a light blush spotted his cheeks. "Why? I didn't do anything."

I grabbed his arm, pulling him into a corner by some lockers. My hand traveled to his chest, resting there as our eyes locked onto one another.

"Benjamin Toves, you are so much more than you give yourself credit for," I murmured, repeating his words to me from the other night.

He cocked his head slightly, his eyes thoughtful as they observed me. Questions cluttered my brain as rationality tried to tell me not to do what I was about to do, but I tuned it all out. Instead, I bit my lower lip then gently pushed him back until he was up against the side of the locker. I leaned forward, tipping my head back as I approached him. His eyes lit up as he realized what I was doing. He brought his hands to my waist as he leaned down and—

"Get to class!" a teacher snapped as she passed by.

"Damn it," Ben growled as we both straightened up, and I squeezed my lips together in an effort not to laugh.

"Third time's the charm," I said lightly before turning around and walking away without giving him a chance to respond.

I looked over my shoulder before entering class and saw him watching me from the same spot where I'd left him. A goofy smile lingered on his face, and when our eyes met, he gave me a wink. I let my hair fall over my face as I blushed. He was turning me into a hot mess.

* * *

Felicity texted me when they were on my street, per my request. Dad was working on a project in the back yard, so I quickly jumped out of my chair and slid my purse over my shoulder.

"Bye!" I called into the living room as I passed, not stopping.

"Be safe, honey," Mom replied from where she sat doing a puzzle with Dawn.

"Have fun!" Dawn yelled.

I blew them a kiss as I stepped out the door then jogged to the end of the driveway as a dark-grey Honda Accord with tinted windows pulled up to the curb. The driver's door opened, and Matthew stepped out wearing a long-sleeved, button-up shirt that matched the color of the car. It was weird seeing him in something other than his typical black T-shirt, but I had to admit he looked good.

"Robin," he said, walking around the car.

"Matthew."

He gave me a side-eyed look that resembled amusement then opened the back door for me as I blinked in surprise.

"Thank you," I managed to say as I slid into the leather interior.

Felicity was turned around in the front seat with a smile on her face as Matthew shut the door. Her lightly tousled hair and subtle makeup gave her a young look, and her dark-green sweater highlighted her eyes, which were bright with excitement.

"You look great," I told her.

"Thank you!" she responded. "This is going to be so fun."

Matthew got back in the car and began driving. "Where are we eating?"

"I was thinking Patisserie Boissiere," Felicity said with a perfect French accent, and I made a face.

"That's a bit fancy for my taste, Felicity. At least for a group outing," I said.

"For any outing," Matthew agreed, giving her an apologetic look.

She pouted for a quick second then shrugged. "Fine. What do you guys want then?"

"How about Brighton Bistro?" Matthew suggested.

"Oh, I love that place!" I exclaimed.

"I do as well," Matthew said, looking at me in the rearview mirror. I smiled, and he nodded his head once—a motion I was coming to learn meant he approved. "Felicity, is that okay with you?"

"Sure. Who doesn't like a good bistro every now and then?"

"Brighton Bistro it is then," Matthew said, turning down Main Street.

He parked in front of the restaurant's windows—through which people passing by could check out the charming décor—before getting out and going around to Felicity's door. I exited the car as he held his hand out to her. She grabbed onto it, and I let them walk ahead of me as I observed them from behind.

Matthew still had Felicity's hand in his, and she leaned into him as they walked. She looked so petite next to him, but they actually made a cute couple. When we got to our table, Matthew pulled Felicity's seat out for her, and she looked down timidly as she sat.

"Thank you," she told him.

"Of course." He looked towards where I'd already sat down. "I would've gotten your chair for you as well."

"That's very kind of you," I replied, not sure what else to say.

"I told you he was chivalrous," Felicity said as she fawned over him.

He watched the table intently, and I thought I could detect a little bit of color rising to his cheeks. Felicity certainly knew how to bring out the normal teenager in him.

After we placed our orders, Felicity charged into a conversation. Matthew and I nodded at appropriate times but seldomly responded, so she finally crossed her arms and pursed her lips as she stared us down.

"I didn't come to dinner by myself you know," she said. "I'm not going to do all the talking."

"Sorry," I replied. "I'm just not sure what to say."

"Just talk." She raised her arms before letting them fall onto the table with a thud. "Both of you. It's not that hard to have a conversation. You do it when you're alone with me all the time."

"I believe the problem is that Robin and I aren't comfortable around one another yet," Matthew said. "We aren't purposely trying to be uncivil towards one another. It just isn't . . ."

"Natural," I filled in when he couldn't seem to find the right word.

"Yes, exactly. I'm sure once we know each other better, it'll be easier like how it is between you and I."

"But that's a little hard when you've been told not to ask personal questions," I commented.

Matthew furrowed his brows. "I never said you couldn't ask personal questions."

"No, I know," I replied. "Felicity asked me not to since you don't like talking about yourself."

"Well, that is true." He pressed his lips together, then took a deep breath before letting it out in a huff. "Felicity, I appreciate you trying to look out for my feelings on that and, Robin, I appreciate you respecting it. It means a great deal that you'd both even try. However, Robin is right. None of you can get to know me if I'm not willing to talk about myself at all."

"You don't have to though," Felicity said, placing her hand on his arm.

"I know, and there's many things I won't discuss. But I'm open to answering some simpler questions." He looked at me expectantly, folding his hands on top of the table. "Go ahead."

I glanced at Felicity, who was biting her lip, and could tell she was nervous this might turn out badly. Matthew nodded when I turned my gaze back to him, so I decided to appease them both by asking the most mundane of questions.

"Okay. What's your favorite color?" I asked.

"That's what you want to know?" he questioned, cocking one brow as Felicity mouthed the words 'thank you' in my direction.

"For now," I replied. "Enjoy the easy ones while you can."

"Noted. Okay, favorite color would have to be black."

I snorted. "Big surprise."

"It's neutral and doesn't draw attention—exactly to my liking."

"Noted," I said, purposely copying him. "Favorite number?"

"Is that a thing?"

"Yes."

"Well, I don't have one."

"Neither do I," Felicity told him. "Robin is just a weirdo."

"I resent that," I said with a grimace before asking, "Favorite season?"

"Fall."

"Mine too!"

"You guys are crazy. Summer all the way," Felicity said.

"Too hot for my liking," Matthew replied.

"Agreed. Give me falling leaves and a cool breeze any day," I said. "Favorite board game?"

"Don't remember ever playing any," Matthew said. Felicity and I both stared at him, slack jawed. "What?"

"You've never played a board game?" Felicity asked, tilting her head quizzically.

"Not that I can recall." His eyes jumped back and forth between us. "Is that really so uncommon?"

"Yeah, actually, it is," I replied. "Where did you grow up that you never played any kind of game?"

His jaw tightened, and his temples pulsed as he ground his teeth together. "Never mind that."

"You're going to shut down the conversation just because we hit a sore spot?" I asked, somewhat rudely. "It's not even anything serious. Why does something like that of all things make you switch off?"

"Robin," Felicity said in a warning tone.

I glanced at her, and she shook her head as Matthew continued to stare past me bleakly. I tightened my eyes and opened my mouth, but she shook her head again, this time with more conviction. I pressed my lips into a tight line as annoyance crept through me.

"Favorite animal?" I asked despite wanting to press the issue of his bizarre behavior some more.

He thought about it for a moment before saying, "A wolf, I suppose."

"Why a wolf?" Felicity asked as she rested her chin on her hand and watched him with fascination in her eyes.

"A wolf symbolizes instinct, intelligence, and a lack of trust," he replied.

We waited for him to elaborate more but when he didn't, I asked, "Do you just like what it represents or is it because you relate to those traits?"

"Both."

"So it's your spirit animal."

"My what?" Matthew's brows pulled together.

"Your spirit animal," Felicity said. "It's basically a spirit that you share characteristics with who guides you through life or problems or whatever."

"Is that a real thing?" Matthew asked, his confusion turning to skepticism.

"In some cultures, yes," I replied. "For us it's more of a fun pastime to talk about though."

"I see."

"Yeah. Never heard of that either, huh?"

"Obviously not," Felicity answered for him, shooting me another sharp look.

I pursed my lips as the conversation lulled then started fidgeting with the tablecloth as I waited for someone else to say something. But no one did. Before the moment could become too strained, our waiter came with our food, and we all focused on our plates. The only sound was the clanking of our utensils as we ate, and I didn't dare look up in fear of risking awkward eye contact.

"That was good," Felicity said, breaking the silence when we had all finished eating, and Matthew and I mumbled unintelligible words of agreement. "This was fun! Right?"

We stared at her with the same expression, our brows arched and the corner of our lips twitching with amusement.

"I wouldn't exactly call it fun," Matthew replied, "but it was certainly interesting."

"Interesting is good too," Felicity said, unbothered by our lack of enthusiasm, then bit her lip. "Actually, I have a confession to make."

"What's that?" I asked.

"I thought this was going to go way worse than it did," she responded, and I laughed once.

"Really? Because it went just as bad as I expected it to." I glanced at Matthew. "No offense."

"None taken," he said. "I was expecting a tense evening as well."

"But it really wasn't that bad!" Felicity exclaimed earnestly. "I mean, sure, it wasn't great, but I feel like you both were more friendly than usual."

"Only for your benefit," Matthew told her.

"Agreed," I said.

"Hey, it's a start," Felicity replied. "Soon enough you'll be best friends! I just know it."

Matthew and I exchanged a look, and I could see the amusement in his face that mirrored my own.

I grinned and shrugged. "Maybe so."

"A definite possibility," he said.

Felicity narrowed her eyes slightly. "Don't patronize me."

A laugh escaped me as Matthew smiled at her.

"We do it because we love you," I told her.

"We'll see who's laughing when I turn out to be right."

"Guess so."

The check came, interrupting our banter. Matthew pulled out his wallet and put a credit card on the table before Felicity or I even had a chance to look at the total owed.

"I can pay for mine," I said.

"Me too," Felicity agreed.

"That's okay. I don't mind," Matthew replied.

"Well, I do," Felicity said. "It's not like this was a date."

Matthew shifted uncomfortably, glancing my way.

"Unless it was?" I asked, wiggling my brows.

Felicity looked at Matthew with scrutiny. "Was it?"

"No, of course not," Matthew replied, focusing his attention on her. "You'll know when it's a date."

"Does that mean you plan on us having an official date then?" Felicity pried, but he hesitated, no doubt uncomfortable by my presence.

"Yes," he finally admitted. "I do. If you say yes when I ask you, of course."

"I doubt you'll have to worry about her saying yes," I remarked more to myself than them since they were too busy staring at one another.

"When are you going to ask?" Felicity pushed, her grin reaching from ear to ear.

"As soon as we don't have a third party around," he answered, smiling at her gently, and I made a face at the table as the awkwardness finally became too much.

"I can leave you two alone now if you like," I said.

That snapped them out of their moment, and they turned towards me.

"No, don't," Felicity said, grabbing my hand from across the table. "I'm sorry if we made you feel uncomfortable."

"When Ben joins us, it can be a double date so no one is left out in the cold," Matthew added. I let out a snort, causing Matthew's brows to furrow. "Are you two not together?"

"Let's just say he hasn't asked me out on an official date either," I replied.

Matthew nodded, but his expression still held a hint of confusion. "You appear to be an item," he said, causing Felicity to laugh, and I narrowed my eyes at her.

"Well, so do you and Felicity but you're not," I told Matthew, and he cleared his throat.

"Yes, I see your point," he said. "I apologize for the assumption."

Luckily, our waiter came back with a receipt for Matthew, ending our conversation. After thanking him for his service, we headed out, walking up the street to the movie theatre.

I charged ahead of Matthew and Felicity, getting to the ticket booth so I could pay for myself.

"Stubborn, isn't she?" I barely heard Matthew say to Felicity as I veered towards the concession stand.

When we settled into our seats, I stuffed my mouth full of popcorn as Matthew and Felicity discussed movie preferences. Unsurprisingly, Matthew retained very little knowledge of popular blockbusters.

*Was he living off the grid all his life? Why is he so peculiar?*

As the movie started, I pushed all thoughts of him out of my mind, letting the picture on the screen keep my attention. When it ended, the three of us talked about what we thought of it.

The conversation lasted as we got in the car and drove to my house, not allowing for any extra small talk or awkward lulls, which I was grateful for. When we reached home, I said a quick goodbye with the promise of seeing them both the next day.

When I opened up our front door, my parents were arguing in the living room, their voices low but angry. I snuck through the hall into my room and leaned against the door after closing it. Their muffled words still reached me, and I sighed heavily, hating that this was our normal. Mom deserved better than the erratic relationship Dad gave her, and I just hoped he could straighten himself out for her and Dawn.

I wondered, not for the first time, if things would get better after I graduated and left the house. I always had this nagging feeling I was the reason he spiraled. He curried favor to Dawn the moment she was born, ousting me almost immediately, and he wasn't subtle about it either. For some reason, he didn't want to be around me—he didn't want me in his life. He didn't want to be my dad and he didn't want me to be his daughter.

I swallowed around the lump forming in my throat. I'd dealt with this reality for years, so you'd think it wouldn't affect me so heavily anymore. But it did. It hurt. It hurt to be unloved. It hurt to be unwanted. And it hurt even more because I saw how much he loved and wanted Dawn. He was a good father to her, so why did he hate me? Why love one daughter but not the other?

I took a deep breath, letting it out slowly as I sat on the edge of my bed. I'd probably never get answers to any of my questions, and I needed to accept that. I didn't need his love anyway. I was fine without it.

# CHAPTER TWELVE

"My parents are so excited you're coming over," Ben told me during free period as he watched me do my homework.

"I'm excited too," I replied, writing in an answer on my paper. "I've missed them. And your little brothers."

"They aren't so little anymore," he said. "Mahka is taller than you now and Dakota is probably close."

"Nu-uh!" I gasped in disbelief, looking up from my work. "They're like what? Fifteen and twelve now?"

"Yep. Looks like they got my dad's tall genes just like I did."

I shook my head. "Your parents bred giants."

"Definitely," Ben agreed with a grin. "You ready to get out of here?"

"Just one second." I finished writing out another answer before packing up my books and slinging my bag over my shoulder. "Did you want me to meet you at your house closer to dinner time?"

His face fell slightly. "Actually, I thought you'd come over now and hang out for a while."

"Oh, okay."

"You don't have to if you don't want to."

"No, I definitely want to," I assured him, and he lit up again, smiling from ear to ear. "But I do have to run home first."

"That's fine. I can take you and wait."

After a quick debate in my head, I decided my dad probably wouldn't be home. Before Ben could take my hesitation as another sign I didn't want to be around him, I said, "Sounds good to me. I'm sure my mom and Dawn would love to see you anyway."

"Great! Let's be off then, shall we?" He offered me one arm while the other gestured in front of us, and I laughed as I placed my hand on his bicep.

He smiled down at me softly, his eyes taking me in, and I ducked my head, rubbing my lips together and pulling my hand back to my side as heat rushed to my cheeks.

"I missed that," he said.

"Missed what?" I asked as we walked.

"How easy it is to make you blush."

I pressed my lips together in a tight line before grumbling, "Wow, thanks."

A loud laugh escaped his mouth, and I couldn't help but giggle in response. When we stepped outside, the sun was barely peeking through the clouds, and we rushed to his car to avoid the dropping temperatures. He opened the passenger door for me, and I arched my brow.

"Taking lessons from Matthew?" I asked.

"Excuse me, but I learned this from my father," he replied playfully. "Had you let me take you anywhere before this, you would know that."

"Well, shame on me." I shook my head.

"Honestly though." He winked before shutting my door and getting in on the other side.

The drive to my house was quick, and we both got out of the car and crossed the lawn. He nudged me with his shoulder, nearly causing me to fall over, and I shoved him back, letting out a grunt of annoyance when he didn't shift at all. Suddenly, loud voices made their way to my ears, and I stopped in my tracks as I realized what we were about to see.

"What's wrong?" Ben asked.

I bit my lip, too ashamed to answer. The yelling got louder as my parents made their way out the front door. My usually composed mom had tears running down her cheeks and daggers shooting from her eyes at my dad, whose face was red with anger. I stood there, paralyzed at the scene as they screamed profanities at one another.

Ben put a hand on my shoulder, and I fought back tears as my heart sank. This is exactly what I didn't want him or anyone else to see.

"I can't believe you're being so selfish! You're going to tear our family apart over nothing! What the hell is the matter with you?" Dad yelled as he stomped over to his bike.

"She isn't nothing! And you did this to yourself, Mark!" Mom replied angrily. She paused when she saw me, and sorrow filled her widened eyes. "Oh, Robin . . ."

I rushed over to her. "Are you okay?"

"I'm so sorry you walked in on this," she replied, ignoring my question.

"Don't baby the girl," Dad growled, stepping back towards us. "She should know what's going on. She should know what you're doing and who caused it!"

"Stop it, Mark!" Mom snapped as he came closer.

"She should know!" he spat out again. Ben walked over briskly and stepped between us, his arm raised slightly towards me in an idle attempt to block us from my dad's rage. "Tell her, Rebecca. Tell her or I will!"

"I think that's enough, Mr. Hayes," Ben said, and Dad glanced at him with a sneer.

"You think I'm going to listen to you just because you're bigger than me?" He scoffed, turning his nose up in disgust. "What are you going to do? Hit me?"

"No, sir," Ben replied as serious as could be.

"Then butt out," Dad said, stepping up to him with a glare.

"I'm not going to do that."

"You need to mind your own business."

"It became my business when I felt like you were threatening people I care about."

"Would you rather I threaten you then?" Dad asked, a gleam in his eyes I didn't recognize.

My eyes darted back and forth between the two as my heart raced. Dad poked Ben in the chest roughly, and a protective feeling washed over me, followed quickly by a surge of energy through my veins. The sensation was both foreign and familiar, reminding me how I'd felt at lunch the day the water cups fell over and spilled.

Dad took one final step towards Ben, just inches away now. I huffed angrily, and the odd feeling of energy worked its way through my body before pushing outward through my hands. The sprinklers in the yard came to life then, spitting water directly at my dad. All four of us jumped back in surprise as the sprinklers continued to spray in that one spot.

Dad muttered incoherently as he shook the water from his hands and face. He scowled at us, shaking his head as he gave Ben a once over, then headed back to his motorcycle. He started it up, revved the engine, then peeled out of the driveway without giving us another look. Ben turned towards me and put his hand on my back. I could see the concern in his eyes, but I turned to my mom, ignoring the questions that he was throwing my way.

"Are you okay?" I asked Mom again as she took deep, calming breaths.

"I should be asking you that." She sighed and rubbed her hand over her face. "I'm so sorry you had to be involved in that. Both of you." She looked at Ben with furrowed brows. "He had no right coming at you like that. I'm sorry."

"It's okay, Mrs. Hayes," Ben replied.

"No, it isn't. But thank you for being so gracious."

"Where's Dawn?" I asked, knowing they wouldn't be fighting like that around her.

"She went home with a friend after school," Mom answered.

"At least she wasn't here. What happened anyway?" I asked.

"Your father and I are taking some time apart," she said. "He has problems he needs to get figured out before he can be a good husband and father again. Until then, I can't keep letting him be around us and cause such friction in our home."

"I'm sorry, Mom," I murmured.

I was proud of her for finally protecting herself and us from his toxicity, but I knew how much she must be hurting. I only hoped he could become the man we'd once known and loved, for her sake.

"It had to be done," she responded quietly.

"Is that what he was talking about?" I asked. "What he wanted you to tell me?"

She hesitated before responding. "Yes."

I cocked my head to the side. She was lying.

"Well, anyway," she said, shutting down the conversation as she turned to Ben and wrapped him in a hug. "It's good to see you again, Ben."

"You too, Mrs. Hayes," he replied with a radiant smile.

"We're going over to Ben's house to hang out until dinner," I said as we walked inside. "We just stopped by so I could finish my physics project and email it to Mr. Garcia."

"Sounds good," Mom said. "I'll entertain Ben while you finish."

"I'll only be about ten minutes," I told Ben.

"Take all the time you need," he replied, following Mom into the kitchen.

I crept up behind her and whispered in her ear, "Please don't embarrass me."

She shot me a wink, and I let out a groan before going into my room. I quickly finished what I needed to do and sent it off, wanting to separate Ben and Mom before she said something I could never live down. I heard them laughing and stood to intervene. Before making it out the door, I paused to look at myself in the small mirror next to the closet.

I patted my hair into place, gently pinched some color onto my cheeks, and straightened my collared shirt and necklace. I smiled in appreciation then shook my head at my reflection and let out a laugh, feeling ridiculous. Ben saw me every day. How silly was it to start caring about how I looked in front of him now?

"She never told me that!" Ben was exclaiming as I exited my room and came into view of them.

"Who never told you what?" I asked, eyeing them suspiciously.

"Nothing," they said simultaneously with straight faces and wide eyes. It was actually a humorous sight.

"Liars," I accused, crossing my arms as they started to laugh again.

"Are you ready to go?" Ben asked, standing up from the table.

I nodded and went to give Mom a hug. "I love you," I told her.

She squeezed me tightly, holding on longer than usual, before letting go and kissing my cheek.

"You guys be safe," she said, her voice thick.

I could see her fighting back tears, so I rushed Ben out the door so she could be alone.

"Bye, Mrs. Hayes," he called over his shoulder with a wave.

We got back in his car, and he blasted the heater to fight off the cold that had enveloped us on our short commute from the house. He tightened his grip on the steering wheel slightly and let out a slow breath before turning my way.

"Are you okay?" he asked, watching me closely as I traced a pattern on my jeans. "Robin?"

I finally looked up at him, my stomach flip-flopping when I saw the concern written all over his face. "I'm fine. I hate that it came to this, but my dad dug his own grave."

"Has it been bad?" he questioned with an underlying tone in his voice that I couldn't quite place.

I shrugged indifferently. "No worse than it's been in the past. He goes through spurts. Sometimes he's great, and he'll have a steady job and be really involved with us. Well, them—Dawn and Mom. Other times, not so much."

Ben hesitated, then pressed his lips together as he looked me over inch by inch.

"What's wrong?" I asked, shifting in my seat as he continued to scrutinize me.

He took a deep breath, then hit me with a question I wasn't expecting.

"Is he hurting you?" he asked through clenched teeth.

My eyes widened at the thought, and I immediately understood why he was so upset. "No!"

"Robin—"

"Ben, it's nothing like that. I promise. He's never laid a hand on me," I insisted. "Or my mom or Dawn as far as I'm aware. He might be considered emotionally abusive, but that's it."

Ben continued to observe me, his gaze intense. He must have seen the unwavering truth in my eyes because he finally relaxed a little.

"That's not okay either but I'm glad he isn't hitting you," he said quietly. "I don't think I could've stayed passive if I found out differently."

I put my hand on his arm and offered him a half smile. "Thank you for caring. But don't ever lose who you are out of anger."

"I wouldn't under normal circumstances."

"You shouldn't under any circumstances."

"Easier said than done. The thought of something happening to you . . ." He stared at the ceiling as he shook his head then glanced at me with his forehead scrunched tight. "It may not be my place, but I feel very protective of you. I don't think I could just sit by idly if someone was hurting you."

I rubbed my lips together as I watched him struggle to speak. Butterflies fluttered in my stomach at his words, and a part of me relished on them. I realized I *wanted* him to be protective of me. I liked knowing he cared.

"I really don't know what to say," I told him after a moment of silence lingered, knowing I couldn't voice my thoughts.

"You don't have to say anything. I'm sorry if I made you uncomfortable."

"No, you didn't. You did the opposite actually."

We stared at one another, a plethora of unsaid words traveling between us. There was so much I wanted to tell him, so much I wanted him to know. I bit the inside of my lip, fighting the urge to reach out and touch him.

His restraint must not have been as strong as mine because he brought his hand up and lightly brushed a strand of hair away from my face. My throat grew dry, and I rubbed my sweaty palms against my pants. Just as I was about to open my mouth to spill my feelings, he dropped his arm and laughed nervously.

"Anyway," he said, taking my hand in his. I cleared my throat and ducked my head as he began driving. "What was your dad talking about when he kept telling your mom to tell you something?"

"You caught that too?" I asked, giving him a sideways glance. "You're more perceptive than you look."

"Ha. Ha," he said dryly. "But really, what was it about?"

I lifted one shoulder in a shrug. "I honestly don't know. Whatever it is, my mom clearly doesn't want to tell me. She lied straight to my face."

"I'm sorry," Ben said.

"Thanks," I replied, despite it not being his fault at all, but I didn't know what else to say.

We drove the rest of the way to his house in silence as a country station played songs for us. After a final left turn, we headed down a straight, gravel driveway that led to a two-story, brick home sitting a distance away from the other houses nearby. Ben parked in the muddied side of the driveway, and I took in the familiarity of what had been my second home growing up.

The chimney let out puffs of gray smoke that matched the hue of the sky, and the peeling porch rails and white window shutters still had Christmas lights hanging from them. Dead trees and bushes littered the yard, which had become more mud than grass from the winter weather. Ben came around and opened my door before helping me out to avoid the wet patches on the ground. Two figures emerged from the side of the house and an energetic whoop of greeting met my ears.

"How you doing, chica?" Mahka yelled, embracing me in a tight hug and twirling me around in a circle.

I laughed lightheartedly at the welcome and grinned up at him.

"You are *not* only fifteen!" I exclaimed as I looked him over. He was easily half a head taller than me and was well on his way to being as muscular as Ben.

"Only in number, baby," he replied with a wink.

Ben rolled his eyes then shoved him playfully in the chest before saying, "Get out of here."

Dakota peeked around the two of them to give me a small wave. He was a lot skinnier than his brothers and could best be described as tall and lanky. His twelve-year-old body was definitely in the middle of an awkward puberty stage, but the resemblance between the three of them was still uncanny. They had almost identical features, just at different points of maturity. The biggest difference between them was in their eyes, each a different hue of brown.

Dakota sauntered next to me as Ben pulled Mahka into a headlock, beginning a full-on battle. I snorted, shaking my head as Mahka ended up on the ground, then gave Dakota an awkward side hug. His blush was ferocious, and I fought back a grin. He was definitely the most reserved of the bunch.

"Benjamin. Mahka. That's no way to act in front of a lady," Kiona chastised, appearing on the front porch. Her voice was stern, but her amber eyes were full of love as she watched them pull away from one another and look up at her sheepishly.

"Sorry, Mom," they sang in unison.

"Bring that girl up here for me to see," she said with a wide smile.

Ben and I walked up the stairs and stood in front of her. She took my hands in her own and looked me up and down.

"Oh, my. You've grown up!" she exclaimed. "Such a beautiful young woman you've turned into. Inside and out from what Ben tells us."

"Thank you," I replied with a blush as Ben stuck his hands in his jacket pockets and cleared his throat pointedly at his mom.

"Yeah, you're all he talks about these days," Mahka said. He clasped his hands together and batted his eyelashes as he swayed back and forth. "Robin this, Robin that, oh Robin's so amazing!"

"I do not!" Ben denied, his face as red as a tomato, and I bit my lip in an attempt to keep from laughing.

"Robin, please, put me out of my misery and marry me!" Mahka continued dramatically before making kissy faces towards his older brother.

"Mom!" Ben whined, looking mortified.

A laugh escaped me. I covered my mouth to try to contain it, but more quickly came. I bundled over, shaking uncontrollably as my laughter filled the air. Mahka and Kiona joined in. I wiped tears from my eye and grabbed my stomach as it spasmed from the force of my laughing fit. Ben glared at the sky above him and crossed his arms in a huff.

"Okay, Mahka, that's enough," Kiona finally said with a smile still on her face. "Go find something to do and leave Ben and his guest alone."

"Yes, Ma," Mahka replied, saluting her. He left us with a parting kissy face, then jumped down the stairs to chase after Dakota.

Kiona turned her attention back to us and ran her hand over Ben's hair in a loving gesture.

"We only tease because we love you," she told him, but he only shook his head, his lips pressed together tightly. "Dinner will be ready in an hour. I'll keep your brothers away from you until then, and I'll try to keep Mahka in line at the table, okay?"

"Thank you, Mom," Ben replied, finally seeming to shed his annoyance, and she went back inside.

I took a step to follow her, but Ben stopped me.

"Wait," he said. "I want to show you something."

He grabbed my hand, then led me down the porch steps and around the side of the house to their unfenced backyard. A detached, two-car garage sat on the far right and a large fire pit consumed the middle with an assortment of chairs surrounding it. I looked to the left, expecting to see the small, rundown barn Ben and I used to claim as our clubhouse but was shocked to see it had been completely revamped.

I stared at the renovated building, completely amazed as we ventured closer. Its weather-warped siding had been replaced with new, bright-red paneling, and windowpanes filled the once empty holes. Two heavy-duty, white doors sat in place of the creaky, broken ones that used to be there, and the roof no longer sat concave. It resembled a house more than a barn now.

"Wow," I murmured as I admired it, running my hand along the wood. "Who did this?"

"I did," Ben replied proudly.

"Really?" I asked, my surprise obvious.

He nodded as he looked over the building. "Mom and Dad wanted to tear it down, but I just couldn't let go of it. So I convinced them to let me keep it as a project instead. I had to pay for all the supplies myself, but it was worth it."

"Seems like it would've been more trouble than it was worth," I said, remembering how disheveled it was.

"Not to me."

"Why's that?" I could only imagine how much money it cost him to fix it up, not to mention the time.

He looked down, shoving his hands in his pockets again. "It was the one thing I had left from our friendship. Tearing it down seemed like I was saying you were out of my life for good and, well, I just really didn't want that to be true."

"Oh." I rubbed my lips together to hide the smile that threatened to creep onto my face. It brought me an odd sense of joy knowing he wanted to salvage something from our past in order to save our future. It didn't make any sense, but emotions never did.

"Yeah."

"Well, I, for one, am really glad you saved it," I said, hoping he'd catch my underlying meaning.

He easily understood and smiled. "I am too. Want to go inside?"

"Of course!"

He unlocked the door, and we stepped into what I could only describe as a cozy man cave. A black, leather couch faced a small TV mounted to the back wall. On the opposite end of the room sat a mini fridge, a foosball table, and a dartboard. Soft white Christmas lights hung around the ceiling, enfolding us in their calming embrace.

"This is amazing!" I exclaimed, soaking it all in.

"It is pretty great," Ben agreed with a grin as he pulled two sodas from the fridge.

The harsh wind rattled the window, and I realized the room wasn't even slightly cold.

"How is it so warm?" I asked, sitting on one side of the couch with my legs pulled up beneath me.

"I insulated the walls," Ben replied. "I wanted to be able to enjoy it in here all year round."

"I would too. I can't believe this is the same place we used to play in."

Ben plopped down next to me and reached out for my hand. Before he touched it, though, he hesitated then picked-ed up the remote instead and turned on the TV.

"What's wrong?" I asked, my brows furrowing.

"Nothing."

I eyed him for a second then grabbed the remote from his hand and clicked the TV off.

"Come on. I know that's not true," I said, trying to get him to look at me.

"It's just . . ." He trailed off, and I could see him struggling to continue.

"Just?"

He sighed and turned towards me with a frown. "When I tried to tell you how I felt about you, you stopped me and basically set boundaries in order for us to remain friends."

"True," I said, stretching out the word as I voiced it slowly.

"And I was okay with that because I don't want to lose you. I've tried to be respectful of what you wanted."

"Also true."

"But it seems like you started breaking those boundaries the same day. So I guess I'm a little confused. I feel like you want to be more than just friends, even though that's not what you told me. Your actions aren't matching your words, and I don't know what's okay for me to do and what isn't."

I rubbed my lips together and nodded slowly. "You're right."

"About which part?"

"All of it." I took a deep breath and tried to ignore the nerves that filled me as I let myself open up to him. "I'm sorry I've been giving off mixed signals. When I set those boundaries, I meant them, but I knew they would be hard to follow."

"Because you thought I couldn't control myself?" he asked, frowning deeper.

I shook my head. "No, because I thought I couldn't."

He scratched the back of his head and said, "I don't understand."

I wiped my palms on my jeans. "I know . . . I'm not very good at this."

"Good at what?"

"Relationships."

"Then I bet you're glad we're not in one," he said, trying to sound light-hearted.

"No, actually."

His eyes widened slightly, and his Adam's apple moved up and down as he swallowed. "No?"

"No."

"Care to elaborate?"

I faced him head on and met his gaze, ignoring the voices that yelled at me not to become vulnerable with him. We both felt the same way about one another. Why fight it any longer?

"Over the years, you've played a lot of roles in my life, and I've always cared about you in some way—as a playmate, a brother, a best friend. You've always meant the world to me." I paused as my voice cracked, then cleared my throat, surprised at the emotion trying to break through.

"But then you changed. You started to drift away, and I could tell I was going to lose you." I stopped again to take a deep breath, letting it out shakily before continuing. "That was hard to come to terms with. But you know what was worse than that?"

He shook his head but didn't speak.

"When my best friend—the person I thought I meant everything to, the person I thought would never hurt me—told me he wished I was dead."

Ben's sorrow filled eyes hardened, and he clenched his jaw. "I can never apologize enough for that. I'll never not hate myself for it."

I held up my hand to stop him from saying more. "I don't want another apology. You already apologized and I forgave you. The only reason I'm only bringing it up is to help explain what I'm feeling."

He licked his lips and nodded, but his fists were still bunched up at his sides, so I reached out and placed my hands over them. He slowly relaxed, and I smiled softly before continuing.

"I, obviously, held onto a lot of resentment towards you for that for a long time, and I just grew to accept the fact that we were done. Or so I thought. But when we reconnected . . . it filled a void in me I didn't realize I had. It was like a part of me had been missing and . . . You brought it back." I glanced down at my hands, embarrassed by how cheesy it sounded. I'd already come this far, though, so I kept going. "And it was so easy to get back to what we were before. It was like nothing had changed. Except something had. Something *did*. Something important."

I trailed off, biting my lip as Ben sat waiting for me to continue.

"What changed?" he finally asked, sounding as nervous as I felt.

I peeked around the hair that fell in front of my face. "My feelings for you." A hint of a smile began to creep onto his face as I rambled on. "But I didn't want to admit that because I was scared of messing it up and losing you again and I don't want that to happen. That's why I tried to fight it."

"And now?"

"Well . . . Now I'm not so scared, and I don't want to fight it." I sat up straighter, looking him dead in the eye as the nerves were replaced by a sudden wave of confidence. "And I'm done pretending that I'm not in love with you. Because I am." I smiled softly. "I'm in love with you, Benjamin."

He brushed my hair behind my ears before cupping my face in his hands. My heart pounded loudly in my chest as I waited for him to say something.

"I'm in love with you too, Robin," he murmured.

My heart skipped a beat, and I forgot how to breathe.

*He loves me.*

He leaned in, and I happily met him halfway, stopping just before our parted lips could touch. Our foreheads rested against one another, and his hot breath washed over me. My eyelids fluttered shut, then his lips were on mine, brushing against them lightly.

They were soft, yet strong, as they gently guided me into a deeper embrace. His scent filled my nose, and his warmth encompassed me with our close proximity. All my senses were glued to him as a slow burn worked its way through my body.

Too soon, he pulled away. I kept my eyes shut as he pulled me into his chest, enjoying the sound of his heartbeat as I took in the moment. It was everything I'd expect from Ben—a simple but passionate kiss overflowing with the raw, untapped emotions that'd built up inside us over the years. It was a sealing covenant of a new chapter for us. A chapter I was more than ready to begin.

# CHAPTER THIRTEEN

"I can't tell you how happy we were to hear about your and Ben's reconciliation," Kiona told me as we passed around the food.

"We missed you around here," Jeremiah, Ben's dad, said in his deep voice, the wrinkles around his eyes deepened by his smile.

"I missed all of you too," I replied, scooping mashed potatoes onto my plate. "It's been too long."

"Maybe now Ben won't cry all the time," Mahka commented with a smirk.

Ben shrugged his shoulders, letting the comment roll off him effortlessly. "Crying is a healthy outlet for one's feelings."

"Yes, it is," Jeremiah agreed, looking at Ben proudly before turning his gaze to his middle child. "You can't appreciate the meaning and importance of things around you if you aren't in tune with yourself."

Mahka rolled his eyes as Jeremiah began lecturing him, and I glanced at my plate. Ben grabbed my hand under the table, running his thumb along the back of it. He smiled at me, and I returned it, feeling lighter and happier than I had in a long time. When I looked away from him, I noticed Kiona watching us with pleased adoration. She met my eye, and I couldn't help but blush.

"So, tell us what you've been up to," she said.

"Oh, nothing too exciting," I replied. "School, sports, helping my mom with Dawn."

"How old is Dawn now?"

"Six going on sixteen."

Kiona chuckled. "I'd love to see them again."

"I'm sure they'd like that too."

"Then I'll be sure to give Rebecca a call to set up dinner plans."

"Okay," I replied with a nod.

"Ben told us you've become quite the athlete," Jeremiah said, folding his hands under his chin as he gave me his attention.

I raised my brows at Ben and said, "You've been talking about me, huh?"

"And you thought I was joking," Mahka muttered under his breath, and Ben cleared his throat as he shifted in his chair.

"Only when we've asked about you," Jeremiah said, coming to his eldest son's rescue. "You grew up here after all. You were a part of our family. We liked knowing you were doing okay even if you weren't around."

"Well, I really appreciate that," I said quietly, my heart swelling with emotions.

I'd spent countless hours in this house—even at this very table—so many of my childhood memories involved the Toves family. Then after Dawn was born, they became my safe haven—a place I could hide from my dad's sudden impatience for me.

I remembered joining them on vacations, inviting them to important school events, and having my own little corner with a bed so I could spend the night on a moment's notice.

I remembered them taking me to powwows to learn about their culture and Jeremiah teaching me how to fish and ride a bike. I remembered Kiona showing me how to cook and comforting me every time I cried about feeling replaced by Dawn.

As much as I love my sister now, there was a time when I blamed her for ruining my relationship with my father. If it weren't for Kiona's interference, I would probably still resent her being born, and that thought made me feel physically ill. Kiona is the only reason I was able to have as much affection for Dawn as I do. I owed Ben's family so much, and here they were still caring about me even when I wasn't around.

Ben noticed my prolonged silence and squeezed my hand before launching into a story about one of my basketball games. I was grateful for the intervention so I could compose myself because I hadn't just lost Ben when I chose to betray him—I'd lost my second family as well and it took many emotional, sleepless nights to come to terms with. Being back here with them was something I used to think about a lot, and now that I was, I couldn't be happier.

As dinner passed, I enjoyed watching them interact with one another. Their dynamic was as genuine, fun, and filled with love as I remembered. Dakota sat as quietly as I did unless asked a direct question, but the others were all boisterous with conversation. When we all finished eating, Jeremiah instructed the boys to help him clear the table as Kiona pulled me into the living room.

"You were awfully quiet at dinner," she said.

"I was just taking everything in," I replied, sitting next to her on the couch.

"Having a lot of mixed emotions?"

"Sort of," I admitted, unsurprised that she could still read me like an open book. "Mostly happy ones though. I just started thinking about everything you guys used to do for me. I mean, I honestly owe you so much. I wouldn't be who I am today without you."

She placed her hand on top of mine and said, "You owe us absolutely nothing, but we owe you *everything*."

My brows furrowed. "What do you mean?"

"You may not be who you are today without us, but Ben wouldn't be here at all without you."

"Oh," I murmured, realizing what she was referring to.

Her eyes brimmed with tears as she drew in a shaky breath. "I know how much heartache you went through after everything happened, and I wish you didn't have to. But my son is alive because of it, so as horrible as it may be, I'm still glad you chose to come to us."

"It isn't horrible," I replied softly. "I understand, and, honestly, I'd do it again in a heartbeat, even knowing I'd lose him."

"I hope you know we tried so hard to get him to apologize to you. For months, we tried. He just . . . Well, he just couldn't."

"It's okay. I don't blame you. I don't even blame him." I paused before adding in, "Not anymore at least."

"You always were a forgiving person," she said with a smile.

"Not really. I'm no saint," I responded, looking down at my hands. "I held a grudge for a long time. Too long."

"But you both came around eventually. That's all that matters."

I glanced up to see her still smiling, her crinkled eyes sparkling with adoration, and I returned it timidly.

"What's going on in here?" Ben asked playfully as he walked into the room.

"Just catching up," his mom replied.

"Talking about you," I said.

"All good things I hope," he responded.

"Oh, definitely not," I responded with a sly grin, and he made a face in return. "How mature."

He chuckled then said, "I hate to say it, but I need to get you home if I'm going to have time to get my homework done."

"You didn't do it during your free period?" Kiona asked, disapproval heavy in her tone.

Ben scratched the back of his head, avoiding her stare. "I got distracted."

"By what?"

"Robin."

"I bet Robin finished her homework."

"Yes, ma'am, I sure did," I said, smirking at Ben's grimace.

"Suck up," he muttered.

"We'll talk about this later, Benjamin," Kiona warned before standing.

She followed us to the front door, and I waved goodbye to Dakota and Mahka as we passed by them. Jeremiah and Kiona both hugged me tightly with the promise of seeing me again soon. When Ben and I were back in his truck, he patted the middle seat and wiggled his eyebrows.

"Don't you want to sit closer to your boyfriend?" he asked, and I twisted my face in confusion.

"Is that what you think you are?" I questioned.

"Aren't I?"

"I was thinking more of a friends-with-benefits thing." I shrugged nonchalantly, and he scowled. A laugh escaped me before I scooted over and brought my hand up to his face, caressing it with my fingers. "I'm only joking."

Ben put his hand on top of mine, holding it against his skin. "I know. But just so there's no confusion, would you do me the honor of being my girlfriend?"

His eyes twinkled mischievously as I smiled widely at his words. "Of course, I would," I said.

He leaned down and gave me a soft kiss, awakening a collection of butterflies in the pit of my stomach. When he pulled away, he gave me a long kiss on the forehead then sighed contentedly.

"Do you know how long I've wanted to be able to do that?" he asked against my hair.

"No," I murmured as a smile crept over my face, the idea of him thinking about it exciting me.

"A hot minute."

"That long, huh?"

"Oh, yeah," he replied, grinning down at me. "And now I can do it whenever I want."

"So can I," I said, already yearning for another encounter with his lips.

"I suppose you can."

We both started to lean in, then I saw his parents step onto the front porch, so I cleared my throat and sat back.

"What's wrong?" he asked, his lips turned down in disappointment. I nodded my head towards his house, and he looked over. "Ah."

"I'd rather not make out in front of your family."

"That makes two of us," he replied as he started the car. "I'm sure they're already planning on having a talk with me when I get back."

"About your homework?" I asked coyly, scooting over to the passenger seat.

"Yes. Definitely about my homework," he replied sarcastically, and I grinned.

"You enjoy that."

"Not even a little bit. But I'll tell you what I will enjoy."

"What's that?"

"Finding another time to kiss you."

I ducked my head as my cheeks burned crimson. A few weeks ago, I never would've imagined that I'd be having this conversation with Ben. Yet here we were—happy and in love.

* * *

"Finally!" Felicity exclaimed, clapping her hands at my summary of the past day's events. I looked around, apologizing to the people who were glancing our way at her volume. "This is absolutely perfect. I'm so happy for you guys."

"I am too," I replied, unable to contain my smile.

"I can tell," she said softly, her eyes shining.

"What about you?" I asked, wanting to be as happy for her as she was for me. "Didn't you spend yesterday with Matthew again?"

"I did," she replied with a grin. "And we have our first official date on Saturday."

*"Official,"* I echoed, grinning back with a roll of my eyes. She shrugged in return, unbothered. "You guys are basically already an item."

"I know, but it's kind of fun doing it the proper way. It's so different than how I usually work."

"You mean just jumping into bed with them?" I asked. She scowled at my blatancy but nodded. A thought popped into my mind and a feeling of relief started to creep over me. "Does that mean we aren't going to the bonfire?"

"Of course, we are!" she replied, shattering my hopes. "Matthew and I are doing lunch and bowling, so we'll still have plenty of time to go and for us to get ready together beforehand."

"Great," I muttered.

"Don't worry. You'll have fun. Plus, it'll be a great way to let people know that you and Ben are the new hottest couple."

"Even better." I groaned internally, already dreading the attention we were going to get, but Felicity only smirked at my misery.

As it turned out, I didn't have to wait for the next day for that ship to sail. All it took for the news to spread like wildfire was one person seeing Ben come up and kiss me on the cheek in the hallway. I spent the rest of the day dodging questions and hiding behind Ben so he could deal with the majority of the brewing curiosity. He was such a sociable person and as eager as anyone else to let our status be known, so it worked out well. At the end of the day, I leaned into him and sighed.

"This was an exhausting day," I muttered, closing my eyes.

"I thought it was pretty great," Ben replied, putting his arm around my shoulders.

"I'm so glad you had fun with all the attention."

"It wasn't about the attention. It was just nice to get to call you mine and show people how much I care about you."

I had to smile at that. Butterflies flew around my stomach again at his interpretation of the day, and I wondered if I'd ever stop feeling this way about him.

"Not to mention that I've staked my claim now," he continued with a grin, despite the face I made. "Which means I won't have to listen to other guys talk about you anymore."

I gave him a look. "What do you mean?"

"Just typical locker-room trash." He shrugged. "You're a hot topic."

"I am not!" I gaped in horrified embarrassment.

"Unfortunately, you are." He looked less than pleased as he grimaced.

"Why?" I asked. I meant it rhetorically, but Ben looked down at me and shook his head slightly.

"You really don't see how beautiful you are," he said, and I glanced down as he continued. "But don't worry. That'll stop now. The guys may be pigs, but they're respectful when it comes to someone else's girlfriend."

"At least they have that going for them," I muttered sarcastically, not liking this newfound information.

Ben smiled and kissed my hand before starting the drive to my house. "Do you want to do something with me before the bonfire tomorrow?"

"I was actually going to spend the day with Dawn," I replied, disappointed a bit by the missed opportunity to see him. "Then Felicity wanted me to come over to her house so we could get ready together."

"That's fine. I bet Dakota will want to do something with me if I ask. Am I picking you up from Felicity's?"

"I think she wanted all four of us to go together. Matthew is supposed to come over around six thirty."

"That's fine. I'll see you tomorrow at six thirty then," he replied happily.

When we pulled up to my house, I put my hand on the door to get out, but Ben stopped me. He turned me towards him and wrapped his arms around my waist, pulling me forward until he was kissing me. My hands found their way around his neck as his fingers got tangled in my hair. I became lightheaded as he pulled me even closer, his lips moving with a sudden eagerness I hadn't expected. All I could feel was him, and all I wanted was more. But just as he'd done every other time, he pulled away, his breath hot on my face as we both tried to refill our lungs.

"Tomorrow night can't come fast enough," he said softly, tickling my ear. "Goodnight, Robin."

"Goodnight, Benjamin," I replied, giving him one more quick kiss before exiting the car and going inside.

"You two are good for one another," a quiet voice said in the darkened house, and I jumped in surprise. I turned to see my mom standing by the window. "I'm happy you found each other again."

"Me too," I responded. Just as I was about to get onto her for spying, I noticed how sad she looked, and I knew she was missing my dad. "Are you okay?"

"I will be."

"Want to stay up late and watch some chick flicks?"

"Can we have ice cream too?" Dawn yelled as she ran around the corner to hug my legs.

"You were supposed to be asleep, young lady," Mom scolded her.

"But I'm not tired," she responded with a pout.

Mom looked down at her for a second, then sighed, seeming like she didn't have the energy to fight. "Okay, fine. Just this once, you can stay up with your sister and me."

Dawn squealed with delight, her hair falling into her face as she jumped up and down. I picked her up and swung her around, and she giggled.

"You two go choose a movie," Mom said. "I'll get the ice cream."

"Yay!" Dawn shouted as I took us into the living room.

We made a makeshift bed on the floor with pillows and blankets, then the three of us settled in to start our first movie. Dawn ate half a pint of ice cream before passing out on top of me halfway into *Bride Wars,* and I was quick to follow, not making it to the end of the movie.

* * *

I woke in a panic, the dream woman's screams echoing in my ears. Sweat dripped down my back, and I groaned, pushing loose hairs away from my face. It'd been almost a week since I'd last had the dream, and I'd been hoping it was gone for good, but I guess not. I just wish I knew what it meant and why it was always the same.

Dawn woke up not much later, and she managed to keep my mind off it all morning as we played dress up and practiced our cartwheels. We were in the middle of a game of Candy Land when Felicity texted me saying I could come over whenever I was ready. So after finishing the game, I headed out. When I got to her house, Annie opened the door with a radiant smile on her face.

"Hi, Robin," she said before handing me a plate full of cookies. "Felicity is upstairs. Mrs. Turhune whipped these up special for you two, so don't let them go to waste."

"Oh, we won't," I assured her, breathing in their heavenly scent as my mouth watered. I marched up the stairs and plopped myself down on one of Felicity's couches, stuffing a cookie into my mouth as she walked out from her bedroom.

"Cookies!" she squealed with delight, coming up to grab a handful before sliding onto the rug.

"How was your date?" I asked between bites, and she instantly went starry-eyed.

"It was amazing," she said, looking at me around the bangs that fell in her eyes. "He kissed me."

"No way!" I gasped, and she nodded, her grin reaching both ears.

"It was really sweet. And then he asked me to be his girlfriend," she added sheepishly.

"What did you say?"

"I said yes!"

"That's great," I said, surprised that I found myself meaning it. "Look at us go, getting boyfriends at the same time."

"I know. It's going to be a blast!"

I could already see her imagining all the double dates she'd get to plan.

"Guess you're the one who's going to be in the spotlight tonight," I commented, pleased by that idea.

"Probably so. Matthew isn't going to like it very much."

"No, he definitely won't," I agreed, feeling badly for him as I pictured his discomfort. I made a mental note to help him get through the night as much as I could.

"Let's start getting ready. I want to straighten your hair, and we both know that's going to take forever," Felicity said, jumping up from the floor.

She turned on her radio and a pop-rock song blasted through the speakers as she sat me down at her vanity. Per my request, she kept my makeup simple and natural, then began working on my hair—a feat that took thirty minutes. When she was done, it flowed down to my midback in a luscious curtain, and I kept playing with it, not used to how soft it felt. She tossed a bag my way, and I opened it in surprise.

"What's this?" I asked as I pulled out a beautiful beige jacket with fluffy brown cotton sewn along the cuffs and neckline.

"It was supposed to be your Christmas gift, but the shoes didn't get here in time, so I got you something else. Then I forgot about it," she admitted as I pulled out matching boots and earmuffs.

"They're gorgeous!" I exclaimed, the soft fabric smelling of fresh laundry detergent.

"I figured I better give them to you before it starts to warm up, and tonight is the perfect night for them since it'll be on the colder side," she said as she began changing into warmer clothes.

"Well, thank you," I replied, sliding off my shoes and trading them in for the boots. "I love them."

"I knew you would!"

Felicity monopolized the conversation as she did her makeup, and before I knew it, the doorbell was ringing. We slid on our jackets with gloves and earmuffs stored in the pockets then headed down the stairs where the boys were waiting for us with Felicity's parents.

Matthew watched Felicity in adoration, a small smile playing at the corners of his lips. Despite our recent track record, I felt a sense of pride. I don't think I could've asked for anyone better for her than someone who looked at her like she was his whole world. My gaze shifted to Ben, who was grinning with his hands pushed deep in his pockets. I smiled back as we reached the bottom step.

"You guys have a good time," Felicity's dad told us all. "Please be smart and stay safe."

"Of course, David," Matthew replied. I was surprised that he was already on a first name basis with Felicity's parents. But, then again, he'd been spending a lot of time with them all according to Felicity. "We'll have them back by eleven."

We said our goodbyes and headed for Matthew's car.

"That coat looks good on you," Ben whispered to me as we walked.

"You don't look too shabby yourself," I replied, motioning towards his thick brown hoodie and snow pants with a smirk.

"Latest fashion, don't ya know?" he asked with a wide sweep of his hand. He opened the back door, and we both slid in while Felicity sat in the passenger seat next to Matthew.

"You guys ready to party?" Ben asked loudly as we began driving.

"Oh, yeah!" Felicity replied, just as pumped up.

Matthew met my eyes in the rearview mirror, and I shook my head before making a face. He grinned for a split second then looked away as I sat in shock at the gesture. Talking on our way to our classes had slowly paid off, both of us finally warming up to the other. It also helped that we could bond over a mutual enemy: socializing.

We parked behind a long line of cars at the base of a small, wooded area. A large, Tudor-style home sat up on a hill overlooking the vast grounds, and I guessed it was as big as Felicity's. When we exited the vehicle, smoke filled my nose, and I could hear laughter and music in the distance.

"Whose house is that?" I asked curiously.

"Tucker Mills," Ben answered as we walked down a dimly lit path through the trees.

I pulled my earmuffs on as the cold threatened to overwhelm me already.

"His family owns about ten acres of land," Felicity added, taking Matthew's hand, "and they don't care if he throws parties as long as they can't hear it, which makes this the perfect spot to hold them."

We came into a large clearing lined with tiki torches. Two separate fire pits were already ablaze with light, and chairs sat scattered all around. Someone had stacked blankets next to a table filled with a mixture of hot drinks, beer, and finger foods.

"Hey y'all!" Tucker yelled as he approached us. "Glad you could make it."

"We wouldn't miss it," Felicity said with an alluring smile.

Tucker's gaze lingered on her for a moment too long, and Matthew cleared his throat as daggers shot from his eyes. Tucker glanced over at him then at their intertwined hands.

"Oh, y'all came here together?" he asked, sounding disappointed.

"We did," Felicity confirmed, letting Matthew pull her closer in agreement.

"Cool, cool. Well, y'all have fun. Get a drink. Make some s'mores," Tucker said, scratching the back of his head as he tried to brush off his failed advancement on Felicity. He held up one hand in a wave then walked away to greet more people coming up behind us.

"Ben!" voices called out and we looked over to see Juan and Tom beckoning for us.

"We're going to get some blankets and drinks," Felicity told me and Ben. "Meet us by the fire pit?"

"Sure," Ben agreed before taking my hand and heading over to where a group of guys from the basketball team stood.

A couple of them were laughing obnoxiously, and I could tell they were drunk. I tried to hide my disdain, but it was difficult. I knew what could result from excessive drinking.

"I'm surprised you're here," Juan said to me as we came up. "I don't usually see you at these things."

"It's not really my scene," I replied as a gust of wind gently moved my hair along my shoulders.

"Nothing wrong with that," Juan responded with a smile, and I returned it with appreciation as Ben got pulled away from me.

He started roughhousing with Tom as the other guys hollered at the brawl. I shifted from one foot to the other with my hands clasped together in front of me, not sure what to do. Luckily, Juan continued to converse with me, so I focused on him instead of standing idly.

"So you two are an item now?" he asked as he took a swig from a Styrofoam cup.

"Yeah," I answered. "We are."

"I'm happy for you guys. Ben's been head over heels for you for a long time."

Heat rose to my cheeks, but I couldn't help but grin. "He wouldn't like you telling me that."

"I know," Juan replied slyly in a way that made me giggle.

Ben came up behind me, his cheeks flushed.

"Here I was worried you'd be missing me," he said with a shake of his head, "but you're already laughing it up with another guy."

"Well, Juan *is* pretty great. You might want to watch out," I teased.

Juan gave Ben a wink, so Ben pointed at his eyes then at Juan's in the international *'I'm watching you'* sign. We hung around with the guys for a bit—until they got too rowdy with their drinks—then decided to look for Matthew and Felicity. We found them sitting on a blanket near one of the fire pits, surrounded by some of Felicity's friends from the drama club. Ben got a blanket for us and laid it out next to theirs before going to grab us some hot chocolates. At that same time, Felicity got up with the rest of her drama club friends, which left Matthew and me alone.

"You doing okay?" I asked him.

"I'm surviving," he replied. He got that twinge of a smile on his face again and amusement filled his eyes.

"What's so funny?" I questioned.

"The idea of me not surviving a high school party. It's laughable when I've survived so much worse before."

I didn't know how to feel about his answer, but curiosity and concern were battling for first place. "Want to talk about it?" I offered, but he shook his head.

"No," he replied flatly. He looked over at me, his hard expression softening slightly. "But thank you."

"You're welcome. But if you ever change your mind, we're here for you."

"I appreciate it," he said, looking down at his hands. "I might take you up on it one day. I might have to."

I didn't know what he meant by that, but I could tell he was uncomfortable, so I changed the subject instead of pressing the matter. "I wonder where Ben ran off to."

Matthew glanced around, then pointed and said, "Looks like he's being held hostage by some of the cheerleaders."

I looked to where he pointed. Ben was standing in the middle of a group of girls, laughing at something that was said as they giggled and twirled their hair with their fingers. He caught my eye and smiled sheepishly.

"Does that not bother you?" Matthew asked me suddenly, his brow furrowed.

"Not really," I replied with a shrug.

"How?"

"I trust him."

"He's being flirted with."

"Yes he is."

Matthew's brows scrunched even more. "So how are you not bothered by it?"

"Because he's not the type to cheat, even if he *is* flattered by the attention. Like I said, I trust him."

Matthew eyed me with a look that made me squirm self-consciously.

"What?" I asked.

"You're not like most teenagers."

"Yeah, I've been told that before," I admitted with a humorless smile.

"It's not a bad thing."

"Well, thanks," I said in a tone that made him chuckle.

"Can I ask you a question?"

"Sure," I replied.

"You seem happy."

I waited for more, but he only sat there, so I said, "That's not a question."

"Well . . . Are you? Happy?"

"I mean . . . Yes?"

"And your life is good?"

My brows furrowed. "It has its problems but yes. I'd like to think my life is good."

He nodded slowly. "Would you change it if you could?"

I rubbed my lips together as I thought it over. "I guess there's a couple things I wish were different but, at the same time, I am who I am because of those things so maybe not."

"So you wouldn't want to leave?"

"Leave Milton?" I asked. "Well, sure. I'll leave for college, and I'd love to travel some."

"No, I mean your family. Your life. All of your problems."

"No, of course not," I replied earnestly. "I love my mom and sister. Even after I graduate, I'm going to be around as much as possible. I can't imagine my life without them. And there's problems no matter where you go. You can't just run away from them."

"I see," Matthew said quietly.

I opened my mouth, then shut it again. This wasn't the line of questioning I'd expected.

"Are you okay?" I finally asked. "Is your life . . . Not good?"

"I'm fine. Sorry if I was intrusive."

"No, it's okay." I looked him over as he sat stone faced again. "I'm just getting a little worried about you."

"You don't even like me."

"That's not true," I said, and he cocked one brow. "I'm serious. Sure, we may not be best friends or anything, but I've definitely warmed up to you."

The corner of his lips turned up. "I've definitely warmed up to you too."

"Gee, thanks," I replied, and he chuckled before we melted into silence again.

The night continued in much the same way—with Felicity and Ben being pulled every which way while Matthew and I sat quietly with occasional snippets of conversation sliding in.

"You want another drink?" I asked Matthew as I stood to get myself one.

"I'm fine, but thank you," he replied.

Before I could take a step, I heard someone call my name. I looked over my shoulder and saw a drunken Zack heading our way.

"Robin!" he yelled, despite being five feet away from me. He came up and threw his arms around me in a sloppy hug. "Robin!"

"Hi, Zack," I greeted him, trying not to fall over as he leaned his weight on me.

"Robin! You wanna go on a date?" he slurred, his hot breath wafting over me.

I cringed, immediately repulsed by the heavy smell of tequila. Matthew stood up, standing close as he watched the scene unfold.

"No thank you, Zack," I said.

"But why not?" he whined, one arm still slung around my shoulders and pulling at my hair.

"Because she has a boyfriend," Ben responded, coming up next to Matthew. His face was lighthearted, but his voice sliced the air with an angry bite.

"Haven't you ever heard of an open relationship?" Zack loudly whispered to me, followed by an obnoxious laugh.

I tried to wiggle out from under his arm, but he only tightened his grip, his fingers digging into my arm.

"Let me go, Zack," I told him sternly, continuing to push at him.

He laughed harder, almost knocking us both over.

"Zack!" Ben yelled, his face no longer friendly as he stepped closer.

Zack finally got over his laughing fit, his smile twisting into a scowl. "What?"

People standing nearby began to stare, and a couple guys hovered cautiously, trying to figure out if they should intervene.

"Get your hands off her," Ben demanded, the ice in his voice causing me to shiver. "Now."

"Fine," Zack said with a grin.

Suddenly his weight was off my shoulders and on my back. He shoved me away from him with such force that I fell to the ground with a thud, scratching up my hands.

"What the hell man?!" Ben shouted as he and Matthew knelt down next to me.

"Are you okay?" Matthew asked as they both looked me over.

"I'm fine," I assured them, taking their outstretched hands and letting them help me up off the ground. "Just a little muddy."

Zack was still snickering as we turned his way. Ben stood in front of me in a protective stance as he glared at him, almost shaking with anger as his hands clenched into fists.

"You're lucky I don't believe in using violence to solve problems," he said through clenched teeth.

Zack feigned a look of terror then took a swig of his drink, uncaring of anything going on around him.

"Yeah, well, I do," Matthew announced, swinging his fist into Zack's face with an angry grunt. Zack fell to the ground in a messy heap, his nose gushing blood as Matthew towered over him. "I told you to learn some respect."

Zack shakily stood up and tried to stumble towards Matthew, but Tom quickly intervened.

"Back off man," Tom said, pushing Zack in the opposite direction.

After a couple more shoves, he complied, and we were left standing there alone. Ben wrapped me in a hug, and I laid my head against his chest.

"Are you sure you're okay?" Matthew asked quietly, and I nodded.

"I'd like to go home though," I told them.

"Of course. I'll get Felicity and meet you two at the car," Matthew said. He tossed Ben the keys then turned around to find his date.

"Hey," Ben called out. "Thank you."

Matthew glanced over his shoulder and nodded slightly. "It's what I do."

I wasn't sure what he meant by that, but neither of us pressed for an explanation. Instead, we headed to the car.

"Are you sure you're okay?" Ben asked, just like Matthew had moments before, as he looked me over.

"I just answered that," I pointed out.

"I know. But I'm asking again." He picked up my hands, observing the small cuts.

"I'm fine. Really." I moved my hands to where they were holding his. "I just want to forget about it."

"I'm sorry."

"For what?"

"Leaving you alone."

"I wasn't alone. Matthew was good company."

"Yeah, but maybe if I'd been there Zack wouldn't have approached you."

I stopped walking and placed my hand on his arm. "Zack's drunk. He would've done whatever he wanted no matter who was there. It wasn't your fault, okay?"

He nodded, then sighed and wrapped his arm around me. "I love you."

"I love you too."

# CHAPTER FOURTEEN

It was an unusually warm February day, so we were eating lunch outside, soaking in the sun. Our usual group of four sat on one of the few picnic tables, while many other students opted to sit on the grass, even though it was damp with mostly melted snow.

"I am so ready for summer," Felicity announced, stripped down to her tank top and jeans. Her fair skin was blinding as the sunlight reflected off of it.

"Me too," I said. "I can't wait for swim season."

"You swim?" Matthew asked, cocking his head slightly.

"Does she ever," Ben answered for me. "Fastest swimmer in the region."

"She is," Felicity said.

"I am," I added with a grin, not ashamed of that accomplishment.

Matthew kept looking at me, his brow furrowed as he sat, seeming deep in thought. I was used to his strange reactions to things now, so I didn't pay him any attention.

"I'm ready for volleyball," Felicity said. "The sand in my toes and the sun on my skin."

"Don't forget about baseball," Ben responded, mimicking a bat swinging with his arms.

"All the best sports are in summer," I said as I pulled my hair into a ponytail to ease the sweat on my neck.

Matthew excused himself quietly as we continued to yearn for the warm days to come, then came back just as quietly about a minute later. Loud squeals met my ears, and I glanced around just in time to see a stream of water about to hit us. I threw my hands up to block my face, and the icy hot feeling traveled through my arms, but the water never came. When I looked again, the water had passed us by. Somehow it missed us and continued on to hit other students, who were jumping up, trying to avoid getting soaked by the rogue sprinkler.

I noticed Matthew watching me intently, his usually neutral eyes full of concern. I didn't have time to worry about it, though, because my mind was already swimming with my own unsettling thoughts. How had the water missed us? I looked at my hands, frowning. Had I made it miss us somehow?

*Delusional,* I thought. *Not possible.*

This was real life, not a work of fiction. But it wasn't the first time something strange had happened when I was around water. How many times could I insist on there being a logical answer when there was never one to be found?

Ben and Felicity laughed at the other kids who were dripping wet as Matthew and I continued to stew in our own thoughts. He disappeared right before the sprinkler randomly sprung to life. Was he the reason for that? And if so, why?

"What's wrong?" Ben asked me, finally noticing my silence, and I wrestled with whether or not I should say something. "Robin? What's up?"

"I'm just having an inner crisis is all," I replied lightly, trying to brush it off.

"What kind of crisis?" Felicity pried.

"Nothing. It's silly."

"Maybe it isn't," Matthew said faintly, as if he wanted to hear what I was thinking too.

"Tell us," Felicity insisted.

I licked my lips, trying to figure out how to articulate my uncanny thoughts. "I just can't help but notice that lately . . ." I trailed off with a sigh. I kept looking for words that wouldn't make me sound crazy, but I finally gave up and spoke the words I was thinking. "Lately, I've noticed that some weird, almost unnatural things have been happening when I'm around water."

Matthew closed his eyes, his lips pressed together tightly, while Ben and Felicity watched me, one looking confused and the other amused.

"What do you mean by unnatural?" Ben asked, and I lifted my hands in exasperation then let them fall loudly into my lap.

"I don't know. Calm water bubbling up, water cups falling over, sprinklers hitting—or not hitting—exactly where I need them to."

Felicity let out a snort, and I shot her a look that deflated her amusement.

"Wait, you're serious?" she asked in surprise.

"I know it sounds insane but . . . yes. Every time something happens, it's like a cold burn spreads through me. It's like I'm doing something to make the water react," I explained, praying they didn't admit me into a psyche ward. "And then there's that dream. I'm still having it."

"What dream?" Matthew asked with an unexpected intensity.

I explained my dream to him, and his eyes widened slightly.

"Is it always the same?" he questioned, and I nodded my head.

"Mostly. Sometimes it's a little less intense, and the woman isn't so horror-movie like though," I answered. "I know you guys think I'm crazy, but this isn't in my head. I know it isn't."

"I get that you *believe* that," Felicity told me, her tone light, "but you've been so stressed lately. It's easy to mix-up imagination and reality."

"I'm not imagining it," I insisted.

"Robin—"

"I believe you," Ben said, cutting her off and putting his hand on my arm in a comforting gesture. "So let's figure out what you think is happening, okay?"

His tone was calm and sincere, but I couldn't tell if he really believed me or was just placating me. I hung my head down in defeat; I should've just kept my thoughts to myself.

"Hey," Ben said gently, placing his finger under my chin to guide my eyes towards him. "It's going to be okay."

I nodded, unconvinced. The bell rang, ending both the conversation and my humiliation. Ben gave my hand a quick squeeze before he took off inside with Felicity, who offered me a small, apologetic smile. I sighed, putting my head in my hands as I tried to brush off my embarrassment. When I looked up, Matthew was still sitting next to me in quiet observation.

"You ready to go to class?" I asked, but he didn't answer, his expression slightly withdrawn. "Matthew? Are you okay?"

"No," he finally answered, his voice faint. "I need to tell you something."

"Okay," I replied, puzzled as I stayed next to him and waited.

"I don't know how to tell you this," he said. He gripped the edge of the table on either side of him so hard that his knuckles turned white.

I awkwardly patted his back in a futile attempt at comforting him. "It's okay. It can't be that bad."

"But it is," he whispered. "I'm not who you think I am."

"What do you mean?"

"I—"

"Get to class," a teacher called over to us.

"We better go," Matthew announced abruptly, getting up and walking away.

I looked after him in surprise then jumped up and followed, trying to keep up with his rapid strides. "Wait, what about what you were going to tell me?"

"Never mind," he replied bluntly, his ever-changing attitude giving me whiplash. "Forget about it."

"But—"

"Forget about it," he repeated sharply.

I stopped in my tracks, startled by his tone, and watched him walk away. I slowly replayed the events in the courtyard, trying to figure out what he could've wanted to tell me but remained stumped.

*I will never understand that guy.*

Matthew didn't speak to me for the rest of the day; he was too busy solemnly stewing in his own thoughts. He perked up enough to greet Felicity when school ended but parted ways with her quickly after, claiming he had errands that needed attending.

"He seems a little more broody than normal," Ben commented as we settled in at the library.

"He's been like that all afternoon," I said. "He told me he needed to tell me something then just shut down."

"Weird. What do you think he was going to tell you?" he asked as he chewed on some beef jerky.

"I have no idea. But I think it had to do with our conversation at lunch. It's the only thing that makes sense."

"Speaking of which," Ben said, staring at me with a pointed look, and I glanced away. "I'm going to be completely honest with you. You sound crazy."

"I know," I said quietly, my heart sinking at his words.

"But that doesn't mean you don't have valid points," he continued, and I peered over at him.

"Meaning?"

"I've been around when a couple of those incidents you mentioned happened, and, individually, they could easily be brushed off as some sort of coincidence. But . . ." He paused, contemplating his next words. "A wise man named Deepak Chopra once said, 'I do not believe in meaningless coincidences. I believe every coincidence is a message, a clue about a particular facet of our lives that requires our attention.'"

"Okay?" I responded with raised eyebrows.

"What I'm trying to say is that, even if there are such a thing as coincidences, they happen for a reason."

"And that reason is?"

"To help you figure out something in your life," he replied simply. "Maybe even to find your destiny."

"You know, sometimes your thought process makes no sense to me," I said, rubbing my temples. The conversation had confused me even more than I already was.

"It's the Native American in me," he replied with a grin. "Nature, spirits, destiny; they're all things we believe in."

"So you're saying I'm finding my destiny with all these 'coincidental' water events?" I asked, trying to make sure I was understanding him.

"Maybe so."

"But what could that be?" I asked, more to myself than him.

He shrugged. "I couldn't say."

"But do you think they really are just coincidences?"

"That's the easy answer. But honestly," he hesitated slightly, "I don't see how they could be. Not with how many times something strange has happened."

"So do you think I could actually be controlling it somehow?"

I could tell he was fighting with himself, just as I was, torn between our reality and the possibility of something more. He finally sighed. "I don't know, Robin," he said.

I laid my head on my arms on the table and matched his sigh. Maybe I *was* crazy.

"You could always test it out," he said.

"What?"

"See if you can control the water." He motioned to the fountain across from our table and I made a face at him.

"No."

"Why not?"

"Because now I just feel stupid."

"You never know until you try."

I scrutinized him for a quick moment, taking in his expression.

He was serious.

There wasn't any hint of humor. He wasn't mocking me. Even as ridiculous as the notion was, he was simply trying to be understanding and supportive.

"Fine," I finally agreed.

I gazed over at the fountain and swallowed before focusing on the water pooling at the bottom of the bowl. I stared at it, squinting my eyes and scrunching my nose. After a minute of complete silence, nothing happened.

"You look like you're taking a dump," Ben remarked, and I gasped as I turned towards him, my concentration broken.

"Ben!" I exclaimed, shoving him away from me. He let out a bellow of laughter as I tried to squander a smile. "Don't tease me right now."

"Sorry," he said unapologetically as he continued to grin.

"I did look pretty stupid, didn't I?" I asked, leaning back in the chair.

"Only slightly."

"Maybe I am crazy," I murmured out loud, feeling defeated.

"We're all a little crazy in our own way. But you can't give up so easily."

"I appreciate you humoring me."

"I'm not humoring you. I think you're exploring your own reality, and I'm here to support it—support *you*—no matter what that entails."

A million emotions flooded through me, and I stood up and walked around the table towards him. "You are truly one of a kind. You know that?" I said.

"I know that I love you," he replied with a smile, the look in his eyes speaking to the truth of his words.

"I love you too." I leaned down, giving him a kiss. "But that's enough reality searching for one day. Want to come over for dinner?"

"Always," he said, returning my kiss. "Let's go."

# CHAPTER FIFTEEN

As the weeks passed, my bizarre outburst was dropped from conversation. Life proceeded as normal, despite the nagging suspicion lingering in the back of my mind as even more events occurred. I kept them to myself, but Matthew always seemed to be more on edge when they happened around him. It was as if he knew something wasn't right, but neither of us brought it up. Him, Felicity, Ben, and I became close to inseparable, one of us always with another, as basketball season drew to a close.

"I can't believe we won! We're the champions!" Alli squealed for the tenth time as we celebrated on the court, passing around the trophy.

"There was no way anyone else was taking home that title!" Felicity replied proudly.

"Or that *trophy!*" Tamika yelled, taking her turn holding it as random hoots and hollers still rang out from the stands.

"Let's get your picture for the paper, girls," said a man with a camera, motioning for us to line up.

I knelt next to Amara and Felicity and smiled with unwavering excitement as the man captured our team's accomplishment. After a couple more minutes of celebrating, people began to slowly make their way to the doors of the gym as we headed towards the locker room. Before we reached it, feedback from the announcer's microphone crackled around us.

"Testing, testing, one, two, three," said a familiar voice. I stopped and turned towards the announcer's table to see Ben standing there with a large poster-board sign. "If Miss Robin Hayes would be so kind as to step forward, I have a question for her."

My stomach dropped to the pit of my stomach as people stopped and stared. Felicity pushed me ahead of her since I made no attempt to move on my own. Ben grinned when he saw me and turned his sign around for me to see. Pictures of basketballs lined the outside edge of the paper, framing bold orange letters that read: "I finally got the balls to ask, so take a shot with me at . . ."

"At what?" I asked out loud.

"Glad you asked," Ben responded, throwing a real basketball my way. I caught it with ease and turned it around to see one word written in black glitter: Prom. I glanced up at Ben, who was walking across the court to me. "Will you go to prom with me?"

Exhilaration filled me, but I pursed my lips and twisted my face into a thoughtful expression. I looked behind me at all my teammates, who were nodding their heads, then at the spectators who were watching the scene with eager anticipation. I finally turned back towards Ben, who was now nervously fiddling with the pockets of his jeans as he awaited my answer. He raised his eyebrows questioningly, and I prolonged replying just to see him squirm more.

"Of course, I'll go to prom with you," I finally said.

The look of relief on his face made me laugh. He came up and hugged me, and I buried my face in his chest as the onlookers applauded.

"You kinda had me worried there for a second," he admitted.

"Yeah, well, that's payback for pulling a public stunt like this," I replied.

"You know you loved it," he teased.

"No."

He chuckled and gave me a kiss on the cheek. "I'll see you after you get changed."

I turned around and was swarmed by squealing teammates, all offering their congratulations. I couldn't help but get wrapped up in their girly ways as we ran to the locker room, gossiping about prom the entire time we showered and changed. I pulled on my dark jeans and a red blouse before clasping my necklace around my neck. Then Felicity and I walked arm in arm out of the gym to find our parents and Dawn talking with the boys.

"Congratulations!" Dawn hollered when she saw us, running up and clutching both of us in a hug.

"Thanks, sunshine," I replied, hugging her back.

She ran back to the rest of the group, her arms stretched towards Ben. He scooped her up and sat her on his hip.

"Ben said we could go to the park again tomorrow," she told me.

"Again?" I gasped. "We've gone almost every day this week!"

"Ben said yes," she replied seriously, and we all laughed. "And Matthew said he'd come too."

"He did?" Felicity asked with brows raised high, mirroring my inner surprise, but he only shrugged.

"She's very hard to say no to," he offered up as an explanation, coming over and wrapping his arm around Felicity's waist.

"That she is," I agreed.

Dawn had us all wrapped around her fingers, and she knew it too.

"Congratulations on your big win, ladies," Felicity's dad told us.

"We're so proud of you," my mom said, giving us both a hug.

"It was a team effort," I said with a smile.

"We were thinking of throwing a celebratory dinner party tonight," Annie said. "We could invite all the girls on your team, and the boys' team, and anyone else you feel like having over."

"That sounds great, Mom!" Felicity clapped and jumped from one foot to the other.

"We thought you'd agree." David said with a grin. "We'll plan it if you do the invites."

"Deal," Felicity agreed, giving her dad a double thumbs up. She turned her head to look at me, Ben, and Matthew. "Hey, do you guys want to come to a party at my house tonight?"

I rolled my eyes at her as Ben answered for the three of us. "Consider us RSVP'd for attending."

Matthew and I gave each other a knowing look, already prepared to be each other's wingman as we were dragged into their social plans once again. It'd become a comfortable routine for us.

"Until then, who wants lunch at Lou's Barbeque?" Mom asked.

"Yes, please!" I answered, my mouth watering at the idea.

"Count me in too," Ben said.

"Guess that makes me three," Matthew added.

"We appreciate the offer," David said, "but we should head home and start the party planning. We're already short on time with how last minute it is. Next time?"

"Of course," Mom agreed. "Felicity?"

"I'd love to, but I think I'll go home with my parents to make sure their taste is up to par," she replied, with a wink thrown at her mom.

"Alright then." Mom laughed before turning to me. "Lizzie is going to meet us there. Want to ride with us?"

"Sure," I replied, grabbing Dawn from Ben. "We can play *I Spy* on the way."

"Okay," Dawn agreed happily.

"We'll see you two over there," Mom told Ben and Matthew before we parted ways to head to our separate cars.

* * *

"This looks amazing," I said, my jaw dropping open as I walked through the Larson's den.

The theme was black and orange and it showed in every detail. There wasn't a space left untouched by balloon arches, streamers, flowers, or some other form of decor. Three large tables lined the far wall with a variety of food and beverages already being devoured by the teens that filled the room.

"Well, it helps to have party planners on speed dial," Felicity said, looking around proudly. Her hair was pulled up in two top buns, held in place by black and orange scrunchies, and her black cocktail dress was adorned with an orange sash and orange shoes to keep with the color scheme. Spotting new people in the doorway, she called out, "Oh, hi Katie!" And with that, she took off with Matthew in tow to greet more guests.

"Poor Matthew," I remarked as we watched him trying to converse with the girls.

He smiled politely and interjected at all the right places, but you could tell he'd rather be anywhere else.

"He's gotten a lot better in social situations," Ben said.

"How could he not when he's dating the queen of social?" I asked, and Ben chuckled. "He really has come a long way though."

"I think we were good for him," Ben said, holding my hand as we walked towards the food.

"I do too."

It seemed like a lifetime ago that I'd thought he could be dangerous. I couldn't imagine myself seeing him that way now. He still had an air of mystery about him—which I questioned—but I was grateful for his companionship and the sense of completeness he'd brought to our circle. Despite not knowing anything about his past, I knew he was a good person, and that's all that mattered.

"Congratulations on the win, Robin," Tom said, throwing a high-five my way.

"Thanks!" I replied.

"Season high scorer. Not too shabby," Juan added, spilling the beans on what I thought was my well-kept secret.

"No way!" Tom exclaimed. "Keep that up and you'll get a scholarship next year for sure!"

"That would be amazing," I said.

"You didn't tell me you were the season high scorer," Ben accused.

"I didn't tell anybody," I responded with a shrug, and Ben shook his head as a smile played on the edge of his lips.

"No recognition for anything, huh?" he asked.

"You know me so well," I replied sarcastically, giving his hand an affectionate squeeze.

"Well, it won't be a secret anymore, I'm afraid" Juan said, motioning towards Tom who was already doing the rounds with his newfound knowledge. "Sorry about that."

"It's fine," I told him. "Everyone would've found out at the award's assembly anyway. I just don't like the attention."

"She's too humble for that," Ben added, kissing the top of my head.

Unfortunately for me, people began making their way over to voice congratulations and opinions of my success. I plastered a smile on my face and accepted the praise as best I could. After an hour and a half of nonstop conversing, Matthew walked up behind me, interrupting the person who was speaking to me.

"Want to get some air?" he asked, offering me an escape.

"That sounds great," I told him, relief flooding through me.

I excused myself from the conversation and followed him through the crowd to the French doors that led to the Larson's backyard. We walked past the large patio and planted ourselves on the outside couch that sat between two marble fountains. The night air was chilly, but not unpleasantly so, and we relaxed in its tranquil embrace.

"Thanks for the save," I said as I turned on the gas fire pit in front of us.

"Anytime," he replied, stretching his arms above his head before relaxing into the cushions. "I thought you'd had enough attention for one night."

"That was enough attention for a lifetime," I corrected, pulling my hair out of its ponytail and letting it run wild on my shoulders.

Matthew grinned at my response. "Why don't you like attention anyway?"

"I'm an introvert," I replied with a shrug. "It just feels suffocating. I'd rather be observing than be the one observed. You of all people should understand that."

"I do. I was just curious about your mindset. So I take it you didn't like Ben's 'prom-posal?'"

"It was sweet, and I'll treasure the memory," I answered without answering.

"But?"

"But I definitely would've preferred something less public."

"And Felicity would've preferred something a little more public than me just asking her on our date, I'm sure," Matthew said, and I snorted as I remembered Felicity's rant about it the other day.

"Opposites attract."

"That they do," Matthew agreed with a shake of his head. "It doesn't make much sense, though, does it?"

"No, it really doesn't. Then again, nothing with you really does."

Matthew nudged my arm with his shoulder. "Hardy har-har."

"So he *does* know the art of sarcasm," I said, raising my eyebrows in feigned shock, and he made a face at me.

The wind picked up slightly, throwing a handful of dirt our way. I held my hand over my face to protect it from being sprayed with the debris, but something managed to make its way into my eye, and it began to water.

"Ugh," I moaned, rubbing at it. "Of all the rotten luck."

"Let me look," Matthew said. He leaned in close with one hand under my chin as I blinked incessantly. "Would you stop blinking?"

"I can't," I muttered.

He sighed and held my eyelid up with his thumb as the rest of his hand rested on my cheek.

"Hold still," he instructed. His finger lightly brushed over the side of my eye, the unnatural feeling giving me goosebumps. "There. It was just a piece of a leaf."

"O-m-g-!" I heard from behind us as my eye slowly stopped burning.

I turned to see Julie and Annette standing nearby with two seniors, all of them staring at us.

"My, my, my," Annette murmured disapprovingly. "What do we have here?"

"Looks like a scandal to me," Julie answered, eyeing us with pleasure.

"What are you talking about?" I asked.

"Wait until everyone hears about you two," Annette replied.

"Excuse me?" Matthew said, sounding as confused as I felt.

"I didn't take you for a cheater, Robin," Annette continued, and my mouth dropped open. "Then again, who could resist Mr. Blue Eyes here?"

"I don't know what you think you saw, but you're wrong," I told her, standing up and folding my arms over my chest.

"Are we though?" Julie questioned with a coy smile. "Because we all saw you two huddled up nice and cozy there. I think I even saw you kissing."

"We were not!" I yelled, appalled.

"Your eyes deceived you, Julie," Matthew said, standing up next to me, but she only shrugged.

"I don't think Felicity or Ben will be very happy once it gets back to them," Annette said, forming her lips into a pout.

"Don't you dare go making up rumors about us," I said, agitation filling me. They were the dynamic duo of spreading lies—lies people often believed.

"Who said anything about making stuff up?" Julie asked innocently. "We're just going to tell it how we saw it."

"You two are a real piece of work," I snapped as my irritation switched to anger.

I glared as heat coursed through my body, leaving me with the tingling sensation I'd now come to expect. Matthew put his hand on my shoulder, and when I glanced over at him, his eyebrows were drawn tightly together.

"Calm down," he told me quietly.

I heard a camera click as a photo was captured and whipped my head back towards Annette and Julie.

"You can't deny your little fling when you can't even keep your hands off each other," Annette scoffed, her phone pointed towards us.

"Can't deny what we have proof of either," Julie added in with a laugh, looking over Annette's shoulder at the picture she'd taken of us.

My usual even-temper was thrown out the window as rage boiled in my bones.

"You shallow, low-life, lying bimbos!" I yelled, but they ignored me as all four of them stared at the phone.

Without realizing what I was doing, I pushed my hands outward, letting the energy of anger course through my body and leave through my outstretched arms. As the feeling bolted out of me, the water from the fountains hurtled their way. All four of them let out different levels of screams as they were soaked to the bone.

"Where did that come from?" Julie cried.

I dropped my arms, shell shocked, and the water splashed to the ground. Annette and Julie ran away with their dates on their heels as I stared at my hands, open mouthed.

"Please tell me you saw that," I whispered, feeling a range of emotions spanning from terror to enthralled.

"Robin," Matthew said in a strangled voice. I gazed up at him as he licked his lips and rubbed the back of his neck with his hand.

"Matthew?"

"Sit down," he instructed quietly. "We need to talk."

# CHAPTER SIXTEEN

"You know something, don't you?" I accused softly. "You know what's going on with me."

"I do." Matthew sat down heavily, as though he were carrying the burdens of the whole world on his shoulders.

"Tell me," I insisted, sitting next to him as my heart beat faster at the idea of getting answers.

After a moment of silence, he sighed and turned towards me. "What you believe to be true . . . is."

"No, don't do that," I told him sternly. "Don't pull your usual cryptic crap. Not now. Not about this. Just give it to me straight. *Please.*"

He observed me for a quick second, then started again. "You possess what we call 'hydrokinesis.' You can control water."

"Excuse me?" I heard myself say, trying to figure out if I'd heard him correctly.

"You can control water," he repeated.

My head clouded as I struggled to decide if he was joking or not, disbelieving despite everything. "You're kidding, right?"

"No. I'm very serious."

"That's impossible," I stated with a near hysterical laugh.

"You just saw proof that it isn't."

He was right, I had.

*This is real.*

I struggled to get my bearings as questions surged through me. My heart skipped a beat as I attempted to get words through my lips. "H-How is that possible? What-what does it mean? And who's 'we?' How do you even know this?" I stared him directly in the eye, my voice growing hoarse. "Who are you, Matthew?"

"I'm going to answer all your questions, I promise," he replied. "But it's not going to be easy to hear. Or believe. So just listen with an open mind and don't interrupt me, okay?"

"Okay," I agreed, my voice barely a whisper.

"The life you know isn't the life you were born into," he began, looking into the distance at nothing. "You and I both come from an underworld society called Garridan—a society made up of people with an array of supernatural powers. Among them, there are a select few who specialize in the elements: fire, air, earth, and water."

He looked over at me when he said 'water' and I pointed to myself with raised eyebrows. He nodded slightly before continuing.

"We call those people the Keepers of Balance. They're in charge, and they do exactly what it sounds like—keep the peace in the community and keep the elements in balance for the entire world to prosper. But, like any civilization, Garridan isn't perfect. There were some people who were unhappy with hiding from the Norms and wanted glory for their perceived superiority in the larger hierarchy."

"Norms?" I questioned, breaking my vow of silence.

"Normal people," Matthew answered, and I made a face at the lack of creativity. "Anyway, those who disagreed with the way things were done gathered enough followers and broke away from Garridan to create their own base of operations. They called themselves the Cyfrin. After that, war raged, and they began to target the children of Garridan, believing they should be raised with the mindset that they're superior to the Norms.

"To protect them, the Keepers of Balance made the decision to send all the children fourteen and under to live in hiding amongst the Norms where they'd be safe. They stripped them of their powers first with the intention of returning them once they were brought back home after the war. However, it took them *much* longer than expected to bring the Cyfrin down.

"By the time they finally did, and they began trying to get their children back, a lot of them had already been adopted or shuffled around so much in foster care that they couldn't be easily found. They also discovered that, from the day those children were sent into hiding, the Cyfrin had been hunting them down, kidnapping them and moving forward with their plans. It's been sixteen years now since the kids were sent away, and Garridan has only gotten back about sixty-five percent of them. The rest are either with the Cyfrin or still missing."

He stopped talking and eyed me, taking in my rigid posture and bewildered expression. "You alright?" he asked.

I swallowed loudly, the dryness in my throat making it difficult to talk. "Just processing."

I chewed on my bottom lip as I tried to remember to keep breathing. A secret world full of people with supernatural powers seemed absurd, but I couldn't deny I had at least some proof it wasn't impossible. My power over water was certainly real, which meant he likely wasn't just pulling my leg and everything he was telling me was the truth.

"If that's all true," I said faintly, "that means . . . I'm adopted."

"That's correct," Matthew replied simply. I let out a humorless chuckle and leaned back, staring into the night sky as he continued watching me. "You don't seem surprised."

"I'm not," I admitted, running my fingers through my hair. "I don't look like either of my parents or my sister, and a lot of people have joked about me being adopted before. It's always been a nagging question at the back of my mind to be honest. I just don't know why my mom never told me."

"I couldn't say."

My mind reeled, trying to wrap itself around my adoption, while also replaying Matthew's story. I had many questions but struggled to settle on specific ones to ask.

"What about my family?" I asked.

"Well, I suppose it's up to you if you want to tell them or not."

"No, I mean my other family," I replied quietly. "Who are my real parents? Do I have any siblings? What are they like? Should I try to find them?"

"I can't answer any of that for you, unfortunately," Matthew said in an apologetic voice. "I can take a guess about one thing though. Most elemental powers stay within certain bloodlines, which means the odds are good that one or both of your parents have it as well. If that's the case, your parents are Keepers of Balance."

"Which means they're important."

Matthew nodded. "If you decide you want to find them, I think I can help."

"Thank you. But I'm gonna have to think about it. *A lot.*" My emotions were running high at the thought of how betrayed my mom would feel if I brought any of this up to her.

"Understandable."

"So you're from there too?" I asked. "What's it like?"

Matthew hesitated before answering. "I don't really know. The last time I was there was before I was sent away with the rest of the kids, and I was only almost two at the time . . . so I don't remember it at all."

"What do you mean?" I questioned, my lips turning down. "If you were never brought back there, how do you know about it?"

"Because once upon a time, *I* was one of the children hunted and kidnapped by the Cyfrin. I grew up with them. Training, learning, being molded." A hint of anger was evident in his tone.

This newfound information explained a lot about him, and the dots began to connect in my mind. His demeanor with other teenagers, his hesitancy to share details about his childhood, the way he could fight . . . It all made sense now.

"Then how did you end up here?" I wondered out loud.

"I—" Matthew stopped, seeming torn about whether to answer, but I had little patience.

"You just told me my whole life is a lie and that I have supernatural powers. What could be worse than that and so bad that you think you have to hide it?"

"Nothing," he replied, though I caught a glimpse of the old Matthew in his cold expression. "I ran away from them a while back. I wanted to live a normal life where I wasn't being treated as an assassin or used as a pawn in some bigger power move. Me ending up here was pure coincidence."

"You know, Ben doesn't believe in coincidences," I said, getting a vibe that he wasn't being completely forthcoming. He didn't react to my comment, his face remaining stone-faced, so I decided to move on as my curiosity grew stronger than my suspicion. "How did they find you?"

"They have a man named Arthur. He has the ability to locate power sources. If someone uses their powers, even accidentally, it makes a tracer for him to latch onto and follow. It's how they were able to take so many of the kids," Matthew explained, his tone lighter than it'd been before.

"But I thought you said the kids were stripped of their powers," I said, and he nodded.

"They were. At least the ones who had already come into their powers. But there was nothing to take away from those whose powers hadn't manifested yet. The Keepers of Balance couldn't do anything about that except hope the war would be over before of any of them did."

"But some of them did?"

"Yes. There's no set time when powers surface, but most kids get them before they're five. There were many of those young ones who ended up discovering them accidentally and that was all it took for them to pop up on Arthur's radar."

"How come I didn't know I had powers until now then?"

"When you're not raised in an atmosphere that normalizes it, it's easy to ignore the signs," he answered. "You probably came into your powers a long time ago. But if you don't accept them or practice controlling them, they fade away in a sense—lying dormant and waiting to be utilized. Your case is a bit different though."

"How so?"

"Your abilities are rare and powerful. They could only sit stagnant for so long. Since you weren't making use of them yourself, they used your emotions to assert themselves to try to get you to take control."

"You say that like they're alive," I said, raising my eyebrows.

"Not alive. Just a big part of your genetic makeup. No different than any of the organs functioning inside of you."

"So how do I learn to control and use it?"

"Lots of practice and training. I can help you with that though."

"Really?"

"Really. It wouldn't be the first time, and I'm very good at it."

"Wait, what's your power?" I asked, intrigued by the possibilities.

"I'm a petrifier. I have the ability to petrify anything, living or not."

I eyed him, a chill running up my spine. "You know, that explains why you're so scary."

"Scary?" he asked in surprise. "You're scared of me?"

"No." I shrugged. "But I was when you first got here."

"Why?"

"Because you gave off an aura of danger. Not to mention that you glared at me all day, and I got this weird, cold feeling when you were around."

"Ah. That would be the pull of the powers."

"The *what?*" I asked, making a face.

"Our powers can sense when others with abilities are near. When you're around them all the time, you don't notice the feeling they give off. But when you're not, it's very prominent."

"Oh . . . You know, this all keeps getting stranger and stranger the more you explain."

"Not strange. Just not *your* idea of normal."

I nodded my head slowly, everything feeling muddled. "Why didn't you tell me all this sooner?"

"Because I wanted to be a normal kid," he responded quietly, refusing to look at me, "living a normal life, and telling you would've made that impossible . . . But that doesn't excuse it, and I apologize for leaving you in the dark."

"It's okay," I said. I couldn't imagine being in his situation or having his upbringing. I couldn't blame him for hiding it. "I mean, it would've been nice to know I wasn't going crazy a little sooner, but I understand your reasoning."

"I appreciate that," he said, finally glancing up at me. "You're a highly compassionate individual, and I don't deserve it, but I'll accept it."

I smiled at him, then sighed. "So what now? Where do I go from here?"

"If it were anybody else, I'd say it's up to you. But with your particular powers, I don't think there's anything for you to do but accept that you have them and perfect your use of them. That being said, the rest *is* up to you. You need to decide if you want to tell people closest to you or not."

"That one isn't just my choice though."

"Why's that?"

"Because telling Ben and Felicity would blow your secret too."

He nodded slowly, then said, "That's okay with me."

"Really? You want to tell them?"

"If I plan on keeping Felicity in my life, I can't keep lying about who I am," he replied. "And I'm hoping she's in my life for a long time."

"I think she will be," I replied, putting my hand on his arm.

He smiled bigger than I'd ever seen from him before, and a new light shined in his eyes. Telling me our backstory unlocked a whole new side to him—a side I was eager to get to know.

In that moment, as we stared at one another, I knew we'd reached a new level of friendship that bonded us together in a way most people would never experience. His mysteries were starting to be unraveled, and I was excited to learn more.

"Does this mean vampires are real too?" I asked.

Matthew threw me a disgusted look, and I broke out in laughter. I leaned against him, trying to compose myself, but more giggles erupted. I'd just learned I wasn't going crazy, but now I was losing my mind. What a night.

# CHAPTER SEVENTEEN

"You and Matthew are causing quite the stir," Ben said as he drove me home.

I rolled my eyes, imagining the rumors, then looked at Ben to assess his feelings on the matter. He didn't look upset, which was a good sign.

"You know there's no truth to it, right?" I asked.

He glanced over at me, then grabbed my hand and squeezed it.

"Of course I know that," he replied, bringing my hand up to his lips. I sighed in relief. "I never believe anything Annette or Julie say. Plus, I trust you and I trust Matthew. I don't think he would ever hurt Felicity."

"No, he wouldn't," I agreed.

I continued to watch him, biting my lip in contemplation. Should I tell him what I'd learned tonight? I knew he'd believe me. He was always so supportive, especially of what everyone else would call crazy. But it was for that exact reason that I decided not to tell him yet. I needed time to process and come to terms with it, just in case I didn't want to accept this as my new reality.

"What has you so far away?" he asked.

"Nothing," I replied with a smile. "I'm just thankful for you."

"Well, I'm thankful for you too," he responded as he pulled up in front of my house. "Do you want to meet at the park at noon tomorrow? We can have a picnic with Dawn."

"Sounds great. I'll text Felicity and let her know so they can meet us."

"Alrighty. Sleep well, Robin."

I gave him a kiss then jumped out of the car and waved as he drove away before going inside.

"How was the party?" Lizzie asked from the couch.

I sat on the floor in front of her and Mom, but when I glanced at Mom, a pit of emotion grew inside me.

"It was fun for the most part," I told them as they sipped glasses of wine.

"I know that look," Mom said, eyeing me. "What happened?"

"Just mean girls being mean," I responded. Telling only part of the truth would hopefully keep her from catching on to the fact that anything else was bothering me. I couldn't bring up what I'd learned about myself tonight. I wasn't ready, and neither was she.

"Annette and Julie tried to accuse Matthew and me of being an item and cheating on Ben and Felicity," I continued. "And then they went and told everybody and their mother about it."

Lizzie's mouth fell open. "Those little bi—"

Mom smacked her on the arm, and she grinned sheepishly as I held back a laugh.

"What did Ben have to say about it?" Mom asked.

"He said he didn't believe them and that he trusted us," I replied, making her smile.

"You got a winner with that one," she said, and I looked down at my hands.

"Yeah. I think I did."

When I looked back up at her, she was gazing at me with adoration, and my heart broke a little. I didn't care that I was adopted. She was the woman who raised me and taught me right from wrong. She'd always loved me unconditionally and, even though I wasn't her blood, she made me part of her family anyway. I could never repay her for any of that, and I was so grateful for her. I didn't care in the least that I was adopted.

But I was still hurt because she kept the truth from me. She kept it a secret, hiding one of the most important parts of my life from me. It didn't seem right or fair.

"I'm going to go to bed," I said as I stood. "Enjoy your wine."

I gave them both a hug as they said goodnight to me then headed for my room. When I closed my eyes, I fell asleep instantly, but the night left me tossing and turning as I jumped from one bad dream to another. To top it off, it ended with the screaming of the woman who haunted my subconscious.

* * *

At lunch the next day, we all laughed about the night before and how pitiful teenagers could be. Felicity was just as dismissive of the rumor as Ben, so there was no tension between any of us. Dawn ran around playing with other kids, periodically being intercepted by one of us. Even Matthew got in on the fun, chasing her around and pushing her on the swings. It was a strange but nice change to see the effect

Dawn's energy had on him. A couple hours later, Felicity announced she had to leave.

"I can take you," Ben offered as he stood up. "I promised my brothers we'd go hiking, so I probably shouldn't stay any longer anyway."

"Cool, thanks," Felicity said. She looked over at Matthew and me and stuck her finger out at us. "Now don't you two be getting all lovey-dovey while we're gone."

"Ha. Ha," I said dryly, narrowing my eyes. She let out a giggle then waved as she and Ben walked to his car. "I should probably get Dawn home too."

"What are your plans after that?" Matthew asked as I called for Dawn.

"Nothing exciting."

"Want to start your training?" he asked, causing me to snort.

"Sorry," I apologized when he cocked one brow. "It just sounds like something from a bad spy movie."

"To some," he replied, unfazed. "Is that a no?"

"No, it's not. It's a 'yes' and an advanced 'thank you' for your patience," I said, already anticipating his need for it.

He gave me a small nod of acknowledgement as Dawn ran up to us, her face flushed and hair wild.

"Ready to go, silly girl?" I asked her.

"Yep," she replied. "Thanks for playing with me, Matthew."

"Any time," he told her with a gentle smile.

He joined us on our walk home with Dawn tugging his arm the entire way. After dropping her off with my mom, we walked back to the park to pick up his car.

"Where are we going?" I questioned as he drove further away from the city towards the wooded terrain.

"A place with a water source where no one will be around," he replied. "First rule: Never let anyone see you using your abilities. Our people have remained a secret for so long because of their caution."

"Don't get caught." I nodded. "Check."

"Not unless you want to be locked up by some crazy government scientists."

"Wait," I said, suddenly remembering something important. "You said that man, Arthur, could find me if I use my powers."

Matthew nodded slowly. "Yes, that's correct. But odds are you're already on their radar because you've been using your powers without knowing. Which means, at this point, it's better to keep using them to train so you're prepared to defend yourself in case they try to come for you."

My stomach dropped. "Do you think they will?"

Matthew's lips hardened into a tight line. "Yes. They will. Especially if they find out you're the daughter of a Keeper of Balance. But that's why I'm going to help you learn how to protect yourself."

I bit my lip and focused on the scenery we were passing. My normal, carefree life had been ambushed, and I wasn't sure I would like the results. But it was too late to turn back now. If Matthew was right, I needed to be capable of protecting my family, as well as myself, just in case things took a turn for the worse. I wouldn't let my mom or sister pay the price for my origins, and I certainly wasn't going to let some creeps try to turn me into a pawn in their games.

Matthew parked the car on a small dirt path that stopped at the base of a hill. I followed him through the overgrown brush, hiking up and over the hill. As we walked down the other side, I admired the small lake lying comfortably between the rolling land as it was brightened by the reflection of the sun above us.

"This is beautiful," I said softly.

Matthew smiled as he looked around. "Yeah, it is. I came across it by accident and come back whenever I need to take a step back and think."

"I see why. It's peaceful. I could fall asleep here with no worries."

"Still having nightmares?" he asked, and I nodded.

"Mainly just the screaming woman."

"I think I know how to fix that."

"Really? How?"

"It sounds like you're experiencing a visit from a telepathic dreamer. It's someone who has the power to transport people into the dreams of others," he explained. "But they can't communicate correctly until both parties are willing and open, which is why the woman is being perceived by you as screaming."

"That's wild," I almost whispered, my eyes wide. "How do I let them talk to me?"

"Just accept them. Don't be afraid or hesitate in any manner, otherwise they'll be yanked from your dream like they have been," he replied. "They can physically touch you, but they can't use their powers and they can't hurt you. So, even if it's someone dangerous, you'll be safe."

"Okay. I guess I'll hope she comes back then. I wonder who it is."

"I couldn't say. But until we know, let's focus on you." He walked towards the water, beckoning me to follow. "The first and most important thing you need to do is connect with your power. Close your eyes and search for it within you."

I followed his instructions and closed my eyes. I could feel my heart beating and my blood flowing through my veins. My stomach gurgled and my throat contracted as I swallowed. After a moment, I opened one eye and saw Matthew staring at me.

"I don't feel anything," I told him.

"Because you're not looking closely enough," he said, and I sighed. This sort of thing seemed easier in movies. Matthew grabbed my hand and pulled me down until we were sitting at the edge of the water. "Water speaks to you. All you have to do is listen. So let's try again. Close your eyes and take a deep breath. Listen to the water lapping the ground, the way it smells. Let it surround you and invite it in with every sense."

As he spoke, my mind slowly focused. Thoughts of everything aside from the liquid reservoir in front of me faded away. I breathed in its fresh, natural odor, and heard the waves gently caress the place where dirt met water. A small tingle worked its way through me from my head to my toes.

"Focus on it," Matthew instructed quietly, as if he could sense my feeling.

Everything faded away as the tingling amped up to the icy burn I'd felt before, running through my veins like lava. I could see it behind my closed eyes, leaving a glow in the darkness as it danced around.

"Now grab a hold of it. See how it moves. How it shifts when you touch it."

I did as he said, reaching towards it in my mind. It was a bright twinkle, flickering with energy, and the closer I got, the more it radiated. It seemed like it was reacting to me and slowly began to mold itself to my body. The rope of light wrapped around me perfectly, fitting to my every curve, and I let out a small gasp of pleasure as it attached to me.

Then, just like that, we were one and the same.

Matthew's voice broke through my stupor. "Now use it."

"How?" I whispered, my eyes still closed as I savored the power's invitation.

"It's very simple. Just think about what it is you want to do and be open-minded to your powers performing it."

"Okay," I murmured.

I licked my lips as my eyes opened and gazed at the translucent water in front of me, focusing on the buzz it gave off. When I did that, I suddenly realized it really *was* speaking to me. Not in a conversation type of way but communicating with my very soul, as though we were kindred spirits. It'd been trying to get through to me for so long, but I never knew.

I redirected my focus to the water and thought about a small stream rising from it in a thin line, bending around itself like a DNA molecule. Then I released the energy built up inside of me, letting it escape through my hands. As I did, the water rose just as I'd imagined, twisting itself as my thoughts became reality. I let out a shocked laugh and slowly moved the water from side to side.

"That's amazing," I said, awestruck.

"Yes, it is," Matthew replied, watching the water alongside me. "Now try something bigger."

"Like what?"

"Anything you want. Your only limit is your imagination."

I thought about it for a second then directed the water into a human profile, staring at us as if alive.

"Is that supposed to be me?" Matthew questioned with a raised brow.

I grinned over at him. "Pretty accurate, isn't it?"

"It is. You're very powerful."

I dropped my hand, the water falling with it in a splash that ricocheted drops onto us. "Why do you say that?"

"It takes time to develop a power. Wielders start out small, barely capable of anything. After lots of practice, one can start getting more creative, and the powers grow along with them in strength," he replied. "Being able to replicate my figure so precisely right at the beginning shows a lot of skill. But I'd already guessed as much from other things I've seen."

"Cool," I said gleefully, thrilled by that thought.

"I suppose," Matthew replied, suppressing a smile. "However, they weren't wrong when they said that with great power comes great responsibility. If the Cyfrin finds out about you, you'll never be safe on your own. Being related to a Keeper of Balance is one thing, but being powerful is a whole new level for them wanting you."

"Guess I'll just have to make sure they never find me."

"I'm afraid it isn't that easy," he said with a shake of his head. "They can infiltrate your life from the inside, and you'd never even know until it was too late. Your life is never going to be the same again, Robin, and you *have* to be careful. You can't trust anyone."

"That's not true. I have my mom and sister. And I have Ben and Felicity. And I have you."

Matthew's face flickered with different emotions, seeming unsure which to land on. Some of them I saw didn't make sense: anger, shame, fear. His eyes glazed over slightly, but he quickly blinked it away and turned his back to me.

"I haven't earned your trust," he told me gruffly.

"Yes, you have," I responded, putting my hand on his shoulder. "And I'm thankful to have you in my life, especially this new one I've just been introduced to."

He glanced over. "I'm thankful for you too. But you really shouldn't trust me."

"And why not?" I crossed my arms.

He rubbed his lips together then said, "You just shouldn't."

"Well, I do. So if you can't give me a reason not to, then I guess you'll just have to deal with it."

His eyes tightened slightly, and a moment passed before he said, "Okay."

"Okay." I smiled, then changed the subject to let him off the hook. "Show me how to do more."

He nodded, going back into teacher mode, but he seemed distracted. I soaked in everything he said but couldn't help but wonder what had caused him so much distress. Why did my trust in him strike such a nerve? I knew there were things he was still hiding, but I didn't think they were anything nefarious. He was a good person. He had to be.

# CHAPTER EIGHTEEN

"Are you sure?" I asked Matthew one last time as Ben and Felicity came into view.

They were leaning against the hood of her car, and I wondered how she'd gotten it there. I followed the tire tracks and saw a barely visible dirt road tucked in between some of the hills. That would've been nice to know before making the trek over this tall lump of land again.

Matthew paused, his brows furrowed deeply as he reconsidered what we were about to do.

"Matthew?" I put my hand on his shoulder.

He took a deep breath then pressed his lips together with a less than confident nod of his head. "Let's do this."

"Together," I reminded him, trying to reconcile him with the idea that we were both about to completely expose ourselves to the people we cared about most.

"Together," he repeated, wiping his hands against his jeans.

"Hey, guys!" Felicity said as Matthew gave her a peck on the cheek.

"Hi," I replied, my stomach turning in knots as I leaned into Ben for a hug. "Sorry we're late."

"Not a problem," she said. "Ben was just trying to help me choose the curtains for prom."

I grinned at him. "I'm sure he's having a blast with that."

"He's actually got great taste. I wish I could rope him into the prom committee, but he refused." Felicity pursed her lips as Ben winked at us. "So what's up? I have a million things to do for prom, so I really can't stay long."

"And why did we have to come all the way out here?" Ben asked, looking around the terrain. "Not that I mind. It's gorgeous."

"Well, Matthew and I have something we wanted to tell you," I said, unsure how to proceed.

I glanced at Matthew, but he stood stiffly, staring past Felicity's head, and I came to the conclusion he would be no help in explaining this.

"What? Are you really secret lovers after all?" Felicity asked, snorting as she stared at her phone.

"Uh," was all I managed to get out. Felicity's head snapped up, and Ben narrowed his eyes at me.

"What the hell? Are you?" Felicity cried out almost angrily.

"No! No, of course not!" I exclaimed, my hands held up in front of me defensively.

"You're doing *great*," Matthew muttered sarcastically as our better halves relaxed, though only slightly.

"Well, I don't see you jumping in," I replied, glaring at him.

"Robin," Ben said sternly. "What's going on?"

I sighed as I rubbed my hand over my face, trying to figure out where to start. "Remember a couple of weeks ago when I told you something weird was going on with me . . . and water?"

"You mean when you said you were controlling it?" Felicity asked, crossing her arms. "You aren't over that yet?"

"No, I'm not," I told her. "Because it's true."

"Robin," Felicity sighed, rubbing her temples. "I love you, but please stop messing around. That's not possible, and I really don't have time for this."

"Hold on just a minute, Felicity," Ben said, holding his hand up. He watched me intently, looking into my eyes as he scrutinized me. He must've been satisfied with whatever he saw because his expression softened. "Show us, Robin."

I nodded, once again thankful for how open-minded he was. I faced the water I'd practiced shaping and molding for hours the day before and breathed out slowly. Lifting both my hands out in front of me, I pulled a wall of water up from its home and let it stand before us in a dramatic display of proof. Felicity and Ben stared at it with wide eyes and open mouths.

"What the hell?" Felicity whispered, stepping back slightly.

I gently lowered the water back down, watching it send ripples across the top of the lake then waited. No one said anything for what seemed like an eternity, and I shifted uncomfortably as I was stared at.

"How?" Ben questioned, sounding awed.

"It's a long story," I replied as I inspected him. He didn't seem distressed as he stepped closer to me, so I relaxed slightly.

"I have time," he assured me, curiosity blossoming from his every pore.

I glanced at Felicity to see her face frozen in shock.

"Do you?" I asked, unsure how she was processing things, but she turned her gaze to Matthew and ignored me.

"How do you fit into this?" she demanded.

"I'm like Robin," he told her quietly.

"You can control water too?" she asked, sounding near hysteria.

"Not exactly. I'm a petrifier. I can petrify things."

"I'm sorry, what?"

Matthew glanced around then walked away. When he came back, he held a flower with a caterpillar on it. His eyes jumped to the three of us then back down to the items he'd retrieved as he moved one hand over them. As it passed by, what looked like a concrete coating began inching its way across until they were fully covered in the hard substance. We all stared with wide eyes as he moved his hand in the opposite direction, and the flower and caterpillar returned to normal.

"Wow," I breathed, amazed at seeing someone else perform a power.

The thought of there being a whole population that could do different things like that astounded me. I wondered, not for the first time, what it would be like to go there and be with other people like me.

"Explain," Felicity said, her voice barely audible. "Now."

Matthew and I launched into our tale, taking turns explaining the things I'd just barely learned myself. Per my request, we excluded the part about the Cyfrin wanting to come find me. I couldn't see the point in worrying or possibly scaring them when they'd already been hit with so much. The further into the story we got, the more emotions played on Felicity's face and none of them were good. When we finished, we stood there waiting for one of them to say something.

"That's insane," Ben said, running his hand through his hair as he blinked rapidly.

Felicity pressed her lips together and began shaking her head, her eyes brimming with tears.

"No, *you're* insane." Her gaze skipped back and forth between Matthew and me. "You're both insane."

"Felicity," Matthew said, his tone pleading, as he took a step towards her.

She backed up and raised her arms out in front of her as she continued to shake her head. Matthew's face filled with pain as he watched her cry.

"No," she whispered, the tears overflowing onto her cheeks. "No."

She turned and jumped into her car, ignoring our protests as she peeled out and drove away without ever looking back. I stared after her, slightly heartbroken by her reaction.

"I should go after her," Matthew said, unable to hide the hurt in his voice.

"No." I walked up and put my arm on his shoulder. "Give her time. She just needs to process."

He nodded slowly, mimicking the feelings I was having. "I'm gonna go. You two need to talk and . . . Well, I just don't want to be here."

He turned around without another word and started back the way we'd come. Ben came up behind me and wrapped his arms around my stomach. I leaned into him, letting his warmth overtake me.

"Do you think she hates me?" I asked, trying not to cry.

"Of course not," Ben replied, tightening his arms around me. "She's just freaked out. She'll come around."

"Yeah. I really hope so." I sniffled. "For my sake and Matthew's."

He pulled me closer, and we stood quietly for a long moment before he spoke again. "So, you're adopted after all. Did you tell your mom you know?"

I shook my head. "No, and I don't know if I will. She must've had her reasons for keeping it from me, even if I can't understand them."

"It might help you process all the hurt you're feeling," he replied, sensing the emotions I was trying to ignore.

"Maybe," I agreed, watching the small waves in front of us. "But I just don't know if I can do it."

"That's your decision," he said, grabbing my hand. "But I think you'll wind up wanting to."

I stayed silent. I was already struggling enough with how I felt about it without another person's opinion factored in. I knew he meant well, but it wasn't something anyone else could understand unless they were in the situation themselves. I pointed my fingers at the water and made it trickle upward in a line, letting it calm me down. How had I gone so long without this feeling of completion?

"Wow," Ben said breathlessly, and I turned my head back to look at him, smiling at his mesmerized expression.

"Why aren't you freaked out about all this?" I asked, guiding the water over his head.

He reached up and touched it, letting drops of it run down his fingers.

"Oh, trust me, I'm a mess on the inside," he replied. "I have so many questions. Plus, some concerns and thoughts, but you haven't known about this much longer than me so I'm assuming you can't help with much of that."

"No, probably not," I said, surprisingly saddened by the thought of not knowing enough about my heritage to answer questions about it.

"I can't believe everything we thought was imagination is real."

"Not *everything,*" I replied with a shrug. He raised his eyebrows in question, and I grinned. "Matthew assured me that vampires do not exist."

"Well, isn't *that* a relief," he replied sarcastically. "But all jokes aside, how are you doing with all this?"

"I'm okay. It's hard to put into words. There are so many different emotions fighting for a front spot, and I'm not sure which one is winning. Anger, sadness, fear, excitement . . . It's a lot to work through."

"I can imagine."

"You can't though," I told him, trying to hide my frustration. "How could you? This isn't anything you've ever experienced before. I'm a supernatural being that was sent away from my home because of a civil war, adopted and never told, and not even remotely the person I thought I was. I feel so alone because, let's be honest, who could possibly understand what I'm going through?"

Ben was silent for a long minute, his hair rustling in the breeze as he stood as still and tall as a tree. I looked at my feet, embarrassed by my outburst.

"I'm sorry," I murmured. "I didn't mean to lash out at you like that."

"Don't apologize," he said, still not looking at me. "You're right. I don't know what you're going through, and it was stupid of me to say otherwise. But you are wrong about one thing."

"What's that?" I asked, and he finally met my gaze, his expression soft.

"There *is* one person who can understand what you're going through. Someone who may even have so much knowledge that *you* can't understand everything *they're* going through," he replied, once again being the voice of reason for me.

"Matthew," I said quietly.

"Matthew," he repeated with a nod. "As much as I hate it, he's clearly better suited to help you with this than I am. And honestly, I think he needs you right now as much as you need him. But just know I'm here for you, too, no matter what."

I blinked back tears for the second time as I wrapped my arms around him. "How are you always so understanding about everything?"

"It's the result of effective therapy."

"Maybe I need some of that."

"If you do, I know a guy." It sounded like a joke, but I knew he was serious.

"Thank you. For everything."

"You're welcome." He rested his head against mine.

"So you still love me even though I'm a freak?" I mumbled against his shirt.

His chest bounced as he chuckled, then he pulled back to look at me. "I still love you, and I'll always love you no matter what. Besides, you've always been a freak."

I scoffed and pushed him away, but he held me tighter in his arms so I couldn't squirm out of his grasp. He eyed me slyly then bent down and gave me a kiss that melted everything away.

"So," he said when we parted for air. "Will you show me again?"

I couldn't help but smile at his excitement, which reminded me of a little kid on Christmas morning. I nodded and pulled him down onto the ground with me, eager to share this new part of myself with him and relieved he wanted to be a part of it with me. I only hoped that Felicity would come around and feel the same way in the end.

# CHAPTER NINETEEN

"She completely ignored me," I said, not sure if I was more angry or sad about Felicity's behavior.

"What about in art class?" Ben asked, taking a bite of a banana. "She sits right next to you. She couldn't have just said nothing."

"She came in and talked to Ms. Meers then left. Probably because she didn't want to be near me." My voice wavered between bitterness and loss.

Matthew played with the uneaten food on his plate. He was more withdrawn than he'd been in a long time. Felicity's rejection left an imprint on him that I hoped could be undone.

"You two need to relax," Ben told us. "Give her some time. This isn't an easy thing to blindly accept, so just let her think. Unlike you, she's only human."

Matthew and I both glowered at him, unamused by his joke, and he grinned sheepishly.

"Too soon?" he asked.

Matthew got up from the table, huffing as he walked away.

"Too soon," I confirmed.

The bell rang, so I stood to follow Matthew to Spanish. I caught up with him as he was rounding a corner, but he stopped dead in his tracks, causing me to bump into him. I looked past him to see what his abrupt halt was about and saw Felicity standing a few feet away, looking back and forth between the two of us. Matthew took a half step towards her, but she quickly turned around and rushed away in the opposite direction. Matthew let out a breath, his eyes trailing her every move.

A rambunctious group of freshmen pushed past us, knocking into our arms with no remorse. Matthew grabbed the closest one by the collar and swung him around, pushing him forcefully into one of the lockers.

"Watch where you're going," he hissed in the kid's face, staring him down with a look that could kill.

The boy's face drained of color, and his eyes were wide with fear.

"Matthew," I said, pulling at his arm. He kept staring the kid down, so I tugged his arm even harder. "Matthew! Let him go. *Now.*"

He glanced at me, annoyance dancing in his eyes, then shoved the kid towards his friends, who were all watching with looks of horror. I pushed Matthew away, hoping none of them would say anything as we left. I didn't think I could stop him a second time.

"What was that about?" I asked, but he ignored me. "Look, I know you're upset about Felicity. I am too. But you can't go beating people up to get your feelings out, especially younger kids."

"Whatever," he replied as he walked ahead of me.

"Hey," I called out. He stopped but didn't turn around. "Want to get out of here?"

He slowly rotated his body towards me. "Yeah. I do."

"Let's go then," I said, walking towards the side door exit. My eyes skirted around, trying to make sure no faculty members were around.

"When you're doing something wrong, you're not supposed to act suspiciously," Matthew said. "It draws attention."

"Well, excuse me for being nervous," I muttered as we stepped outside. "I, for one, don't skip class. Let alone a whole half of the day."

"And you're insinuating that I do?" Matthew asked with a raised brow, and I shrugged nonchalantly. "Ouch."

We walked along the back road, away from traffic and anyone that could rat us out for cutting class. The sun beat down but it mixed with a cool breeze to create the perfect temperature as we walked in silence, both absorbed in our own thoughts.

"If you thought I was dangerous when I first started at school, why did you interact with me? Why did you even attempt to be my friend at all?" Matthew suddenly asked, watching me with curiosity.

"Because of Felicity," I answered.

"That's a big negative feeling to push aside though. Especially just because someone asked you to."

"She's my best friend," I responded, as if that was explanation enough because, to me, it was.

"You really love her, don't you?"

"Of course, I do." I glanced his way as I decided to voice a hunch. "So do you."

He ran his fingers through his hair and chuckled nervously. "Yeah. I do, actually."

"I thought so," I said, smiling softly.

He sighed, looking sad again. "Not that it matters now."

"Of course, it does!" I exclaimed, but he shook his head.

"How? She's scared of me," he growled, frustration masking the pain. "She looked at me like I was a monster. Hell, maybe I am."

"You're not a monster!"

"How would you know?" he asked bitterly. "You've only known me a few months. You have no idea who I am or what I've done."

I twisted my hands, hating the idea that this is what he thought of himself.

"I may not know all the skeletons in your closet, but I *do* know you," I said. "You're protective and caring and chivalrous. You stand up for what's right, even when the rest of the world is against you. You're a good person, Matthew. You're not a monster."

He shoved his hands in his jacket pockets and stared straightforward bitterly. "You can't say that when you don't know my past."

"I don't care about your past. All I care about is now, and as far as I can tell, you're a good person. You're good enough to be my friend and good enough to love Felicity."

"Even if I do love her, it means nothing if she doesn't love me back," he said, hanging his head down.

"But you don't know that she doesn't," I pointed out, but he just shrugged again.

"At this point, I may never know."

I didn't have a response to that, so I stayed quiet. She would come around. She had to.

We lounged around a while longer before deciding to drive to the lake, making use of our time by exploring the extent of my powers. After confirming I could shape the water into any form I wanted, Matthew pushed me to learn defensive skills.

"We're going to start with reflection. If you can learn to reflect people's attacks—both physical and power related—you'll have greater protection for yourself and others. But it isn't easy, and it takes a lot of practice and energy," Matthew warned.

"That's okay. I'm up for it," I replied, nodding my head and jumping from one foot to the other.

"Calm down," he instructed, so I stopped bouncing and sheepishly held my hands behind my back. "We're going to start small. I'll throw some things at you, and I want you to use the water to block them."

"Okay, sounds easy enough."

Matthew looked skeptical, which I didn't understand, then threw a stick right at my face. It scratched my cheek, and I flinched away.

"Hey!" I shouted.

"I told you to block it," he said, unfazed.

"You didn't tell me you were starting though," I shot back. He threw a rock my way, and I leaned to the side, barely missing getting struck in the face again. "Matthew!"

"You have to learn to expect the unexpected. You have to be prepared at all times, otherwise you've already lost," he said, tossing another rock that I ducked away from. "Use your powers. You can't just duck away from a lightning bolt or a car thrown your way."

He continued to throw items at me, and I finally pulled the water up, slowing them down before they came through the other side.

"Good," he said. "Now try to stop them completely *inside* your water shield. Let the water grab onto them. If you can hold items in there, it'll be a greater asset."

"Why?"

"Because that means you can hold people in there as well, and that'll be a great defensive skill."

"Wouldn't that drown a person?" I asked, uneasy at the thought.

"Essentially. If you don't release them soon enough."

"I don't think I want to learn that," I said quietly, and Matthew's face softened slightly.

"Look at it this way: Every skill you learn can be used in different ways depending on the situation you're in. Good and evil exist in our world as much as it does everywhere else, and almost all of our powers and abilities can be deadly in one way or another. But that doesn't mean they have to be. You need to learn everything you can about your powers, and then it'll be up to *you* to choose who you are and how you're going to use them.

"This skill right here is a perfect example," he continued. "It's easy if you're using it to hold inanimate objects. But if the time comes when you need to hold an animal or human back, you have to decide when enough is enough, and that'll determine a lot about you. Do you understand what I'm saying?"

I nodded. "We get to choose if we use our powers for evil or good."

The corner of his mouth lifted slightly. "That's a very summarized version, but yes. Exactly my point. So, let's try it, shall we?"

He began tossing things my way again. I lifted my shield of water in front of me and attempted to expand it as three logs pierced the front. I clenched my jaw as they pushed their way through the water, trying hard to get a grip on them. I managed to stop one, the water molding its way around it in a vibrant hue of blue, but the other two found their way through.

"Not bad for your first try," Matthew said.

"Try again," I insisted through clenched teeth as I kept my focus on the log.

Matthew agreed and threw two rocks my way. When they hit the water, I split my concentration and poured out two more lines of energy towards them. A bead of sweat dripped from my temple, but I managed to grasp all three items in their watery cell simultaneously. I bit my lip as my concentration started to fade and the edges of my vision blurred. When I couldn't take it anymore, I dropped my arms, everything falling to the ground with them, and panted as though I'd just ran a mile.

"Are you okay?" Matthew asked. I lifted my thumb up towards him, trying to catch my breath. "That was impressive. You catch on quick."

"I was barely able to hold three things. And for like twenty seconds. I don't see how that's impressive."

"Robin, you've only been doing this for three days," he pointed out. "It typically takes beginners a month or so to be able to do even one thing with their powers well. What you just did would be considered advanced by anyone's standards. The only other person I know who's that powerful was one of the leaders of the Cyfrin, but he'd been practicing for decades."

"Wow," I said, unable to think of anything else to say. "What does that mean though?"

"It means you're *very* powerful," he replied, staring at me with furrowed brows. "I wonder . . ."

"You wonder what?" I pressed.

"Come with me," he said, walking away without any explanation.

I jogged to catch up with him as he led us away from the water and into the sparse area of trees.

"Where are we going?" I asked, trying to keep up with him as he continued further into the small forest. He didn't answer but finally stopped walking and turned towards me.

"Stay here," he said before marching around and gathering up different sized rocks, sticks, and wild mushrooms. He backed away from me, then threw one my way, smacking me on the hand.

"Ow," I said loudly, even though it didn't actually hurt. "What are you doing?"

He threw something else, and I sidestepped it. "Block it."

"This is sounding awfully familiar," I grumbled.

"Block it," he repeated as I avoided a stick.

"With what? There's no water here!"

"So? Block it," he said once again, his face as neutral as ever.

"*How?*" I yelled in annoyance as a mushroom slapped me in the face.

He continued throwing his assortment of goodies, not allowing me to think or ask any more questions. I tried to avoid everything he flung, but he was being relentless, throwing them harder and faster. A sharp rock dug into my cheek, drawing blood, and I let out a yell of frustration as a new wave of coolness ran threw me.

It entered my body from every pore then banded together to form a tight ball. This energy wasn't what I was used to though. It was different—it was more powerful, more consuming. It threatened to overtake me, so I pushed it up and out of my palms in a strong wave. A thick wall of water formed in front of me, repelling the objects that hit it and ricocheting them back towards Matthew.

He jumped to the side as they burrowed into the trunk of a tree then stared at them with wide eyes. The water dissipated as I lowered my arms, and Matthew stared at me, his face a mask of shock.

"Holy crap," he whispered as he gaped at me.

"What just happened?" I asked, enthralled at the feeling of satisfaction that lingered in my body.

"You conjured water from the moisture around us," he explained in awe.

"Isn't that what you were trying to get me to do?" I asked, confused by his reaction. "Can't all people with hydrokinesis do that?"

"No! I mean, that *is* what I was trying to see if you could do, but no, they can't all do that. There are only about ten people in our entire society who are gifted with hydro-kinesis, and I only know of two who can do what you just did. They're two of the most powerful people in our world."

"So what are you saying?"

"That you're going to have a very special place in Garridan if you ever choose to go there."

"Special as in?"

"As in holding a seat amongst the Keepers of Balance." He continued to gaze at me with new eyes, as if I'd suddenly changed into a respectable figure, and it made me antsy.

"How is that even determined?" I asked curiously.

"So, like I said before, elemental powers are a rare gift. Each element is inhabited by only a handful of people at a time. The largest group at one time in our entire history was fourteen pyrokinesis users at once. Each person who possesses an elemental power is part of Garridan's government in one way or another, but lineage and power level determine who sits on the panel of the Keepers of Balance," he explained, giving me a look into the structure of where we'd come from.

My interest piqued, though I tried to reign in my inquisitiveness. "How many Keepers of Balance are there?"

"There's a total of sixteen: four water, four earth, four air, and four fire."

"And you think I could be one of them?"

"Your power level alone would get you a seat amongst them."

It blew my mind to think not only was I apparently very powerful but that, in our world, I could also be the complete opposite of who I was now. I could be a leader, someone with authority.

"Well, luckily I'm here and not there," I settled on saying, and Matthew looked at me, confused.

"You wouldn't rather be there, ruling over an entire population of people?"

"No. I wouldn't. I love my life here, and I'm happy. I couldn't ask for anything more than that."

"I understand. But man, what I wouldn't give up to be in that position and make a difference. I've seen firsthand what can happen when we use our powers for the wrong reasons, and it isn't pretty."

I looked at him with sympathy, wondering what all he'd had to bear growing up with the Cyfrin.

"Why don't you go there then?" I asked. "You could tell them what you know about the Cyfrin and help Garridan take them down once and for all."

He hesitated then shrugged his shoulders, not uncaringly but almost defeatedly. "It's complicated."

"I'm sorry . . . Do you want a hug?"

"No," he replied, scrunching his nose in disgust.

I grinned and walked over to him anyway, wrapping my arms around his waist. He stiffened for a moment, then relaxed slightly and put one arm around me. I stepped back and smiled.

"See, that wasn't so bad, was it?" I teased. He rolled his eyes and grunted, making me laugh. "Come on. We should head back now. My mom's expecting me after school."

"Okay," he replied as we ventured out of the forest. "And hey . . . Thank you for the distraction today."

"You're welcome. Do you want to come over for dinner?"

"I'd like that."

His disheveled hair fell into his eyes as he moved, and I noticed the stress in them. Felicity's reaction had taken much more of a toll on him than it had on me, and I was worried what would happen if she decided not to accept this new us.

# CHAPTER TWENTY

"This was delicious, Mrs. Hayes," Matthew told my mom as we started to clear the dishes. "I appreciate you letting me stay when you weren't expecting me."

"You're welcome here any time, Matthew," she said with a warm smile. "And how many times do I have to tell you to call me Rebecca."

"Sorry, ma'am, I'm just not used to it," he replied.

She shook her head, then patted his arm. "We'll work on it."

After the dishes were done, Dawn roped us into playing Candy Land.

"No, Matthew!" she huffed with a pout as she was sent all the way back to Plumpy. "There's no way I'm going to win now."

"Winning isn't everything," I reminded her gently as she glared down at the board.

"Besides," Matthew said, "don't ever count yourself out. The only true failure is when you stop trying."

"Whatever," she grumbled, picking up a card.

I shrugged at Matthew as he grinned. "She's only six," I said as a knock came from the front door.

A minute later, my dad walked into the room behind Mom.

"Daddy!" Dawn exclaimed, jumping up and running to him. He scooped her up and hugged her tightly. "I missed you, Daddy!"

"I missed you too, Dawn," he murmured into her hair, giving her a kiss on top of her head. He looked over at me with a nod of acknowledgement. "How are you doing, Robin?"

"I'm fine," I replied, looking him up and down. He was dressed nicely with a freshly shaved face and neatly trimmed hair. His eyes were full of life, and there was no trace of impairment anywhere on his person. "You look good."

"Thank you," he said with unusual sincerity. "I *feel* good."

"That's good." I bit my bottom lip then realized Matthew was sitting rigidly. "Oh, uhm, this is Matthew. Matthew this is my father, Mark."

Matthew stood up to shake his hand. "Nice to meet you, sir," he said, polite but cautious.

"You too, son," Dad replied before turning to Mom. "I was hoping I could take Dawn out for a little while then come back and talk."

"That's fine," Mom said. "Just not too late. It's a school night after all."

"Of course," Dad responded, setting Dawn down and grabbing her hand.

Mom followed them out the door, and I began cleaning up the game. Matthew slid back to the floor across from me, staring at me with a look I was all too familiar with.

"Go ahead and ask," I said.

He didn't need any more encouragement. "Okay. What's his story?"

"He's an alcoholic. He's had his ups and downs with it ever since I can remember, but my mom finally kicked him out a couple weeks ago because he put Dawn in danger. From the looks of it, he's sobered up now, though, so I'm guessing he's going to ask to come back home."

"Will your mom allow that?"

"I'm not sure," I replied with a shrug. "She's made excuses for him for a long time, but I think she hit her limit when he left Dawn alone. And we're doing great without him so . . . I don't know. Guess I'll find out."

"You don't like him very much."

"It's not that simple." I had to admit it was true though.

"He doesn't like you."

I chuckled humorlessly, then furrowed my brows as the dots connected. "Huh."

"What?"

"It never made sense to me before, but now it's clear as day."

"What is?"

"Why he doesn't like me. I always wondered how he could dislike his own daughter. Or, better yet, how he could love one daughter but not the other." I rubbed my lips together, shaking my head as I realized the truth.

"Because he never considered you his," Matthew murmured, seeing what I was getting at.

"Because I wasn't. I'm not. Because I'm adopted."

"I'm sorry," Matthew said, but it didn't help the growing wound I felt on my heart.

"Why would they adopt me if one of them didn't even want me?" I asked, thinking out loud. "What kind of life could they offer a baby that was going to grow up unloved?"

"But you weren't unloved," Matthew pointed out. "Your mom gave you enough love for both of them. And what about Dawn? That little girl adores her big sister."

"That's true," I admitted softly.

"I know it wasn't a perfect situation but look at the person you've grown up to be because of it. You said the same thing when I asked you if you would change your life. You've been shaped by every experience, and that's made you who you are today—a pretty amazing person in my opinion."

A tear ran down my cheek, and I wiped it away in annoyance. I hadn't even realized my eyes were pooling with emotion. My childhood traumas were nothing compared to his, but he still somehow found a way to be sympathy-etic to my situation. This probably seemed like spilled milk next to what he'd endured, but he didn't act like it, which made me feel even worse about crying to him.

"Thank you," I said, rubbing at my eyes forcefully before another tear could get out.

He sighed dramatically and held out his arms. "Come here."

"What?"

He gestured for me to approach. "Come here," he repeated, so I scooted over to him, and he wrapped his arms around me.

"Two hugs in one day," I teased as I rested my head on his shoulder.

"Only because it's been an emotionally damaging day," he replied snippily, causing me to grin. "After today, no more of this ooey-gooey mushy crap."

"Oh, definitely not. We wouldn't want to ruin your reputation or anything."

"Exactly."

I pulled away, and when we made eye contact, we both broke out in a fit of laughter. We were a mess but at least we were a mess together.

Someone cleared their throat, and I turned to see Mom standing at the door with a frown on her face.

"It's starting to get late," she said. "Matthew should probably head home."

"It's seven thirty," I replied in surprise. "And you just sent Dawn out, and she's way younger than us."

"That's okay," Matthew cut in, standing up and adjusting his wrinkled shirt. "I have homework I need to get done anyway."

"Okay," I said, wondering why Mom was giving us a subtle look of disapproval. "I'll see you tomorrow. And hey, thanks for today."

"Anytime," he replied. "I can show myself out. It was nice seeing you again Mrs. H—" He stopped. "I mean, Rebecca."

"You too, Matthew," she told him. To anyone else, she would've sounded sincere, but I could see past her facade too easily. Something was bothering her. "Come back soon, okay?"

"Yes, ma'am," he said before heading out the door.

After he was gone, I turned towards my mom, who had crossed her arms. "What's wrong? Is it Dad?" I asked.

"No, it's not your father," she replied. "It's you."

"Me? What did I do?"

"What's going on with you and Matthew?"

My brows furrowed. "What do you mean?"

"Are you . . . Are you two . . . *Together*?" she struggled to ask.

My mouth dropped open, and I stared at her, stunned. "*What?* No! We're *friends!*"

"Robin, I saw the way you two were in here cuddled up and laughing," she said, her hands flying up. "Don't get me wrong, I like the boy, but I thought I raised you better than this. Can you imagine how Ben will feel when he finds out? When did this even start? When Annette and Julie saw you at Felicity's party?"

Her words were like a slap in the face and hurt deeper than any physical harm could've. "I am *not* cheating on Ben!" I cried out. "I love him, and I would never hurt him like that! Matthew and I are *just* friends. That's it."

Mom hesitated before asking, "Are you sure?"

"Yeah, I'm pretty sure," I replied, the bite in my tone almost masking the sarcasm. "How could you even accuse me of that? Don't you know me at all?"

"Yes, of course I do. I'm sorry if I'm jumping to the wrong conclusion, but—"

"No 'if' about it" I cut her off. "You are."

"Then I'm sorry. You two just seem much closer than you used to."

"Because we are," I replied hotly. "Unfortunately, there are some things in my life that only Matthew understands and can help me with. We're connected through something I can never share with anyone else so that's resulting in a close relationship. But luckily, unlike you, my boyfriend and possibly ex-best-friend trust me enough to be okay with it!"

It was her turn to look flabbergasted as I basically spat out the last words.

"There are so many questions about all that I'm not even sure where to start," she said, putting her fingers against her temples.

"Don't bother. I don't feel like talking anymore," I replied with an attitude that almost never made an appearance. I stomped towards my room then stopped and turned around, unable to contain throwing more sass her way. "Oh, by the way, we weren't cuddling. He gave me a hug because I started crying when I told him about how my father never loved me."

"Robin," Mom murmured, her eyes filling with pain.

"Speaking of which, are you planning on letting him waltz back into our lives again?" I asked. "Just want to know if I need to prepare myself to be the adult of the family again."

"Robin!" she exclaimed, hurt evident in her voice.

I knew I needed to stop while I was ahead, but my own hurt topped hers and made me continue lashing out.

"What? It's true! We both know you're a pushover and you'll let him come in and destroy us again!" I snapped, waving my arms angrily in the air. "But, come on, do you even care? Because from over here, it looks like you'd rather seek his approval than protect your own children!"

"Robin Elizabeth, you need to watch your tone. I am your mother, and I will not—"

"Are you?" I asked.

She retracted as if I'd slapped her. "W-what?"

I swallowed around the lump in my throat, instantly regretting my words. "Nothing," I whispered.

I turned around and ran to my room.

"Robin, come back here now!" she cried after me, but I ignored her and slammed my door shut.

I leaned against it as a sob tore through my chest. My hands covered my face as all the emotions that had built up over the last couple days finally broke free. The pain, the fear, the anger, and everything else that had been brewing was being evicted from my heart and shown to the emptiness of my bedroom.

I could hear my mom crying in the opposite room, and a new round of tears flowed down my cheeks as I was hit with the shame of my words to her. How could I have brought up my adoption like that? What was wrong with me?

I wanted to go apologize but didn't have the energy to deal with anything more tonight. Instead, I crawled into bed fully dressed and closed my eyes, willing sleep to come over me so the day would come to an end. Luckily, sleep came quickly, and I succumbed to its sweet embrace as it freed me from all the feelings I wanted to forget.

* * *

"Robin," the woman whispered, causing me to tear my gaze away from the calming waves that were bringing peace to my soul.

She slowly took a step towards me. The air turned cold, and ominous grey clouds appeared as the ocean's current grew stronger. I remembered Matthew's advice, so I breathed out slowly to calm my fear then walked towards her, hoping she wouldn't disappear like she had every other time. The storm clouds stayed in the distance, but the wind encased us in huge gusts, and my hair slapped me in the face repeatedly.

"Robin," she repeated.

Her distinctive blue eyes—my eyes—were filled with hope as we slowly closed the distance between us. She lifted her hand out to me like she had before, only this time, I took it with no hesitation. The instant our hands met, the clouds disappeared, taking the wind and current with it and leaving nothing but a beautiful night sky in its place.

I glanced around, amazed by the sudden change. When I looked back at the woman, her eyes were brimmed with tears, their already bright blue color becoming almost unnatural. She studied me intently, taking in every feature until she reached my face.

"Hello, Robin," she said, beaming from ear to ear. "I've been waiting for this moment for a very long time."

I rubbed my lips together. "Uhm, I'm sorry, but who are you?"

"My name is Adriana Caldwell. I'm . . . Well, I'm your mother."

My mouth opened and closed a couple times, but no sound came out. She squeezed my hand, watching quietly as I faltered for words. There was no way for me to prove her claim but something inside me believed her instantly. Our uncanny resemblances made sense now.

We looked alike because I'd inherited her features. I was her flesh and blood. I was her descendent. I was her daughter.

"I, um, I—" I stopped, blinking away tears. Finally, I just said, "Hi."

She pulled me in, and I gladly accepted her embrace, wrapping my arms tightly around her. She caressed my hair gently as we both cried against each other. After a few minutes, she pulled away, holding my face in her hands and wiping my tears with her thumbs.

"I've waited for this moment for a very long time," she repeated. "My sweet Robin. You've grown up into such a beautiful young lady." She swallowed loudly. "I'm so sorry your father and I weren't there to witness it."

"My father?" I asked, sniffling unattractively.

"Yes," she replied with a warm smile. "Elijah. You look so much like him."

"Really? Because I think I look an awful lot like you," I replied, and her eyes filled with tears again.

"I'm so sorry we had to send you away," she whispered.

"It's okay." I could see the pain she was feeling, and wished I could make it go away. I'd never thought about how difficult it must've been for them to give up their children, even if it *was* for their own safety. "From what I understand, you didn't have any other choice. And I was lucky. I grew up loved."

"Yes, it would seem so, and I'm very thankful for that. I just hate that we didn't find you sooner. I hope you can forgive us for it someday."

"There's nothing to forgive," I said. I bit my lip, knowing it was true as realization slapped me in the face. "I'll never know the things I missed out on by not being raised in my birthplace. But I do know what I have because of it, and I'm grateful for that. I have good friends and a good life and an amazing sister and . . ." I paused before quietly finishing. "And a mom who loves me."

Adriana looked at me without a hint of sadness on her face. "That's all your father and I ever hoped for you—that you had a full and happy life."

"I do. I really do."

"Oh, sweet girl," she murmured, looking at me with adoration in her eyes. "I want to hear all about it, but unfortunately, we don't have the time. Dream projection can only be done in short spurts."

"But I have so many questions!" I exclaimed, dread forming in the pit of my stomach at the thought of her leaving.

"I know, honey," she replied, looking as pain stricken as I felt. "I do too. But there are things I need to tell you before Jamal has to pull me out of here."

"Okay," I whispered.

"You aren't safe," she told me intently. "The Cyfrin know where you are and they're coming for you. They may already have someone watching you."

"How do you know that?"

"We have a spy on the inside. Once Arthur located you, we knew. It's the only reason I was able to be dream projected to you. But they've been watching your power surges, and our intel tells us they're strong. Very strong. Can you tell me what you've been doing?"

I looked down at my feet. "I've been practicing."

"Practicing what?" she asked, gently.

"Using my powers. I literally just found out I had them, and Matthew's been helping me learn how to use them. He said I needed to be able to protect myself."

"Who's Matthew?"

"He's a friend of mine. He's from Garridan too."

"How long have you known him?" she asked with narrowed eyes.

Before I could answer, a loud crack of thunder sounded, causing us both to look up at the clouds that were rolling in once more.

"No, no, no! Not yet!" Adriana cried out. She looked back at me, slightly panicked, which caused anxiety to course through my veins. "Robin, what are your powers?"

"Hydrokinesis."

Despite her panic, she managed to smile. "Just like me."

Exhilaration filled me but before I could answer, a clap of thunder rang out so loud that I covered my ears. A flash of lightening zapped through the dark sky and sand blew into our faces as the wind rolled around us loudly.

Adriana held her hand up to protect her eyes as she said, "If the Cyfrin finds out about that, it'll put you in even more danger. You need to come home. It's the only place you'll be safe. We can send someone to get you right away."

I stared at her in shock, not expecting that. "I-I can't do that!"

"Robin, please," she said, yelling to be heard over the roaring of the wind. "Your father and I can't lose you again. Not to the Cyfrin. We need you with us."

"I can't," I cried out loudly. "I'm sorry . . . but I already *am* home."

She looked down and rubbed her lips together. Tears trickled down her face when she brought her eyes back up to me. "I understand. We won't ever force this life on you. We'll figure out some other way to keep you safe."

She pulled me into another hug, and I clung to her frantically. "Don't go. Please!"

"I'm sorry, Robin," she said, holding me tight. "But I'll come back."

"When?"

"Whenever Jamal can break through again. Dream projection isn't easy, but we'll keep trying!"

"Why can't you just come to me in person?"

"It's complicated," she replied.

She opened her mouth to continue but disappeared before my very eyes. My arms fell to my sides as the darkness of the storm washed away the dream and my first true encounter with my birth mom.

# CHAPTER TWENTY-ONE

"I met my mom last night," I blurted out as I walked up behind Matthew and Ben, who were chatting in a secluded spot outside the school. They both turned to look at me with confused looks, so I quickly clarified. "My birth mom."

"What? No way!" Ben exclaimed in disbelief. "How? Where?"

"In my dream," I replied, fidgeting with the hem of my shirt. "She was the woman in my dreams this whole time, trying to get through to me."

"Huh?" Ben asked, confusion filling his face again.

Matthew quickly explained the concept of dream projection to him, then—as Ben stood there looking stumped—turned his stoic expression my way.

"How do you know it was her?" Matthew asked, as cautious and untrusting as ever.

"Because she told me so," I answered, which got me a disapproving look from both of them.

"You can't believe everything people tell you," Matthew said.

"It wasn't just that," I assured them. "I can't explain it exactly, but I know she wasn't lying. She's my birth mom."

"I mean, that's amazing then," Ben finally said. "What was she like?"

"More importantly, what did she say?" Matthew asked.

"She seemed really sweet," I replied, answering Ben's question first. I smiled, remembering her. "Her name is Adriana, and I look a lot like her. She didn't get to stay long, though, because I guess that's just how dream projection works. But she apologized for them not finding me sooner and said she was happy that I've had a good life regardless. She wanted to know more about me, but she started getting pulled away, so she asked about my powers then told me I wasn't safe."

"What do you mean not safe?" Ben asked, scrunching his forehead.

"Turns out Matthew was right. She said the Cyfrin have been monitoring my power surges, and since my powers are so strong, they're going to want to come get me. She said someone may already be watching me." I felt sick to my stomach.

Matthew looked away, his eyes tight as he stared at the front doors of the school.

Ben crossed his arms and asked, "What do you mean Matthew was right?"

I bit my lip and looked away, knowing he was about to be very upset at me.

"Matthew already warned me about this when he found out what my powers were and then again when he saw how strong they were," I explained. "That's why he's been pushing me so hard to train. So that I can protect myself from the people who want me."

Ben's face hardened, his expression angrier than I'd seen in a very long time. He narrowed his eyes then closed them altogether and took a deep breath.

"Why didn't you tell me this before?" he asked, trying hard to keep his voice steady.

"I didn't want to worry you over nothing."

"Nothing?" he repeated, his eyes opening to stare at me. "Some people, who I'm going to assume are very dangerous and powerful, are going to come after you, and you think that's *nothing*? You didn't think it was worth mentioning?"

"We don't know that they're going to come after me for sure."

"Yes, we do," Matthew spoke up quietly, and I shot him a glare. So much for calming Ben down. "Your birth mom only confirmed what I already knew to be true. They've seen how powerful you are, so it's only a matter of time before they try something. They'll want you to join their side willingly, but if you won't . . . Well, it won't be good."

Ben let out a slow breath, his jaw tensed. "So what do we do?"

"*We* don't do anything," I said before Matthew could answer. "It's too dangerous for you. Matthew is teaching me how to defend myself, but there's no way for you to do that. You're no match for someone with powers."

"I'm not going to sit on the sidelines and do nothing while the girl I love is being threatened," he replied with a scowl. "And if you expect me to, you're crazy."

"Benjamin—"

"Don't 'Benjamin' me! I've been darn well under-standing and supportive over the last couple days, but this is where I draw the line! I can handle this weird, super-natural world I've been exposed to, and I can handle the two of you bonding over it and becoming so close. What I can't and *won't* handle is being belittled or omitted from things for any reason. You have to keep me in the loop, even if you think I can't help in any way, and you have to let me at least *try* to help before you deem me useless!"

"I don't think you're useless, Ben. I just don't want you to get hurt!"

"Then how do you think *I* feel?" he asked loudly as he towered over me.

Matthew put his hand on Ben's shoulder and said, "I understand how you feel. Truly, I do, but Robin's right. You're no match for someone like us."

"So I'm supposed to just accept that and hope for the best?"

"For the time being, yes," Matthew responded. "I'll do everything in my power to keep her safe, and, even better, teach her how to keep *herself* safe. All you can do for her right now is keep giving her the support and understanding you've already been so generous with. She's going to need it."

I watched their exchange with mixed emotions. I hated being the reason Ben was so upset, but I hoped he would listen to what we were saying. His fueled emotions lit a fire in me, and I knew my training had to be my number one priority so I could keep him and everyone else I loved safe.

He finally looked back at me with troubled eyes. "Fine. But I'm not happy about this."

"Thank you," I told him quietly, trying to smile, but he glanced away.

"Did your birth mom say anything else?" Matthew asked, and I shook my head absently.

"No. I mean, she asked me to go to Garridan with them because I'd be safe there, but I told her I couldn't do that." I was still torn about it though.

"If you'll be safe there, you should go," Ben said.

"I can't do that," I replied.

"Why not?" Matthew asked.

"Because my life is here. I have my family and my friends and school," I explained, emotion rising in me. "And I don't even know those people. I've never been to Garridan. Heck, I didn't even know it existed until a few days ago. As much as I want to learn about my history, I can't just toss this life away for that one."

"Even if it meant you'd be safe," Ben muttered, and I couldn't tell if he was angry or sad about it.

"I'm not going to live my life in fear."

"Even so, it wouldn't hurt to think about that option a little more," Matthew said. He opened his mouth to say something else then paused, seeming torn. But finally, he voiced his thoughts. "I could even go with you. We could learn about our histories together, and you wouldn't be completely alone."

I looked back and forth between the two of them, feeling ambushed, and shook my head. After a long moment, I said, "I can't."

"At least talk with your birth mom more if you can," Matthew replied, a hint of disappointment in his voice. "Get to know her. We can always reevaluate her offer later."

"How long do you think it'll be before the Cyfrin try something?" Ben asked.

"It's hard to say," Matthew responded. "When they go after someone, they take their time to learn about them.

They don't just rush in with powers blazing. They're careful and articulate about it."

"Why?"

"Because they want to try to coerce that person to join them. Like Robin's birth mom said, they typically send someone in to watch and observe their target. They'll even plant someone in their lives to get close to them before they make their move. Because of how powerful Robin is, I would assume they'd take extra precautions, which means more time."

"Hopefully enough time for her to rethink going to the one place where she'll be safe," Ben said with crossed arms.

My eyes narrowed as I became more annoyed that he wouldn't let it go. If I went to Garridan, I would be leaving him behind. Why didn't he care about that?

"Does it not bother you that, if I left, we don't know when we'd see each other again?" I snapped, frowning at Ben as my feelings started to get the best of me.

"Of course, it bothers me!" he exclaimed. "But not as much as you being forcibly taken away and *never* seeing you again!"

I glared at him, and he glared right back, neither of us giving an inch or even a hint of willingness to back down. Matthew eyed us both, unsure whether or not to intervene. Just then, the bell rang, so our fight didn't get a chance to escalate.

"I gotta get to class," Ben muttered before turning on his heels and stalking away.

I watched after him, feeling defeated. Matthew cleared his throat awkwardly, and I glanced over at him. His look was slightly disapproving, which made me defensive all over again.

"What?" I growled with my hands on my hips.

"You can't fault him for caring about you," he replied, unfazed by my attitude.

"You think I'm wrong?"

"Not entirely. You're right that he can't help protect you in any way. He would just get hurt. But you're wrong for being angry at him. Imagine if the roles were reversed. You wouldn't like the idea of being helpless either, and you'd want him to go to the one place where he'd be safe."

I looked down at my feet, knowing he was right.

"Ben loves you, Robin. Not many people would be as accepting as he's been," he continued, sounding sad when he said it, and I could tell he was thinking about Felicity. "If all he wants is to be in the loop and have an opinion, I think you owe it to him. And I think you owe him an apology."

"Seems like I owe a lot of people an apology," I murmured, thinking of my mom and how harsh I'd been with her too.

"What do you mean?" he asked.

I briefly explained to him what had happened the previous night, leaving out the fact that she'd thought we were an item.

"My emotions are getting the best of me, and I don't like who I'm becoming because of it. I'm usually so calm about everything but now . . . I'm just a mess. In less than twenty-four hours, I've pushed away two of the people I love most. I don't want to keep hurting anyone."

Matthew listened with his full attention, taking what I was saying seriously. "You need to find an outlet for your feelings. This is a lot for anyone to handle, and you just need a way to process everything."

"How?"

"I'm sure we can think of something," he replied as we walked to class.

"When did you become the voice of reason?"

"That is a very good question," he responded, half serious, and I realized none of us were the same people we'd been at the beginning of the year. I wasn't sure if that was a good thing or not though.

Ben avoided me for the remainder of the day, and I couldn't say I blamed him. I tried to catch him during free period, but Juan told me he'd skipped out early. I decided to be bold, or intrusive, and go find him at his house.

Matthew lent me his car, and I drove to the outskirts of town as soon as the final bell rang. I pulled into the Toves' long driveway and saw his car parked on the side of the house. When I got out of Matthew's car, I noticed Dakota walking through the fields.

"Hi, Dakota," I called over to him, and he offered me a timid smile as I made my way towards him.

"Hi, Robin."

I gave him a side hug, and we continued onward together. "How was school?"

"It was good. I had the highest spelling test score."

"Way to go!" I exclaimed, causing him to blush. It was crazy how different all three of the Toves brothers' personalities were.

"Well, hello there," Kiona said as we came through the door. She gave Dakota a hug as he was taking off his backpack then set a snack down in front of him. "Would you like anything to eat, Robin?"

"No, thank you," I replied. "I was actually looking for Ben."

"He's in his hideout. He came home in a pretty bad mood."

"I'm afraid that's my fault," I admitted with a sigh.

Kiona patted my hand. "But you came to fix it which is all that matters. Good luck."

"Thank you," I replied before heading out the back door.

I rehearsed what I was going to say as I walked to our clubhouse. Nerves raced through me, and I could only hope he'd forgive me. When I made it to the door, I hesitated. I usually walked right in, but I wasn't sure if I should knock this time, just in case I wasn't welcomed. I contemplated it for a moment then lightly knocked and waited.

When Ben opened the door, I gave him a half smile. "Hi."

"Hi," he replied.

His eyes were rimmed in red, and I could tell he'd been crying at some point. We stared at each other, both of us clearly hurting.

"I'm sorry," we said simultaneously.

Relief flooded through me as he pulled me in for a hug, and I held him tight, listening to the beat of his heart in his chest. He led me to the couch, and we sat down facing one another.

"I was out of line earlier," he started, but I held up my hand to silence him.

"No, you weren't. You were right," I told him. "You're one of the most understanding and supportive people I know, and I'm so thankful you've stuck by my side as all this craziness has happened. I know this isn't what you signed up for."

"Hey, I signed up for *you*. And that means all of you. Even the weird, witchy side," he said, trying to lighten the mood.

"Oh, thanks," I replied with a roll of my eyes. "But in all seriousness, thank you. Thank you for being my rock through all this and thank you for caring about me so much."

"You're welcome."

"I promise to tell you everything going on from here on out. It's only fair for you to know if you want to."

"Of course I want to."

I nodded. "Okay, but on that note, you *have* to understand that you can't do anything to protect me," I said. His face clouded over, but he stayed quiet. "I know how hard that is to hear, but it's just the way it is."

"It's not hard to hear. It's unbearable," he said through clenched teeth. "What's worse is that I know you're right, and it's killing me. I feel helpless. I can't even think about someone hurting you."

"I know," I whispered, grabbing his clenched fist and trying to smooth it out. He looked at me with such sorrow that I instantly cuddled up next to him.

"Will you at least consider going to Garridan?" he asked into my hair.

I licked my lips, knowing I couldn't give him the answer he wanted. "I'll get to know Adriana as much as I can and go from there. But I can't just disappear. It would kill my mom, and I don't even want to think about what it would do to Dawn."

"You could go when school lets out. Tell your mom you have some kind of summer-long camp."

"That's . . . actually not a bad idea. We'll see, okay? That's all I can offer you right now."

"Okay."

I could tell he was still upset, but he didn't say anything else.

"Want me to show you a trick?" I asked, trying to distract him.

We spent the next hour playing with my powers, conjuring water from nothing and getting soaked in the process. We laughed like we were ten years old again, and it was a nice change of pace while it lasted.

# CHAPTER TWENTY-TWO

"Hi, Mom," I said, wiping my slick palms on my pants as I came into the living room. "Where's Dawn?"

"Your father took her out for a while," she replied, putting down the book she'd been reading. I rocked side to side, unable to look at her. "Would you like to talk?"

I nodded but remained silent.

"You know," she said quietly, and I nodded again.

The ticking of the clock on the wall was the only sound brave enough to speak as Mom and I struggled with what to say to one another. The air was thick with tension, and I blinked away tears, wondering if I ruined our relationship. We'd never not been able to talk, and I didn't like it. My chin quivered and waterworks sprang from my eyes.

"Oh, Robin," Mom whispered. "Come here, sweetie."

I flung myself into her outstretched arms, leaning against her as sob after sob tore through me. She ran her fingers through my hair, rocking us back and forth as she shushed me. Her own tears spilled down her face onto me, and I held her tighter.

"I'm so sorry, Mom," I said around a hiccup before pulling away and running my arm against my nose. "I'm so sorry. I didn't mean it, I swear."

"Yes, you did," she replied, a sad smile covering her face. "And I can't exactly blame you."

"It just came out."

"You wanted to hurt me."

I rubbed my lips together, realizing she might be right. "Yes. I think so."

"How long have you known?" she asked as she blotted a tissue against her cheeks.

"Not long."

"How did you find out?"

"Someone told me."

"Who? Your father?"

"No, definitely not," I replied with a roll of my eyes. Suddenly, another dot connected. "Wait. The other day when Ben and I saw you two fighting and he kept telling you to tell me something . . . Was this it?"

Mom lowered her gaze. "I'm afraid so."

I frowned, more realizations hitting me. "He blames me for everything, doesn't he? Your guys' problems, his drinking, all of it."

"No, of course not!" Mom exclaimed, but my no-nonsense look made her rethink her lie. She sighed and brokenly said, "Yes. He does."

"But why? What did I do to make him hate me so much?"

"He doesn't hate you, Robin."

"Well, he definitely doesn't like me," I said, and her silence told me it was true. "I don't understand. Why did you guys adopt me if he didn't want me? Do you think that was fair to me? Or him?"

"He *did* want you."

"Mom—"

"No, really, Robin, he did." She looked down at her hands and rubbed her lips together. "We tried to have a baby for a long time, and it just never happened. The doctors told us your father couldn't have kids and it destroyed him, but we both agreed we still wanted a family, so we decided to adopt." She looked up at me and smiled softly. "Then we saw you and we fell in love."

I swallowed around the lump in my throat, still trying to come to terms with the idea that I was adopted. Hearing it confirmed by her made it all the more real, which made me all the more torn apart inside.

"You made us so happy, and you filled a void in our lives. You meant everything to us," she continued.

"So what changed?"

She took a deep breath and blew it out shakily. "I got pregnant."

I closed my eyes, the confession only confirming what I already thought. But it was still agonizing to hear. "Of course," I murmured. "Why would he want a child that wasn't his if he could have one that was?"

"Unfortunately, those were his exact thoughts."

"But how?" I asked, my voice cracking slightly. "He loved me for an entire decade before Dawn came along. How could he just lose that? How could he just . . . stop?"

Mom reached out to me, but I pulled away, not wanting to be touched. My fake dad's rejection still hurt more than I liked to admit. Mom placed her hands back in her lap.

"He had a hard time coping with the idea of never having a biological child," she said.

"No, don't make excuses for him," I said sharply.

"I'm not. I'm trying to answer your question."

I eyed her suspiciously but saw nothing that indicated she was lying. "Okay. Sorry. Keep going."

"Thank you. So, because of all that, he saw himself as less of a man and it made him hate himself, which drove him to start drinking."

"That's what started his alcoholism?" I asked, and she nodded.

"But when we made the decision to adopt, he stopped drinking entirely. He was sober until the day Dawn came."

My brows furrowed. "No, he drank when I little too."

"No, Robin, he didn't. He was sober for ten years."

"Are you sure? I swear I remember him drinking back then."

"I think you're just blurring the timeline," she said gently. "But you were still pretty young when he started, so I'm not surprised you think he's always done it."

"Huh," I said, knowing she must be right but not being able to think of a time when he didn't drink.

"Anyway, once Dawn came, he was so happy, and I think he blamed you for not having her sooner."

"Why?"

"Because we stopped trying to have kids when we adopted you."

"But the doctors are the ones who said you couldn't have any."

"Correct."

"Then how does blaming me make any sense?"

"It doesn't," she said. "But in his mind, if we didn't have you, we would've kept trying regardless of what the doctors said."

"That's stupid," I replied bluntly, narrowing my eyes slightly.

"It is," she said softly. "It is."

"So he blamed me—a ten-year-old—for not having a 'real' kid sooner and decided to take it out on me for the rest of his life?" I blew air out my nose as I shook my head. "I hate him."

"No, you don't!" Mom exclaimed.

"Yes, I do!" I cried out. "He's *not* my father. He's a horrible person, and I hate him."

Mom's lips pressed into a tight line as her chin started to quiver and more tears fell down her face. "Does that mean you hate me too?"

"What?" I asked, shocked. "No!"

"But I'm not your real mother."

I grabbed her hands and waited to speak until she looked at me. "You may not be my biological mother, but you *are* my real mom, and I love you."

"Even though I hid this from you?" she asked, her red-rimmed eyes full of sorrow.

"Yes," I replied. "I hate that you did, but it doesn't make me love you any less. And how I feel about . . . *Him* doesn't make me love you any less either."

She pulled me into her, sobbing uncontrollably, and I rubbed her back. As hard as this was on me, I knew it was just as hard on her. I could easily blame her for allowing him to treat me the way he did but I didn't—I couldn't.

"I love you so much, Robin," she whispered, clutching me like I was about to disappear.

"I love you too, Mom."

"I'm sorry I didn't tell you that you were adopted. I thought I was doing the right thing." She pulled away and swallowed loudly. "That's a lie. I did it because I never wanted you to resent us . . . I did it for selfish reasons, not for the right ones."

"It's okay," I replied, trying to comfort her with a smile.

"You're not angry at me?"

I hesitated then said, "I'd be lying if I said no. I am a little. And I'm hurt."

"I'm sorry."

"We'll get past it. It'll just take some time."

She pushed my hair over my shoulder. "I hope so."

We sat quietly for a moment then I asked, "Are you letting him come home?"

"No. I'm not."

"Really?" I asked, my eyebrows raising to my hair line.

"Really." She cupped my face in her hands and stared at me intently. "I don't appreciate how you spoke to me last night, nor how you chose to express your anger. However, you were justified in what you said. I wish I could've been stronger and stood up for us before, but I wasn't, and I'm sorry you had to deal with the repercussions of that."

"It's okay," I said softly, knowing she was as much of a victim as I was in this situation.

"You father—" she stopped and cleared her throat, "Mark, I mean, is trying very hard to get his life turned around. He's been sober since I kicked him out, he's going to AA meetings twice a week, and he's got a good job that he's doing well at. But we've seen that before."

"Yes, we have," I replied as she absentmindedly played with my hair.

"As happy as I am for him, it doesn't change things." She took a deep breath then let it out slowly. "So, I've filed for divorce. He wasn't happy about it, but he's lost the right to be a part of our lives. He did ask to keep seeing Dawn, though, and as long as he's doing well, I have no reason to say no."

"I understand," I replied, slightly dumbfounded. I never thought she'd take that step. "Dawn needs him as much as he needs her."

"Yes, I agree. Later on, we'll have to work out some sort of custody arrangement, but for now, he's agreed to after school visits here and there. We'll deal with the rest when the time comes."

She looked wary, as if she were afraid he'd try to get full custody, but I knew she wouldn't have to worry about that. All the evidence pointed to her being the more suitable parent.

"I'm proud of you," I said, leaning my head against her shoulder. "But I'm sorry. I know this isn't how you wanted it to turn out."

"Definitely not. But thank you."

"And I'm sorry for last night."

She rested her head against mine. "I forgive you."

"So we're okay?"

"We are more than okay."

"I love you, Mom."

"I love you too, Robin. So much."

I gave her a long and much needed hug. Everything was out in the open now, and I felt better for it. We still had things we'd have to work through but, for now, this was good. This was enough.

We spent the rest of the evening watching movies, mocking all the bougie characters and charming love interests. When Dawn raced through the door, she was a hyper mess, so I offered to get her ready for bed while Mom talked to Mark—the man I could no longer call my father. It took me nearly two hours to get her calm enough to crawl into bed, but as soon as she was asleep, I went to bed as well, hoping to have another visit with Adriana.

* * *

"Do you want to come to the lake with us later?" I asked Ben as we walked hand in hand towards the food court in the mall. It was slow for a Saturday, making it more enjoyable in my opinion.

"Sure," he replied. "I don't think I'll ever get enough of seeing you do what you do."

I smiled bashfully. Since I participated in highly spectated sports, I was used to people watching me when I did things, but this seemed more intimate, and it made me nervous. Despite that, I couldn't deny I was proud of my abilities, and I fought the urge to use them every second of the day.

"Have you talked to Adriana again?" he asked.

"No," I sighed in disappointment. "It's been four days. I don't understand why dream projection is the only way we can communicate. Are there not phones in Garridan?"

"I couldn't say," he said with a shrug. "But maybe it's just the only safe way."

"What do you mean?"

"Maybe they're being monitored every other way they could reach out to you."

"Maybe. Whatever the reason, it sucks. I have so many questions I want to ask her, and I want to meet Elijah."

"I know, Robin. Just try to be patient."

"I have been patient," I muttered with a pout.

"Ben!" a familiar voice called out from behind us.

I glanced back to see Felicity approaching us with a smile. When she saw me, she stopped in her tracks, her face falling.

"What are you doing here?" she asked me quietly.

"Having lunch with Ben," I replied.

"But *I'm* supposed to be having lunch with Ben," she said, and I shot an accusatory look his way.

"I have to go get something," Ben said, as though he hadn't orchestrated this coincidental meeting. "Bye."

He turned and briskly walked away, nearly running over an elderly couple in his haste. I shifted from one foot to the other as Felicity wrung her hands together and bit her lip.

"You have every right to be mad!" she blurted out as I stared at her.

"I'm not mad," I said, my brows furrowing. "I mean, I've had my moments when I was, but I'm more hurt and confused than anything else."

She didn't reply, so we stood there in awkward silence as people made their way around us.

"Do you want to sit down?" I finally asked.

"Okay," she said, sliding into the seat closest to her.

I sat across from her and folded my hands on top of the table.

"Do you want to talk?" I asked, unsure what to do as her silence continued.

"Yes," she said but didn't offer up anything else as she picked at her fingernails. After another minute of silence, I pushed my chair back to leave. "No, wait!"

"I'm not going to sit here if you aren't going to talk," I said. "I'd love to have a conversation with you, but it has to go both ways."

"I want to talk. I do," she insisted. "I just don't know what to say."

"How about we start with whether or not you still want to be my friend."

"Of course I do!" she exclaimed, sounding hurt.

"Well, you aren't acting like it."

"I know," she replied softly, looking ashamed. "And I'm really sorry. I've been out of line this week . . . with both of you."

"I understand that you're freaked out about me and Matthew. It's a lot to work through. Trust me, I get it. But that doesn't excuse you blatantly ignoring us and being rude. You have to choose if you want to have us in your lives anymore, because if you do, you have to accept who we are."

"I know that."

"You know, Matthew thinks you're scared of him," I said. "He's been really shaken up over this whole thing, and he thinks he's going to lose you."

"I don't want that," she whispered, blinking rapidly.

"Then what *do* you want?" I asked in frustration.

"I just . . . I want to live in a normal world," she said, her voice barely audible in the noisy environment.

"Well, you don't. None of us do. So get over it."

"You're awfully testy," she said, raising an eyebrow.

"Yeah, well, I have bigger problems on my plate than your inability to accept change," I said dryly.

"Like what?" she asked curiously, sounding more like the Felicity I knew.

"It's classified," I responded curtly.

"Robin," she whined.

"Felicity," I whined back. We looked at each other with pathetic faces for a moment before cracking up in fits of laughter. When we got control of ourselves, I smiled at her reassuringly. "See? Nothing has changed."

"You can control water," she said, blank-faced.

"Besides that," I replied, waving my hand dismissively. "I'm still the same person you know and love."

"I know you are."

"Then why are you still scared?"

"I'm not scared of you guys, Robin. I never was." She sighed, shaking her head and looking down. "Honestly, I was just being shallow."

I cocked a brow. "How?"

"Because my life has always been perfect, and I didn't want that to change. I wanted it to stay the same easy, carefree, picture-perfect way it's always been, but that obviously can't happen with what you told me. So I thought I could just pretend you two didn't exist, which would keep my life the way I wanted it."

"And how did that work out for you?" I asked, not extremely surprised by her explanation.

"Not great. I've been miserable. I realized I'd rather have a screwed-up life that you two are a part of than a perfect one that doesn't include you."

"Good."

"Good?" she repeated incredulously.

"Good. It's only fair that you were as miserable as we were."

"Wow. Jerk."

"Takes one to know one," I replied. "I'm glad you've come to your senses and realized we're worth ruining your life over."

"That's *not* what I said!" She threw an empty cup at me with a scowl, and I laughed. It was good to have her back. "So how much does Matthew hate me?"

"He doesn't hate you. He's just sad and hurt like I was."

"Do you think he'll forgive me?"

"I think there's a pretty good chance," I said with a smile. "Do you want to find him now?"

"No, that's okay. I want to catch up with you first. I'll call him and beg him to meet me when we're done."

"You're going to make him really happy," I told her, already imagining the heartache being lifted from him.

"I hope so. But anyway, catch me up on what's new with you," she said. I gave her a look, and she raised her brows. "What?"

"It's been a crazy week full of very abnormal things."

"That's okay," she assured me, putting on a brave face. "I can handle it. I promise."

* * *

"So, how much trouble am I in?" Ben asked me when I met him by his car.

I reached up and gave him a kiss, long and slow.

"None," I murmured, pulling away just enough to talk. "Thank you for interfering."

"If this is the thanks I get, I'll interfere more often," he said, his hot breath wafting over my face before my mouth found his again. His hands traveled down my back, pulling me closer as our kiss deepened. I bit his lip teasingly, and he let out a low moan of pleasure.

"Get a room!" someone yelled, and we quickly pulled apart.

Some of Ben's teammates from baseball were walking by and he flipped them off. I pursed my lips as heat spread through me, and Ben grinned before giving me a quick peck on the lips.

"How did it go anyway?" he asked when we got in his car.

"It was good. Awkward at first, but then it was like nothing had even happened. I'm assuming you already know why she was ignoring us."

"Yeah," he admitted with a halfhearted shrug. "Can't say I blame her. She was just trying to preserve her own reality."

"Do you think she'll really be okay with everything going on?" I asked, still a little worried about it.

"You tell me. How did she take everything you told her?"

"She seemed a little freaked but really interested."

"I think she'll be okay then. Soon enough, she'll be asking so many questions you'll wish she would go away again."

"Probably," I agreed with a grin. "Oh, we aren't meeting Matthew anymore. Felicity got ahold of him, and they're going to go out and talk tonight."

"That's good! In that case, do you want to come to my house for the rest of the day? We have a bonfire planned with members of the tribe. Amara will be there too."

"Are you sure that's okay?" I asked, not wanting to intrude.

"Of course."

"Then I accept."

After a long, emotional week, things were finally seeming to get back on track, and I could only hope it stayed that way. I knew I had a knife hanging over my head, and none of us knew when the Cyfrin would make their move, but I didn't want to think about that. All I wanted was to fine-tune my powers, get to know Adriana, and enjoy the rest of the school year with my friends.

# CHAPTER TWENTY-THREE

"Robin!" Adriana called out, and I ran to her with a wide smile. She embraced me tightly, and I could smell a hint of morning dew on her scent.

"Why didn't you come back sooner?" I asked. I could hear the sad, accusing tone in my voice and saw it reflected in her sorrowful expression.

"Dream projection is a very tricky skill," she replied. "It's a hit-or-miss type of situation every single time you try it."

"Why can't you talk to me some other way then?"

"Our forms of communication are limited outside the walls of Garridan," she said. "We have all the modern technology you do, but as a safety precaution, it only works within our own radius. On the rare occasion we have to communicate with someone on the outside, we rely on powers, such as telepathy or dream projection."

"What do you mean by 'walls of Garridan' exactly?" I asked. "Literal walls?"

"Not literal, no. Garridan is surrounded by an impenetrable force field."

"No way!" I found myself exclaiming, and she smiled.

"Yes way. It camouflages us to outside eyes and protects us from external attacks or from outsiders accidentally stumbling in. It also acts as a barrier for our two worlds when it comes to technology. Imagine it as two separate radio channels. We can't contact anyone outside the wall, and no one on the outside can contact us."

I snorted. "No spam."

"What?"

"Nothing," I replied quickly. "Where is Garridan anyway?"

"Nowhere, Oklahoma."

I gave her a look. "I'm all for sarcasm, but don't I have a right to know?"

She let out a wholesome laugh that made me smile. "No, it's literally located right outside of a small town in Oklahoma called Nowhere."

I raised my brows in disbelief at the name. I could just imagine the looks residents got when they told people where they were from: *"Nowhere."*

"And no one knows there's a whole city right under their noses?" I asked, mind blown.

"Not a soul."

"That's crazy. Can you come visit me here then? Oklahoma isn't that far away."

"No, honey. I can't," she said sadly.

"Why not?"

"For one thing, we have strict rules in Garridan. It's not a place where you can just come and go as you please. We leave for only a few very specific reasons. That's one of the reasons we've been able to remain a secret for so long."

"Does that mean that, if I go there, I couldn't leave again?" I asked, my mouth turning down in a frown.

She contemplated her answer for a moment. "Your situation is a little different. If you decided you wanted to come here, your father and I *might* be able to pull some strings to make it just a visit and not permanent.”

“Because you’re both Keepers of Balance?”

“That’s right,” she answered in surprise. “How did you know that?”

“Matthew. He’s been trying to teach me as much as he knows, but it’s not a lot. He actually offered to go to Garridan with me so I wouldn’t be alone, but I think there’s a part of him that really wants to see where he came from and who his family is.”

“Does he know his birth given last name?”

“I’m not sure if it’s his birth given one, but his last name is Alastair. Why?”

Her face lit up. “That’s Malachi and Susan’s boy!”

“You know Matthew’s parents?” I gasped, and she nodded.

“We know his whole family. The Alastairs have a long family history of serving and protecting Garridan. Malachi is part of our guard, and Susan works very closely with us. Their eldest son just joined the guard as well.”

“Matthew has siblings?” I asked, my smile reaching from ear to ear.

“A brother and a sister,” Adriana replied. “They’re going to be so thrilled when I tell them the news. His parents never got over not finding their youngest.”

“I can imagine.”

“Does that mean you want to come here after all?”

“Not exactly,” I responded, and her face fell slightly. “I was thinking I could visit for the summer once the school year is over. That way I could get to know you and Elijah beforehand, and I wouldn’t just be abandoning my family.”

"That sounds like a fair compromise," she agreed, her eyes soft and understanding. "If that's the case, I'll see to it that it's allowed."

"But you'll keep coming to see me until then, right?" I asked, feeling that slight panicky feeling again. I didn't want to lose any more time with her than I had to.

"I'll try every day."

"I have prom in a couple weeks," I said out of nowhere. "I wish you could be a part of it."

"Oh," she said, bringing her hand up to her chest. "I do too. But you can bring pictures when you visit. Do you have a dress?"

"Not yet." That had been the last thing on my mind lately.

"How about a date?"

I smiled timidly. "My boyfriend, Ben."

"Ah, young love." She sighed happily. "Does he treat you right?"

"Very. He's amazing. You'd like him."

"I wish I could meet him," she said as the wind picked up, letting us know our time was just about done. "I wish I could meet everyone in your life. Especially the people who raised you."

"I do too," I replied, averting my eyes at the mention of my parents. "I told my mom I knew I was adopted."

"You didn't know before?" she asked, her brows furrowing.

"No. She, uh, she never told me."

"Why not?"

"She said it was for selfish reasons. She didn't want me to resent her."

"I can understand that," Adriana murmured.

"The funny thing is, I always wondered if I was adopted since I look so different from them, but I never knew for sure until Matthew."

A strong breeze slammed into my face, nearly knocking me over, and a crash of thunder sounded right above us.

Adriana looked up, her face twisted unhappily. "I want to know all about that, but before I'm pulled out of here, I have to ask: Where did Matthew come from?"

"What do you mean?"

"You said he's been helping you practice, but how does he know how to?"

"Oh, because he grew up with the Cyfrin."

"He *what?*" she exclaimed, her eyes wide.

"Yeah, he ran away from them a while back," I said, not understanding her reaction.

"No, Robin, I don't think that's true," she replied frantically, grabbing onto my arms.

"What? Why not?"

She opened her mouth to reply, but nothing came out before she disappeared, and I was left standing alone as my dream world faded into nothing.

* * *

"We have to go prom dress shopping this weekend," Felicity said as we walked down the hall. "My mom wants to fly us to New York to check out her favorite boutique."

"That's really sweet, but you know I couldn't afford anything like that," I replied.

"And you know my mom wants to pay," she shot back, her bangs falling into her eyes. She pushed them away, looking at me pleadingly. "Please. She *wants* to do this for you and your mom."

"I don't know how my mom would feel about that," I said, not wanting to humiliate my mom in any way.

Felicity grinned. "That's the best part. Your mom already agreed to go as long as she can pay for half the dress."

"Then why are you even trying to convince me?" I asked, rolling my eyes.

"Because I want you to *want* to go."

"Of course I want to go!" I exclaimed, knocking into her with my shoulder. "How could I pass up a free trip to New York?"

"That's the spirit! Ugh, I'm so excited!" She started talking about dress styles and colors, and I realized I was in way over my head. Who knew dress shopping could be so complex?

"Felicity," Matthew said as he came up behind her, wrapping his arms around her waist.

She turned her head to plant a kiss on him, and I smiled, relieved everything was right between us all again.

"You're just in time," she said to him. "Don't you agree that Robin would look hot in a mermaid-style dress?"

Matthew met my eyes, suppressing a grin as I shot him a look. "You would look beautiful in anything," he told me.

"What a sweet answer!" Felicity exclaimed, turning her attention to him.

I trailed behind them as we walked to class, thinking of Adriana's last words to me. What was she going to say about Matthew? Why didn't she believe what he'd told me?

"Robin?" Felicity said, waving her hand in front of my face.

I blinked up at her in surprise. "What?"

"You're off in la-la land. What's up?"

"Uhm," I looked over at Matthew then slowly said, "It's actually kind of sensitive. Do you mind if I talk to Matthew alone?"

"Oh," Felicity said before nodding. "Yeah, okay. Sure. Uhm, I'll just see you in class."

She looked between us then walked away with a small half wave.

"What's wrong?" Matthew asked when she was gone. I pressed my lips together, wondering how to start. "Robin?"

"Yeah, sorry," I said. "Nothing's wrong, I don't think. It's just . . ."

"Just?"

"I talked to Adriana again."

"That's good. Isn't it?"

"It is."

"Then?" he pressed.

"Well, we talked about you some," I admitted, and his eyes instantly grew guarded. "I told her you were helping me practice my powers and you knew how to because you grew up with the Cyfrin. I also told her you ran away from them a while back and . . ."

I bit my lip as he narrowed his eyes and asked, "And what?"

"She didn't seem to think that was true."

"Why not?" he asked coldly.

I furrowed my brows at his reaction. "I'm not sure. She got pulled out before she could elaborate." He stared at the ground with a frown, and I asked, "Why do you think she thought that?"

"I couldn't say."

"Are you sure?"

"What's that supposed to mean?" He scowled as his steps became close to stomps.

"Nothing. But you're getting pretty defensive, so now I'm wondering if maybe she's not so far off the mark."

He stopped walking, and I stood stationary by his side, scrutinizing him. His throat contracted as he swallowed, and his hands balled into fists at his sides before relaxing. He licked his lips, staring at me with upturned brows.

"Do you trust me?" he asked quietly.

I frowned as I contemplated my answer. I trusted him before, so were Adriana's words enough for me to change my opinion of him? No. They weren't. But when paired with his odd reaction to them, it made me hesitate.

"Yes," I finally murmured. "I do."

Relief showed on his face as he let out a breath. "Good. Then please believe me when I say there are some things I've kept hidden for good reason."

"Okay."

He rubbed the back of his neck, his posture still rigid. "I want to tell you everything—I really do—but I can't. Not yet."

"Okay," I repeated.

"Really?" he asked. "Just like that?"

"Just like that."

"Even if your biological mom thinks you can't trust me?"

"Even then."

"But why?" he asked, sounding dumbfounded.

"Because you haven't given me any reason to doubt you. So, unless you do, I'm going to keep trusting you. Besides, I know nothing about Adriana, so her word doesn't mean much to me right now."

His gaze grew soft as he watched me. "Thank you. You don't know how much that means to me."

"You're welcome." I offered him a tight smile, praying I was making the right decision by putting faith in him. "But the things you can't tell me right now, you'll tell me one day, right?"

"Yes. When I can. When I know it'll be okay to."

"Okay. That's all I ask."

"Did Adriana say anything else?" he asked.

"She did actually."

"What was it?" His jaw tightened slightly again.

"Nothing bad. She knows your family."

"W-what?" he stammered, his eyes widening.

"Apparently your lineage is well respected in Garridan."

"I have a family," he stated, though it almost sounded like a question.

"You have a family," I confirmed with a smile.

"Well, who are they? What do they do?"

"Your parents' names are Malachi and Susan. Your dad works for the guard, and your mom works in the government."

His eyes were full of wonder as he ate up my words. "What else?"

"She said you have an older brother and sister."

The corners of his mouth turned up. "I do?" he asked, and I nodded. "What are their names? How old are they?"

"She didn't say," I answered quietly, and his look of disappointment made me wish I knew more. "All I know is they were sent away with the rest of the kids from Garridan, but they were lucky enough to be found."

"Good . . . Good," he murmured, his brows creased together. "I have a family."

"You have a family."

"I have a family," he repeated, swallowing loudly.

I couldn't tell what was going through his mind, so I stood there silently, letting him collect his thoughts. Suddenly, he walked away from me, and I ran to catch up.

"Where are you going?" I asked. "Class is that way."

"I have to do something. It's going to take me a couple of days, but I'll be back."

"Wait, what?" I asked incredulously, trying to get in front of him. "You're leaving?"

"I'll be back soon. Monday at the latest," he said without slowing down. His face was twisted into the impenetrable look of mystery he used to wear all the time.

"What am I supposed to tell Felicity?" I tugged at his arm, trying to stop him.

He sighed and paused to look back at me. "Tell her not to worry and that I'll call her as soon as I'm back. I'm sorry, Robin, but I have to go."

He strutted away, ignoring me when I called his name. I stared after him, wondering what could've been going through his mind. The only thing I knew for certain was that Felicity was going to bite his head off.

* * *

"You look stunning!" Mom exclaimed as I walked out in a form fitted, yellow dress.

"It complements your skin tone," Annie said as she looked me up and down.

I turned towards the mirror and stared at my reflection. The dress was beautiful—as all of them had been—and it hugged my hips in just the right places, but I couldn't make myself like it.

"Maybe we should try another one." I headed back to the rack Felicity had filled with options for me. I rifled through them, and Mom came up behind me, placing her hand on my back.

"Robin," she said, turning me towards her. Her eyes were gentle as she assessed me. "What's the matter?"

"What makes you think anything is the matter?"

"Because I know my daughter," she replied.

I looked back at the dresses to hide the sadness that worked through me. I was enjoying the day with her, Annie, and Felicity, but a small seed of grief kept trying to creep in because I wanted to experience this with Adriana too. I'd already missed out on so many milestones with her, and this was just one more to add to the list. But I couldn't tell my mom that.

I was also distracted with worry for Matthew. He hadn't reached out to any of us, and we were all going stir crazy wondering where he was. He said he was coming back, but I'd stressed myself out thinking it was a lie. If he didn't return, I think I'd be lost. He was the only person who understood what I was going through. I needed him and his guidance.

"I just don't feel like any of these dresses are me," I ended up saying, which was true.

"Maybe that's because *you* didn't choose any of them," she said. "Felicity did."

"That's true."

"We should go look for some ourselves. Okay?"

"Okay," I replied, forcing a smile onto my face.

Felicity walked out of her dressing room in a short, red ensemble that barely covered her chest. It closely resembled outfits she'd worn to other dances when she was trying to get someone's attention. She fiddled with the bottom of it, biting her lip and staring at herself with distaste.

"Ugh, I just don't know," she groaned.

I wrapped my arm around her. "Can I make a suggestion?" I asked.

"Please do."

"Matthew's going to think you look beautiful no matter what, but he's a very classy guy. You don't have to dress like a sl—" She shot me a glare, so I corrected my words. "You don't have to dress provocatively to get his attention. He's already head over heels for you."

She stared at herself a moment longer then sighed. "You're right. I know you're right. I guess I'm just used to needing a reason for a guy to stick around. Him taking off like he did didn't help."

"I know," I said, grimacing. For as confident as she was, it always surprised me how little self-esteem she had when it came to her relationships. "He's coming back, though, and I'm sure he'll explain when he does."

"I hope you're right."

"I am." I rubbed her arm and tried to smile. "Now forget about him and pick a dress that *you* like. I'm gonna go to do the same."

I turned around and walked arm in arm with Mom to one of the building's far corners. We rifled through the dresses, picking out things I actually liked, before bringing a whole new rack to the dressing rooms.

Felicity and I shoved our problems to the back of our minds so we could enjoy the rest of our shopping adventure. After another hour of searching, we both settled on dresses we loved.

"We absolutely must stop by a jewelry store before heading home," Annie said. "I would love to buy you both some accessories. Earrings, necklaces, the works."

"That's so nice, but I was planning on wearing this necklace," I replied, touching the heart around my neck.

"Come on, Robin," Felicity said, shaking her head in disapproval. "This is *prom*!"

"A nice set of pearls would look lovely with your dress," Mom added.

"I don't know," I replied hesitantly. "I don't want to hurt Dawn's feelings."

"Dawn will be fine," Mom said with a wave of her hand. "In another year, she won't even think twice about those necklaces."

"Wow, thanks," I muttered. "In that case, a set of pearls it is."

When we boarded the Larson's private jet later that evening, we were six bags heavier with our perfect dresses, matching shoes, and accessories. We were done shopping for prom, and I was actually excited about it. The next three weeks couldn't pass by fast enough. Or so I thought.

# CHAPTER TWENTY-FOUR

"I can't believe you won't tell me anything!" Felicity yelled.

Matthew averted his bruised face, refusing to look at us. He was back Monday morning, just as promised, but he was holding onto a vow of silence. Despite our continual probing, none of us got any information about his trip.

"Just respect that I can't answer your questions," he said, wincing slightly at the way the cut on his bottom lip was bothered by the movement.

"Respect? You want to talk about respect?" Felicity scoffed. "Where was the respect when you took off out of nowhere without a word? Where's the respect now when you come back with a broken face and won't tell us what happened?"

"A black eye and split lip are hardly a broken face," Matthew said, void of emotion, and Felicity glowered at him.

If looks could kill, Matthew would be a goner. She opened her mouth, no doubt to yell some more, but Ben jumped in first.

"Maybe we should all just take a deep breath and reassess," he said, holding his hands up between them. "We're all worried and, let's be honest, super curious about where you've been and why you're coming back looking like that."

"Don't forget pissed," Felicity muttered with a scowl. Ben gave her a warning look, and she rolled her eyes but didn't continue.

"It's his right not to tell us," Ben told her. "As much as we may not like it, he probably has his reasons, and we just need to accept that. Do you tell him everything you do?"

"Well, no, but—"

"No buts," Ben said, cutting her off. "Don't be a hypocrite."

Felicity huffed, and Matthew grabbed her hands in his own. She tried to pull them away, but he held on tighter, looking at her intently.

"I would tell you if I could, but I can't," he said in a hushed tone. "Please don't be angry at me for that."

Felicity stared at him, unhappily contemplating her next words. She grimaced then said, "Fine. But I don't like it."

"I know," he acknowledged, giving each of her hands a kiss. "I'm sorry."

"I don't forgive you," she replied curtly.

Ben patted him on the back. "We're here if you change your mind."

"I know. Thank you." He glanced over at me, as if assessing my feelings about his secrets.

I offered him a tight smile, which he returned, but I sensed an aura of guilt around him. Wherever he was, whatever he'd been doing, he wasn't proud of it, and it only piqued my curiosity even more.

After lunch, when Matthew and I were alone, he pulled me aside and backed me into a deserted corner of the hallway. "We need to train every day," he said. "And not just your powers. You need physical training as well."

"What? Why?" I asked, confused.

"You aren't safe," he replied, his face as serious as a heart attack.

"So I keep being told."

"This is serious," he snapped, grabbing onto my arms too hard.

"Let go!" I demanded, raising my hand and forcing him back with a torrent of water. I left it hovering between us as I assessed his attitude.

"I'm sorry," he murmured, taking another step back from me. "I didn't mean to hurt you."

I glanced around and quickly flicked the water out of existence before anyone walked by and saw. "What's going on?"

He licked his lips and exhaled slowly. "You don't understand the significance of the situation you're in."

"Yes, I do," I replied, fighting the urge to roll my eyes. "I get it, okay? I'm in danger. I need to protect myself. Yada, yada, yada. The Cyfrin are going to come for me one day, but we have time, and when summer comes, we're going to Garridan, and we'll be safe there."

Matthew growled and threw his fist into the wall next to him as I stared on in shock. He ran both his hands through his hair and shifted his weight from one foot to the other, breathing deeply. He finally turned back towards me, his eyes pleading.

"Robin, please. This is important. Just trust that I know what I'm talking about and humor me. Please."

I didn't understand his sense of urgency, but I knew he wouldn't be pushing me like this for no reason. If he thought I needed to train more than I already was, there was a reason, and that left me feeling unsettled.

"Okay," I finally said. "Okay."

"Thank you," he said with apparent relief. "Meet me every day right after school, and we'll go straight to the lake."

And that's exactly what we did.

Every day, he hounded me, barking orders and demanding perfection. His overbearing demeanor resulted in new breakthroughs with my powers. My previous abilities were polished to perfection while new ones made themselves known. I barely had to think as my powers grew. They seemed to just know what I wanted to do, and it happened effortlessly. Despite that, Matthew showed no mercy as he continued pushing me to my limit, not just mentally but physically as well.

He insisted that I learn basic fighting techniques to ensure I could defend myself if my hydrokinesis failed. My athletic build was used to high-intensity workout routines, so I didn't mind the sit-ups and push-ups he forced me to do. I thrived under high pressure, which made it easier to handle—enjoyable even.

However, the boxing he forced me into was another story. He continuously avoided my attacks while I consistently failed to block his. When the weekend rolled around, my body was sore and bruised. I definitely wasn't a fighter.

"Okay, I humored you all week long, but we both deserve a break," I told him on Saturday morning. "I appreciate you caring so much and helping me out, but can we please just have a relaxing weekend?"

He contemplated it, then nodded. "Fine. I'm sure Ben and Felicity would've insisted on it anyway."

"Thank you!" I exclaimed, leaning back in my chair with relief.

"How about we call them up and meet by the lake."

"I'll pack lunch," I replied before heading to the kitchen while he made the phone calls.

An hour later, we were lying on top of two blankets we'd spread out, the remains of our food scattered about. My head rested on Ben's arm, and I soaked in his warmth, trying to ignore the cool breeze. I closed my eyes, enjoying the picturesque moment. The water lapped calmly at the shore and the sun rose high in the sky, offering us a bit of comfort from the chill.

"I can't wait to be underwater again with the sun shining above me," Felicity said.

"You can jump in now," Ben replied.

"No way! It's still too cold. I'd rather not freeze my poor little tootsies off."

"Your poor little tootsies?" Ben repeated, cocking one brow.

"Yes, my poor little tootsies," she shot back, unashamed.

As they went back and forth, an idea popped into my head, and I smiled mischievously. With barely a flick of my finger, I raised some water from the lake and wrapped it around us so we were lying beneath a dome of liquid. Sun beams pierced through, highlighting the beautiful shades of blue as it rippled around us.

"There," I said. "Now you're under the water with the sun shining above you, and your poor little tootsies are safe."

"Wow," Felicity breathed, slack jawed at the sight.

"Look, a fish!" Ben exclaimed, pointing at a little minnow swimming around in circles.

"This is incredible," Felicity whispered, the look of awe on her face threatening to become permanent.

"It's hard to believe it's real," Ben murmured, his eyes trailing the minnow as it went from one end of the dome to the other.

"I know," I said, staring at the beauty I'd created. "Sometimes I think I'm dreaming and it's all going to disappear when I wake up."

"You'd miss it, wouldn't you?" Felicity asked.

I breathed in deeply then let it out slowly as I thought. "I would. I really would."

"Why don't you ever show us *your* powers?" Ben asked Matthew.

"It's not as impressive as this," he replied with a shrug.

"Can you petrify anything?" Felicity asked.

"Just about," Matthew said.

"How about water?" I asked, sitting up and wagging my eyebrows.

He eyed me for a second then reached for my dome. The same grey, concrete-like substance I'd seen once before climbed its way around us. It made a strange noise as it progressed, almost like buttons snapping quickly and repeatedly into place. Soon the entire dome was encased, enveloping us in darkness. I reached out and knocked on the wall, causing it to echo slightly.

"So you really can petrify anything," Ben said, sounding impressed.

"Just about," he repeated, a smile in his voice this time.

"This is cool and all, but it's pretty dark in here," Felicity said.

Matthew chuckled. Instantaneously, the concrete disappeared, revealing the dome of water right before it collapsed and soaked us all to the bone.

"Robin!" they all yelled as we jumped up shivering.

"What?" I cried out. "I didn't know he was going to undo it!"

We quickly picked up our mess and ran for the cars, turning the heaters on full blast so we could warm up. Ben pulled off his wet shirt, revealing his well-toned chest, and I bit my lip as I stared at him, taking in his shape.

"Like what you see?" he asked with a smirk before pulling on a dry shirt from his backseat. Heat rose to my cheeks as I looked away. "It's okay. You can tell me you think I'm sexy."

"Whatever," I muttered with pursed lips as he braided his long hair.

He shot me a wink, and I rolled my eyes as I pulled my own thick hair into a bun.

"Do you want to go see a movie tonight?" he asked. "We can hang out at my house until then."

"Sure. But we'll have to stop by my house first so I can change."

"I don't know," he said, eyeing me up and down. "I kind of like the wet look."

"I bet you do," I replied, folding my arms over my chest as a blush worked its way to my face again. "Now drive and drive fast, Old Man Toves."

"Yes, ma'am," he replied with a salute before heading towards my house.

"You're wet!" Dawn exclaimed with wide eyes when I walked in.

"Yes, I am," I replied.

"So are you!" she said to Ben. "Well, your pants are."

"Very observant," he responded, rustling her hair.

"What happened to you two?" Mom asked as she dried her hands on a towel.

"None of us could wait for summer," I said, and Ben snorted. Mom's brows furrowed, but I shook my head. "Don't ask. I'm gonna go change real quick."

I peeled off my wet clothes and pulled on dry ones. My hair fell out of its bun in the process, and I made a face at how crazy it looked. I ran my hands through the damp wildness, but it did little to help, so I yanked it back atop my head. I threw my damp apparel into the dryer then sauntered back into the kitchen.

"Ben said you're going to see a movie later," Mom told me.

"Yep, that's the plan," I replied. "Is that okay?"

"Of course. Just be home by curfew."

"I will, I promise." I kissed her on the cheek, told Dawn bye, then walked with Ben to his car again.

When we arrived at his house, he received similar questions about his pants.

"It looks like you pissed yourself," Mahka said.

"Mahka, language," Kiona scolded.

"Sorry, Ma," he replied with an unapologetic grin. He lowered his voice and said, "But really, did you have another accident? I know it happens a lot."

"Shut up," Ben said, shoving his shoulder.

Mahka looked at me and asked, "Do you really want to be with a guy that still wets the bed?"

I suppressed a grin as Ben pushed him harder. "I said shut up." He looked at me then said, "I do *not* still wet the bed."

"Hey, it's nothing to be ashamed of," Mahka said.

Ben shot him a glare, but before he could reply, Kiona said, "Mahka, enough. Leave your brother alone."

"But it's just too easy," Mahka replied with a wiggle of his brows.

"Listen to your mother," Jeremiah said without looking up from his card game.

Mahka sighed heavily, shot me a wink, then ran outside.

"Such a nuisance," Ben muttered, and I laughed. "I'll be right back."

He went upstairs to change, leaving me alone with his parents.

"Those boys enjoy getting on each other's nerves too much," Kiona said with a shake of her head.

"It's what brothers do," Jeremiah responded.

"It's what *siblings* do," I added. "Sometimes I want to wring Dawn's neck."

Jeremiah chuckled. "I remember those days."

"What do you mean?" Kiona asked. "You and your siblings *still* act like that."

"We do not!"

"You definitely do."

"You don't know what you're talking about."

"Uh huh. Okay."

I rubbed my lips together to hide my amusement as Kiona rolled her eyes at me.

"What do you two have planned today?" she asked me.

"Just hanging out then a movie later tonight."

"Sounds fun." She stepped closer and whispered, "But really, did he wet his pants again?"

My hand flew over my mouth as I giggled, and she winked as Ben came around the corner.

"What's so funny?" he asked suspiciously.

"Nothing," Kiona and I said simultaneously before sharing an amused look.

"Why do you hate me?" Ben asked with a heavy sigh.

She patted his cheek. "We *love* you, Benjamin."

"Oh, yeah. I sure feel the love."

Kiona smiled before walking into the kitchen, and Ben motioned for me to follow him out the door. We made our way into the clubhouse only to see Mahka and Dakota sitting on the couch.

"Out," Ben said, pointing to the door.

"Aw, why?" Mahka whined.

"Because Robin and I want to be alone."

Mahka arched a brow. "Alone, huh?"

I blushed as Ben scowled and said, "Out!"

"Fine. Enjoy your alone time." He paused before stepping outside. "But don't enjoy it *too* much."

"Mahka!" Ben yelled as his little brother ran out the door laughing.

"You know, he wouldn't bug you so much if you didn't give such a reaction all the time," Dakota said as he stood. "You only add fuel to his fire."

"Yeah, I know," Ben muttered. "But I can't help it."

"Yes, you can. Just stay quiet."

"Easier said than done, kid."

"I do it all the time."

"Because you never talk anyway," Ben said.

Dakota shrugged. "Works well for me."

"I'm sure it does."

"Hey, can we play Scrabble later?" Dakota asked as he clutched his book to his chest.

"Sure. After I get home from the movies, okay?"

"Okay!"

He ran off as I plopped onto the couch.

"Sorry about all that," Ben said as he sat next to me.

"It's okay. It's entertaining," I replied with a grin.

"It's annoying."

"You love him," I said, knocking into him with my shoulder.

"Depends on the day." I smiled wider, and he narrowed his eyes. "What?"

"Do you remember when we were, like, eight and you kept calling him your 'teeny tiny little friend?'"

He grimaced and pushed his hair away from his face. "I don't remember that at all."

"Really?" I cocked one brow, knowing he was lying. "I do. You always wanted him to follow you around. When he didn't, you'd cry to your mom that he didn't like you anymore."

"I did not."

"Did too."

"Did not."

"Did too!"

Ben let out a grumble and crossed his arms. "Okay, fine, I did."

I smirked at his annoyance. "My how the tables have turned."

"Just wait until you don't want Dawn around."

"I don't think that'll happen."

"Oh, it will." He paused, his brow furrowing. "I mean, unless you aren't here anymore."

"What?" I asked, feeling blindsided. "What do you mean?"

"It's just . . ." he trailed off and picked at his fingers.

"Ben?" He looked at me and I repeated, "What do you mean?"

He licked his lips then finally said, "I just can't help but wonder what's going to happen in the future. Will you be here? Will you be in Garridan? Will you be with the Cyfrin?" He swallowed loudly then whispered, "Will you be dead?"

"Ben!" I exclaimed, shocked. "How could you say that?"

"Because it's a possibility," he replied loudly, and my eyes widened. "And you can't say it isn't. There's a chance the people from the Cyfrin come here and—when you won't join them—kill you."

"That's not going to happen," I managed to say around the lump in my throat.

"You don't know that." He blinked rapidly and grabbed my hand. "And it's all I can think about."

"Ben," I murmured, my heart ripping apart at his tortured expression.

"I lay in bed at night, and all I see when I close my eyes is the different ways you're being hurt. And since we're dealing with people with supernatural powers, the options are kinda limitless." He shook his head. "I see you tortured. I see you fight back and lose. I see you scream for mercy.

"I see you die hundreds of ways every night then I see your funeral. I see the casket. I see the flowers on your headstone. I see the picture for the program. And worst of all, I see your mom and Dawn and Felicity falling apart with grief—on their knees completely broken."

"Ben," I whispered, tears silently falling down my cheeks as his voice broke.

"Can you imagine that?" he asked, barely audible.

My chin shook as I shook my head. I had no idea that's where his head was. Plagued by these thoughts, day in and day out, and I didn't know. How did he manage to keep a smile on his face during the day?

"I'm sorry," I managed to say, leaning into him.

"Me too."

"I don't want you to have that kind of burden on your shoulders."

"I don't either but, unfortunately, it's there."

"And it's my fault."

"Yes. It is," he said quietly.

"I'm sorry," I repeated.

He licked his lips and glanced around the room. "I wish I could say it's okay, but it's not."

"I know. I don't expect you to forgive me."

"If everything turns out okay, I can forgive you for this, Robin. I can forgive you for the pain you've inadvertently caused."

I sniffled and wiped my arm across my face. "You're too good of a person."

"No, I'm not."

"Yes, you are. You'd forgive me for anything."

"Not anything," he replied bitterly.

A voice in the back of my head warned me not to ask, but I ignored it. "What wouldn't you forgive me for?"

He looked down at me, his eyes tight with pain. "Dying."

My brows furrowed together. "You'd be angry at me for dying?"

"I'd be angry at you for dying when you could've done something to prevent it."

"Oh," I murmured, averting my eyes.

"Just imagine if the roles were reversed. Would you forgive me for not doing the one thing I could've done to not get hurt?"

"No. Probably not."

"Not even just me. What if it were Felicity? Or your mom or Dawn? You'd want them all to choose safety, so why do you think you're the exception? It's just hypocritical."

His words sliced through me along with a mixture of grief and anger. My fingers dug into my thighs as I said through gritted teeth, "Please don't say stuff like that. It's hard enough thinking of you or Felicity being hurt. But Dawn? No. That's unimaginable."

"I'm sorry," he said, rubbing his hands over his face before interlacing them behind his neck. "That wasn't fair of me to say. I'm just-I'm just so-I'm just so . . . Ugh!"

"Angry?" I murmured.

He nodded. "Yeah. Angry."

We sat quietly for a long time, both of us wrapped up in our own thoughts. I could see how much I was hurting him, and I hated it. Everything he said was true. I was being a hypocrite. But I still couldn't bring myself to change the decision I'd already made.

Did that make me a bad person?

Maybe.

"Hey," he suddenly said, forcing a smile. "Let's play a game."

He pulled me up as I tried to force our conversation out of my mind. I didn't want to think about how much torture I was putting him through anymore.

* * *

"Robin," she said, greeting me like she always did, but she seemed distracted as she wrapped me in a hug.

"Hi, Adriana."

"How's your training been going?"

"It's been great on the hydrokinesis side," I replied proudly. "Physical combat, not so much."

She let out a chuckle and ruffled my hair. "You take after me then. Luckily, your powers are more than suited to keep an attacker at bay."

"Good thing." I looked her over, noting the simple crease between her eyebrows and her forced smile. "Is something wrong?"

"Not necessarily."

"But something *could* be wrong?" I asked with raised brows.

"Possibly."

"What is it?" She hesitated, so I crossed my arms and said, "I think I deserve to know."

After a moment of careful consideration, she said, "Our intel suggests that the Cyfrin are going to make a move soon. We don't have any specifics, but we're worried you might be their target."

"But there's a chance I'm not?"

"Correct. There are still quite a few children from Garridan who haven't been located, but the Cyfrin have the advantage in finding them because of Arthur. You aren't the only one on their radar right now, so there *is* a possibility they're going after someone else."

"If you know where these other kids are after your intel tells you, why don't you just go get them so the Cyfrin can't?" It seemed simple enough to me.

"Because, like you, they have lives of their own," she replied. "When they were younger, it was easier, but now they're almost all adults or in their last years of school. We can't just steal them away from the only life they've known. We only intervene if we have to, like in your case."

I looked down at my hands. The people of Garridan were extremely selfless. Not only did they give up their children to protect them, but now some were giving them up a second time so they could live a happy life with their new loved ones. I couldn't imagine the heartache of finding your child after so many years only to decide to stay out of their lives.

"That's very honorable," I said to Adriana.

"We must do right by our loved ones," she replied. "Your father and I had decided to stay out of your life when you were found, but the Cyfrin made that choice impossible to follow through with."

"Well, if I'm being honest, I'm pretty happy you had to interfere," I said softly. "I love my mom and little sister, but it's nice to know where I really come from. And it's *really* nice to know I wasn't the ugly duckling of the family for no reason."

"You are not ugly!" she exclaimed, sounding like a mom.

I grinned. "It's just an expression."

"Even so. Don't talk about my daughter that way."

An odd sense of pride filled me. I was her daughter. This strong, selfless woman was my mother.

"So," I cleared my throat, fighting off the emotion that wanted to surface. "When will you know what the Cyfrin are up to?"

"Probably not until it happens, unfortunately." She sighed, clearly bothered by this. "Our inside person isn't high enough on the totem pole anymore to get any details about that sort of thing. So, just in case, please take extra precautions over the next couple of weeks. Don't let your guard down and stay safe."

"I will. I promise."

My palms were slick with sweat, but I knew I had nothing to be nervous about. Matthew would stay by my side twenty-four seven once I told him what she said. I guess his insistence at extra training might pay off sooner than I'd imagined. I'd have to remember to thank him for his uncanny timing.

"Is something else wrong?" I asked as she twiddled her thumbs.

"I'm just worried about you," she replied. "I talked to Susan and Malachi, Matthew's parents, and they're afraid he isn't being truthful about when he left the Cyfrin either."

My stomach flip flopped. "Why would they think that? They don't even know him."

"No, but I just found out that our spy on the inside gave them updates on him every now and then."

"They knew where he was and never tried to rescue him?" My frown bordered on becoming a full-on scowl. "That's messed up."

"Don't be too hasty to judge. It's not that simple."

"Oh, it never is," I replied, crossing my arms as a wave crashed into the shore, spraying us with water.

Adriana glanced around and said, "Please don't take this the wrong way, but you need to calm down."

"Excuse me?" My eyes narrowed.

"Your attitude," she said gently, beckoning around. "It's going to shatter the dream projection."

I looked around and realized the storm clouds had moved closer, bringing the wind with them. I dropped my arms and grimaced.

"Sorry. I didn't mean to," I said.

"I understand. But we should probably leave that conversation for a later time—when we aren't in the dream realm," she suggested, squeezing my shoulder, and I nodded.

"Okay. Can you at least tell me why his parents think he's lying?"

"Because the last time they were updated, he was still very much doing the Cyfrin's bidding."

"How long ago was that?"

"About a year."

A gust of wind slapped me in the face as my concern dissipated. "Oh, so not anytime recently."

"Well, no, but—"

"But nothing." I waved my hand dismissively. "A lot can happen in a year. Just because he was still a part of their organization then doesn't mean he didn't leave after."

"I know that, honey. So do they. We're just a little wary is all. The timing seems too convenient."

"I understand. I really do." I dug my toes into the sand as I shrugged. "I've had my doubts about him a couple times myself. But he's done nothing but help me since we became friends. Why would he do that if he was going to help the Cyfrin take me? Why would he teach me about my powers and self-defense?"

"I see your point, but it doesn't really alleviate my concern."

I smiled. "That's just your mom side coming out."

"Maybe so," she replied softly. She pulled me into a hug as rain began to pelt us. "Just promise me you'll watch your back."

"I promise," I said, holding her tightly. "I'll be okay."

Thunder rumbled around us, rattling my bones, then my arms fell to my side as she was once again pulled away from me.

# CHAPTER TWENTY-FIVE

"Why aren't you dressed yet?" I asked Dawn, picking her up and setting her on the kitchen counter.

Her fine hair was full of static, hovering above her head like a weightless astronaut in space, and her pink pajamas sat wrinkled from a good night's rest. She had one finger in her mouth, messing with a loose tooth.

"I'm going to the children's museum!" she replied excitedly.

"Oh, really now?" I questioned with raised brows as I shook cereal in a bowl for us to share. "What about school?"

"It's a teacher workday so she's off," Mom said as she came into the kitchen wearing faded jeans and a T-shirt.

"How fun. I'm assuming you're taking her?"

"What makes you say that?" she asked, pouring herself a cup of coffee.

"That isn't exactly work attire," I replied with a grin.

She looked down at herself and nodded. "I can see why you came to that conclusion."

I let out a snort before pinching the side of Dawn's cheek lightly. "Well, you two have fun. I want to hear all about it when I get home."

I scarfed down my food and did the dishes before going into the bathroom to brush my teeth. My fingers yanked through my tangled hair, trying to tuck down the crazier pieces, then I grabbed my backpack and coat. Mom kissed my cheek and Dawn nearly knocked me over with a bear hug before I headed to the door.

"Love you both!" I called out to them.

"Love you, little birdy," Dawn yelled after me, and I couldn't help but smile.

Felicity was waiting in her car for me when I opened our front door. I ran over and hopped in with a cheery hello that was barely audible over her loud music. She made no effort to turn it down, so we rode to school with a mini-jam session, turning heads as we hit the parking lot.

We greeted people with big smiles, rejuvenized by our exuberant car ride over. Our cheery demeanors seemed to be an ongoing theme as the morning passed. The teachers were in good moods, so our homework load was nonexistent. We even got to watch videos in government instead of having our usual pop quiz.

*If every day could be like this, I'd enjoy school a whole lot more.*

When lunch rolled around, the temperature had risen enough to be inviting, so we sat outside in a huge circle with other people. I watched the fluffy, white clouds slowly moving overhead, covering us in their shadows as they paraded past the sun. Every now and then, someone would ask me a question and I'd jump back into the conversation, but I was enjoying the peaceful feeling the weather was giving us.

Felicity gossiped with Jordan and Alli about some prom-posal that had gone embarrassingly wrong while Matthew and Ben were in a heated debate about sports with some of the guys. I noticed Amara and Juan were sitting close together, completely captivated by their own conversation, and I grew happy at the idea of them together. They'd make a cute couple. I relaxed into Ben, and his arms tightened around me as he gave me an absentminded kiss on the top of my head. Today was pure bliss.

"Ms. Hayes," I heard. I looked over and saw our school counselor, Mrs. Bailey. "Can you come with me, please?"

"Okay," I replied, wondering what she could need me for.

I stood up and stretched, shrugging at the curious glances thrown my way before following her inside. We walked down the hall and through the front office where her office awaited. The principal stood with a serious-looking woman in a dress suit, and beside them was Lizzie, whose eyes were red and puffy beneath slightly smudged makeup. I could see the room was full of sorrow but didn't know why.

"What's going on?" I asked. Mr. Peterson motioned for me to sit, and I looked Lizzie up and down. "Are you okay?"

She nodded but didn't speak. The tension was palpable, and no one seemed to want to be the first to talk, so I repeated my question more firmly as my stomach churned. "What's going on?"

Lizzie took a seat opposite of me and grasped both my hands in hers. I'd never seen her look so upset, and it rattled me because I knew whatever was wrong, it was bad.

She swallowed a couple times and cleared her throat then finally spoke, her voice heavy with emotion. "I'm afraid there's been an accident."

"What kind of accident?" I asked, my mouth going dry.

She glanced over at Mrs. Bailey, who nodded ever so slightly, then let out a shaky breath. "Your mother and sister were involved in a car accident earlier today."

My eyes grew wide, and I gripped the armrests of the chair. "Are they-are they okay? W-what happened? What hospital are they in?" My pulse raced as I struggled to control my ragged breathing. "I want to go see them!"

The deafening silence that followed told me everything I needed to know.

"Say it," I whispered as my heart thumped wildly in my chest, trying to fight off the creeping darkness that threatened to overwhelm it. "Say it!"

"I'm so sorry, Robin," Lizzie managed to say around broken sobs. "They didn't make it. They're gone."

"They're . . . *dead?*" I breathed, saying the one word she was tiptoeing around.

"Yes," she replied, reaching for my hands again, but I pulled them away. "They're dead."

My throat thickened, and I clutched my chest with trembling fingers as I tried to breathe. My stomach churned, and I put my head on my knees, trying to keep my lunch down.

"How . . . How did it happen?" I asked, my voice barely audible.

"It, uh," Lizzie faltered, and I could hear her trying to force the words out. "The police think it was foul play. They were run off the road."

*Foul play? Run off the road? Someone did this intentionally? How? Why? Who?*

My mind jumped to the conversation I'd just had with Adriana. She said an attack was coming. Was this it?

*Did the Cyfrin just kill my family?*

If they did, this was all my fault. Their blood was on my hands. I choked back a sob and held in the tears that wanted to escape. My heart couldn't take the raw emotion my brain was so desperately trying to process. I could feel them both starting to shut down.

"Robin," said the lady in the corner. She walked over to me and knelt down. "I am so very sorry for your loss. My name is Katarina Spelzie, and I work for social services. Even though your parents were starting the process of divorcing, custody of you would go straight to you father, but . . ." The woman looked as though she'd rather take early retirement than continue with her news, but in the end, professionalism won out. "Your father has chosen not to take responsibility for you and has waved his custodial rights."

"Of course he did," I murmured, unsurprised and uncaring. He never wanted me anyway.

"However," she continued, "some time ago, your mother had a legal document drawn up naming Lizzie your legal guardian in the case that both she and your father were to pass away. As such, custody falls to her, so she'll be taking care of you until your eighteenth birthday."

"Okay," I said, feeling thoroughly numb.

Lizzie offered me a tight smile, but I couldn't return it. She'd always been family, and I would choose her over my father in a heartbeat. But in this moment, I was incapable of showing any sort of affection.

"Uhm, this may not be the right time," Lizzie said, drumming her fingers on her leg before reaching into her pocket and pulling out a small, clear bag. "But there may never be a right time so here. This is for you. Your father didn't want them, but he told the police I could take it. It's the personal items they retrieved from Dawn and Rebecca. I thought you might like to have them."

I looked down at the bag in my hands, horrified. There were only three things in it: Mom's stud earrings and Dawn's necklace. I pulled out the necklace with quivering hands and stared at the familiar half-heart adorned with emerald circles. But the emeralds weren't all green anymore; some of them were dark red, stained by the unmistakable presence of dried blood.

The darkness finally won. I couldn't think, couldn't see, couldn't breathe. The voices around me became nothing more than a low buzz as the ringing in my ears intensified. The urge to cry vanished and in its place was a hollow, deadened void that made all the feelings disappear—an emptiness that filled every inch of my body and reached deep down into my soul.

Suddenly, I was running out of the office and down the street. My feet thumped along the ground as my limbs cried out for me to slow down. But I didn't. I couldn't. I ran with no destination in mind and no will to stop. Maybe if I ran fast enough or far enough, I could outrun the demons that had just latched onto my life.

I couldn't feel the sun on my face or the wind in my hair. I couldn't feel the aching in my feet as they blistered. I couldn't even feel the fire in my lungs as they screamed for relief. I couldn't feel anything at all.

* * *

"I found her!" someone yelled. Hands touched my face, pushing my hair back. "Robin, it's okay, I'm here."

Ben knelt in front of me on the floor of our clubhouse, his face clouded with worry. Footsteps thudded outside, coming closer. I didn't divert my eyes from the wall above the TV. I didn't care who was here or what they wanted.

"Is she okay?" Felicity asked, her voice thick.

I wasn't sure what time it was, but the sun had gone down ages ago as I laid there on the couch. I must've scared them.

"She doesn't look hurt," Ben said, his hand still on my cheek. "Robin, are you okay? Can you hear me?"

*Yes*, I thought, but the word didn't reach my mouth.

"Robin," Kiona said, squeezing my hand. "Can you sit up?"

*No.*

"Why isn't she answering? What's wrong with her?" I heard Mahka ask, sounding scared. It was a strange tone to hear from him.

"She's grieving," Jeremiah said.

"Should we call a doctor?" Felicity asked, sitting by my feet and putting her hand on my leg.

*No doctor.*

"No," Jeremiah replied. "She just needs some time."

*Yes, time. Time will help . . . Right?*

"I'll call Lizzie," Kiona said, pulling Mahka away with her.

"What should we do?" Ben asked his dad.

"Just stay with her," he replied. "She needs all the support she can get."

Felicity ran her hand down my back a couple times then stepped back outside.

"She's probably calling Matthew and some of the others to tell them you're safe," Ben told me, running his thumb across my chin. "We've had half the class looking for you all night. We were so worried, Robin."

He watched me closely, his eyes begging me to talk. I wanted to reach out to him—to ask him to help me escape from this—but I wasn't in control of my body anymore. It didn't belong to me; it belonged to the grief that held me down and made it impossible to function. I was a prisoner in my own body. I couldn't fight it, so I decided to embrace it and let it pull me into a bottomless slumber where I could have peace.

* * *

"She can't stay here forever," Felicity said in a hushed tone.

"She can stay as long as she needs to," Ben replied.

"No, I'm afraid she can't, Ben," Jeremiah told him, his stern voice sad. "It's been two days. She needs to accept what's happened and learn how to cope with it. If we let her continue this way, I'm afraid she may never recover."

*Two days. Has it really been two days?*

"She just needs more time," Ben insisted.

"No amount of time can fix what's hurt her," his dad said. "We need to do what we can to help her through this, but letting her lie on the couch, clinging to that necklace, isn't the answer."

"She still hasn't talked?" Matthew asked.

"No," Ben replied. "Not a word. She hasn't even cried."

"She might be afraid to," Jeremiah said.

"Why?" Felicity asked.

"She might think once she starts, she won't be able to stop."

*No. That's not it. There're no tears to cry because there's no pain. Only numbness.*

I could feel them all looking at me, so I kept my eyes shut. They continued to talk softly as I drifted back to sleep again.

* * *

"Robin, please," Felicity said as my hollow eyes stared past her. "Lizzie and Ben's parents are talking about having you committed. You have to snap out of this."

*Snap out of this? But why? Mom and Dawn aren't coming back. I killed them.*

"Do you want to go to the looney house?" she asked.

"It's a hospital," Ben said, his voice sharp. "Not a looney house."

"Might as well be. They're just gonna dope her up on medication."

"They're going to *help* her."

"Yeah, 'help.'"

"Felicity!" Ben yelled. "She hasn't moved in three days. She's sitting in her own urine. She won't eat, won't drink. Would you rather us just do *nothing* and let her die on that couch?"

"Ben," Matthew murmured, placing his hand on his shoulder.

Ben shook it off. "No. She needs to face reality. Robin needs help. Help we can't give her."

"So you'd rather hand her off to some strangers?" Felicity cried out, her voice breaking. "Let them deal with the burden?"

"We don't think she's a burden and you know it!"

"Could've fooled me!"

*No. Don't fight. Please don't fight.*

But they couldn't hear me. Their voices became louder as Matthew tried to get between them.

*This is all my fault.*

Ben threw something against the wall then fell to his knees with his head in his hands.

*They're hurting because of me.*

Felicity covered her mouth with her hand as tears streamed down her face.

*There's been enough hurt already. I have to stop this.*

My mind began kicking into gear.

*Mom wouldn't approve of this.*

She'd never shut down a day in her life, even at the worst of times. She always persevered and pushed through the pain because she wanted Dawn and I to have a good life.

*I'm failing her when I should be honoring her.*

I needed to accomplish everything in life she wanted me to—it was the only way to let her live on through me. But to do that, I had to get up. Which meant I needed to climb out of this dark hole and face the emotions I'd suppressed.

*I can do it.*

For my mom and Dawn, I had to do it.

*Come on, Robin . . . just do it!*

I slowly sat up on the couch, and the room went dead silent. I blinked a couple times as they stared at me with wide eyes. I opened my mouth, but nothing came out, so I cleared my throat and tried again.

"They're dead," I managed to get out, my hollow voice raspy. "My family is . . . dead."

A broken sob tore through my chest, and I brought my hand up to my mouth as they continued. Ben rushed over and wrapped me in a tight hug, holding me together as I threatened to fall apart completely. My eyes were blurry with uncontainable tears, and I leaned into him as I poured out my sorrow. He ran his hand up and down my back, shushing me as his own tears spilled down his cheeks.

"It hurts," I whimpered into his chest as a thousand swords stabbed into my heart.

"I know it does," he murmured.

"They're gone." The anguish that overtook me was as intense as a typhoon, unforgiving and intimidating.

"I know. I'm sorry, Robin. I'm so so sorry."

"I-I don't know . . . I don't know w-what to do. I don't know how to be okay."

"You don't have to be. No one expects you to be."

"I peed my pants," I whispered, the humiliation drowning in the grief.

"That's okay too."

"I need a shower," I said around sobs as snot ran down my nose.

"Let's go take a shower then," Ben replied softly.

"I can't get up." My body was too malnourished to move, and I broke down all over again as my stomach rumbled.

*How could I let myself get like this?*

I remembered Lizzie trying to pull me up to go to the bathroom, but I couldn't get my legs to work. After the first accident, they'd placed puppy pads beneath me. I remembered Kiona putting food in my mouth, but I couldn't swallow. They tried to coax it down my throat, but I just threw it up. No wonder they were about to get professional help.

Ben continued to hold me as I cried, resting his head on mine and whispering comforting words. By the time my tears finally stopped falling, I was shaking uncontrollably, and my brain pounded against my skull. My eyes and throat burned too, but I didn't care. Anything was better than the numbness.

"Kiona made you food," Felicity said as she and Matthew walked through the door.

I hadn't even noticed they were gone, but I was grateful they'd given me privacy to mourn. I could only imagine how much of a mess I looked like after lying on a couch for so long then bawling my eyes out. My stomach churned at the sight of the food she placed before me, and it took everything in me not to puke.

"Maybe we should start with water," Matthew suggested, seeing my nauseated expression.

I tried to pick up the glass, but my hands shook too much to bring it to my mouth. Ben grabbed it from me and held it to my lips, letting me take small sips.

"You ready to try some food?" Felicity asked gently, and I nodded.

She spoon fed me a couple bites before I was able to do it myself. It was a slow process but, eventually, I managed to eat everything on my plate.

"How are you feeling?" Ben asked.

"Better," I replied, my tired eyes meeting his. "But I'd really like a shower."

"Of course. Let's go inside," he said.

He and Matthew each took one of my arms and carefully pulling me to my feet. I wobbled slightly then leaned into Ben for support as we walked.

"I'm, uh, I'm really sorry I ruined your couch," I said, intense heat rising to my cheeks. The embarrassment almost made me cry again.

"Don't apologize. It can be cleaned," he said.

I opened my mouth to argue, but Felicity cut me off. "Can I just buy you a new one?" she asked.

I could tell Ben was about to decline, but Felicity motioned towards me and shook her head. She knew I'd never be comfortable sitting there again. Ben must've understood too because he nodded and forced a smile onto his face.

"Sure," he said. "But only if it comes with heated seats and cup holders."

"I'll see what I can do," Felicity replied sarcastically, and I actually cracked a small smile.

"Look at that," Ben said softly. "You can still feel happiness."

"Yeah. I guess I can," I murmured, the thought sitting funny. Mom and Dawn were dead. Was it okay to find joy without them?

As if reading my thoughts, Felicity said, "You don't have to feel guilty for it."

I swallowed and looked at my feet. "But I do."

"That's okay," Matthew said. "You can be happy and sad at the same time. You can be angry. You can feel whatever you need to in order to get through this."

I nodded, needing to hear the validation. "Thank you."

We slowly walked out of the clubhouse, and I winced at the brightness outside. Kiona and Lizzie met us at the door, taking Ben and Matthew's places beside me so they could help me up the stairs.

"I can shower alone," I said when we reached the bathroom.

"Are you sure?" Lizzie asked, her wide eyes full of worry. "We don't mind helping."

"No, I'm okay," I replied, staring at my feet. I'd had enough humiliation. "Really. But thank you." I looked at Felicity and asked, "Will you stay in the bathroom with me though?"

"Of course," she said. "You don't have to be alone until you're ready."

I looked down at the bloodied necklace in my palm. My chin quivered and I breathed in deeply, the breath coming back out in shaky, broken waves. I swallowed and held it out to Lizzie.

"Can-can you take this and clean it?" I asked her, blinking away tears.

"Yes," she replied, her own voice hoarse. "I'm so sorry for giving it to you. I should've known better."

"No, it's okay. I want it." I tried to smile but it resembled a grimace more. "I *need* it. Just not with . . ."

I trailed off and Lizzie nodded her head vigorously. "I understand. When you're done in the shower it'll be good as new."

"Thank you."

She pulled me into a hug, her snot staining my shirt as we clung to one another.

"I'm afraid to let go," she whispered in my ear.

"I know," I replied just as quiet, hearing the underlaying words—she was scared of losing me too. "But I'm okay. I'm still here."

"Thank God," she said, holding the back of my head to her fiercely. Finally, she let go and wiped her cheeks. "Go. Get clean. We'll be downstairs waiting when you're ready."

Kiona nodded in agreement, her red-rimmed eyes watching me with uncertainty. She was afraid for me too. They headed down the stairs, and I turned towards the bathroom. Felicity had a bundle of clothes in her hand, and my brows furrowed.

Before I could ask, she said, "Lizzie brought them over a couple days ago. We thought you'd get up and want to change but . . ." She stared at her feet and rubbed her lips together.

"I'm sorry," I said, seeing the pain she was feeling.

Her eyes flashed to me, suddenly angry. "Don't you dare apologize. You haven't done anything wrong. Okay? I'm just—" She stopped and swallowed. "I was just so worried about you, Robin, and I didn't know how to help. I still don't."

"I don't think there's any way you can," I replied. "But just being here for me . . . That's enough."

She threw her arms around me, and I hugged her back as the tears started all over again. I sniffled and pulled away, needing a reset as my head thumped against my skull. I stepped into the shower, letting the hot water burn into my skin.

When I closed my eyes, the image of Dawn's face lingered there—petrified, crying, screaming—as Mom desperately tried to keep control of the wheel.

I leaned against the wall with my head in my hands, letting out a muffled shriek. My palm slapped the wet tile, over and over, as my voice grew hoarse from yelling. Anger. Pure anger. That's what I felt now.

* * *

"I want to go to my house," I said as I rubbed Dawn's necklace between my fingers.

"Are you sure?" Ben asked, his face telling me he didn't like that idea.

I nodded, pulling my knees to my chest.

Lizzie exchanged glances with Jeremiah and Kiona. "I'm not sure that's a good idea, sweetie," she said.

"I have to eventually," I replied, resting my chin on my legs. "All my stuff is there."

"Someone else can do that for you."

"No." I shook my head. "Please. I need to go. I need to see it."

"Why?" Felicity asked. "It's just going to hurt you more."

I picked at my fingers. "Maybe. But it's something I need to do."

Jeremiah slightly nodded his head at Lizzie. She rubbed her lips together, pushed her faded orange hair behind her ear, then sighed.

"Okay," she said. "I'll take you."

"Actually, can you not?" I asked quietly. "I'd rather go alone."

"Now *that* really isn't a good idea," she replied. "No."

"Please?"

"Absolutely not."

"What if I go with her?" Ben interrupted. He looked at me and asked, "Would that be okay?"

Lizzie watched me as I chewed on my bottom lip. I didn't want anyone with me, but I really didn't want to argue anymore so I nodded.

"That's fine," I said.

"Okay," Lizzie replied, placing her hand on my shoulder gently. "Ben can take you, but I want you to come to my house after. We need to get you settled in."

My stomach churned.

*I have to move in with her. I'll never go back to the home I grew up in. This is real. Mom and Dawn are gone.*

"Robin?" Ben asked, gripping my hand in his own.

I blinked rapidly and nodded. "Let's go."

# CHAPTER TWENTY-SIX

I stood in front of the house I called home for most of my life. It hadn't always been my safe place, but it was still a home filled with plenty of love and happy memories. As I stared at it, I was hit all over again with the fact that my family was gone.

I would never again see Dawn run out that door to greet me with a big hug and contagious smile. I would never again walk inside and see my mom standing in the kitchen making us pancakes on Monday morning. All the love and happy memories were now reminders of my loss. It placed a weight on my chest, threatening to break me again.

I took a deep, shaky breath and let it out slowly, fighting back the tears.

"I'll be right back," I said softly.

"We can go inside with you," Ben offered as Felicity and Matthew nodded in agreement. They'd followed behind us in their car, despite my objections, and I was still annoyed about it. No one was listening to me.

I shook my head and pulled away from them. "No. I just need a minute alone."

I walked away and could feel their eyes on my back as I made my way to the door. I unlocked it then placed my hand on the doorknob. I swallowed back the anguish I felt and pushed the door open, stepping through the threshold slowly.

Despite my entire world shifting, everything in the house was the same as it'd been when I'd left for school Monday morning. The stack of magazines that no one read were still on the table; the morning dishes were still soaking in the now cold, soapy water; Dawn's stuffed animals were still scattered around the living room, wishing for her to come play with them.

I walked to the bedroom I'd shared with Dawn and stared at her messy bed. The whole house was on pause, just waiting for us to come back, but we never would. A tear trickled out of my eye, and I sniffled, wiping it away immediately. I pulled out my suitcase from the back of the closet and quickly loaded it up with my clothes, toiletries, and the few personal items I couldn't live without. After I zipped it up, I sat down on my bed and let my eyes roam across our room. What would happen to everything else?

*Thump.*

I glanced towards the door. Had someone come in? The thumping continued, followed by a low moan and a hiccup. I peeked out of my room. When I didn't see anyone, I walked towards the kitchen. The living room came into view, and there was a hunched-over figure, who had apparently knocked over an empty bottle of rum.

"Where did you come from?" I asked with disdain.

The man I used to call Dad turned around, nearly falling over, and burped.

"What are you doing here?" he muttered before guzzling a beer.

"I think the better question is what are *you* doing here?" I crossed my arms.

He tripped over the coffee table and cursed as I glared at his drunken stupor.

"This is my house," he drawled out slowly. "I don't gotta tell you nothing!"

"Why are you drinking? I thought you were sober," I said, disappointed—not for me but for him. He was choosing to throw his life away again.

"Didn't you hear? My wife and daughter died." He stepped closer to me, his eyes burning with rage. "It's all your fault, you know. Everything is your fault. I never wanted ya, but Rebecca insisted. But I knew! I knew you weren't good for us."

I pursed my lips as I tried to hold it together. His drunken honesty cut through me as he admitted what I'd always suspected—he never wanted me. He never loved me because I was adopted. He'd fooled Mom but not me.

"Whatever." I glared at him. "You're the one who wasn't good for us. I may not have been their blood, but I was a part of this family more than you were."

I turned around, ready to leave him in my past, but he scurried after me as I walked away.

"You didn't deserve them!" he yelled, causing me to pause. "They were *my* family. *Mine*! You hear? You stole them from me! They should've been with me. *With me*!"

He broke off, sobbing messily into his arm, and I almost felt bad for him. Then he looked at me, his teary eyes full of hate. "They're better off dead than here with you."

My jaw dropped, and I stared at him, horrified, as he knocked back another beer. Slowly, my horror turned to something else. I was breathless from the anger. An unqu-

enchable energy formed in my veins as I watched him struggle to open another bottle.

Pure instinct took over, and I harnessed every drop of
energy within me. My hands hovered over the water in the
sink and the murky liquid lifted easily. Without a second
thought, I hurled it towards him, shaping it over his face as
the force knocked him into the wall.

I held it there, fire burning my core, as he struggled to
break free of the watery grave I'd cast upon him. My lips
pressed together, and my nostrils flared. Why were they
dead while he lived? It wasn't fair. It wasn't right! The front
door slammed open, and footsteps thumped towards me.

"Robin, stop!" Matthew yelled.

I ground my teeth together before hitting Mark with another wave of powerful energy as it trickled off my fingertips. The water tightened around him, and he clawed help-
lessly at his throat.

"This isn't you! I know you're angry and hurt, but this
won't make you feel any better. Do *not* give in to these feelings! Control it, Robin," Matthew said.

I lifted my chin in defiance. Did it really matter what happened now?

"Robin?" a small voice said.

I glanced over my shoulder. Felicity and Ben were standing by the door, watching the scene in horror. The fear in
their faces managed to break through my heated exterior,
and the anger deflated just enough for reason to set in. My
lower lip quivered, and Matthew slowly walked towards me
with his arms raised.

"Don't become the monster he is," he told me, his voice
gentle. "Be the girl your mother and sister knew and lov-

ed—the girl your mother raised to be kind and compassionate."

Hot tears streamed down my face as I turned back towards Mark, whose face was turning blue beneath the layer of water coating it. I let out a shaky sob and stared at him a moment longer then released the water, letting it fall to the ground.

Mark coughed violently as he tried to draw deep breaths into his lungs. His reddened eyes looked suddenly sober and followed me with fear as I backed away.

"I'm-I'm sorry," I whispered before turning around and rushing past everyone. I sank to my knees outside and shuddered as I puked in the bushes against the house. My mind whirled, unable to process what I'd just done.

"Are you okay?" Matthew asked, kneeling next to me, and I shook my head as I wiped my mouth and leaned back.

"I almost killed him," I choked out, appalled by what I'd done.

"But you didn't," Matthew said, as if that made it okay.

"He just-he said some terrible things and I-I got so angry," I stuttered, tripping over my explanation.

"Hey," Matthew said, turning me towards him. "You're going through something extremely traumatic right now. Your emotions are all over the place because you're trying to find a way to cope. Shutting down didn't work and neither did getting angry, but it's okay that you tried both."

"I just don't know how to exist in a world where they don't," I whispered.

"I know. But one day you will." He looked up at the sky, his jaw tense. "It won't be easy, but eventually you'll start to hurt less. You won't stop grieving, but you'll learn how to deal with the loss."

Ben and Felicity walked out of the house with my suitcase in tow. Neither of them looked our way, and I glanced down, ashamed.

"Are they scared of me?" I asked Matthew quietly.

"No," he replied, picking me up off the ground with him. "They're a little freaked out, but they know that's not who you are. They won't bring it up unless you do."

"I'd rather not think about it ever again."

"You may not want to, but you need to."

"Why?"

"Because you need to remember this feeling if you're ever put in another situation where your anger could get out of control. It's good to know who you are and who you don't want to be."

I nodded, his words ringing in my ears. I never wanted to be like that again.

* * *

"Hey, sweetie," Lizzie said after my luggage and I were dropped off.

"Hi," I replied, standing awkwardly.

"Are you okay?"

"Yeah, I guess. Just don't really know how to act."

"That's okay," she said with a small smile. "It might be a little weird at first, but we'll get used to it. Okay?"

I nodded as I looked her over. Her hair was a mess, and her face looked oddly naked with no makeup on. I could tell she was in pain, but she tried to hide it.

"So, this is your house?" I asked, wondering why I'd never been there before as I looked at the contemporary and sleek home. The outside was dark grey with wooded accents and sleek lines. Large windows covered much of the front, and it was lined with greenery. It was very much Lizzie's style.

"Sure is," she replied. "And it's yours now too."

"Only for a little while."

"You're welcome to stay as long as you want, Robin."

"I know, and I'm really grateful but . . ." I wasn't sure if I should mention Adriana and Elijah.

"But what, honey?"

I hesitated then decided to just go for it. "Did you know I was adopted?" I asked, and she winced.

"I did."

"Did Mom tell you I found out?"

"Yes."

"Well, she didn't know this part, but I found my birth parents, and I've been in contact with them. As soon as school's over, I want to go visit them for the summer."

"Oh, Robin, I don't know," she said, her eyes going wide.

"Please. I really can't explain it, but I have to go. I'd like your permission, but I'm going to go either way."

She rubbed her lips together and lifted her shoulder. "I suppose I can't stop you. You're almost an adult, and I trust you to make the right decisions. But I'd like to talk to them at some point before you go."

"Okay," I replied, knowing there was no way she could do that.

"Okay," she repeated, nodding with a bit more confidence. "Just for the summer though, right? You'll come back for your senior year and be here with me."

The automatic 'yes' I was going to say got stuck in my throat. Of course I wanted to finish my time in school where it had started. I wanted to experience all the events reserved for seniors with Ben, Felicity, and everyone else I'd grown up with. But what I wanted and what was best were two entirely different things, and I didn't know if it was best for me to put anyone else in harm's way.

Lizzie noticed my hesitation and held out her hands. "We can talk about that later. For now, let's go inside and get you all set up. I'm sure you want to unpack that bag."

"Definitely." I hated living out of a suitcase.

"Okay. While you do that, I'll whip up some food and hot chocolate. You can eat it in your room if you want to be alone, or we can pop in a movie," she said as she dragged my luggage up the front steps.

"A movie sounds perfect," I told her.

Despite having people around me the entire time, I'd never felt more alone than I had the last few days when I withdrew into myself. Being alone was the last thing I wanted anymore. I only hoped everyone would be patient with me as I clung to them while I learned how to live with my grief.

# CHAPTER TWENTY-SEVEN

"Tomorrow's the funeral," I told Adriana as she sat next to me on the rocks. "I'm afraid I won't be able to keep it together."

"No one expects you to," she replied, wrapping her arm around my shoulder. "You're a seventeen-year-old girl who lost her family. You have every right to break down."

"But what if I lash out again?" I whispered, thinking of Mark.

"You won't," Adriana said confidently.

"How do you know?"

"Because you are a loving, compassionate person who is *good*," she replied. "You made a mistake, but it doesn't define who you are. If anything, it helped you see how easy it is to lose control, which will make your control all the stronger."

I leaned my head against her. "I miss them."

"I know, sweetheart. I wish I could take away your pain."

"Is there a power for that?" I asked, only half joking.

"Physical pain, yes. Emotional, I'm afraid not."

"I couldn't get that lucky, could I?" I sighed.

"That pain—the grief—it's there to remind us of what we lost. You don't want to forget it. I promise."

I nodded, knowing she was right. Forgetting it would mean forgetting how much I loved Mom and Dawn, and I didn't want that.

"Did you ever find out if the Cyfrin were behind their car being run off the road?" I asked.

I didn't call it an accident like everyone else because it wasn't. There was video footage showing a black SUV ramming into their car more than once. My mom kept control the best as she could, but in the end, she lost. Their car was pushed into the column of a bridge, breaking through it and crashing down into the rocky canyon below.

"I'm afraid so," Adriana said quietly.

I closed my eyes. "So it *is* my fault."

"No, it is not!" Adriana exclaimed.

"They killed them because of me. How is that *not* my fault?" I spat out, my teeth grinding together.

"They did it because they're bad people and they do bad things," she told me harshly. "And, honestly, this tragedy could've had absolutely nothing to do with you anyway."

"What do you mean?"

"The Cyfrin don't typically operate this way. They don't go after people's loved ones unless they're denied what they want. Since they haven't even made contact with you yet, it doesn't make sense for them to target your family."

"Then why did they?" I asked, not at all comforted.

"I don't know that. Yet. But I promise you we're going to find out. Okay?"

"Okay."

"I don't ever want to hear you say this is your fault again."

"Okay," I repeated.

She pulled me back to her, and we sat silently until she was taken away from me once more.

* * *

It was a beautiful day for a funeral. The sun shone bright, and there wasn't a cloud in the sky as we stood before the graves. Lizzie made all of the arrangements because I hadn't been able to bear leafing through the endless options of caskets, headstones, and flower. Everything she chose was pleasing to the eye, and I had no complaints as I took in their final resting place.

My yellow dress looked out of place amongst the sea of black, but I didn't care; yellow was Dawn's favorite color. I held onto the two hearts that dangled side by side on my chest as people took turns speaking. A large photo of them stood on an easel in between their headstones, and my eyes lingered on it. I longed to hear their laughter again as I had when I'd snapped that picture. They were so happy.

Anger coursed through my veins during the service. To whoever said time is a thief, I disagree entirely. The real thief is death itself. Because for some people, not enough time has passed. Yet there death is, still ready to steal the life right out of them—the people who haven't had enough time.

As the caskets were being lowered into the ground, I grasped a hand on either side of me to keep from falling over as I wept. My legs trembled beneath me, threatening to give out. Ben wrapped his arm around me, supporting my weight as I cried into his shoulder. Lizzie squeezed my hand, letting me know she was there, and I could hear her sobbing softly, as were many other people. Time passed in a blur as friends and family members made their way to me to voice their condolences.

*"They're in a better place."*
*"It happened for a reason."*
*"You'll see them again someday."*

I wanted to smack every single person who thought they were being supportive saying things like that. It didn't help. It didn't make me feel better. In fact, it made me feel worse.

When most everyone had cleared out, I sat down on a chair, completely worn out. My eyes burned as I stared at their headstones covered in sunflowers and daisies. I knew Mom and Dawn would've approved of the selection and wiped away a lone tear.

"How are you holding up?" Matthew asked, sitting down next to me.

I shrugged, not looking his way. "As well as can be expected."

"I'm sorry," he said softly, and something in his voice caused my gaze to shift towards him. Dark circles sat under his eyes, and worry lines seemed permanently etched into his face.

"Are *you* okay?" I asked, and he leaned forward with his elbows on his knees, resting his head in his hands.

"I know I didn't know them for very long, but I grew attached," he replied. "Your mom treated me like I was part of the family and for someone who never had a family, that meant a lot. And Dawn . . . well, I'm sure she captivated everybody she ever met."

"She sure did," I agreed with a half-smile.

When he continued, his voice was sadder than I'd ever heard. "I have to tell you something, and after I do, I think our friendship will be over."

I was taken aback, and I'm sure the shock showed on my face. "What makes you say that?"

"Because I don't know if you'll ever be able to forgive me." He swallowed, and I watched as he looked everywhere but me.

"It can't be that bad."

"But it is," he responded.

When he didn't continue, I asked, "Well, what is it?"

His lips turned white as he pressed them together, then he said, "Your family is dead because of me."

My blood ran cold, and I froze. "Excuse me?"

"I haven't been entirely forthcoming about my past," he said, his voice hard as steel. "Everything I've told you about me has been true except for one thing . . . one very important thing."

"Which would be what?"

He rubbed his hand over his face. "I didn't run away from the Cyfrin, and it was no accident that I ended up here. I was sent here by them on a mission."

*Adriana was right.*

I felt like I'd been punched in the gut. My mind ran amuck as I struggled to get my bearings. He lied. The enemy wasn't coming . . . It was already here. My eyes widened as some of his past words ran through my head.

"You once told me they could infiltrate someone's life and that person would never even know until it was too late," I slowly said, piecing things together. I thought back on some of his hesitant answers when I'd asked his opinion about the Cyfrin finding me and the change in his demeanor when we talked about why he hadn't told me about my history sooner. Everything clicked together all at once, and I let out a faint gasp as I stared at him accusingly. "You're it. *You're* the person they sent to infiltrate my life . . . the person already watching."

As soon as I said it, he looked away, and I knew it was the truth.

"You came here to help the Cyfrin get me."

"I'm afraid I did."

"So it was all a lie then?" I asked harshly, feeling exposed. "Everything that happened between us? Our friendship? Your love for Felicity?"

"No!" he exclaimed, sounding genuinely shocked. *"Everything* we went through was real. I've *always* hated the Cyfrin, but I had nowhere to go where they couldn't find me, so I stayed. When they sent me here, I was already torn about what to do, but the second Felicity approached me, everything changed. I wanted a normal life and to just be a kid in high school. I wanted friendship and acceptance.

"I knew I couldn't hide it from you forever, but I didn't know how to tell you. I knew it would mean losing you and possibly everything else I'd gained since coming here. So, instead, I did what I could to prepare you for what I knew was coming. The training, the lectures, all of it was to keep you safe because I care about you!" He gripped my hands tightly. "Our friendship was *never* a lie, Robin. I swear! You're important to me. You're *all* important to me; you have to believe that."

Seeing him so openly emotional, so raw, gave me very little room to doubt his sincerity. His eyes glistened with unshed tears, and it pulled at my heart. I wanted to tell him it was okay, that we were okay, but I couldn't. The hot fire of betrayal burned too high for me to show him any compassion.

"Why did you say what happened to my mom and Dawn was your fault?" I set my jaw, ignoring his pleas.

He sighed heavily and shook his head, looking down. "Remember when I disappeared for a couple days?" he asked, and I nodded. "I went back to the Cyfrin's compound to tell them I wanted out. I told them I wasn't going to bring you in and that I'd stand next to you against them if they attempted to come for you."

I was startled by this revelation, my feelings even more divided.

"They told me I would regret defying them," he continued, "and if I cared about you so much, I better watch you closely because they were going to destroy your life." He sniffled and set his jaw, his eyes blazing. "I thought they were still talking about trying to abduct you, but I was wrong. They went after your family instead."

I looked up and blinked rapidly to ward off tears. I wanted to scream. I wanted to hit him. I wanted to use my powers against him so he would hurt the way I did. But I couldn't bring myself to do it. Despite some of his dishonesty, I knew he'd just been trying to protect me, and I believed he didn't know what the Cyfrin were planning. I could see the truth in his bloodshot eyes.

In that moment—as I remembered Adriana's words—I made the almost impossible decision to not blame him for the horrible consequences of his actions. I reminded myself who was truly to blame, and that Matthew had never personally harmed me or treated me badly. Our friendship might've been built on a lie, but I could tell his feelings were genuine.

I knew our friendship meant something to him, as did the chance for him to have a normal life. He'd been terrified of losing us—of losing the one good and safe place he had. Could I really fault him for that? The only thing he was truly responsible for was lying . . . but that was bad enough.

My chin quivered as I stood to walk away from him, but he quickly followed and grabbed my arm to stop me.

"Robin, please. I'm *so* sorry," he told me fervently, his eyebrows pinched together. "You have to believe me."

"I do believe you," I said hoarsely. "I believe you meant everything you just said, but that doesn't change the fact that you lied—that you've been lying this whole time. Not just to me but to Ben and Felicity too! You came here to help *abduct* me for crying out loud. I don't know if that's something we can get past. How do you expect me to ever trust you again? How do you expect me to feel *safe* with you?"

"I don't know," he mumbled. We stood in silence, staring at one another. "Is this it then? Did I lose you?"

I rubbed my lips together and lifted my shoulders slightly. "I don't know."

"I'm sorry," he whispered again.

"I know you are." I looked away, not wanting to see the hurt in his eyes any longer. "But I need some time." He didn't try to stop me as I walked away. After a few steps, though, I stopped, let out a slow breath, then softly said, "Their deaths weren't your fault. Don't blame yourself."

I could hear his knees hit the ground, but I didn't look back. He needed to find a way to forgive himself, and so did I.

# CHAPTER TWENTY-EIGHT

The following week, I finally found the confidence to go back to school. I ignored the whispers and stares as best as I could, but sometimes they got the best of me. Some people were brave enough to come up to me and convey their sympathy, but most kept their distance, treating me like an exhibit.

"It'll get better," Ben said as he escorted me to class.

I leaned into him, grateful for the unending support he'd been giving me. "I know. I just wish it was over already."

"Until it is, Felicity or I will be with you at all times, as long as you need."

"Thank you," I told him as sincerely as I could manage. He leaned down and gave me a kiss. I hesitated for a moment then voiced the thought that had been on my mind. "How's Matthew?"

"He's . . . okay," Ben answered slowly.

Matthew had gone to Ben then Felicity after talking with me, admitting his truth and asking forgiveness. We all wanted him to be a part of our lives, but we each had to come to terms with how to do that after his deceitfulness. Unsurprisingly, Ben offered him grace the moment he apologized. Felicity, on the other hand, punched him in the face and made him wait a couple days before she accepted his apology. I was the only one who hadn't spoken with him again, but no one was pressuring me to. They knew I needed to do it in my own time and in my own way.

"Is Felicity with him now?" I asked since I hadn't seen either of them in class.

"I think so," Ben answered. "She called me this morning and told me they'd be late, but she didn't say why."

I looked down at my watch. "It's almost fourth period. They're a little more than late."

He shrugged. "Your guess is as good as mine."

We stopped in front of the door to my government class, and he dropped me off like a kid on the first day of school. I walked in and sat down, watching the door.

"It's good to see you, Ms. Hayes," Mrs. Helena told me, patting my shoulder as she walked by.

I offered her a weak smile then turned my gaze back to the door as she called the class to order. I tried to listen as she started the lesson, but I couldn't stay focused. I kept glancing at the door, waiting for Matthew to walk in, but he never did. The hour passed without him showing up, and I was a little disappointed.

Ben met me by my locker after class, and we walked to the lunchroom. After grabbing our food, we found seats outside to enjoy the fresh air. About halfway through, I saw Felicity's car pull into the parking lot.

"Well, look who finally decided to show up," I said, pointing her out to Ben, and we watched as she made her way to us. When she got closer, I noticed her cheeks were rosy and her eye makeup was slightly smeared.

"He's gone," she said when she reached us, sitting down and putting her head in her hands as she sobbed.

Ben and I shot each other a confused look then rushed to comfort her.

"Who's gone?" I asked, though I already knew.

"Matthew. He left," she answered, wiping her tear-covered cheeks.

"Why? Where did he go?" Ben questioned, rubbing his hand along her back. I offered her a napkin, and she took it gratefully, blowing her nose.

"I don't know where he went. He said he didn't want to keep putting Robin in a position where she'd have to be around him if she didn't want to be," she explained. "He didn't want to put her through any more than he already had."

Guilt flushed through my system. I didn't want him to leave.

"Is he coming back?" I asked softly, and she shook her head.

"He-he said he was going t-to make things right," she stammered.

I looked up at Ben and exhaled sharply. "He went back to the Cyfrin. He's going to try to stop them."

Felicity snapped her head up with wide eyes. "He'll get killed!"

I didn't have any comforting words to say to her because she was right. If they caught him, I was sure they wouldn't welcome him back with open arms.

"What do we do?" Felicity asked desperately. "We have to do something!"

"I'm afraid there's nothing we *can* do," I told her, hating that fact. We might not have been on good terms, but I still cared about him. He was family. "I don't know where the

Cyfrin's compound is. Even if I did, I couldn't just walk in and demand him back."

"What about Adriana?" Ben asked, and I bit my lip with a nod.

"Next time she gets through to me, I'll ask her. Maybe there's something they can do for him."

My words seemed to bring hope to Felicity, and I prayed I was right.

"He'll be okay," Ben assured her, and she nodded eagerly as I shot him a look.

I could tell he knew Adriana was a long shot, but he wanted to make Felicity feel better. I voiced profanities in my head, wishing Matthew could hear them. He thought he was making amends, but he didn't realize the new problems he had created. Felicity couldn't handle losing him, and, honestly, neither could I.

* * *

Adriana promised to do all that she could, so we clung to the hope of seeing Matthew again. Unfortunately, I knew she might not be able to do much. I kept Felicity distracted by helping her with the last-minute prom planning that needed to be done. It wasn't something I would typically enjoy, but it kept me distracted too and that was something I needed.

"I can't believe it's prom day!" Felicity squealed as we pigged out on the breakfast her cook prepared.

I'd stayed the night with her, so we were rocking fuzzy pajamas and bedhead while the TV played softly in the background.

"It's gonna be great," I said around a mouthful of toast. "You put a lot of work into it."

"I know." She sighed dreamily. "It's been my baby, and now it's all grown up."

"You're so weird."

"Nevertheless, you love me," she replied with a sly smirk, and I snorted.

She threw a pillow at me, accidentally hitting the plate of food off the bed, and I gasped in surprise then started laughing. She joined in, both of us cackling like maniacs. When we finally got our bearings, she bit her lip and looked away, but not before I saw her demeanor change.

"What's wrong?" I asked.

"Nothing. It's just . . . That's the first time I've heard you laugh since . . ." She trailed off.

"Since my mom and Dawn died," I finished for her, and she nodded, looking guilty for bringing it up. "It's okay. You can say it."

She continued without repeating my words. "It's just nice to see you happy again."

"It's nice to *feel* happy again," I admitted quietly. The sadness was always there but not as prominently as before. It was a slow process, but I was learning how to live my life without them in it.

I cleared my throat then asked, "Did you ever get another date?"

"No. Some people asked, but I just couldn't say yes."

"I'm sorry."

"It's okay." She looked down at her plate and sighed. "I miss him."

"I know. I do too."

"I just wish we knew if he was okay," she said, her voice wavering.

"He's smart. And skilled. I'm sure he's fine."

"Do you think we'll ever see him again?"

"I hope so."

"Me too," she murmured. She suddenly jumped up with a forced smile on her face. "Anyway, what time do you want to start getting ready? I need plenty of time to get us both prom worthy."

"I was going to go visit my mom and Dawn for a little while, but I'll come back right after, then I'm all yours."

"Perfect!" she exclaimed gleefully.

As soon as we finished eating, I got dressed and headed to the cemetery, stopping by a shop to pick up fresh flowers on the way. When I got there, I arranged the flowers in the ceramic vase that was set into the ground between their headstones.

"Hi, guys," I said, kneeling in front of them. I wrung my hands and bit my lip. "I miss you both so much. And Matthew. We still haven't heard from him, and I'm really scared something bad happened to him. I feel so useless. I wish I could tell him to come home and that he doesn't have to make anything right for me. I don't know what I'll do if he dies because of me . . . I could really use some of your comforting advice right about now, Mom. Or even just a hug from you, Dawn. You always could melt away all my problems."

I smiled softly and sniffled. "So, anyway, prom is tonight. I'm pretty excited about it, but I wish you two were here to see me off. Lizzie's doing a good job with me though. She's been giving me dance lessons all week, so hopefully I won't step on Ben's feet too much. Oh, and I've decided not to wear the pearls, Mom. I know we agreed on it but . . . I can't take off our necklaces. They're the only thing I have to keep you both close to me. I hope you're not mad."

The wind rustled the grass around me, and I breathed in the fresh air, letting the breeze dry off my cheeks. I knew cemeteries got a bad rep for being spooky, but I found a calming ambiance here. Maybe it was because I sensed my family was near. Whatever the reason, I enjoyed the peace that settled over me while I visited. I talked to them for a while longer then headed back to Felicity's.

"How was your trip?" Annie asked me when I walked through the front door.

"Calming," I answered with a smile, and she gave me a tight hug as Felicity raced down the stairs.

"Ben and his family are coming over an hour before the promenade for pictures, so we have to get started. Are you ready to be pampered?" she asked.

"As ready as I'll ever be."

She pulled at my arm and rushed me upstairs with her, setting me down in front of her vanity. "Let's do this," she said, hitting play on the remote for her radio.

Two hours later, I was primped and prettied with golden-brown eyeshadow and crimson lips. The top layer of my hair was pulled back in an artistic messy bun while the rest flowed down my back in tamed waves. I lounged on Felicity's bed as she worked on herself, which was a much faster process since her hair was so fine and short. She quickly teased it into a bump and flared up the ends before coating her face with a light blush and applying peach lipstick and green and gold eyeshadow.

"You look stunning," I told her, appraising the work she'd done.

"Just wait until that dress gets on," she replied with a wink, as humble as ever.

We helped each other into our dresses, and I admired mine in her floor-length mirror. It was a lovely turquoise color with flowy tulle at the bottom and a navy lace appliqué on top of the illusion neckline. It was alluring and sensual, reminding me of the mystery of the sea.

I looked over at Felicity and let out a low whistle of approval. She was a knockout in a trumpet-style, olive-green dress that was completely covered in sequence. It had a one-shouldered full sleeve and a small cutout in the middle of her chest, showing off the top of her cleavage.

"You look hot," I said.

"And you look gorgeous," she replied with a smile.

"Robin, Felicity!" Annie called up to us. "Ben's here."

"You ready?" Felicity asked, grabbing her clutch.

"I'm actually a little nervous," I admitted as my stomach flip-flopped.

"Don't be. You look great. Ben is going to love it. I'll go down first, then you can follow so we both get a dramatic reveal."

"Just what I've always wanted!" I exclaimed, clasping my hands together and batting my eyelashes.

"Ha. Ha," she said dryly, nudging my shoulder as she shuffled out of her room.

I heard oohs and aahs as she walked down the stairs and could only imagine how stunning she looked gliding down them.

*I should've gone first.*

"Robin, you coming?" I heard Felicity ask.

I took a deep breath then headed down, taking one step at a time so I wouldn't trip in the low heels. As I rounded the curve, I saw the foyer lined with all the members of both the Toves and Larson family, as well as Lizzie. They stared at me in awe, and I blushed as my eyes darted to Ben, who was standing at the end of the stairs. His radiating smile lit up his face and his eyes sparkled. When I reached the bottom of the stairs, he held his hand out for me, and I took it graciously.

"You look absolutely beautiful," he told me quietly, slipping a corsage onto my wrist.

"And you look completely dashing," I replied with a smile as I took in his black suit with its turquoise tie and vest that matched my dress. His hair framed his face nicely, highlighting his cheekbones.

"Okay, picture time!" Lizzie declared, holding out her camera.

We spent the next twenty minutes doing every combination that was requested of us: Felicity with her family, Lizzie and I, Ben and I with his parents, the three of us, and so many more that I lost count.

Afterwards, I fought back tears when I remembered I'd never share these special moments with my mom and sister again. But I quickly shook off the thought, knowing they wouldn't want me to be sad tonight.

We were sent off with well wishes to have fun and be safe while everyone else stuck around for dinner. Ben helped us both into his car, carefully tucking in the bottoms of our dresses so they wouldn't get caught in the door, before getting in himself.

"You guys ready for the best night of our lives?" he asked with a grin as he started the engine.

"Let's do this thing," Felicity said, her determined look making me laugh.

Despite all the things that'd gone wrong, this was still going to be a good night.

# CHAPTER TWENTY-NINE

The walls of the banquet hall were lined with moss, flowers, and fairy lights. Green tulle spread across the ceiling in large arches with a chandelier planted in the very center, sparkling beautifully in the dim room.

"Wow," I said breathlessly as I walked through the woodsy arches at the front door. To the left, a makeshift pergola sat with a swing positioned beside it. A dark, moon-lit night backdrop hung behind them to create a picture-perfect spot. The dinner tables were on the right, decorated with flickering lanterns and flower arrangements.

"You guys definitely got the garden theme right," Ben told Felicity as he admired the setup.

"Everything looks amazing," I added.

"Thanks," she replied, taking in her handywork with bright eyes. "I'll be back."

She strutted away, the lights dancing off her sequenced dress, so Ben and I walked over to a table.

"You really do look gorgeous," he murmured in my ear, sending shivers up my spine.

"Thank you," I replied as he pulled a chair out for me. After getting settled, my eyes flickered around the room, landing from one person to the next.

"I'm sorry he's not here," Ben said, and I looked back at him with raised brows.

"What? Who?"

"Matthew. You were looking for him, weren't you?"

I frowned, realizing he was right. "I guess I was. I don't know why though. I know he's not here."

"Because you wish he was."

I nodded as I played with the bottom of my dress. "Yeah, I do." I hesitated then asked, "Does that bother you?"

"Of course not," he replied, placing his hand on my leg. "I know you guys are just friends, and I know you need some stability in your life right now. You've lost enough people already. You don't want him gone for good too."

"No. I really don't. I miss him."

"I know. And you miss having someone here who understands what you're going through."

"That too," I admitted with a small shrug. "I feel like a freak knowing there's no one around like me."

"You're not a freak," Ben said sternly.

"Close enough."

"You have *superpowers*. That doesn't make you a freak. It makes you a superhero!"

A snort escaped me. "Yeah, okay."

"I'm dating a super hot superhero!" he called out, causing heads to turn.

I giggled as I pressed my hand over his mouth. When he pulled away, he was smiling softly.

"There's that laugh I love so much," he said. "I've missed it."

"Felicity said the same thing."

"Because it's true. It's nice to see you happy again."

I averted my eyes as guilt tried to consume me. As much as I still missed my mom and Dawn, I was finding myself enjoying life again. Without even realizing it, I was healing, and that was okay. They would want me to.

I glanced around the room and, when I was sure no one was watching, I collected the smallest amount of water from around me and flung it towards Ben. It hit him in the face, and he jerked back in surprise, his eyes wide.

"How dare you," he said, pulling me towards him. He held my head to his chest, and I squirmed around as I tried to push myself away.

"My hair!" I cried out, still trying to shove him away as he laughed.

Finally, he let me go, and I let out a playful huff as he grinned. He cupped my face in his hands and brought his lips to mine. I inhaled his sweet scent, enjoying the way his lips tasted, then his teeth grazed my bottom lip and I sighed contentedly.

"Alright, alright. That's enough," Felicity grumbled.

Ben and I pulled apart as my face flushed red. "Sorry," I said with a guilty smile as she plopped down beside me.

The announcer called for everyone to take a seat so the waiters could bring out our meals. Ali, Jordan, and their dates chose seats across from us, while Amara and Juan ended up next to us. A local band played softly in the background as we ate and chatted merrily. Soon enough we were hustled outside to enjoy some games while the tables were put away, clearing room for the dance floor. A DJ invited us back in with classic songs that no one could resist dancing to.

"This has been so great!" I exclaimed as Ben and I took advantage of the photobooth.

"I'm glad you're having fun," he replied.

"I am too."

"And I'm *really* glad that in ten years I'll be able to tell people I went to junior *and* senior prom with my childhood crush."

"Bold of you to think I'm going to prom with you next year," I said, cocking one brow.

"How could you resist?" he asked, motioning towards himself. "Just look at me."

I laughed as he nudged me with his shoulder, then I stopped and stared straight ahead with wide eyes as I broke out in a cold sweat. I shivered as a chill ran up my spine. It was an all too familiar feeling, and I whipped my head around excitedly.

"Are you okay?" Ben asked.

"Matthew's here," I replied, still looking around to find him.

*He's alive.*

"How do you know that?"

"The pull of the powers," I said with a wide smile.

"The *what?*" he asked incredulously.

"It's hard to explain, but I can sense him. Come on, we have to go tell Felicity and find him."

We ran back into the banquet hall and looked around, frantically trying to spot Felicity. Ben put his hand on my arm and pointed. My heart fluttered when I saw what he did—Felicity and Matthew in a deep embrace. I smiled up at Ben and he returned it before wrapping his arm around me and pulling me close as we watched them.

"He's alive," I murmured out loud, relief filling me.

"Let's go say hi," Ben said, and we walked into the middle of the dance floor to join their reunion.

"Matthew," I said.

He turned around, and I was shocked to see his face covered with aged bruises and still-healing cuts.

"It's good to see you, man," Ben told him, shaking his hand and patting him on the back in typical male fashion. "We missed you."

"I missed you all as well," he said, returning the back pat. Then he hesitantly turned his gaze towards me and licked his lips. "Robin I—"

"Oh, come here you," I cut him off, wrapping my arms around him. He clung onto me tightly, and I could feel his tension melt away.

When he finally drew back, his eyes were glassy with unshed tears. "I'm so sorry," he said.

"Hey, this is no time for apologies," Felicity said, gluing herself to his side. "This is a celebration!"

"Actually, it's not," Matthew replied.

"What do you mean?" Ben asked, his voice layered in worry.

"I failed," he answered, gritting his teeth. "I wasn't able to stop the Cyfrin. I tried. So hard. But I'm no match for them. Not even close."

"Hey, don't beat yourself up over it," Felicity told him.

"Yeah, someone else already did it for you," Ben teased, drawing a minuscule smile from him.

"You're only one person," I added in. "None of us expected you to stop them. So let's just be happy you're back safe and enjoy the party."

"I'm afraid we can't do that," Matthew said grimly. "The Cyfrin are coming."

"Well, yeah. We've known that for a while now," Felicity said.

"No, they're coming *now*," Matthew responded, and fear paralyzed my body.

"Now? Now as in *now* now?" Ben asked, looking around as if he'd see a threat.

"Now as in any time in the next couple days," he answered. "I was able to get away from them right before they were set to travel here." He looked at me, his eyes tight. "We're out of time."

"You two have to go to Garridan then," Ben said urgently. "Now."

"I-I don't know," I stuttered, putting my hand on my forehead. I wasn't ready for this.

Ben grasped the top of my arms gently and stared at me with a no-nonsense look. "You don't have another option anymore. If you stay here, they'll take you."

"He's right," Felicity finally chimed in quietly, her voice cracking. Matthew pulled her to him, and I felt lightheaded. "You aren't safe here anymore. Neither is Matthew."

I pressed my lips together and closed my eyes, trying to think, but every road led to the same answer. There really was no other way. This was it. We couldn't very well fight them and win, which meant Garridan was the only place I'd be safe.

I looked from Matthew to Felicity to Ben and my heart skipped a beat. Adriana had said she and Elijah would try to get the other Keepers of Balance to allow me to come back to Milton after the summer, but there was no guarantee since they had such strict laws. But now, staring into their faces, I knew I could never come back. Not for good, at least.

The Cyfrin wouldn't stop hunting me. They'd know when I was away from Garridan's protection. They'd come back, over and over. And each time, everyone I loved would be in danger. I couldn't allow that. I had to keep them safe. No one else could die because of me.

"Okay," I finally said. "Okay. You're right."

"Okay, then let's go," Ben urged, pulling at my hand.

"No. Not tonight," I replied. "We can leave first thing tomorrow morning."

"Robin—"

"No! They've already taken enough away from me. I'm not letting them ruin my perfect prom too. I want to enjoy this last night with all of us together, so that's what we're going to do. We'll go tomorrow morning."

The three of them glanced at one another unhappily, but they all finally agreed with different levels of enthusiasm. A slow song began playing, and I turned towards Ben.

"Now ask me to dance," I demanded, holding out my hand to him.

"Yes ma'am," he replied softly. He smiled sadly but grasped it and pulled me to him as his other hand sat against the small of my back. I wrapped my free arm around his neck, and he held onto me tightly, savoring the moment just like I was.

"I'm going to miss you," I whispered, resting my head on his chest.

"I'm going to miss you too," he murmured, leaning his chin against my head. "But I'd rather you be safe than selfishly keep you with me."

"I don't know when I'll see you again." *If ever.*

"After summer," he replied, but he didn't know I'd already decided that wasn't going to happen. He didn't know this was one of our last moments together.

I nodded half-heartedly then dropped the subject so I could enjoy my time with him. We spent the next hour dancing and laughing the night away with all of our friends, who were oblivious to the lingering threat. Matthew and I strayed to a back corner to drink some punch as Ben and Felicity continued to boogie on the dance floor.

"They have never-ending energy," I said, shaking my head as I watched them.

"That they do," Matthew replied with a grin.

I leaned against the back of my chair and let out a groan. "My feet are killing me."

"I bet. Those heels look like death traps."

"Imagine how Felicity feels," I replied, staring at her stilettos.

"I don't know how she does it," he said, watching her with adoration. "She's amazing."

"She is," I agreed with a smile, then I looked at him, observing his cuts and bruises again.

He must've sensed it because he glanced at me and shifted uncomfortably. "What?" he asked.

"Nothing. I just—" I stopped and bit my lip. "What happened over there?"

His eyes grew wary. "You don't want to know."

"I do though. You went back there because of me and got hurt."

"This was not because of you," he replied sharply. "Everything that happened was my own fault. I needed to right my wrong, even if it meant dying."

"Dying?" I basically yelled, and he shushed me. Quieter, I asked, "What do you mean dying?"

He shrugged. "The Cyfrin is very unforgiving."

I swallowed down the bile that rose in my throat. "You were willing to die for me?"

"I was willing to die to fix my mistakes. I've made a lot that I can't make up for, but this was one I could."

"I don't like that," I murmured, rustling my tulle with my foot.

"I know. It's why I didn't tell any of you what I was doing. You would've tried to stop me."

"Of course we would've! We love you, Matthew."

The corner of his lip turned up. "I love you guys too." He let out a shaky chuckle as he ran his hand along the back of his neck.

"Does that embarrass you?" I asked as my brows raised into my hairline.

"A little bit, yeah," he replied, his cheeks the faintest shade of pink.

"Well, get used to it. Think of all the emotions you'll be on the receiving end of when we get to Garridan."

His eyes widened slightly. "Crap. I didn't think of that." I laughed loudly as he suddenly turned into a nervous nelly. "Do you think my family will, you know . . . Want to hug me and stuff?"

I snorted. "I'd say there's a good chance, yeah."

"What if they don't like me? What if they hate the monster the Cyfrin created?"

My amusement washed away as I stared at him. He was actually scared. I placed my hand on his arm and waited until he looked at me to talk.

"You're not a monster, and they're going to love you," I said. "Adriana said they've basically been killing themselves trying to get things ready because they want everything to be perfect. They feel so guilty for the life you were forced to live, and they don't blame you for anything you did under the Cyfrin's leadership."

"They can't say that and mean it until they know what all I've done," he replied, hanging his head.

"That's not true. I don't know everything you did, but I don't care. It doesn't change who you are to me, and I truly mean that. So do they."

"What about everyone else in Garridan?" he asked. "I don't think they'll be as accepting."

"No, maybe not, but who cares?"

"I hate to admit it, but I kinda do." He sighed. "I'm just ready for an easy life, I guess. One without any judgement or expectations. If the council hates me, they could make my life there miserable."

"Well, I won't let them."

"I don't think you exactly have any pull with them to sway their decisions."

"No, but Adriana and Elijah do," I pointed out. "And I know they'll do whatever they can to help your transition there go smoothly. Not just because of me, but because they're close friends with your parents and they want to help them too."

"What are the odds of that?" he asked with a shake of his head. "Our parents being friends."

"Stranger things have happened."

"That they have." His eyes trailed Felicity as she and Ben hopelessly tried to two step. "Are you scared? Of going there and leaving this all behind?"

I swallowed, slowly nodding, then quietly said, "Yeah. I am."

"Are you going to come back?"

I rubbed my lips together, then shook my head. "No."

"I didn't think so."

"How could I? The Cyfrin would just come after me again, right?"

"I'm afraid so."

I watched Ben dip Felicity, nearly dropping her, and they both laughed. Amara and Juan joined in, then Ben pulled Amara into his arms, playfully rustling her hair as she protested. He met my eyes with a wide smile on his face, and I tried to return it. When he looked away, my smile disappeared as my throat contracted.

"I can't be the reason they get hurt," I whispered. "And as long as I'm around, it puts them in danger. So I have to go, and I have to stay gone."

It was Matthew's turn to place his hand on my arm. "I'm sorry I helped put you in this situation," he said.

"I'm not."

"What?" he asked, taken aback as his hand fell to his side.

"The Cyfrin would've come after me whether they sent you first or not," I explained. "But by them sending you, I had someone here who could help me." His brows furrowed as a small smile rose to my face. "You showed me I wasn't crazy. You told me the truth about myself and taught me how to use my powers to protect myself. Without you,

I'd still be oblivious. I'd think I was going insane, and I'd have zero protection against the Cyfrin. So, really, you coming here did nothing but help me."

The hard lines on his face disappeared, his eyes lighting up at my words. "You really think that?"

"I do. I'm glad the Cyfrin sent you." I grabbed his hand. "Little did they know they were sending me a guardian angel."

He snorted. "That's a bit extreme."

I grinned and said, "Maybe so. But they definitely sent me a best friend. Can we agree on that much?"

"I have no objections to that," he replied.

"See, you're already getting better at this ooey gooey mushy stuff, as you call it. You'll have no problem when we get to Garridan."

"We'll see," he grumbled, and I laughed.

I leaned onto the back of the chair and raised my arms to stretch, taking a deep breath in the process. My nose stung as the smell of smoke filled it. I cleared my throat as I looked around.

"Do you smell that?" I asked.

Matthew sniffed and his eyes surveyed the room. "Smoke?"

"But where's it coming from?"

I noticed others starting to lift their noses up, their eyes flickering around like ours were. The smell was getting stronger, and a faint haze appeared. That's when I saw bright orange flames licking at the cracks in the closed entryway doors.

"Fire!" someone yelled, and widespread panic instantly broke out. Screams echoed as the students of Milton High ran around frantically.

"Everybody, calm down!" a chaperone called out, raising his arms to be seen. "File quickly but carefully towards the emergency exit!"

The closest student pushed the door open, setting off an alarm that blared incessantly, then pulled away with a shout as flames rushed towards him through the opening. More screams sounded around me as the walls rapidly caught fire, the decorations fueling it. The dark gray smoke was thick now, and people started coughing as it filled the room.

"What happened to the sprinkler systems?" I asked in horror as they remained inactive.

The crowd of students clumped together, everyone trying their best to stay away from the heat. People clung to the chaperones, but it was useless—they were as trapped as we were. Felicity and Ben pushed their way towards us, fear written across their faces.

"What do we do?" Felicity cried out.

Matthew put his hands on my shoulders, his gaze intense as he got my attention. "You have to use your powers."

"But there's no water!" Felicity exclaimed, tears pooling in her frantic eyes.

Matthew ignored her as he stared at me. "You know what you have to do."

I bit my lip but nodded earnestly. "Yes."

"Draw it from the moisture that's here while there's still some to use. Then aim it at the base of the flames at the door and keep it there for as long as you can."

"Okay."

The smoke was heavy now, and I could barely see more than a few feet in front of me. I closed my eyes, blocking out the terrified yelling, and tried to sense the moisture in the air. There wasn't much but it was all I needed. I let the coolness wash over my body as I drew in all I could. When I had enough, I pushed the energy from my toes to my fingers and water spurted forth. I directed it towards the emergency exit, dousing the flames in that one spot and trying to keep more from encroaching.

"Go!" I yelled, my lips turned down as I struggled to concentrate. "Get everyone out!"

"We aren't leaving you!" Ben exclaimed, coughing.

"I'll be right behind you. But you have to go! Now!"

The three of them took off, directing people towards the only way out. The crowd shuffled forward in a herd, desperate to be free of the inferno. I stayed focused on pulling more moisture from around me, but the heat was licking it up, stealing from me. I tried to find more, but it was gone. My cascade of water fizzled out, and the fire reappeared along the doorframe, re-trapping me and a handful of unlucky people who hadn't made it out in time.

I scanned their faces, relieved when I didn't see Ben, Felicity, or Matthew among them. They all made it out safely.

The fire raged along the ceiling now, weakening the structure more with every moment that passed. My eyes and throat burned as I coughed viciously into my arm, my lungs desperate for fresh air. Hearing a loud cracking noise, I looked up just in time to see the chandelier come crashing into the ground. I blocked my face as glass splintered, flying up and cutting into my arms.

Sobs of terror and cries for help filled my ears. I joined in, just as frightened as everyone else. A portion of the roof began to cave in, and I jumped to the side, but a fiery piece of rubble managed to strike me. I let out a howl of pain as my arm burned from the impact. The tulle on my dress ignited, and I screamed again, hopelessly trying to fight it off.

Someone beat at the flames with their tuxedo jacket, quickly extinguishing them. I looked up and saw Zack standing there with tears streaking his soot-covered face. He offered me his hand then helped me up, supporting my weight.

"We're gonna make it through this!" he yelled over the roaring of the fire.

I nodded briskly just as the sound of sirens made their way to my ears. "The fire department!" I cried out, relief coursing through me.

"We just gotta survive a couple more minutes," he said, more to himself than to me. "Come on."

He gathered up the others who were still in the building, and we huddled together, anxiously watching as water started falling from the sky.

"They're here!" someone exclaimed.

With all the energy I could gather, I inconspicuously directed the water around us for safety then towards the worst parts of the blaze. I struggled to keep my eyes open as the effort drained me. What seemed like an eternity later, the fire was controlled enough for firefighters to come in and rescue us.

Finally emerging outside, I gratefully breathed in the fresh air, then coughed miserably as my nose and throat stung from the motion. My head throbbed and my lungs were uncomfortably tight as I was led to the back of an ambulance and fitted with an oxygen mask.

A police barricade had been formed just beyond the parking lot, and many people watched anxiously from behind it, their formal wear looking like it'd seen better days. I skimmed over the crowd before spotting who I was looking for. Their faces were smudged with soot and their eyes red, but other than that they looked unscathed. I offered them a weak wave, and Ben fell to his knees, his hand flying over his chest.

"Can my friends come over here?" I croaked to the paramedic.

"I'm afraid not, hon," she said. "We're just putting temporary relief on your burns then taking you straight to the hospital."

"How's everyone else?" I asked.

"Burns of varying degrees and lots of smoke inhalation, but it looks like everyone is going to be okay," she answered with a comforting smile. "You all got very lucky."

"Good." I sighed, then started coughing again.

"Okay, let's load her up," the paramedic announced to her partner.

They helped me into the ambulance and laid me down on the gurney, despite my protests. The lady closed the doors, staying in the back with me, and thumped the wall behind the front seat in an indication that they should get going.

"Just relax," she instructed.

I took her suggestion and closed my eyes, focusing on my breathing and wishing for relief from the scratchy burn.

*I could really go for someone with a healing power right about now.*

The movement of the ambulance was peaceful in a way, and I yawned as it began lulling me to sleep. Not long after, the tranquil moment was abruptly interrupted as the ambulance came to a screeching stop.

"What's going on, Tim?" the paramedic asked the driver through the small window, rubbing her head where it had banged against the wall. "Tim?"

The doors in the back ripped open, banging against the metal frame, and the paramedic was suddenly gone, pulled through the opening by some unseen force. My breath caught in my throat as my heart pounded, and warnings screamed in my head. I searched the dark with wide eyes that were still blurry from the smoke. Two shapes materialized in the distance, and I squinted, trying to see them better. As they came closer, I realized the shapes were actually people.

"Hello?" I called out, my voice shaky, hoping it was the paramedics but somehow knowing it wasn't.

"Hello," a woman's voice replied.

An invisible vise-like grip latched onto my throat, yanking me from the ambulance and suspending me in the air. I scratched at it in a desperate attempt to get free as it blocked my airway. An unusual gurgling sound erupted from my mouth as I choked.

"Put her down, Serafina," a man commanded as they both stepped into view.

The black-haired woman looked sickly with her pale skin and sharp features. She pouted her thin, red-stained lips then sighed and waved her hand to release me from whatever force that held me aloft. I fell to the ground and coughed viciously, sucking in as much air as I could despite how it burned my lungs.

"Who are you?" I asked as I struggled to my feet. "Darth Vader?"

"Serafina," she corrected with a glare.

Clearly, she didn't understand the art of sarcasm. The man walked in front of her, looking me over. He had a dark, round face with a large nose and skinny brows that sat high up on his bald head. Unlike the woman, he didn't look menacing. He actually looked inviting.

"Are you Robin Hayes? Daughter of Elijah and Adriana Caldwell?" he asked politely.

I gave him a look and turned my nose up defiantly. "Who's asking?"

"My apologies. I'm Darnell, and, as she said, this is Serafina." He motioned towards the lady. "We're members of the Cyfrin. We're here to take you back with us."

All the air rushed out of my lungs as my worst fears became reality. I'd already figured as much, but having it confirmed terrified me. I'd been worried about this very moment for months and wasn't as prepared for it as I'd hoped to be.

"I'm not going anywhere with you," I said, begging my voice to hold steady.

"I'm afraid you don't have a choice," he replied.

"Like hell I don't!" I pulled moisture from the air and launched it at them.

Serafina easily redirected it with a flick of her wrist and, in that moment, my confidence was shattered. It was one thing to train with Matthew but an entirely different matter to go up against someone who could just dismiss anything I threw their way. I stood no chance.

"Don't worry, I got you," Darnell said softly, waving his hand over me.

My eyes grew heavy and, as hard as I tried, I couldn't keep them open. Within seconds, I was surrounded by a wave of darkness as sleep overcame me.

# CHAPTER THIRTY

I groaned lightly, struggling to open my eyes. My head felt groggy, and a metallic taste lingered on my tongue. I searched around me blindly as my eyes adjusted to the recessed lighting in the small room. When I could finally see, I realized I was lying on a twin bed with gray sheets and one lonely pillow. A toilet and sink were on the opposite wall, and a door stood near the foot of the bed. There were no windows, and the only light flickered above me.

I stood up slowly, fighting off the nausea that came with the movement, and noticed the burn and cuts on my arm were completely gone, as was the pain in my chest. I saw fresh clothing folded at the end of the bed and picked it up. My prom dress was scorched and torn, its beautiful turquoise color barely recognizable. It gave off a strong odor of smoke, so I decided to change out of it. I didn't want it to trip me up if I needed to fight.

I pulled on the black T-shirt and grey pants that had been left for me. They didn't fit perfectly but would do for now. I walked over to the sink and splashed cold water on my face to get rid of the fuzziness in my head then ventured to the door. I tried turning the knob, but it was locked.

"Hello," I called out, slapping the door with my hand. "Is anybody out there?"

The only reply I received was the echo of my hand hitting the door, and I sighed. My heart felt heavy, knowing I was in the Cyfrin compound.

*How long have I been here? Has anyone realized I'm missing yet?*

I sat on the bed, feeling deflated. The only person who knew how to get here was Matthew, but there was nothing he could do on his own. My only hope was that Adriana would visit me so I could tell her where I was.

As the minutes passed and turned to hours, I kept myself busy by playing with the water from the sink, not sure when or if I would be getting out of this room. I was toying with the tulle on my ruined dress when I heard a loud click. I jumped to my feet, instantly on the defensive, as the doorknob turned.

"Hello again," Darnell said when the door opened. He placed a plate of food on the bed, and my mouth watered at the sight of it as my stomach rumbled. "Go ahead."

I shook my head. "No."

"Come on, you have to be hungry."

"How do I know it's not poisoned?" I asked, seriously concerned.

He smiled in amusement then grabbed a piece of food and stuck it in his mouth. "See. It's perfectly safe. And delicious."

I eyed it for a moment longer then dug in, inhaling it to satisfy my hunger. When I'd finished every last crumb, Darnell picked up the plate and headed for the door.

"Wait!" I cried out, not wanting to be locked in here again.

He glanced back at me and motioned me forward. "Come on. You're coming with me."

He walked through the door, leaving it wide open. I hesitated for a moment then slowly followed him into a narrow hallway. We passed by four doors, which I assumed led to rooms similar to mine, before coming into a large kitchen.

Darnell put the plate on a counter and continued walking. It actually seemed fairly domestic, making me think we might just be in a house. We passed more doors then entered a massive foyer with a grand, double staircase.

*Okay, so not just a house then. A mansion? Maybe a castle?*

Darnell led me to a large pair of double doors positioned directly between the two staircases. Two middle-aged men stood on either side of the doors and opened them when we walked up.

My jaw hit the floor as we entered a vast room, the word 'grandeur' popping into my head. Pillars lined each wall, and stained-glass windows sat in between each one. An array of old murals was painted onto the ceiling and an enormous chandelier was in the very center of the raised roof.

Shelves full of books were placed against the side walls. There were tables in front of them with people sitting and reading loose papers. Eight ornate chairs sat in the back of the room on a lifted platform, three of them occupied by serious-looking individuals who were staring directly at me. Darnell led me towards them, and I swallowed around the dryness in my throat.

"Robin," Darnell said as we reached them and stopped. "I'm pleased to introduce you to our Keepers of Balance: Toshiro, Alexander, and Mallory."

*Keepers of Balance?*

I guess it only made sense that they would have them too, but I'd never thought about it before.

"Robin, welcome to our home," Toshiro said, standing up and showing off the sharp business suit he wore. He was middle-aged with shaggy black hair, brown eyes, and an up-turned nose. "We're glad to have you."

"That makes one of us," I replied, setting my jaw as he smiled down at me.

"She's sassy," Mallory said, her curly auburn hair sticking out wildly. She walked closer to me, just as Toshiro had, and I could see freckles lining her ivory skin as well as the nose ring she was sporting. Her brown eyes gleamed with pleasure, and I was shocked by her apparent youth.

"How old are you?" I couldn't help but ask in concern.

"Thirteen," she replied with a malicious grin, and my eyes widened.

*How could someone so young be in charge here?*

"I'm sure you have many questions," Toshiro said, "and we'll answer them all in good time." He chuckled before turning to the boy who was still sitting down. "Alexander, don't be rude. Come greet our guest."

Alexander slowly lifted himself out of his chair and saun-tered over, his brown eyes looking me over with a blazing intensity. He was tall and lean with light brown skin and a tapered mini-afro. Stubble covered his pronounced jawline, making him appear older than I'd initially thought.

"Welcome," he said gruffly, not taking his eyes off me as he stopped next to Toshiro and Mallory.

"We've waited a long time for you," Toshiro told me.

"For *me*?" I questioned, making a face.

"Don't flatter yourself," Mallory said with a sneer. "He just means a water element."

"Precisely," Toshiro replied. "But how lucky are we to have gotten one with such power—such strength? Your power surges have been off the charts." He appraised me with crazed eyes as his hands rubbed against one another. "I can't wait to see you in action."

My gaze jumped back and forth between the three of them, trying to figure out my options. I could stand here and exchange pleasantries with the people who kidnapped me and killed my family, or I could run. The second option seemed the more appropriate response, so I conjured up the moisture around me, letting the energy build up.

"How 'bout I give you a little demonstration then?" I replied.

I released the energy, creating a wall of water that surrounded me completely before pushing it outward. It forcefully traveled like a powerful wave in all directions, knocking everyone in the room off their feet.

The three Keepers of Balance slammed backwards into the chairs, knocking them over, and I took the opportunity to turn on my heel and make a beeline for the doors. I passed into the foyer and ran towards the front door, not knowing what was on the other side. But it didn't matter. Anything was better than being stuck in here with these looney tunes.

Something wrapped around my ankles, yanking them back so I crashed to the ground. I laid there, stunned, then glanced at my feet to see . . . Vines?

Before I could look closer, hands forcibly turned me onto my back, and there sat Alexander on top of me, looking smug as water dripped from his clothes.

"Pinned ya," he murmured. I grunted as I tried to knock him off me, but he pushed me back onto the ground, restraining my hands above my head. "Pinned ya again."

"Did you just quote *The Lion King* to me?" I asked, frustrated.

"It's one of the few movies we get with the awful reception out here," he replied, the corner of his full lips turning up slightly. His hot breath wafted over my face as he exhaled through his nose. His eyes never left mine as he stood, bringing me with him. "This was fun and all, but we should get back."

He pulled me into the other room with a firm grip on my arm. The floor was covered in puddles, soggy papers, and annoyed people wringing out their clothes.

"Excellent demonstration!" Toshiro exclaimed, clapping gleefully as my brow furrowed. For such a dangerous organization, their leaders were strange. Very strange. "Now, how about we sit down and talk."

"I have nothing to say to you," I told him with a glare.

"Robin, we are not your enemy. We fed you and clothed you. We even healed your wounds," he replied, gesturing to my arm. "Surely you have questions you want answers to."

Without letting me reply, I was guided to a wooden chair in front of their own and forced into it. Toshiro moved his wrist in a circular motion around himself, picking up speed as he went along. A warm breeze blew about, and I realized he was drying himself off. I watched in awe as he did the same thing to Mallory then Alexander before the three of them sat down and stared at me.

"As I'm sure you figured out, I possess the element of air," Toshiro said. "Mallory is fire, and Alexander is earth. All we're missing to complete the balance is you."

I remembered Matthew's brief explanation about the rarity of elemental powers, but he'd also said there were four of each in Garridan.

"Why aren't there more of you?" I heard myself ask, and Toshiro sighed sadly, his face almost breaking into a pout.

"There were more of us at one time. Unfortunately, though, our numbers have dwindled rather than risen," he replied. "Twenty years ago, when we broke off from Garridan, there were two of each elemental power. However, we lost many of them in battles along the way, so we had almost no bloodlines capable of producing more. Mallory is the one and only child born from an elemental bloodline in our compound. Luckily for us, it happened before her parents passed."

"So you were one of the original founders of the Cyfrin?" I asked, and he smiled with pride.

"That I was. I've lost many friends along the way, but I know I can rebuild to what we once were." He eyed me with pleasure. "Especially now that you're here with Alexander."

I glanced over at Alexander, who stared at me with tight eyes. It reminded me of how Matthew had stared at me when he'd first come to Milton High School.

I looked back at Toshiro, puzzled. "What do you mean?"

"Well, the odds of having a child with an elemental power are almost certain when both parents possess one."

It took a moment for his words to make sense.

"You're joking," I said, almost laughing at how ridiculous the notion was.

"No. I'm actually very serious," he replied.

I recoiled as much as I could while sitting. "You think I'm going to have a baby with him?!" I exclaimed in shock.

"Not right away, of course. We'll let you two get to know one another first."

"You're a sick bastard," I almost yelled, completely disgusted. "I will *never* agree to that."

Toshiro stood and walked towards me. Gone was his lighthearted demeanor and in its place was one of danger as his eyes burned with anger. "You don't have a choice," he said, his words slow and deliberate. "The only option you have is *how* we do this—the easy way or the hard way. But just remember that the hard way involves more unnecessary loss in your life."

His fingers grazed the necklaces on my chest, and my blood ran cold.

"You have many people back home that you care about," he continued. "Don't ever forget how easy it was for us to take people away from you. People I'm sure you miss deeply. And just look at the tragedy that unfolded at your dance. You got lucky with that one, but it won't happen again."

My eyes widened. They had started the fire. I ground my teeth together as I attempted to keep my emotions under control. This was the type of monster I'd expected to meet here, and I wasn't disappointed. "Screw you," I whispered.

One side of his lips turned up in a smirk. My eyes widened as I realized he was amused then turned to slits as anger blazed in my very core. Unable to contain it, I lashed out, striking him in the chest with a torrent of water. He must've expected it this time, though, because he braced himself against it so he wouldn't fall back.

He flung his hand out and an intense pressure fought against my stream of liquid. I pushed it forward with all my might, but slowly lost ground as Toshiro walked forward, his air more powerful. Sweat poured down my face, but it was no use. He was only a foot away now and I had no strength left.

He brought both his hands back then shoved them towards me as his eyes danced mischievously. A strong updraft ambushed me, knocking my feet out from under me. My chin hit the ground as I fell, and the corners of my vision blurred as the pain traveled through my jaw. I fought the urge to puke as I shakily pushed myself onto my knees. Toshiro grabbed my hair and yanked my head back as I grunted in displeasure.

"You may have a lot of power," he murmured in my ear, "but we have a lot more. I'd recommend you don't try something like that again because you *will* lose and, next time, I don't promise to be as forgiving."

He shoved my head forward, and I barely caught myself from sprawling onto the ground again. I gritted my teeth as Mallory cackled. Alexander continued to appraise me, never making a sound, and I hated him all the more for it.

"Now, how about you go back to your room and think about that," Toshiro suggested, turning away from me. "We'll try this again tomorrow."

He waved his hand, and Darnell stepped forward, ushering me up from the floor. I slowly got to my feet, fighting off the lightheadedness that tried to take over. It took everything in me not to lash out again, and even more not to start bawling. But I wouldn't appear weak in front of these people. I wouldn't let them see me cry.

I made direct eye contact with each of them—unfazed by Mallory's devilish grin or Alexander's hateful stare—then turned around with my head held high as Darnell led me away from the repulsive scene that just unfolded.

# CHAPTER THIRTY-ONE

I spent the night restlessly shifting in my uncomfortable quarters. I needed a way to get out of there, but I knew that was easier said than done. The Cyfrin had already proved I couldn't escape on my own, which meant I would have to sit tight and wait for someone to come for me. Until then, the only thing I could do was play nice to protect everyone back home.

"Toshiro has invited you to brunch," Darnell said after opening my door.

"Joyful," I muttered, and he looked at me with heavy disapproval.

"I'd suggest keeping the sarcasm in line. Toshiro may not approve."

"I don't really care what Toshiro thinks."

"You should."

"Why?"

"Because he can make everyone you've ever talked to disappear."

A shiver ran up my spine, but I didn't let it show. "He doesn't scare me."

"He should," Darnell replied with a small frown. Something in his eyes made me think he was speaking from experience, but I couldn't be sure. "Anyway, come with me, please."

I followed him into a dining room that held a long table. The three Keepers of Balance were already seated and looked up when I entered. Darnell directed me to the chair next to Alexander and I sat down, my body buzzing uncomfortably at our close proximity.

"Good morning!" Toshiro greeted me cheerfully.

"Good morning," I replied dryly.

"I hope you slept well."

"Peachy."

"I suspect you've thought about our parting words yesterday," he said, his pleasant voice layered with the underlying tone of a threat.

"Yes," I told him quietly, looking at the napkin someone placed on my lap. "You'll receive no more problems from me."

"Excellent," he replied joyously as Alexander watched me from the corner of his eye. "Let's eat, and you can learn about our history while we're at it."

"I already know your history. Matthew told me all about it."

"Well, then, that saves us some time now, doesn't it?" Toshiro asked, his eyes narrowing at the mention of Matthew. "Is there anything you don't know?"

I faltered, unsure what to say, so I said the first thing that came to mind. "Why is a thirteen-year-old a Keeper of Balance?"

Mallory pursed her lips, clearly not thrilled with the question, but I ignored her as Toshiro answered.

"A wonderful question!" he said. "We aren't in the habit of letting children hold such monumental roles in our society but, as you know, we are in short supply of them here at the moment, so it couldn't be avoided. Mallory had been training since she was very young, and after her parents died, she was the next and only fire element in line. We were already missing a water element, so we couldn't very well make do without fire as well."

"Why not?" I questioned, spreading butter over a piece of toast.

"The Keepers of Balance are responsible for many things, and when we aren't in balance, neither is anything else. Our lands run dry, our food supply runs low, our weather patterns become unpredictable. It's essential that we rely on one another equally to provide for our people. It doesn't work if we're not in synch."

"I thought we were responsible for keeping balance in the whole world."

"The Cyfrin are responsible for the people of *our* world. People like *us,*" Toshiro corrected with a hint of malice in his voice. "Garridan believes everyone in the world should benefit from our talents and hard work, but we do not. We provide for our own and only our own until we can seize the recognition we deserve."

"And how do you plan on doing that?"

Toshiro let out a laugh. "By taking over the world of course. One day *we* will rule, and all the little people will be put in their rightful places as our servants."

"The world is an awfully big place full of people who fight for freedom," I said. "They won't give in easily."

"They won't have a choice. You see, Robin, we could easily wipe them out of existence without even trying. But we won't do that. It'll be enough for us to make an example out of one country or continent, if need be," he explained, his chipper tone out of place. "The rest of the world will give in out of fear and fear alone."

My stomach knotted at his sadistic objective. He'd kill hundreds of thousands of people to get his point across without giving it a second thought. Darnell was right—I should be scared of him.

"Why haven't you done that already?" I tried to keep my voice steady even though I was trembling on the inside. "You broke off from Garridan a long time ago."

"A revolution takes time," Toshiro responded. "In the beginning, we lost a lot of our people to the war. We've been recuperating ever since. However, every time we seem to be close to a revival, Garridan strikes us down. It's as if they know!"

He was growling by this point, so I stayed quiet, not wanting to be the focus of his wrath.

"Calm down, Toshiro," Alexander told him. "You know we're ahead of them this time."

"That we are," Toshiro agreed, his face smoothing out. "You are quite an asset for us, young lady. It's a miracle we located an unfound child that possesses an elemental power."

"Unfound child?" I repeated.

"Yes. Someone Garridan hasn't found yet," Toshiro replied. "Them not knowing who you are or where you've been is the only thing guaranteeing that this is going to work out so well."

My mind reeled. They didn't know my birth parents had connected with me.

"That's right," Mallory added smugly. "No one will be looking for you, so you're stuck here with us."

I stifled my joy at how very wrong they were, not allowing even a hint of it to show on my face.

"Exactly!" Toshiro exclaimed, hitting the palms of his hands on the table gleefully. "And so, for that reason, our next planned move is foolproof."

"What move?" I couldn't resist asking.

They all turned to look at me with different levels of amusement.

"That's classified," Toshiro said.

"Well, I'm a Keeper of Balance here now, right? Don't I deserve to know what going on?"

Toshiro and Mallory laughed wildly as Alexander grinned ever so slightly.

"Nice try, but we aren't that stupid," Mallory said, and I looked down at my empty plate.

*Worth a shot.*

"Janet!" Toshiro suddenly yelled, causing me to nearly jump out of my seat. His eyes blazed as he stared at a woman standing by the kitchen door. She shrunk back, her face visibly flinching. "There's an eggshell in my breakfast!"

"I-I'm so sorry, sir," Janet stuttered, walking over with her head down.

"Sorry doesn't fix the aching in my tooth," he snapped. He pushed his hand out, and Janet flew backwards into the wall.

She hit it with a loud thump before falling to the ground. Toshiro hit her with another wind gust, gluing her to the ground as she cried out in pain.

"Stop!" I shouted, standing with wide eyes.

Toshiro glanced at me from the corner of his eye, arching one brow. "You think you're allowed to tell me what to do?" he asked.

"N-no," I stammered. Words of anger wanted to burst out, but I bit my tongue, knowing I couldn't cause problems.

"Then sit down."

I did as he said, trying to hide my disdain as I watched Janet begin to cry. Toshiro kept his eyes on me tauntingly as he smirked.

"You don't like seeing me hurt her, do you?" he asked. I stared at my plate, refusing to play into his hands. "But you're showing remarkable control anyway."

"I told you you'd have no issues from me," I said tersely.

He laughed, finally letting Janet go. She whimpered as she shakily stood, hastily making her way out of the room.

"I see the question you're wanting to ask," he said. "Go ahead." I swallowed loudly and he laughed again. "This isn't a trick. Go ahead and ask."

I looked from him to Alexander to Mallory then asked, "Why did you do that? I thought you protected your own people."

"Oh, we do," Toshiro replied, leaning back as he crossed his arms. "But she isn't one of us."

"She's normal?" I asked with wide eyes.

"No, she has powers. But they're useless, so she might as well be normal."

I furrowed my brows. "I don't understand."

"There are some people whose powers are less than adequate," he explained. "They serve no purpose. They're futile. Those people have no spot among us, so they're reduced to servantry."

I eyed the spot that Janet had disappeared into. "You turn your own people into slaves?"

"It's the only spot suitable for their failures."

"But they didn't choose what power they got."

"Nevertheless, they pay for it."

"But that- that's so . . ." I trailed off, flabbergasted. Not only were normal people at risk with the Cyfrin, but so were their own.

"It's how things are done here," Toshiro said. "Be quick to learn it, and don't oppose it. It won't serve you well."

I nodded, staring at the table again as I rubbed my lips together to keep quiet.

"We have a planning session at one," he announced, directing his attention to Alexander. "Until then, how about you show Robin around."

Alexander nodded in acknowledgement and stood. He offered me his hand, but I dismissed it and stood on my own. I could fake being nice, but I wouldn't do anything to encourage the idea they had in mind for us. He walked ahead of me, and I trailed behind wordlessly as he glanced at me from the side of his eye.

"So, you're Robin," he said.

"Same person you met yesterday," I replied, a bite in my tone.

"You really are sassy, aren't you?" he commented with amusement. "I see why Matthew is fond of you."

I stopped cold in my tracks. "What?"

"He wouldn't risk his life for just anyone."

I swallowed around the bile that rose in my throat. "Were you the one who hurt him?"

He glanced at me with furrowed brows. "I would never."

"What's that supposed to mean?" I asked, something in his tone confusing me.

His eyes traveled over me, stopping when they reached my gaze. "You don't know him as well as you think you do."

"I know all I need to."

"Really? What if I were to tell you he's killed many, many innocent people?"

I licked my lips, my stomach twisting. "I don't care."

"How can you not?"

"Because he's different now. That's not who he wants to be."

"But it doesn't change who he was."

"I won't judge him for his past," I said. Alexander continued to watch me, his gaze intense. I averted my eyes, uncomfortable. "What?"

"Matthew chose a good friend."

"What?" I asked, taken aback at his soft tone. What was his deal with Matthew?

Instead of answering, he walked away, and I ran after him as he reached the front doors. A small gasp escaped my mouth when they opened, and I took in the sight. We really were in a refurbished castle, sitting atop a hill that looked over a beautiful garden and a quaint town.

"Where are we?"

"I'm afraid I can't tell you that," Alexander replied.

"Can you tell me who lives in that town?" I asked as we made our way down the front stairs towards the garden.

"Our people. We're minuscule next to Garridan but, from what I'm told, we hold a lot more charm."

"Oh. I've never been to Garridan."

"I haven't either," he replied, and I studied him with furrowed brows. When he finally noticed, he stopped short and stiffened. "What?"

"How old are you?" I asked in reply.

"Nineteen."

"Were you born here?"

"No."

"That means you were sent away from Garridan as a child too."

"That's correct."

"So your parents are still there." His eyes hardened slightly, and I knew I'd struck a nerve. "Do you know who they are?"

"No. Nor do I care," he responded dryly.

"Why not?"

"None of your damn business," he spat, glaring at me with such disdain that I closed my mouth and took a step back. "You're awfully nosy."

I shrugged, not wanting to speak again in fear of what he might be capable of when upset. He scrutinized me, and I squirmed nervously.

Finally, he took a deep breath and let it out slowly. "I apologize for lashing out."

I couldn't tell by his neutral tone if he was sincere or not. His face was tight with furrowed brows, but his eyes were softer than before. He looked genuine enough, but I stayed quiet.

"What else would you like to know?" he asked.

I hesitated before my curiosity won over. "How long have you been here?"

"Twelve years," he responded, leading us past some overgrown hedges to a small fountain.

"How did you end up here?"

"Same way as the other children," he replied with a shrug, as if it were obvious.

"They kidnapped you," I stated, gazing at the water as it splashed over the side of the marble onto the stoned walkway.

"I prefer the word 'rescued.'"

I snapped my head in his direction and scoffed. "They're bad people with bad ideals. They subjected you to a life of evil. That isn't rescuing."

"You'd be wise to remember that I'm part of the 'they' you're speaking about," he reminded me coldly, stopping me in my tracks.

I bit my lip, silently chastising myself. His history was similar to Matthew's—which made me sympathetic—but he wasn't Matthew, and I couldn't afford to forget that. He obviously supported the lifestyle choices here, and that meant he was an enemy.

"You're right," I said through clenched teeth, as I remembered what the Cyfrin were responsible for. He cocked a single brow at my tone, waiting for me to continue. "Which means you're responsible for killing my mom and little sister."

"Not my style." He waved his hand dismissively. "I may be part of this world, but I'm not in charge of the decisions."

I crossed my arms over my chest. "I thought the Keepers of Balance were all equal."

"Ideally. However, Toshiro runs the show here. We act on his say so. Mallory is too young to be trusted with anything, and I just have no interest."

"But—" The loud chime of a bell cut me off.

"Next time, it's my turn," Alexander said as he turned his back to me.

"Your turn to what?"

"Ask the questions," he replied, turning his head around to give me a sly smile. "Feel free to wander around the courtyard, but keep in mind that there's an electric barrier that'll fry your brains out if you try to go too far."

I stared after him, not sure what to make of our conversation. It only left me with more questions. The Cyfrin weren't everything I'd imagined them to be. All I knew was I had to keep my guard up around them.

I wandered around, admiring the well-kept grounds. All the bright colors and inviting decorations made me forget where I was. If I didn't know better, I'd think this was Heaven.

I sat on a marble bench, closing my eyes as I soaked up the warmth the sun was giving. Despite the peaceful atmosphere, my heart was heavy. These people were responsible for the death of my family, the torturing of Matthew, and so much more. They wanted to take over the world and kill anyone who got in their way. They were monsters, and I couldn't stand the thought of being near them any longer than I had to be.

*Someone please take me away from here.*

The sun was setting on the horizon by the time I headed inside. When I walked through the doors, I hesitated, unsure if I should head to my room or snoop around. My decision was made for me when Toshiro walked down one of the stairways.

"Hello!" he said, greeting me like an old friend. "I was just about to send a guard out to get you. We have a surprise."

"What is it?" I asked distrustfully.

"Follow me." He strutted down a corridor lined with full metal suits of armor, and I followed silently. I couldn't keep track of how many turns we made when we began descending down some stairs. We reached a heavy wooden door, and Toshiro turned towards me, his face serious. "Take this with a grain of salt, Robin. Learn from it."

"Learn from what?" I questioned, his words making no sense.

He knocked on the door and a moment later, it was pulled open. He motioned for me to go forward, so I slowly stepped up and peered in. My heart plunged into my stomach, and I ran inside as fear loomed over me.

"No!" I yelled, my hands flying desperately over Matthew's bloodied body, which was hanging from chains. His head was limp, his swollen eyes closed. I gently touched his cheek, begging him to look at me, then whirled around, fire burning in my core. "What did you do?"

"Don't look at me like that," Toshiro scolded. "We only apprehended an intruder."

I clenched my hands into fists and fought back tears. He'd come here for me. Of course, he had. He wouldn't be Matthew if he sat around and did nothing while I was potentially in harm's way. I swallowed away the lump in my throat and looked at his still form.

"Is he dead?" I whispered.

"Not yet," Toshiro replied, and I let out a silent breath of relief.

"Let him go."

"I can't very well do that. He betrayed us. For that, he must be punished. Not to mention, he'd always be a thorn in our sides when it came to you, and we can't have that."

I closed my eyes and rubbed my lips together. "Please."

"No can do. Sorry."

"Why did you even bring me here then?" I shouted angrily. "To torture me? Make me miserable? I told you you'd get no problems from me, so why?"

"Don't be so dramatic," he said, and I scowled at him with narrowed eyes as my nostrils flared. "I just thought you'd like to see an old friend one last time. It's my gift to you."

"*Gift?* You think this is a *gift?*" I hissed.

"It's as close to one as you'll get, so enjoy while you can because soon enough, he'll be gone."

He turned on his heel and left, leaving me alone with two guards stationed outside the door and Matthew's unconscious form. I sat down against the wall nearest him and stared at his broken face with tears trickling down my cheeks, waiting for him to come to. After a while, my head started lolling as I dozed on and off.

"Robin," a muffled voice said.

My head snapped up, and I saw Matthew's eyes on me. I jumped up and gave him an awkward hug as he hung there, unable to contain my relief.

"I'm so happy you're awake!" I exclaimed, sniffling. "I was so worried."

"I'm fine," he responded, his voice gurgling strangely. "Are you okay?"

"I'm okay. My living quarters are only a small step up from yours, but at least I'm not dangling from a ceiling." My chin quivered as I stared at him, trying not to be upset. "Why did you come? You should've known better."

"We have to get you out of here."

"We have to get *you* out of here. They're going to kill you if we don't."

"And what's to say they won't do the same to you?" he asked, clearly bothered by my focus on him instead of myself.

"Trust me, they won't do that." A single, humorless chuckle escaped my mouth, and he raised his eyebrows questioningly.

"What makes you so sure about that?" he asked. "They may need your element with them, but that doesn't mean you're not expendable."

"My element may not make me indispensable, but my uterus does."

"Excuse me?" he asked, taken aback.

"Toshiro needs more elemental bloodlines to live on if the Cyfrin have any chance of surviving."

"And?" he pushed, frowning.

"And you're more likely to have an elemental baby if there's two elemental parents, so he wants me to have children with Alexander," I informed him curtly, staring at my fingernails.

He let out a plethora of expletives, swinging on his chain as he worked up his anger. I pursed my lips, waiting for him to be done.

"Like hell you're doing that!" he roared.

"Don't yell at me!" I shouted back. "I didn't ask for this!"

He took a couple deep breaths and quietly counted to ten before saying, "You're right. I'm sorry. But I will *die* before I let that happen."

"You very well might," I replied, eyeing his chains.

"We have to get out of here."

"Yes, we do. But how?"

He rubbed his lips together as his head slowly shook side to side. "I'm not sure."

"That's reassuring," I muttered. "We do have one advantage over them, though."

"What's that?"

"They don't know that Garridan knows about me. They think no one will come looking for me."

"But someone will," he said, sounding hopeful as I nodded in agreement. "That's it. That's our way out of here."

"But what if no one comes in time? You'll die." My heart skipped a beat at the thought of it.

"Alexander won't let that happen."

My forehead scrunched. Alexander said he'd never hurt Matthew, and now Matthew was confirming it. But why? I opened my mouth to ask, but a knock sounded at the door and Darnell entered.

"Time to leave," he told me, and I looked back at Matthew in a panic.

"Hey, calm down," Matthew told me. "I'll be okay."

"How do you know?"

"Just trust me. Go get some sleep. Try to come back to-morrow."

"Okay," I whispered, hoping I could return. I took one last look at him, offered him a small smile, then turned around and left him hanging exactly as I'd found him.

# CHAPTER THIRTY-TWO

"Robin."

I ran over to Adriana's open arms and clung to her in happy relief.

"I'm so glad to see you!" I exclaimed.

She cupped my face in her hands, and I watched tears well up in her eyes. "And I'm so glad you're okay! Your father and I were so scared when Ak- I mean, when our inside spy told us. But don't worry. We're coming to get you. We'll be there tomorrow, so just hang in there until then."

"You're coming for me?" I asked, the weight of all my stress lifting from my shoulders. I'd hoped they would but having it confirmed was an entirely different feeling.

"Of course we are!" she exclaimed. "But you're coming to Garridan with us. You can't go back home."

"I know," I replied, hanging my head. Going back would only bring a repeat of the events that led us here. "What about everyone there though? Ben, Felicity, their families, Lizzie . . . Toshiro already threatened them. If I go with you, he'll make good on his word. I know he will."

"Don't you worry about that," she said, brushing my tangly hair over my shoulder. "We'll have guards watching over them twenty-four seven for as long as necessary. Okay?"

"The council is okay with that? I thought you had strict rules about leaving."

"We do. But this constitutes extreme measures. We don't want anyone to be harmed, whether they live in Garridan or not. We'll protect whoever we need to against Toshiro and his followers."

I nodded earnestly as tears welled in my eyes. Everyone would be safe. "Thank you," I said, my voice shaking.

She pulled me into a hug and held my head against her shoulder. "It's going to be okay, honey. I promise."

"What about Matthew? You'll get him out too, right?"

"He's alive?" she asked, sounding relieved, and she drew back to look at my face.

I remembered I hadn't talked to her since before prom, so she didn't know. "For now. He got away and came back the night of prom to take me to Garridan—because the Cyfrin were on their way for me—but then the fire happened and—"

"Fire?" she repeated, her eyes wide with concern.

"Yeah, there was a fire during prom. The Cyfrin started it to draw me out, but that doesn't matter." I waved my hand as I brushed it off. "After I was taken, Matthew came for me because he thought I wasn't safe. Now they have him locked up and being tortured. They're going to kill him!"

My voice quivered slightly, and she instantly wrapped me in another hug as she slowly shook her head back and forth.

"That boy risked his life for you," she murmured, and I nodded against her chest. "You don't find friends like that every day. Of course, we'll take him with us. His family has been worried sick. They'll be so relieved when I tell them he's alive."

"Thank you," I whispered, breathing easier.

The only obstacle now was them succeeding in the rescue, but I had no doubt they were capable of it. Soon, Matthew and I would be safe and far away from this awful place, reunited with our families and our real home.

I looked up at her and asked, "Tomorrow I'll get to hug you for real?"

She chuckled lightly. "Yes. And you'll get to meet your father."

"Do you think he'll like me?" I asked, suddenly nervous.

"What a silly thing to ask," she said, watching me with adoration. "Your father loves you. As do I. Soon enough, we'll all be together like we were always meant to be."

I let her words linger in my mind. My mom and Dawn could never be replaced, and my heart would always ache for them. But it was uplifting to know that, even though I'd lost one family, I'd gained another who might love me just as much.

* * *

"Good morning!" Darnell greeted me with his usual smile as he freed me from my room. He was so polite and happy all the time; it made me question what he was doing here.

"Good morning," I replied.

"Did you sleep well?" he asked as he led me down the same route we'd taken yesterday morning.

"I slept remarkably," I told him, smiling inwardly to myself. "Can I skip breakfast and go see Matthew?"

"I'm afraid not. Toshiro had explicit instructions to keep you away from there moving forward. Besides, he's in no shape for visitors after last night."

"What happened last night?" I asked, immediately concerned.

He looked at me with squinted eyes, as if he wasn't sure if I was serious or not. When he saw that I was, he answered bluntly. "Another beating. Worst one yet."

My heart dropped and I bit my lip. I needed a way to let him know he was going to be okay—to give him some hope and a reason to hold on a bit longer.

"Can you give him a message for me?" I asked. He hesitated and began shaking his head. "Please. Nothing that could get you in trouble, I promise. Just a harmless message to maybe, I don't know, comfort him, I guess."

Darnell itched his bald scalp and considered it for a moment. "Sorry. I just can't do that."

I sighed dejectedly, and Darnell gave me a sideways glance, looking like he felt bad for denying my request. I only hoped that Matthew would fight to stay alive until we could get to him. When we arrived in the dining room, I sat down silently to not draw attention to myself. Toshiro and Alexander were in the middle of a heated debate, and completely ignored my entrance. I ate quietly, catching Mallory's eyes from time to time as she refused to look away from me.

"Sir, there's a problem that requires your attention," a man announced to Toshiro.

He stood up with a sigh and followed the messenger out of the room without another word. With him gone, Alexander turned towards me, but before he could say anything, I had a question for him.

"Why can't I see Matthew anymore?"

He cocked his brow. "I thought it was my turn for questions."

I continued to eye him until he narrowed his eyes and scowled, unhappy with my challenging me.

"Trouble in paradise?" Mallory asked with a smirk.

"Shut up, Mal," he said without breaking our eye contact. "If Matthew is going to pose such a problem for you, maybe he needs to be taken care of sooner rather than later."

"No!" I exclaimed. He continued to glare at me, but I held my ground until he stood up, his chair almost falling over in his rush. "Where are you going?"

"To pay a little visit to the person you can't," he replied dryly, walking away without another glance at me.

I stared after him with wide eyes as Mallory snorted. "You really did it now," she said.

"Is he going to hurt him?" I asked, my stomach queasy.

"Nah," she said, rolling her eyes. "He loves him too much for that."

I glanced over at her. "What do you mean?"

"I thought you and Matthew were, like, great friends or something," she replied. "He didn't tell you he and Alexander have a history?"

I shook my head. "What kind of history?"

"They used to be foster brothers before they came here. We got a two for one deal when we found them because they were practicing their powers together."

My jaw dropped open at this revelation. "Are they still close?"

"It's complicated," she said sarcastically.

I stared at my eggs, stunned. It seemed as if there was no end to the surprises of Matthew's life. After breakfast, Mallory instructed me to go back to my room but after much coaxing from me, she escorted me to the library instead. It wasn't as nice as being outside, but it was better than my claustrophobic living arrangements. She left me there with two guards, but I didn't mind being alone. She wasn't very pleasant to be around anyway.

After choosing a book, I made myself comfortable on the only couch in the room. All I had to do was survive today, then I'd be free of this place. Immersing myself in the pages of a story was a safe way to pass the time without having to interact with anyone.

After only a short time, the library doors swung open, and I glanced up from my book to see Alexander walking in. He stopped in front of me, his expression unreadable. When he didn't say anything, I slammed the book closed.

"Can I help you with something?" I snapped as I folded my arms.

"May I join you?" he asked, unfazed by my attitude.

"I'm pretty sure you can do whatever you want."

"Yes. I can. But I'd still like your permission to join you."

I cocked my head at him, unsure if he was patronizing me. "Fine," I finally said.

He sat down on the opposite end of the couch, watching me silently as I went back to reading. After a moment, I looked up hesitantly.

"Will you tell me how Matthew is?"

"He's strong," Alexander replied. "He's gone through worse before. He'll be fine."

"But Toshiro wants him dead."

"It's not the first time Toshiro's had him under a death sentence. I've saved him before, and I'll save him again."

"I don't understand." My brain was fuddled, his words contradicting the sadistic person I pinned him as.

"He's family."

"Care to elaborate?" I asked, wanting to understand not only his thought process but also his relationship with Matthew.

"No. I don't. I do, however, want to know why you care about him so much."

I bit the inside of my lip, contemplating an answer that would suffice, before repeating his own words back to him. "He's family."

"You haven't even known him that long though," Alexander said with a shake of his head. "And he was lying to you most of that time."

"Yeah." I looked down at my hands. "But that doesn't matter to me. Not anymore."

"I don't understand." His eyes were tight as he repeated the words I had just moments ago.

"Join the club."

"What club?"

I rolled my eyes. "Never mind."

His eyes traveled over me again, taking in every feature, every characteristic. I cleared my throat and shifted in my seat, uncomfortable by his stare.

"Why are you staring at me?" I demanded.

"I don't know," he said quietly. "Just trying to figure out what Matthew sees in you."

"What do you mean?"

"He abandoned us for you. Then he came back—not once, but *twice*—for you. Knowing, both times, that he might end up dead." He ran his hand over his lips. "And when I went to see him just now, his only thought was of you. He wanted to know if you were still okay and how I could possibly think of procreating with you. He even threatened to rip my head off."

He chuckled once, then leaned in towards me. "So, tell me. What makes you so special to him, Robin?"

I swallowed and shrugged, his intensity too much to handle. "I don't know."

"Are you two . . . *Together?*" he asked, his eyebrows shooting up on the last word.

"What? No!" I exclaimed, surprised at the thought. "I have a boyfriend."

"I'm well aware."

My eyes narrowed. I didn't like him knowing about Ben. "How?"

"We know many things about you. It's the only way to be efficient in our threats, after all."

He said it lightheartedly, but there was rage in his eyes. I inhaled shakily, his demeanor changes giving me whip lash.

"Matthew and I are close," I said. "He was there for me when no one else could be."

"Which explains why you consider him family," he said, leaning his elbows onto his knees. "But why does *he* think the same of *you?*"

I rubbed my lips together, then quietly answered. "Because I accepted him, flaws and all. He never had to pretend with me because he knew I wouldn't judge him. I'd still see the best in him no matter what."

"And there it is."

"There what is?"

"The answer." He smiled ever so softly, once again changing his attitude. "You're a purist."

"I'm sorry, what?" I asked, almost laughing.

"You're a good person, a *kind* person. Someone who forgives. Someone who would take a bullet for a friend. Someone that sees the good in others, despite all their bad."

"You got all that from my answer?" I questioned, furrowing my brows.

"Yes. I did. And I'm right, aren't I?" He waited for an answer, but I didn't give one, so he murmured, "I thought so."

"You don't know me," I said quietly.

"No, I don't. But I think I'd like to." Silence stretched between us. I didn't know what to say, and just when I thought he wasn't going to speak again, he did. "We're not all bad, you know. The Cyfrin, I mean."

I scoffed and narrowed my eyes. "Yeah, okay. Sorry if I don't believe that considering you kidnapped me to use me as some kind of baby maker."

"Toshiro's views aren't all of ours," he replied.

"Really?" I asked bitterly. "Because I don't see you trying to stop him. Not with this, not with Matthew, not even when he had my mom and sister killed." My voice broke slightly, and I fought to keep my composure as I kept going. "Her name was Dawn, and she was only six. *Six!* You really want to sit here and tell me you aren't all bad when none of you care that you murdered a *six-year-old!*"

"Who said we don't care?" Alexander asked, his face hard.

I tore my gaze away from him, fighting back tears as grief overwhelmed me. "Go away. I'm done talking to you."

To my surprise, he actually stood. Before walking away, he said, "For what it's worth, I'm sorry about your loss."

"It's worth nothing," I snapped.

"Nonetheless, I'm sorry," he murmured before stepping away from me and leaving.

I sniffled, blinking away my tears as I opened the book back up.

*I just have to survive today.*

Some hours later, a commotion made its way to my ears. I tore my eyes away from the page I was reading to watch the door. Loud voices filled the hallway and footsteps thudded past. The guards glanced at each other before standing up and heading towards the noise to see what was going on. Before they reached it, the door burst open, and Alexander walked through.

"Come with me," he instructed when his eyes met mine. "Hurry up."

I jumped off the couch and scurried towards him as he walked away. I had to jog to keep up with him as we headed for what I'd come to think of as the throne room.

"What's going on?" I asked as my heart thumped wildly in my chest, even though I suspected the answer.

"Just keep quiet and don't cause any problems," he said in a low voice.

He led me to the fancy chairs at the back of the room and pointed to the seat next to him. We sat down as people bustled around and lined up along the walls before Mallory and Toshiro strode in angrily. They both took their seats, and I rubbed my lips together nervously.

"Why are they here?" Toshiro hissed through his teeth.

"I don't know, Toshiro," Alexander replied.

"Oh, come on. We all know why they're here," Mallory said as she turned her cold gaze to me.

"They don't know about her!" Toshiro yelled, and I averted my gaze quickly.

"Are we sure about that?" Alexander questioned, and I could feel his eyes on me.

Toshiro continued to seethe as the people in the room came to order and stood tall.

"Bring them in," Toshiro ordered, his gaze set on the door.

They opened immediately and eight guards walked in surrounding four individuals—three men and a woman. I suppressed the urge to run towards the woman I quickly recognized as Adriana. Her long hair was pushed back by a headband, showing off her wrathful glare as she stared Toshiro down.

The man next to her had soft, blue eyes that skimmed the room until they landed on me. His wide lips turned up in a huge smile, leaving crinkles by his eyes. I appraised his slender nose and heart-shaped face with the same olive skin tone that Adriana and I possessed. My heart skipped a beat, realizing he must be Elijah—my birth father. I returned his smile, wishing I could give him a hug, then turned my attention back to the situation at hand.

"To what do we owe the pleasure of this visit?" Toshiro asked calmly with a forced smile.

"We came for our daughter," Adriana announced, her confidence carrying throughout the room.

Toshiro lost his smile, his expression tight. "And who might that be?"

"We're not here to play games, Toshiro," Elijah said with a strong voice. "Hand her over, and we can leave in peace."

"I don't believe we're going to do that," Toshiro told them, his tone condescending. "We aren't as weak as we once were. You can't take us on with just yourselves and two guards."

My eyes traveled to the two men that stood only slightly in front of them. One was middle-aged and sported light-brown hair and blue eyes that burned with rage. The other was young, probably in his early twenties, and he had the same dirty-blond hair and light-blue eyes as Matthew.

*Could they be related?*

"Alone?" Adriana repeated. "Surely you don't think us to be that stupid. We have a hundred guards lined up at the edge of town just waiting for our signal."

"If you don't comply with our demands," Elijah said, "we *will* bring them in, and you know as well as I do that you'll lose."

I wiped my hands on my pants as Toshiro visibly seethed, practically shaking with anger. When he didn't respond, Alexander spoke up.

"You expect us to believe you have your whole army waiting outside?" he asked, sounding bored.

"Do you know us to be liars?" Adriana responded, and Toshiro jumped up from his chair.

"You can't have her!" he yelled, his eyes blazing. "Bring your army in because you have a fight on your hands. She stays or she dies!"

My breath caught in my throat as my eyes widened at his threat. Elijah stared at him calmly then addressed the older man to his right.

"Malachi. Call in the guard."

Malachi nodded as he put his hand to his ear and gave a quiet command into a comms unit. A second later, a loud explosion sounded then a handful more. I covered my ears as they shook the castle and rattled my bones.

"That would be your protective barrier going out," Malachi informed Toshiro.

Toshiro let out a crazed roar and beckoned his guards forward. They simultaneously moved into an attack formation but before they could act, a staticky ball of luminescent power surrounded the four outsiders. I stared at it, mesmerized as it protected them.

"Don't let your ego get in the way," Adriana said to Toshiro. "Your people will die, and their blood will be on your hands."

Toshiro's eyes jumped wildly from one person to the next, his nostrils flaring.

"Toshiro," Alexander murmured, glancing at him. "We've come too far to ruin our chances now. Don't do this. It isn't worth it."

"A pure bloodline is most certainly worth it!" he snapped.

"Not if we don't have anyone to lead," Alexander replied, only loud enough for the three of us closest to him to hear. "They'll crush our numbers, and we'll be back to square one. Do you really want to rebuild yet again when we're so close to a victory?"

"We can find another way to get a pure bloodline," Mallory added.

"Once we destroy Garridan, we'll have unlimited options," Alexander continued as I listened in horror.

*Destroy Garridan? Was that possible?*

Toshiro contemplated their words. Despite his anger, Alexander and Mallory seemed to have gotten through to him. He took a deep breath and gazed out at the four people of Garridan.

"Fine. Take her," he spat. "But just know you'll pay for this confrontation."

Elijah nodded at Malachi, who quickly spoke to whoever was on the other end of the comms. The force field around them disappeared as they all stood tall with unwavering looks of defiance.

"We're taking Matthew as well," Adriana said, and Toshiro set his jaw as he shot daggers at her. "And everyone in Milton is going to have round-the-clock protection, so I advise you to stay away from Robin's friends."

"You little—"

"Anything else?" Alexander cut in, seeing that Toshiro was about to lose what little control he had left.

"Not at the moment," Elijah responded.

Alexander nodded, then addressed a guard. "Go retrieve Matthew."

I noticed Malachi's eyes turn hopeful as the guard disappeared. I looked him over again then held back a smile as his name finally clicked into place in my brain, and I realized who he was—Matthew's father.

Alexander watched my parents thoughtfully. "How did you know she was here?"

"Dream projection," Adriana answered, almost smugly.

Toshiro jumped up, his anger finally winning over. "This was our time!" he screamed at the people around the room. "*Our* upper hand! It only worked because she was unfound, so no one would come for her! How in the hell did we not know that they knew where this girl was?"

"Because you never take the time to create a foolproof plan," Elijah answered, his voice flat. "You just want what you want when you want it and don't think about the implications. Only *you* are to blame for your misfortune."

Toshiro raised his arms with a loud shout, shooting a violent burst of air towards Elijah. Elijah quickly matched his pose, and I let out an inaudible gasp as I realized his power was also the element of air. Their strong winds met midway, rippling out and forming a wind tunnel around the entire room as they pushed back and forth for the upper hand. The effects were as strong as a tornado. People were being blown over and books circled the room, caught up in the gusting air currents. My hair whipped wildly around my head, and I pushed it away as I struggled to keep my chair from tipping over.

The bookcase nearest me fell over, and the scattered shelves got picked up by the wind. One soared towards me at lightning speed. I lifted my hands over my face, hoping to block the worst of it, but Alexander pulled me to the ground and took the hit himself, crouching over me in a protective stance.

Our faces were close together, and I could feel his breath waft over me as his hands lingered near my face. I stared at him with wide eyes as he continued to block me from the debris.

"Enough!" Adriana yelled, creating a wall of water in front of each man, containing their efforts.

They both dropped their arms, glaring at one another, but didn't argue as the people around the room shakily rose to their feet. Alexander offered me his hand, and I hesitantly took it as his eyes scanned me for injuries. When he seemed satisfied that I was okay, he stood us both up and stepped away from me, just as the door opened and Matthew was pushed into the room.

His shirt was torn and stained with the remains of dried blood, but he appeared to be in one piece. I sighed in relief and ran past everyone to get to him, giving him a tight hug. He grimaced at the pain it caused him, and I quickly let go.

"Sorry," I said.

He grabbed my hand and squeezed it as Elijah and Adriana stepped up next to us. Malachi and the other guard wrapped Matthew's arms around their shoulders and helped support his weight as he struggled to stay on his feet. They both appraised him with visible concern, and Malachi's eyes started to shimmer with unshed tears. I could tell he was itching to tell Matthew who he was.

"We'll be on our way now," Adriana announced, putting her arm in mine.

"Just get out," Toshiro snapped through gritted teeth.

Adriana led us through the door, but I took a quick glance back, meeting Alexander's guarded eyes. He gave the slightest of nods in my direction, the corner of his lip barely upturned. My brows furrowed—was he actually happy I got rescued?

I turned back around, trying to push him out of my mind as the front doors were opened for us. Alexander was nothing like Matthew, yet he kept reminding me of him. Maybe, somehow, there was still hope for him just like there'd been for Matthew.

We quickly and quietly made our way through the town, ending on the far side of the barren land that surrounded the Cyfrin compound. A small jet sat there, guarded by a handful of people. I looked around as we began to board and was surprised to see miles and miles of nothing.

"Where's your army?" I asked Adriana as Matthew was gently propped up on a couch.

She grinned and said, "Back home."

"That was all a bluff?" I asked incredulously.

"Of course not," she replied. "Only part of it. We have fifteen members of our guard here, all the most powerful wielders of their respective talents. We knew Toshiro wouldn't risk a fight at this point."

"That seems like a pretty dangerous thing to build a bluff on," I murmured, slightly impressed but even more concerned.

Elijah walked over to us and stared at me in the same way Adriana had when we'd first met in my dreams. His chin wobbled, then he let out a broken sob and fiercely wrapped his arms around me. I leaned into him, taking in his airy scent and letting his hold comfort me. I finally had a father who loved me.

"Hi," he whispered into my hair.

"Hi," I replied just as quiet.

I didn't want to, but I pulled back, matched his smile as we took in each other's features. Adriana was right—I looked like him too.

"Edna, please come take a look at my son," I heard Malachi tell an older lady, who quickly approached.

"She's our healer," Adriana informed me as I looked over at them.

She slowly moved her arms over Matthew as Malachi and the other guard looked on uneasily.

"Who's that with Malachi and Matthew?" I asked Adriana as she and Elijah took a seat on either side of me.

"That's William, Matthew's brother."

My heart swelled. Matthew had a family who'd come for him too. I couldn't wait for the moment they told him who they were. I wondered what his reaction would be to knowing someone loved him enough to come rescue him.

As the plane took off, Adriana played with my hair absentmindedly, and I smiled as I accepted the maternal gesture. Elijah held my hand, and I realized that neither of them wanted to take their hands off me. But I didn't mind. I needed this reunion as much as they did.

"Onward to your new home," Adriana told me with a soft smile.

"Actually." I hesitated. "Can we make one stop first?"

# CHAPTER THIRTY-THREE

When the plane landed, Ben and Felicity were waiting right where I'd told them to. I ran down the stairs and across the field into their arms. They held onto me, their tears soaking into my shirt.

"We were so scared," Ben whispered.

"I know," I replied.

"We felt so useless," Felicity said, wiping her nose on her sleeve. "Matthew said there was nothing we could do and just took off. He said he'd get you back but . . . We thought we lost you both."

I gripped her hand as Ben looked me over. "Did they hurt you?" he asked, his voice strained.

"No. They didn't. They actually healed my injuries from the fire."

"What? Why? I thought they were the bad guys," he said.

"They are. They definitely are," I muttered.

"What happened?" he asked, his eyes narrowed.

In that moment, as they both stared at me, I knew I couldn't tell them. There was no point.

"Nothing," I replied, trying to force a smile. "Let's just forget about it, okay?"

"What? No, that's not okay," Ben said, cupping my cheek in his hand. "I need to know."

"No, you really don't. All you need to know is I wasn't hurt in any way. I'm fine."

Ben opened his mouth to argue more but Felicity cut him off. "Where's Matthew?"

"In the plane. A healer is still working on him," I replied.

"A healer?" Her eyes instantly widened. "Why? What happened? Is he okay?"

I placed my arm on her shoulder. "He will be. The Cyfrin just didn't like him coming back."

"I knew he shouldn't have gone," she said, her hands wringing together.

"So you'd rather he left Robin there?" Ben asked, crossing his arms.

"Of course not!" she exclaimed, her lips setting into a pout.

"It was a lose lose situation," I cut in, holding my hands up between them. "There's no right answer, so there's no need to argue about it. It's done, okay?"

"Okay," they both murmured.

"How's Lizzie?" I asked.

"Pretty torn up," Ben replied. "We didn't know what to tell her, so we just said we didn't know where you were."

"That was the right choice," I said, but guilt ate at me. She must be going crazy.

"Who are they?" Ben asked, staring past me.

I glanced back and saw Adriana and Elijah standing at the bottom of the steps, watching us hesitantly. I smiled and beckoned them forward. When they got closer, I said, "Ben, Felicity, I'd like you to meet Elijah and Adriana—my birth parents."

Both their jaws dropped open as Elijah and Adriana stopped on either side of me.

"It's nice to meet you," Ben said, shaking Elijah's hand. "I'm Ben."

"Robin's boyfriend," Adriana said, foregoing the handshake and pulling him into a hug. "I hear you're quite the catch." He blushed and ducked his head as Adriana turned to Felicity. "And you must be Felicity. I've heard a lot about you too."

"All good things I hope," Felicity replied, returning Adriana's hug.

"Mostly," I said with a grin.

"Ha. Ha," she said, shoving me playfully.

Elijah's nose was rosy, and I realized he was holding back tears. "What's wrong?" I asked him.

"Sorry," he said, laughing shakily. "It's just seeing you. Seeing you with people from the life we missed . . ." His voice caught in his throat as Adriana rubbed his back, her own eyes misty. "We missed out on so much, and I don't know how we'll ever make up for it."

"You don't have to," I said, my heart full of sorrow. "You did what was right for me in that moment, and I don't blame either of you for it. I honestly only have to thank you because I got to live a good life here."

"Adriana told me you said as much," he said with a soft smile. "I'm glad you can see the good in the situation, but, for us, it's all heartache."

"I know." I reached out, grasping onto his hand. "But we'll have plenty of time to catch up now."

"That's right," Adriana said, latching on to my other hand. "We're going to be together just like we always should've been."

Felicity stifled a sob, and my heart dropped again. What was a happy thing for some was a sad thing for others.

"Sorry, sorry," she said hastily as we all looked at her. "I didn't mean to ruin your family moment."

"Nonsense," Adriana said. "You're losing someone you love. Don't apologize for being sad about it."

Felicity nodded vigorously and I pulled her to me. We clung to one another fiercely as tears poured down our cheeks. I glanced up at Ben and saw him blinking quickly as he stared up at the sky. I was breaking their hearts. But I had no choice. I had to leave.

"I wish I didn't have to go," I whispered, "but I do."

"We know that," he said gruffly. "It's just hard knowing we won't see you for so long."

"But then we'll make senior year the best one yet," Felicity said, trying to force a smile onto her face.

Adriana's brows furrowed. She opened her mouth, but I shook my head, knowing I needed to tell them myself. She nodded, and I took a deep breath.

"Actually." I bit my lip, hating the heartache I was about to unleash. "I won't be coming back."

"What?" they both cried.

"I can't," I whispered, my eyes begging them to understand. "If I come back, the Cyfrin will just come after me again. I'll never be safe here, and neither would you guys."

"But-but—" Felicity stammered as Ben closed his eyes. I could see him trying to stay composed.

"Okay," he finally said, and Felicity's eyes nearly popped out of her head.

"What? That's it?" she asked.

He stared at me, his heart exposed as I saw all the emotion in his eyes. "Staying away is the only way she stays safe," he murmured. "Let's not make it any harder on her than it already is."

My chin quivered. I was never more thankful for his understanding nature than I was now. I fell into his chest, sobbing uncontrollably as he gently shushed me. I loved him so much. How could I live without him?

"Matthew!" Felicity called out, and I glanced up just as she crashed into his arms.

I noticed he'd changed out of his bloodied clothes. Between that and his unscathed face, you'd never know he'd just been on the brink of death.

"Look. That's my dad and brother," I faintly heard him telling her excitedly.

I smiled, sniffling away the last of my tears as I calmed down again.

"Are you okay?" Ben asked me, and I nodded.

"I will be."

"We should get going," Malachi said from the door of the plane, his eyes glancing around uneasily.

"We have to make one more stop first," I said to Elijah and Adriana.

"I don't know if we should," Elijah replied slowly. "It's not safe for us here."

"I know, and I wouldn't ask if it wasn't important."

They glanced at one another, then Adriana asked, "Where do you need to go?"

"To Lizzie's." They looked puzzled so I said, "My mom's friend. The one I was living with."

"Oh, right!" Adriana exclaimed. "Yes, I remember now."

"I can't just disappear on her. I have to explain."

"You can't tell her about Garridan, honey."

"I know. I won't." I thought about it for a moment then said, "She knows I wanted to visit you guys in the summer, so we can tell her I changed my mind—that I want to go with you now and stay with you permanently."

"Will she let you go without a fight?" Elijah asked.

I nodded. "I think so. She trusts my judgement, and she won't want to keep me from you."

They looked at each other once again then nodded. "Okay," Adriana said. "But it has to be quick."

"I understand. Thank you."

As they went to talk with the others, Felicity and Matthew walked up. Without a second thought, Ben pulled Matthew into a hug and patted his back before released him.

"I'll never be able to repay you for saving Robin," Ben told him.

"I didn't though," Matthew replied, hanging his head. "Our parents are the ones who did the rescuing."

"But you went. You *tried*. That counts for everything in my book."

"I'd do it again in a heartbeat."

"I know. And that's why I know she'll be okay in Garridan. Because she'll have you." Ben smiled softly. "I'll miss you, man."

Matthew cleared his throat. "I'll miss you too."

"Aw, do I sense a bromance going on?" Felicity asked with a grin, and Matthew scowled as Ben and I laughed.

"But for real," Ben said, "I'm happy you found your family. They look nice."

"They do, don't they?" Matthew replied, glancing over at them.

Adriana and Elijah walked back over. "Alright, it's all settled," Elijah said. "But I'm afraid we don't have a teleporter."

"Oh, uh—" I faltered. Teleporter?

"Felicity and I brought a car," Ben said, seeming just as mystified as I was.

"Excellent," Adriana replied with a wide smile. "Let's go then, shall we?"

The six of us squeezed into Felicity's car. Ben was pressed close to my side, but I didn't mind. I leaned into him as the car moved, enjoying what could be some of our last moments together.

When we arrived at Lizzie's, she was a basket case. After chastising me for a full ten minutes, she calmed down enough to greet my parents, and we all sat down to talk. It took a while, but she finally agreed to let me go with them. I stepped outside while she spoke to my birth parents privately.

Ben and I sat quietly as he played with my fingers, holding both my hands in his. My head rested on his shoulder, and I breathed in his scent, not knowing when I'd smell it again. The door opened and the adults walked out, Elijah carrying my lone suitcase. I stood and faced Lizzie, whose eyes were streaked with red.

"I'm sorry," I told her, fighting back the urge to ask to stay as I gave her a hug.

She held on tight, then pushed me back so she was looking at me. "Don't apologize. You've gone through so much and deserve to be happy. If that's with your birth parents, so be it." She smiled sadly. "Just promise me you'll come back and visit."

"I promise," I said, feeling terrible that I might not be able to make good on that promise.

"Your mom would be so proud of you, kid."

I pressed my lips together as I nodded, unable to speak. Felicity came up behind us with Matthew in tow, and I walked down the front steps. She clutched me firmly, and her body shook as she cried. When she released me, her makeup was running down her cheeks, and she swiped at them quickly.

"I'm going to miss you so much," she said around a hiccup.

"I'm going to miss you, too," I said, my voice cracking.

"Take care of yourself," she said before glancing at Matthew, who was saying his parting words to Ben. "And look after him for me, will ya?"

"Of course. He's family."

"We better get going before it gets too dark," Elijah said softly.

Felicity gave me another quick hug, kissed Matthew with a blazing passion that made us all look away, then went and stood by Lizzie on the porch as the rest of us walked to the car. Ben climbed in the backseat next to me, and I was thankful for the little extra time we had together. As we drove away, I waved to Felicity and Lizzie until they were just small specks in my vision.

Ben wrapped me in his arms, and I leaned my head against his shoulder as we bumped around. The car was silent, filled with the solemn feelings we were all radiating.

Elijah kept glancing at us in the rear-view mirror, his eyes full of concern.

I knew they'd support Matthew and I both as we made this change, but it didn't make it any easier to leave the place where I'd grown up. I wouldn't graduate from Milton High with all my friends or finish out the swim season. I wouldn't play on the basketball team or go to my senior prom. I didn't even know if I'd be back to visit before everyone went their separate ways as adults next year. My time here was over.

The car came to a stop a small distance back from where the plane sat in the empty field. I swallowed around the lump in my throat as we filed out of the car, knowing my hardest goodbye was upon me.

"You're sure you can't write or call?" Ben asked, suddenly desperate.

I looked over at Adriana, who shook her head slightly, then gazed down at my feet. "I'm sure. You heard what they said. Communication doesn't work the same way there. Nothing comes in, and nothing goes out."

"But why can't we plan for you to come visit?"

"Garridan has strict rules about travel," Adriana spoke up when I failed to give an answer. "We don't mingle with the outside world because they'd know we're different. We couldn't keep our land a secret if people came and went as they pleased."

"But you provide *everything* for the outside world," Ben said. "Don't you want that recognition?"

"We don't," she said with a smile. "Think of us as a silent partner. We're there helping and contributing but nobody can know. It's safer that way."

"The rules can't be bent even for you?" I asked.

"No," Elijah answered gently. "As leaders, we lead by example. We can't expect our people to do what we aren't willing to do ourselves."

"You came for me though."

"That was different. It was a rescue mission, and it was a council decision that was voted on," he said. "I'm afraid they wouldn't be very lenient in granting you permission to leave again, especially since the Cyfrin seem so hellbent on getting you."

Ben and I looked at each other.

"So you're saying we'll *never* see each other again?" Ben asked softly.

"If you did, I'm afraid it wouldn't be for a very long time."

"Not unless you're granted a power and join us," Matthew murmured, and we all turned to look at him. He shrugged nonchalantly, not offering any further explanation.

"Is that true?" I asked Adriana, trying hard not to get my hopes up. "Can that happen?"

She and Elijah exchanged a quick glance. "It's very unlikely," she said.

"But it *could?*" I pressed.

They exchanged another look.

"Well, it *could*," she replied, "but it's an exceptionally rare occurrence. We only have five recorded instances of it happening in our entire history."

"How?" I asked eagerly. Any possibility was better than none.

"No one is entirely sure," Adriana replied slowly.

I wondered why she seemed so hesitant to tell me, but it was pressed from my mind as she continued.

"There are legends about a Keeper of Balance with an earth element who wanted to make peace with all the lands for our people. One day he left, and he was never seen or heard from again. Rumor has it that he, quite literally, turned into a tree and lives to this day, protecting nature and balancing our usage of it. It's said that if he's visited by someone from this world whom he deems worthy, he'll grant them a power. Alternatively, if they come from our world and wish to leave, he'll take their power away."

"It's just a silly legend though," Elijah said, but I wasn't listening anymore.

"Wow," I murmured. "That's . . ."

"Crazy," Ben finished for me, shaking his head.

"But if it's true you'd be *more* than worthy to receive one!" I told him earnestly.

His eyes tightened and he frowned. He looked at the others and asked, "Can you give us a moment alone please?"

I stared at him as the others walked to the plane, wondering why he wasn't as excited about this news as I was. When everyone else was out of earshot, he spoke.

"Robin—"

"Ben, we could go find that tree! We could do it. I know we could!"

He shook his head. "No, we can't."

"Why not?"

"For one thing, your parents said it's just a legend. So it may not even be true."

"But if it is, it could solve *everything*." My eyes were filling with tears. "We wouldn't have to lose each other. You could come with me."

"Robin . . ." He trailed off, his voice hoarse. He looked up, blinking rapidly as he tried to find the words to express what he was feeling. Finally, he took my hands in his own, and looked at me with eyes full of despair. "We both know I can't go with you. Just like you couldn't go a couple of months ago when I begged you to. I could never leave my family or my tribe. They need me, and I need them."

"But I need you too," I whispered. My heart seemed to stop beating as it ripped right down the middle. Deep down, I knew he was right, but in that moment, it seemed impossible to accept.

He opened his mouth to say something then closed it again as he clenched his jaw. We stared at one another, both knowing this was the end.

"We might never see each other again," I said, my voice barely audible.

He wrapped his arms around me, and we stood there, motionless, both coming to terms with that heartbreaking reality. I pulled away from him a bit, and he gently lifted my chin so we were staring into each other's glistening eyes.

"I believe we'll meet again," his low voice stated, and I nodded, unable to voice a reply right away.

Finally, I put my hand on his cheek and softly said, "I love you."

"And I will *always* love you," he responded.

His lips met mine as he kissed me firmly. There was an undertone of urgency in the way his lips moved against mine, both of us aching for the life together we'd just lost.

When the kiss finally ended and we pulled away from one another, our foreheads stayed pressed together, neither one of us wanting to accept that this was it. It took everything in me to step back from him, but I did, one hand still in his, our fingers interlocked.

"Goodbye, Benjamin," I murmured, taking another step back.

"Until we meet again, Robin," he corrected as I took one more step and our fingers slid apart.

I turned around and jogged towards the plane, the air unable to dry the tears that streamed down my cheeks. I boarded quickly and took the first seat I came to, looking out the window. The engine sputtered to life, and I could see Ben's hair fluttering in the wind. He lifted his arm in farewell, knowing I was watching, and I put my hand on the window as my heart shattered.

I kept watch out that small window as we lifted into the air and flew away from the life I'd always known. The city where I'd spent my entire life grew smaller and smaller until it was completely out of sight. When I could no longer catch even a glimpse of it, I looked away from the window and took a deep breath.

Matthew sat down next to me and pulled my hand into his. I leaned my head against his shoulder, grateful for his presence. We stayed that way for a long time, silently contemplating how much our lives had just changed. The loss I'd experienced this year was heavy but, as I watched my birth parents laughing at Malachi, I found a glimmer of hope.

Even though one chapter was ending, another was beginning—one where I was a superhero, as Ben had said. A seed of excitement planted in my stomach, and I grasped onto it. I couldn't change anything that was happening, so I decided to embrace the uncertainty that awaited me.

With a heart full of courage and a soul ready to soar, I smiled. This was the flight to my destiny.

Breanne Leftwich is an up-and-coming author with her debut book being *Robin's Flight*.

Books have been a huge part of her life for as long as she can remember, and she can always be found with one in her hand. She's been writing and creating stories since she was a young girl and excelled in English over the course of her academic career. It has always been a dream of hers to write and publish books for young readers so she could provide them with an outlet or escape from whatever difficulties they might be experiencing in their lives.

Aside from reading and writing, Breanne enjoys listening to music and being outside as much as possible. She currently lives in Oklahoma with her husband and daughters.